JULIE KAGAWA

NIGHT *of the* DRAGON

YOUN
ADUL

This novel is entirely a work of fiction. The names, characters and incidents portrayed in it are the work of the author's imagination. Any resemblance to actual persons, living or dead, events or localities is entirely coincidental.

HQ
An imprint of HarperCollins*Publishers* Ltd
1 London Bridge Street
London SE1 9GF

This edition 2020

1
First published in Great Britain by
HQ, an imprint of HarperCollins*Publishers* Ltd 2020

A catalogue record for this book is available from the British Library.

ISBN: 978-1-84845-770-6

MIX
Paper from
responsible sources
FSC™ C007454

This book is produced from independently certified FSC™ paper to ensure responsible forest management.

For more information visit: www.harpercollins.co.uk/green

Printed and bound by CPI Group (UK) Ltd, Croydon CR0 4YY

NIGHT
of the
DRAGON

Also by Julie Kagawa

Shadow of the Fox series

Shadow of the Fox
Soul of the Sword
Night of the Dragon

The Talon Saga

Talon
Rogue
Soldier
Legion
Inferno

Blood of Eden series

The Immortal Rules
The Eternity Cure
The Forever Song

The Iron Fey series

The Iron King
The Iron Daughter
The Iron Queen
The Iron Knight
The Lost Prince
The Iron Traitor
The Iron Warrior

To Tashya, Nick and Misa sensei.
Arigatou Gozaimasu.

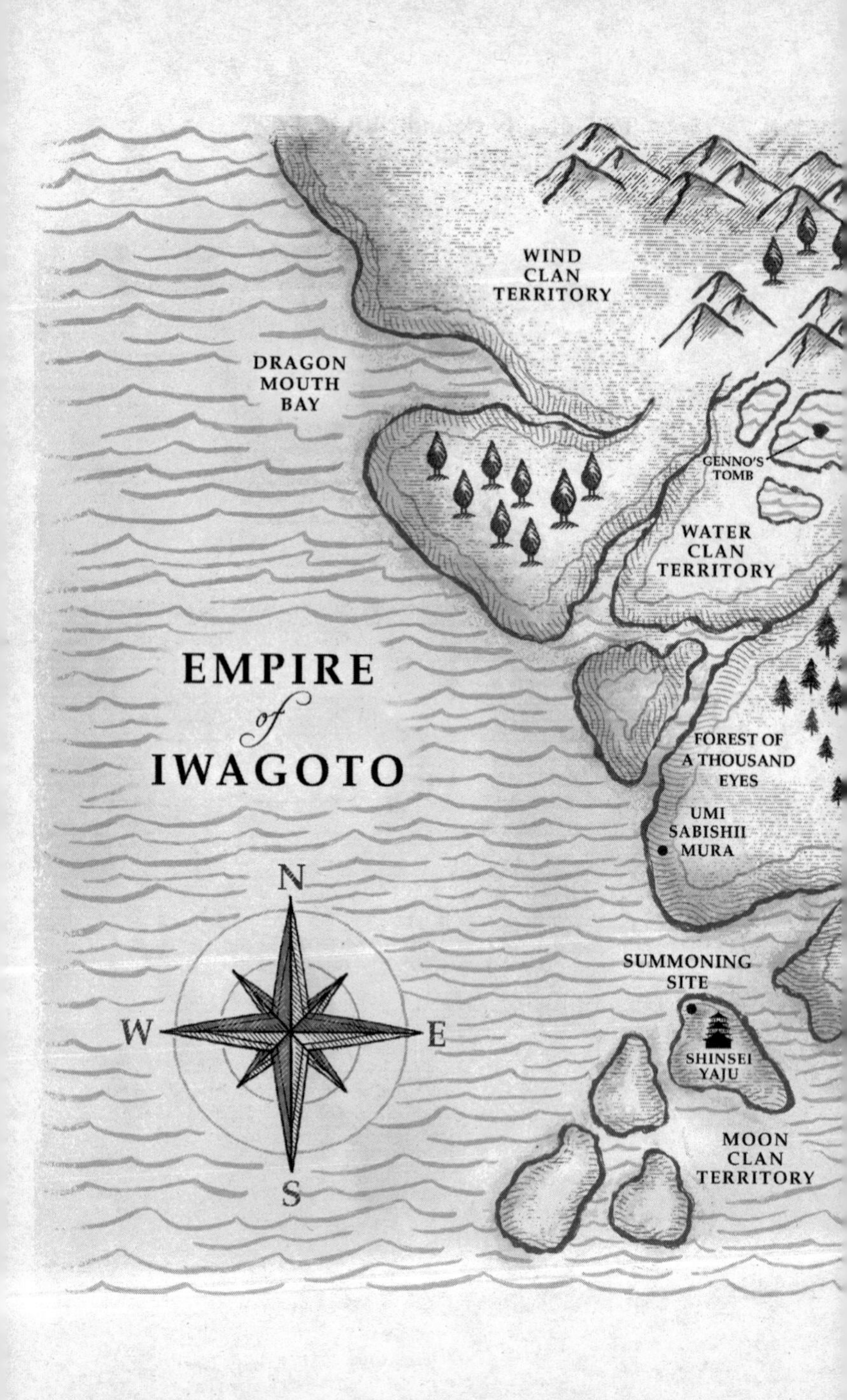
WIND
CLAN
TERRITORY
DRAGON
MOUTH
BAY
GENNO'S
TOMB
WATER
CLAN
TERRITORY
EMPIRE
of
IWAGOTO
FOREST OF
A THOUSAND
EYES
UMI
SABISHII
MURA
N
W
E
S
SUMMONING
SITE
SHINSEI
YAJU
MOON
CLAN
TERRITORY

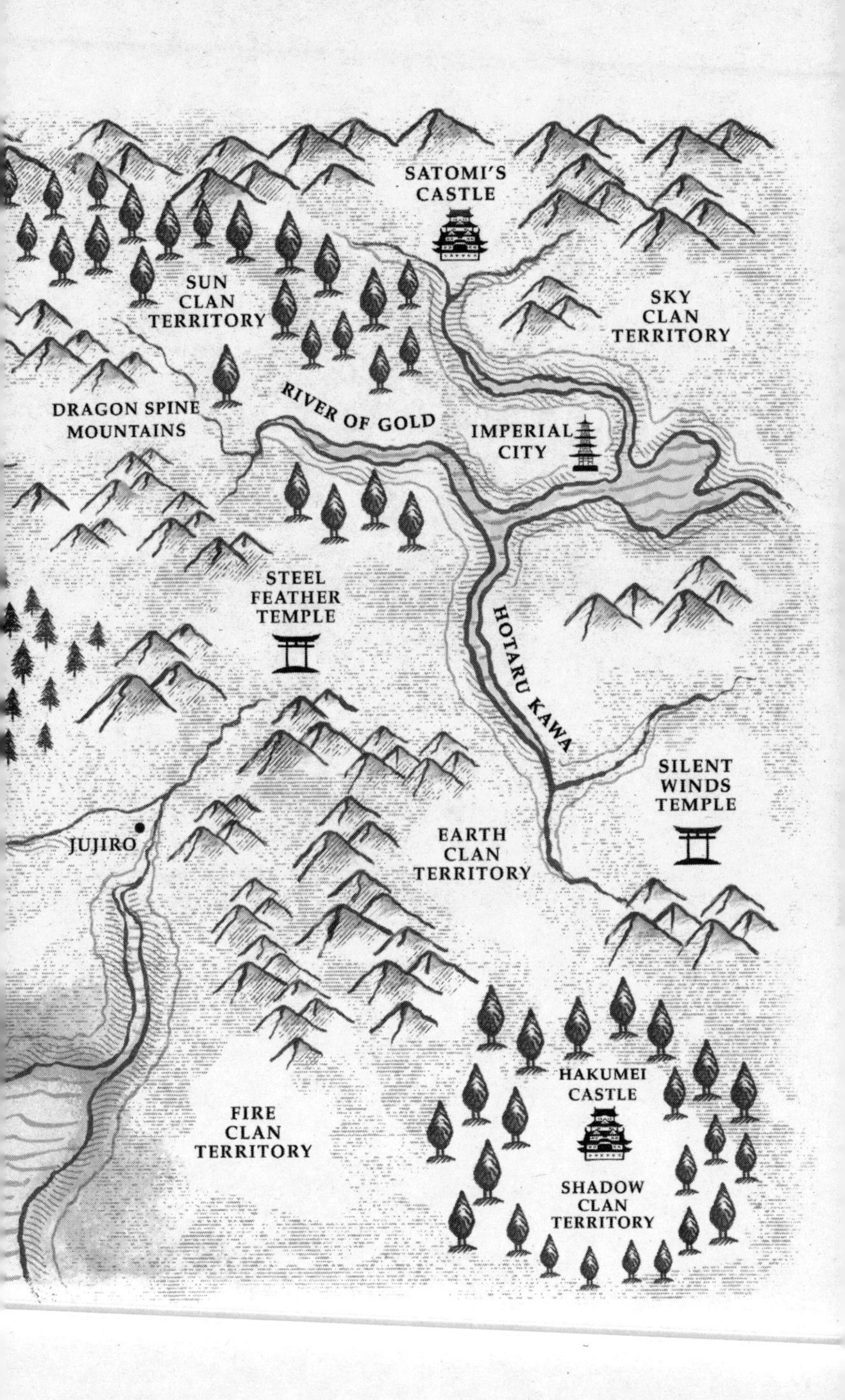
SATOMI'S CASTLE
SKY CLAN TERRITORY
SUN CLAN TERRITORY
DRAGON SPINE MOUNTAINS
RIVER OF GOLD
IMPERIAL CITY
STEEL FEATHER TEMPLE
HOTARU KAWA
SILENT WINDS TEMPLE
JUJIRO
EARTH CLAN TERRITORY
HAKUMEI CASTLE
FIRE CLAN TERRITORY
SHADOW CLAN TERRITORY

PART I

1

Calling on Jigoku

One thousand years ago

In the long years of his existence, the number of times he had been summoned from Jigoku could be counted on one claw.

Other demon lords had been summoned before. Yaburama. Akumu. The oni lords were too powerful not to have some enterprising blood mage attempt a contract with them, though such rituals often ended badly for the arrogant human who thought they could enslave an oni lord. The four of them were, admittedly, a proud bunch, and did not take kindly to an insignificant mortal attempting to bend them to their will. They humored the blood mage long enough to hear what the human was offering, and if it did not interest them, or if the mage foolishly tried to assert dominance, they would rip him apart and do what they pleased in the mortal realm until they were sent back to Jigoku.

It had always amused Hakaimono when a mortal tried to summon him. Especially that moment when they gazed upon him for the first time and fully realized what they had done.

Narrowing his eyes, he gazed around, peering through smoke and ignoring the brief feeling of vertigo that always accompanied being dragged from Jigoku into the mortal realm. A growl of murderous annoyance rumbled in his throat. Already, he was not in the best of moods. Akumu had been scheming again, trying to weaken Hakaimono's forces behind his back, and he had been on his way to deal with the devious Third General when black fire had erupted over his skin, words of blood magic echoing in his head as he abruptly found himself in the mortal realm. Now he stood in the center of a ruin, broken walls and shattered pillars surrounding him, the scent of death thick on the air, and contemplated squeezing the head of the mage responsible until it popped like an egg in his claws.

The stones under his feet were sticky and had a sweet, coppery smell he recognized instantly. Lines of blood had been painted over the ground in a familiar circle, with words and sigils of power woven in a complex pattern. A summoning circle, and a powerful one at that. Whomever the blood mage was, they had done their research. Though it wouldn't save them in the end.

"Hakaimono."

The First Oni looked down. A woman stood at the edge of the blood circle, black robes and long hair seeming to blend into the shadows. She clutched a knife in slender fingers, her pale arm covered in red to the elbow.

A chuckle escaped him. "Well, don't I feel important," he said, crouching down to better see the woman. She gazed coolly back. "Summoned by the immortal shadow herself. I am curious, however." He raised a talon, watching the human over curved black claws the length of her arm. "If you rip off an immortal's head, do you think it will die?"

"You will not kill me, First Oni." The woman's voice was neither amused nor afraid, though the certainty in it made him smirk. "I am not so foolish as to attempt a binding, nor will I ask much of you. I have but a single request, and after that, you are free to do what you like."

"Oh?" Hakaimono chuckled, but admittedly, he was curious. Only the very desperate, foolish or powerful called on one of the four oni generals, and only for the most ambitious of requests. Like destroying a castle, or wiping out an entire generation. The risk was too great for anything less. "Let's hear it then, human," he prompted. "What is this one task you would have me undertake?"

"I need you to bring me the Dragon scroll."

Hakaimono sighed. Of course. He had forgotten it was that time again in the mortal world. When the great scaly one himself would rise to grant a wish to an insignificant, short-lived human. "You disappoint me, mortal," he growled. "I am not a hound that fetches upon command. You could have gotten the amanjaku to retrieve the scroll for you, or one of your own human warrior pets. I have been called on to slaughter armies and tear strongholds to dust. Fetching the Dragon's Prayer is not worth my time."

"This is different." The woman's voice was as unruffled as ever. If she knew she was in danger of being ripped apart and devoured by an annoyed First Oni, she did not show it. "I have already sent my strongest champion to retrieve the scroll, but I fear he has betrayed me. He wants the power of the Dragon scroll for himself, and I cannot let the Wish slip away now. You must find him and take back the scroll."

"One human?" Hakaimono curled a lip. "Not much of a challenge."

"You do not know Kage Hirotaka," the woman said quietly. "He is the greatest warrior the Empire of Iwagoto has seen in a thousand years. He is kami-touched, but also trained in the way of the samurai. His talents with both blade and magic are so great, the emperor himself praised his achievements. He has killed men, yokai and demons in waves, and will be perhaps the single greatest opponent you have ever faced, Hakaimono."

"I very seriously doubt that." The First Oni felt a smirk cross his face as he breathed in the blood-scented air. "But now, I'm intrigued. Let's see if this champion of shadow is as good as you say. Where can I find this demonslaying human?"

"Hirotaka's estate lies outside a village called Koyama, ten miles from the eastern border of Kage territory," the woman replied. "It's not hard to find, but it is rather isolated. Aside from Hirotaka's men and servants, you won't be opposed. Find Hirotaka, kill him and bring the scroll to me. Oh, and one more thing." She raised the knife, observing the bloody, glittering edge. "I cannot have anyone suspecting me of blood magic. Not now, when the night of the Wish is so close." Her black eyes rose to his, narrowing sharply. "There can be no witnesses, Hakaimono. No survivors. Kill everyone there."

"I can do that." A slow grin spread across the oni's face, and his eyes gleamed red with bloodlust. "This will be fun."

He would come to regret those words more than any other in his existence.

2

Familiar Shadows

Tatsumi

The tengu banished us from the mountain.

Letting me live was the last straw, it seemed. Their home had been destroyed, their daitengu killed, and the pieces of the Dragon scroll taken by the enemy. A demon on their sacred mountain was something they could not abide, and when Yumeko had refused to have me slain, they informed us in no uncertain terms that we were no longer welcome at the Steel Feather temple. That the doors would be forever hidden from us, and that, come morning, if they saw the bearer of Kamigoroshi on the mountain again, they would destroy him without hesitation.

And so, with barely enough time to bind our wounds, we left the Steel Feather temple and the home of the tengu, fleeing the mountain and the soon to be vengeful guardians of the scroll. Somehow, we made it to the base of the mountains and, exhausted, wounded and still bleeding, found the entrance to a cave, just as a cold rain started falling. The cave was crowded, with five people and a dog crammed inside, but it was empty and dry, and we had no better option. As the ronin started a fire and the shrine maiden began the arduous task of cleaning and rebinding our battle wounds, I retreated to a dark corner, out of the way of everyone, to ponder what had happened. And to answer the question that had been plaguing me since we'd left the temple.

Who am I?

Was I Kage Tatsumi, or Hakaimono? I didn't feel like either of them, though I knew I had irrevocably changed. When this body had been possessed by Hakaimono, the oni's spirit had completely suppressed the human soul, keeping it trapped and unable to do anything. Until Yumeko had arrived, using fox magic of her own to possess the demonslayer and face the oni from within. She had found Tatsumi's soul, freed it, and together, they had attempted to drive Hakaimono back into the sword. Though the First Oni had proved to be far stronger than either of them realized.

However, before a victor could be determined, Genno had appeared, an army of demons behind him, intent on taking the scroll. He'd betrayed Hakaimono, running him through with Kamigoroshi, and left him to die on the field of battle. To save us both, the souls of Kage Tatsumi and Hakaimono had merged, allowing Hakaimono to use his full power to heal the body and keep it alive. Impossibly, it had worked, and I had been able to kill most of Genno's army before they could slaughter everyone. But in my weakened state, the temple had been destroyed, and Genno had left with all three pieces of the Dragon scroll in his possession.

The Master of Demons had everything he needed to summon the Great Kami Dragon and make the wish that would herald the end of the empire. We had to find Genno and stop him from using the scroll, but it was going to be a long, treacherous journey, and some of us might not survive. Even without the concern that my demon half could emerge at any time and tear my companions apart.

"Tatsumi?"

I looked up. Yumeko had broken from the rest of the group and now stood before me with the firelight against her back, casting her in a faint orange glow. She still wore the elegant red-and-white onmyoji robes from the night she had performed for the emperor, though the billowy sleeves were tattered now, her long hair was unkempt, and dirt stained her face and hands. She did not look like a revered diviner of the future. She looked like a peasant girl wearing a costume, except for the tall, black-tipped fox ears poking out of her hair, and the bushy, white-tipped tail behind her. I knew her fox features were invisible to most humans, but ever since the night she had invaded my soul, they were always visible to me. A reminder that Yumeko was kitsune, a yokai. She wasn't completely human.

But then again, neither was I.

"May I sit with you, Tatsumi?" she asked in a soft voice, large eyes glowing a subtle gold in the flickering shadows. I nodded, and she carefully picked her way across the stones to sit beside me, that bushy orange tail brushing my leg as she settled against the cave wall. Odd that the contact didn't make me shy away like it used to.

"How are you feeling?" she asked.

"I'm alive," I told her in an equally quiet voice. "That's about all I can say for certain." She stared at me, her gaze searching, questioning, and I felt my lip curl in a faint, bitter smile. "I know what you're asking, Yumeko. And I can't answer. I feel…different. Strange. As if…" I tried to find the words to explain the impossible. "As if there's a hidden rage inside me, this…savagery that needs only the barest push to come out."

Yumeko blinked, looking thoughtful. "Like when Hakaimono

was living in your head?" she asked. "You were always fighting him for control—is this the same?"

"No." I shook my head. "We were always separate, two individual souls fighting each other for control of one body. If… if I am still Tatsumi, I feel as if Hakaimono is part of me now. That his viciousness and bloodlust could come out at any time. And, if I am Hakaimono, I feel that Tatsumi has infected me with his human thoughts, fears and emotions." I raised a hand before my face; it looked human enough, but I remembered the deadly talons that had curled from my fingertips the night I fought Genno's army. "Maybe it's best if I take my leave," I muttered. "If I am part demon, none of you will ever be safe."

I shot Yumeko a sideways glance to see if any of this frightened her, but her golden fox eyes seemed only sympathetic. "No," she said bluntly, making me blink at her. "Don't go, Tatsumi… Hakaimono…whoever you are. You promised you would help us find the Master of Demons. We need you."

"And what if I'm not Tatsumi?" I asked, turning to face her. "What if I am Hakaimono? How do you know whose soul is stronger, or if Kage Tatsumi even survived the merging of human and demon? Even I don't know the answer to that."

She continued to gaze at me without fear. Watching her, I felt a jolt of shock as light fingers came to rest on my arm, sending a ripple of heat coiling through my insides. Yumeko smiled faintly, though there was a sadness in her eyes as she gazed at me, a glimmer of longing that I didn't understand, but that caused my heart to give a strange little stutter.

"I trust you," Yumeko said very quietly. "Even if you're not the same, I saw your soul that night. I know you won't betray us."

"Yumeko," called a voice before I could suppress my churning emotions long enough to speak. Near the fire, the shrine maiden was watching us with a grave look on her face, her small orange dog giving me a stony glare from its place at her feet.

The miko's dark eyes glittered with mistrust as they shifted to me. "Kage-san. If you would join us—we're off the mountain and no longer in danger of the tengu's retribution. We need to decide where to go from here."

"Hai, Reika-san." Yumeko rose and padded to the fire, fox tail swishing under the hem of her robes. I stood slowly and followed, noting the dark looks and suspicious glares from the rest of the party. The shrine maiden and her dog watched me with barely restrained hostility and mistrust, as if I could turn into a demon at any moment and leap at them with fangs bared. Taiyo Daisuke of the Sun Clan sat cross-legged by the fire, hands tucked into his sleeves, his expression carefully hidden behind a veneer of decorum. Beside him, the ronin slouched against his pack, looking as unkempt and disheveled as ever, reddish-brown hair coming loose of its ponytail. They were, I noticed, sitting very close for two men of vastly different statuses. I had known samurai who would not deign to be in the same room as a ronin, much less share a fire with them.

Glancing up, the ronin gave me a rueful smirk and a nod as I crouched beside the flames, and his dark gaze flickered up to something on my brow.

"You have a little...something on your face there, Kage-san," he said, motioning a finger at his own forehead. I set my jaw, ignoring the obvious reference to the small but blatant horns curling above my eyebrows. Everything else—the claws, the fangs, the glowing eyes—had disappeared, at least temporarily, but the horns remained. A permanent reminder that I was a demon now. If any normal human saw me like this, I would likely be killed on sight.

"Baka." The shrine maiden stalked up behind the ronin and gave a quick swat to the back of his head. The ronin winced. "This is not the time for jokes. Genno has all three pieces of the Scroll of a Thousand Prayers and is a breath away from summoning the Dragon. We have to stop him, and to do that, we need a plan. Kage…san…" She glanced at me, stumbling over my name. "You said you know where the Master of Demons is headed?"

I nodded. "Tsuki territory," I said. "The islands of the Moon Clan is where the Dragon was first summoned four thousand years ago. The cliffs of Ryugake, on the northern island of Ushima, is where the ritual will take place."

"When?" Taiyo-san asked. "How much time do we have until the night of the Wish?"

"Less than you think," I answered grimly. A quote came to me, though I didn't know from where. Hakaimono's memory was long; he had seen the rise and fall of many eras. *"On the night of the thousandth year,"* I murmured, *"before the dragon stars fade from the skies and concede the heavens to the red bird of autumn, the Harbinger of Change can be called upon by one whose heart is pure."* I paused a moment, then snorted. "As in the case of most legends, not all of it is true. Kage Hirotaka and Lady Hanshou were not entirely 'pure of heart' when it came to summoning the Dragon. That was probably added in the hopes of keeping greedy or evil humans from seeking out the scrolls."

Beside me, Yumeko frowned. "What does it mean by 'dragon stars' and 'red bird of autumn'?"

"They are constellations, Yumeko-san," the noble said, turning to the girl. "Each season has one of the four great holy beasts tied to it. The Kirin represents spring and new life. The Dragon represents summer, for it brings the heavy rains that are essential to the crops. The red bird of autumn is the Phoenix, ready to die and be reborn anew in the spring. And the White Tiger represents winter, patient and deadly as a land covered in snow."

"So, if what Kage-san says is true," broke in the shrine maiden, sounding impatient, "and the Night of the Summoning will be held on the last day of summer…" She jerked up, eyes widening. "That is the end of the month!"

"Less time than we thought indeed," mused the noble, his eyes shadowed. "And Genno already has a head start on us."

"How are we going to get to the Moon Clan islands?" Yumeko wondered.

"Well, hopefully we're not going to swim," the ronin said. "Unless either of you can call up a giant turtle from the sea, I'm guessing we're going to need some kind of boat."

"There are ships in Umi Sabishi Mura that make the journey to Tsuki lands," the Taiyo informed us. "It is a modest village along the coast, but it has quite the impressive harbor. Most of the trade from the Moon Clan islands comes through Umi Sabishi. The problem will not be finding a captain willing to take passengers on to Tsuki lands, but what we will do once we get there."

Yumeko cocked her head. "Why is that, Daisuke-san?"

"Because the Moon Clan is very reclusive, Yumeko-san," the noble replied, "and they dislike outsiders coming to their shores. Visitors need special permission from the daimyo to move freely through Tsuki territory, and we have neither the time nor the means to acquire the necessary travel papers. The Moon Clan is very protective of their land and people, and trespassers are dealt with harshly and without remorse." He raised one lean shoulder. "Or so all the captains will tell you."

"We'll have to worry about that when we get there," the shrine maiden said. "Stopping Genno from summoning the Dragon is our first and only concern, even if we must defy the clan leaders and daimyos to do it."

The noble looked slightly horrified at the thought of defying the daimyo, but said nothing. Beside him, the ronin sighed and shifted to another position.

"It'll take us a couple days to reach the coast," he muttered. "And we have no horses, carts, kago or anything that will make the journey faster. I suppose tomorrow we start walking, and hope we don't run into any demons, blood mages or Kage shinobi still after the Dragon scroll. One assassination attempt was enough, thanks."

I stirred, glancing at Yumeko. "The Kage came after you?"

She looked faintly embarrassed. "Ano… Lady Hanshou asked us to find you," she answered, making my stomach turn. "She sent Naganori-san to find us, and we walked the Path of Shadows to meet with Hanshou-sama in Kage lands. She wanted us to save you from Hakaimono, to drive him back into the sword so you could be the demonslayer again." One of her ears twitched as I raised a brow at her. "I guess this isn't what she was hoping for."

I felt a bitter smile cross my face. Hanshou's relationship with the demonslayers had always been a point of contention in the Kage. It had been Hanshou's decision to train young warriors to use Kamigoroshi rather than have the Cursed Sword sealed away in the family vault where it would tempt no one. The official reason was that this allowed the Kage to manage and control Hakaimono rather than risking the sword falling into the wrong hands. But everyone suspected—though no one would dare suggest—that Hanshou kept the demonslayers around because of the fear they inspired. The Kage demonslayer was trained to be efficient, emotionless and fanatically obedient. A perfect assassin who also shared his soul with a demon. There were whispers in the Shadow Clan that Hanshou kept her position mainly because no one dared challenge her and the pet oni she could unleash at any time.

But even this was only partially true. The real story between Kage Hanshou and Hakaimono went far deeper and was more sinister than anyone could imagine.

"No," I told Yumeko. "This isn't exactly what Hanshou was hoping to achieve. And now that you've failed to contain Hakaimono and find the scroll for her, she'll likely send someone to kill you all."

"Forgive me, Kage-san, but I fear I must ask." The Taiyo

noble turned a solemn gaze on me. "Technically, you are still part of the Kage. Did not your daimyo send you to retrieve the scroll for her? What will you do if that order still stands, or if she commands you to leave no witnesses behind? Will you kill us all to retrieve the Dragon scroll?"

I felt Yumeko stiffen beside me. "I...ceased to be part of the Shadow Clan the moment Hakaimono took control," I told them. It was a sobering realization; I had been part of the Kage my whole life. Since the beginning of the empire, the expectation had been to serve clan and family unflinchingly, without question, for as long as you lived. I'd owed the Kage my loyalty, my obedience, my very existence. If they had given the order to face a thousand charging demons alone, I would have obeyed—and died—without hesitation, as would all loyal samurai. But now I was an orphan. I had no clan, no family and no lord. Like the ronin wandering the empire, dishonored and lost, except I was something even worse.

"My loyalty to the Kage will not come into question," I assured the noble, who still looked concerned. "Lady Hanshou would not risk having dealings with oni, at least not publicly. And I have no intention of returning to the Kage. Not until I find the Master of Demons and make him pay for his betrayal."

The last words emerged as a raspy growl, and a sullen rage flickered to life from within. I was something unnatural and demonic, cast out of my clan, and my existence would either end upon the Kage's blades or with the order to take my own life, but I would kill Genno before I left this world. The Master of Demons would not escape my vengeance; I would track him down and tear him apart, and he would die screaming for mercy as I sent his soul back to Jigoku where it belonged.

"Tatsumi," Yumeko said in a hushed voice as the rest of the circle fell silent. "Your eyes are glowing."

I blinked and shook myself, then gazed around at the others, all of whom looked grim. The Taiyo had gripped the hilt of his sword, and the ronin had eased into a position that would let him spring away and draw his bow. The shrine maiden had reached into the sleeve of her haori, and her dog was bristling and baring his teeth in my direction. I took a slow breath, feeling the rage subside, and the tension around the fire eased somewhat, though it still hung in the air, brittle and uncomfortable.

"Right, no sleep for me tonight," announced the ronin in a forced cheerful voice. Digging in the pack, he pulled out a simple cup and emptied a pair of dice into his open palm. "Who's up for a game of cho-han? It's not complicated, and it'll help pass the time."

The shrine maiden scowled at him. "Isn't cho-han a gambling game?"

"Only if you bet on it."

I rose, causing everyone to glance up at me sharply. "I'll take watch tonight," I said. It was a long walk to the coast, and Genno was far ahead of us. If removing my presence allowed them to sleep, even for a couple hours, so much the better. "Keep doing what you're doing. I'll be outside."

"Wait, Tatsumi." Yumeko started to rise, as well. "I'll come with you."

"No," I growled, and she blinked, lacing her ears back. "Stay here," I told her. "Don't follow me, Yumeko. I don't..."

I don't want you to be alone with a demon. I don't know if I can trust myself not to hurt you.

"I don't need your help," I finished coldly as a flicker of confusion crossed her face. She had done so much and come so far... but it was better if she learned to hate me. I could feel the darkness inside me, a roiling mass of rage and savagery, waiting to be unleashed. The last thing I wanted was to turn on the girl who had rescued my soul.

As I stalked out of the cave into the warm summer night, there was the faintest ripple in the darkness, and the hairs on the back of my neck stood up. On pure instinct, I twisted aside, feeling the disruption of air as something zipped by my face, and *thunked* into the tree behind me. I didn't have to see it to know what it was: a kunai-throwing dagger, the metal black as ink and sharp enough to cut the wings from a dragonfly in flight. I felt blood trickle from a razor-thin gash across my cheek, and annoyance flared into burning, immediate rage.

Glancing into the treetops, I spotted a flicker of movement, a featureless blur drawing back into the darkness, and narrowed my eyes. A Kage shinobi, thinking he could assassinate me from the shadows. Or perhaps intending to lead me into an ambush. I knew my clan. If I didn't take care of this now, more shinobi would follow, like ants swarming a dead cicada, and our nights would constantly be hounded by the shadows.

I curled my lip in a snarl and sprang into the darkness after my former clansman.

I chased him longer than I thought I'd have to, following his scent, the rustle of disturbed branches ahead of me. He was moving fast, leaping through the tree branches with monkey-like grace, barely making any noise as he sprang from limb to limb. On the ground, I was hard-pressed to keep up, so after a few minutes of dodging bushes and tearing through undergrowth, I sprang off a fallen trunk and hurtled into the branches after him.

A trio of kunai came at my face, brief glints of dark metal in the night. I ducked, and one skimmed my shoulder as it flew by and went hissing into the leaves. Growling, I looked up and caught sight of a black-clad figure waiting on another branch, a kusarigama—a weighted chain with a kama sickle attached to the end—spinning in one hand.

I drew Kamigoroshi in a flare of purple light, facing the shinobi across the drop between us. For the briefest of moments, I felt a twinge of reluctance, of regret, at having to kill my former clansman. But the Kage would not relent, and I had sworn to stop the Master of Demons from summoning the Dragon. I could not let them kill me now.

The shinobi waited for me, the kusarigama flashing as he twirled it in an expert circle. It was a deadly weapon, most dangerous at long range; the chain was used to entangle and disarm the enemy while the kama dealt the finishing blow. I had seen them in action but had never faced one myself. They had the stigma of being peasant weapons, something that farmers, monks and assassins would use, not noble samurai. Of course, the Kage shinobi had no such bias.

I narrowed my gaze at the warrior across from me. "Just you, then?" I asked quietly. Something didn't feel right. Often, Kage shinobi were lone operators, silently infiltrating a house or camp to assassinate a target, or to steal important information. However, on extremely risky or dangerous missions, an entire cell would be sent, a whole troop of highly trained spies and killers, to make certain the job was done. Tracking down the most infamous demonslayer in the entire history of the Shadow Clan would certainly qualify as "dangerous." Surely they wouldn't send a single Kage to do the job…

I spun, lashing out with Kamigoroshi, and knocked a pair of kunai from the air with a clang of metal. A second shinobi appeared on a branch behind me, drawing a pair of kama sickles as I turned. At the same time, I felt the cold bite of metal as a chain whipped out and wrapped around my sword arm. The first shinobi pulled the chain taut, drawing my arm back, as his partner leaped at me with both kama raised.

I curled a lip and gave my arm a savage yank. The shinobi on the other end of the chain was jerked off his feet, flew through the air and collided with the second attacker. Both tumbled toward the forest floor, though the first shinobi managed to hang on to the kusarigama, dangling from the chain like a stunned fish. His partner wasn't nearly so lucky, hitting the ground at an awkward angle, and the clear snap of bones cut through the night. He twitched once, limbs flailing, and was still.

With the kusarigama chain still wrapped around my wrist, I

pulled the shinobi up, grabbed him by the throat and slammed him into the tree trunk. He gasped, the first sound I'd heard him make, and I froze. For the voice emerging beneath the cowl and mask was definitely not male.

Reaching up, I stripped away the hood, pulling off the cowl and mask to reveal the face beneath. Dark, familiar eyes glared up at me, and my stomach twisted.

"Ayame?"

The kunoichi stared at me, defiance written across her face, one corner of her lip pulled into a sneer. "I'm surprised you recognized me, Tatsumi-kun," she said in that sardonic, biting voice. "Or, should I call you Hakaimono now?"

I shook my head. Ayame was one of the clan's best shinobi and, a very long time ago, she had been a friend. Perhaps my closest friend. After I'd been chosen to become the new demonslayer, the majutsushi took me away and had me trained in isolation, away from my fellow shinobi and anyone my own age. As the years went by, Ayame and I had grown apart, as children were wont to do, and even after I became the demonslayer we saw each other only in passing. But I still had a few memories of that brief time before, a few recollections even the harsh demonslayer training couldn't stamp out. Ayame had always been eager, defiant and utterly fearless. It made my chest ache that she was my enemy now, that I would very likely have to kill her.

"You were sent after me," I stated. "Did Lady Hanshou order this?"

Her dark eyes flashed, the corner of her mouth curling even higher. "You should know better than that, Tatsumi-kun," she said softly. "A shinobi never gives up their secrets, even to a demon. Especially to a demon." For the briefest of moments, a shadow of pity crossed her face, a hint of the regret that was eating me from the inside. "Merciful kami, you really have become a monster, haven't you?" she whispered. "So this is why the Kage lords are all terrified of Kamigoroshi. I thought *you*, of all people, were too strong to fall to Hakaimono."

Her words shouldn't have stung, but I felt them anyway, like she had jabbed the blade of a tanto beneath my skin. But at the same time, there was a darkness building inside, urging me to kill her, to crush her throat beneath my hands. I could see my reflection in her dark eyes; the red-hot pinpricks of my own gaze, staring back at me. The ends of my fingers had grown curved black claws that were digging into her skin.

"I don't want to kill you," I whispered, and heard the apology in my own voice. Because we both knew death was the only outcome. A shinobi never gave up until its mission was complete. If I let her go, she would only return with reinforcements, putting the lives of Yumeko and the others at risk.

A sad, triumphant smile crossed Ayame's face. "You won't," she said. "Don't worry, Tatsumi-kun. My mission has already been accomplished."

Her jaw moved, like she was biting down on something, and I caught the hint of a sweet, chilling scent that made my stomach roil.

"No!" I squeezed her throat, pushing the kunoichi back into the trunk, trying to keep her from swallowing, but it was already too late. Ayame's head rolled back, and she began convulsing, her limbs twitching in frantic, unrestrained spasms. Her lips parted, and a white foam bubbled out, spilling down her chin and running into the collar of her uniform. I watched helplessly, grief and anger a painful knot in my throat, until the spasms finally ceased, and she slumped lifelessly in my grip, a casualty of blood lotus tears, one of the most potent poisons the clan had at their disposal. A few drops killed instantly, and all shinobi carried a tiny, fragile vial on their person, accessible even if their hands were restrained. Blood lotus tears ensured that the Kage shinobi would never give up their secrets.

Numb, I lowered the kunoichi to the branch and gently leaned her back against the trunk, folding her hands in her lap. Ayame stared sightlessly ahead, dark eyes fixed and unseeing, her expression slack. A trickle of white still ran from a corner of her lips. I wiped it away with a cloth and closed her eyes so it simply looked like she was sleeping. A memory came to me then: the image of a young girl dozing in the branches of a tree, hiding from her instructors. She had been so annoyed when I told her we should go back, and she'd threatened to put centipedes in my blanket if I told our sensei where she had been.

"I'm sorry," I told her quietly. "Forgive me, Ayame. I wish it hadn't come to this."

You really have become a monster, haven't you?

I bowed my head. My former clan sister was right; I was a demon, now. My very nature was to kill and destroy. There was no place for me in the empire, no place for me among the clans, my family and certainly not at the side of a beautiful, naive fox girl who seemed foolishly unafraid of the fact that I could tear her apart with no thought at all.

A breeze stirred the branches of the trees, and I sighed, running a hand down my face. Why had Lady Hanshou sent only Ayame and one other to face me? Ayame was one of the clan's best shadow warriors and answered directly to Master Ichiro, the head instructor of the Kage shinobi. Only the clan daimyo could order such a mission, but Hanshou knew, better than anyone, that a pair of shinobi stood no chance against a demon. And yet, Ayame had said her mission was complete…

I straightened in alarm. Hanshou knew two shinobi wouldn't be able to defeat me, that had never been the objective. Ayame's mission wasn't to kill; she had been a distraction. A ruse to lure me away from Yumeko and the others, leaving them alone in a shadowy cave…

With a growl, I turned and sprinted back through the trees, cursing my idiocy and hoping I wasn't too late.

3

Blades in the Dark

Yumeko

I was worried about Tatsumi.

Not because he was a demon. Or a half-demon. Or had part of a demon soul sharing his mind with him. Actually, I still wasn't sure what Tatsumi was, exactly. And I didn't think *he* knew, either, if he was more oni than human, Hakaimono than Kage Tatsumi. But I wasn't concerned about his demon side. I didn't worry that he would suddenly turn on us in the middle of the night, though I knew his presence made Reika and the others very nervous. None of them, not even Okame, were comfortable having an oni in our midst. Reika would scold that I was being naive, that a demon could not be trusted, that they were evil and treacherous, and that I was foolish for letting down my guard. And maybe I *was* being naive, but I had seen Tatsumi's true soul, the strength and brightness of it, and I knew he would do everything he could not to fall prey to Hakaimono's savagery.

No, I wasn't worried that he would betray us. I worried that his guilt and the fear of what he'd become would prompt him to leave for our safety. That one night, Kage Tatsumi would slip quietly away into the shadows, and I would never see him again. Knowing Tatsumi, he would try to find and confront Genno on his own, and though the demonslayer was incredibly strong, I didn't know if he could single-handedly destroy the Master of Demons and his army of monsters, blood mages and yokai.

Oh, Tatsumi. I would help you, if you would let me. You don't have to face Genno alone. You've been alone long enough.

"Yumeko-chan?"

I blinked and glanced up. Okame sat cross-legged in front of me, one hand on the facedown cup between us, an expectant look on his face. "It's your turn to call," he said.

"Oh." I looked down at the cup beneath his fingers, wondering what to do. I hadn't really been listening when he gave the explanation. "Gomen...what were the rules again?"

"It's easy, Yumeko-chan." The ronin smirked. "You call 'cho' if you think the dice will turn out even, 'han' if you think the numbers will be odd. That's all."

"That's all?" I cocked my head. "This seems like a very simple game, Okame-san."

"Trust me, it's not so simple when there's an empire's worth of coin on the line."

"I don't see any coin. Are we supposed to be using coins?"

"Only if you want to— *Ite!*" Okame winced as Reika reached up and swatted the back of his head again. "Ow, what was that for?"

"Yumeko is capable of turning leaves into money and creating gold from pebbles," the shrine maiden stated calmly. "Do you really want to teach a kitsune about the vices of gambling?"

I had no idea what they were talking about, but suddenly, the hairs on my ears and tail stood up, and a ripple of magic went through the air, cool and dark and familiar. A half second later, the flames in the firepit vanished, like someone had snuffled a candle, and the cave was plunged into darkness.

I scrambled to my feet, hearing my companions leap upright as well, and raised my hand, sending a pulse of fox magic into the air. Instantly, a blue-white flame of kitsune-bi appeared in the palm of my hand, filling the chamber with a ghostly light…

…and revealing the dozen shinobi surrounding us, their dark figures seeming to melt out of the shadows of the cave, blades already raised to strike. For a moment, they froze, as if startled by the sudden flare of light when they had been expecting total darkness. I yelped, Okame shouted and Daisuke spun, his blade clearing its sheath in an instant, beheading the shinobi behind him with his knife raised to cut his throat.

Chaos erupted in the tight confines of the cave. Voices shouted, blades flashed and dark shapes flickered erratically in the light of the kitsune-bi. I threw the ball of foxfire into the air, spun, and came face-to-face with a masked shinobi stabbing down at me with his knife. Jerking back, I collided with someone, hopefully a friend, and threw my hands out toward my attacker. Foxfire roared, and the shadow warrior flinched away, not realizing the ghostly flames couldn't hurt him. Before he could recover, I reached into my obi, grabbed one of the leaves I had stuffed inside and threw it into the air as the shinobi looked up. There was a silent explosion of smoke, and another Yumeko appeared, stepping forward to face the shadow warrior.

The shinobi hesitated a moment, clearly baffled, but then his eyes hardened and he slashed his blade down…at the other Yumeko, who let out a convincing cry of pain before she collapsed, vanishing into smoke as she struck the ground. The black-clad warrior frowned as the illusion writhed away into mist, then glared at me, confusion turning to fury. Raising his sword, he tensed to lunge.

A blade, flaring with purple fire, erupted from his chest, lifted him off his feet and flung him away. I blinked and looked up as

Kage Tatsumi, eyes and horns glowing an ominous red, lowered his sword and met my gaze.

"Are you all right, Yumeko?"

"Help the others," I cried, and he sprang past me with a snarl, cutting another assailant in two, and Kamigoroshi's baleful purple light joined the flickering kitsune-bi on the walls of the cave.

A shout behind me made my stomach drop. I spun, hurling a sphere of foxfire at the nearest shinobi, who had Reika pinned against the wall and was raising his sword. The flames erupted against the side of his head, making him flinch and stagger back, and the shrine maiden thrust an ofuda in his direction with a shout, slamming him into the opposite wall. He bounced off the stones and looked up, just as a glowing blade ripped through his stomach and left him sliding wetly to the floor. Tatsumi continued on, into the midst of the chaos. I tried to follow him, but in the dancing lights, all I could see was frantic movement, the silhouettes of friend and foe darting across the floor, and the flash of metal in the darkness. But, one by one, the shinobi jerked and collapsed, blood spraying the air, as a vengeful demon moved through their ranks like a whirlwind of blades.

The last of the shinobi fell, one sliced apart by Tatsumi, the other beheaded by Daisuke, in the center of the chamber. The two men whirled, still searching for opponents, and their blades met with a screech of metal and sparks. For a heartbeat, they stood there, demon and master swordsman, Tatsumi with his glowing eyes and sword and Daisuke with a blank, glassy expression on his face, both looking entirely dangerous. My heart pounded, wondering, for a split second, if they would continue their fight and cut each other down, if the lure of battle was too much for either of them to resist.

"Uh, Daisuke-san? Kage-san?" Okame's voice broke through the sudden silence. "The fight's over. You can stop glaring at each other anytime."

Slowly, the two lowered their blades and stepped back, though neither seemed eager to relinquish the fight. Daisuke flicked the blood from his sword and nodded to Tatsumi, his expression somber. "You are as fearsome in battle as ever, Kage-san," he stated in a tone of sincere admiration. "Remember, you still owe me a duel when this is finished."

"I haven't forgotten," Tatsumi said quietly, the glow fading from his eyes. "Though are you sure you want to do battle with a demon? Hakaimono is not known for playing by the rules."

"There are no rules in battle, Kage-san," Daisuke replied calmly. "Rules serve only to limit the potential of both swordsmen. When we do fight, please come at me with everything you have."

"Is everyone all right?" Reika demanded, stepping forward with Chu beside her. The dog's hackles stood on end, and his eyes were hard as he glared at the scattered bodies on the cave floor. "We have more important things to discuss than these absurd duels of honor. Yumeko, there's blood on your face. Are you hurt?"

Tatsumi turned swiftly, his gaze meeting mine as I put a hand to my cheek, feeling a sticky wetness against my skin. "No," I said, seeing him slump in relief. "It's not mine. I'm all right. Is everyone else okay?"

"I think we're fine. Though something smacked me on the head pretty hard." Okame stood up, rubbing the back of his skull. He took a step forward, winced and sank to his knees again. "*Ite.* Okay, maybe a bit harder than I thought. Why is the floor spinning?"

Daisuke immediately came forward, concern flicking across his features, to kneel beside him. His long fingers brushed the side of the ronin's face, gently turning his head to the side to reveal a mess of blood at the base of his skull. Okame grimaced, closing his eyes, and Daisuke's concern turned to alarm.

"Reika-san," he said, and the shrine maiden immediately stepped forward and crouched down to peer at the back of the ronin's head. My stomach curled as Reika prodded and examined the wound, making Okame hiss and growl curses under his breath, but after a few moments she straightened with a sigh.

"Nothing life-threatening," she said as I let out a breath of relief. "Lots of blood, but it looks like you took the blunt end of a weapon instead of the sharp one. Not sure how you managed that, but it should heal in a few days. You can be thankful that your head is harder than the palace walls."

"Yokatta," Daisuke breathed, expressing his relief as well, and gave the ronin a faint smile. "You cannot die yet, Okame-san," he said. "Especially not from such a dishonorable, cowardly attack from behind. How are we supposed to meet that glorious death together if you go and die on me before the final battle?"

"Oh, don't worry, peacock." Okame pressed a cloth to the back of his head, grimacing. "It'll take more than that to get rid of me. So far, I've survived a gaki swarm, being eaten by a giant centipede, an oni collapsing a tower on my head and yet another assassination attempt. I'm starting to think Tamafuku himself is watching out for me." He winced, glaring at the still forms of the shinobi in the flickering foxfire. "That *was* a close one, though. Sneaky bastards. Did they come right through the walls?"

"You were lucky." This from Tatsumi, his face grim as he observed the bodies of his former clansmen. "An attack like this is meant to take the targets by surprise and be over in seconds."

"It would have been," Reika said, "if not for Yumeko. Thank the kami that the Shadow Clan weren't expecting a kitsune."

I shivered, observing the bodies on the ground. "I suppose Lord Iesada is still trying to get rid of us," I said, feeling a flare of anger toward the Kage lord. The Shadow Clan noble had sent assassins after us before, when we were on our way to the Steel Feather temple. Reika's mentor, Master Jiro, had been killed in the ambush, and I had not forgiven the arrogant Kage lord for that. If we ever met again, he would come to know the wrath of an angry kitsune.

Tatsumi cocked his head, frowning. "Lord Iesada?" he asked.

"Yeah, the bastard tried this trick earlier," Okame snorted. "You'd think he'd learn, after we slaughtered that unit to a man."

But Tatsumi shook his head. "This wasn't an attack by Lord Iesada," he told us. "Lady Hanshou ordered this."

"Hanshou-sama?" I blinked at him. "But…why? She asked us to find you. She said she wanted us to save you from Hakaimono."

"And you did." Tatsumi nodded. "Your mission was successful…mostly. In her eyes, your usefulness has ended. You know too much about the Shadow Clan now. You've become a liability to the Kage and to her own position."

"So she'll just kill us?"

"Rather than have that knowledge spread to anyone else, yes." Tatsumi gave a grim nod. "Don't let her promises fool you. Hanshou has always been ruthless, willing to do whatever it takes to keep her position secure. She knows you're after the Dragon scroll. That is reason enough to kill you all."

"You don't speak very highly of your daimyo, Kage-san," Daisuke said, sounding as if he wasn't sure if he should be affronted or not. "Such talk would be considered treason among the Taiyo."

One corner of Tatsumi's mouth twisted. "Hanshou and I have a long history," he said, though his eyes flickered like red candle flames, and I knew this was his demon side speaking. "I know things about her that she keeps from her own clan, secrets she hides from everyone. If the Shadow Clan knew all the atrocities she has committed, she would not have lived as long as she has."

I swallowed, deliberately not looking at the bodies strewn about the cave, the blood creeping slowly through the dirt. "So what do we do now?"

"Keep moving." Tatsumi sheathed Kamigoroshi, and the baleful purple light along the sword winked out. "Keep running. Try to stay one step ahead of them. And never let down your guard, especially at night. This won't be the last attack. Hanshou knows where and when the Dragon will be summoned. She'll know we're on our way to Ushima Island right now." His lips curled in a bleak smile, making my stomach churn. "With the night of the Wish so close, she'll be desperate to get the scroll. I expect we'll be dodging the Shadow Clan the entire way to the sacred island."

4

Village of Curses

TATSUMI

I smelled death on the wind before we ever reached the coast.

From the foothills of the Dragon Spine Mountains, it had taken us several days to reach Umi Sabishi Mura, a midsize fishing village at the edge of the Kaihaku Sea. There had been no more attacks from Shadow Clan shinobi, though because of my…appearance, we had to avoid the many villages and settlements we came across on our journey to the edge of the empire. Water Clan territory was lush and fertile, filled with lakes, streams, rivers and rolling hills, and the ruling Mizu family was known for their pacifism and peaceful nature. They were healers and caregivers, skilled in the art of diplomatic negotiation, and the emperor himself had been known to call on the Water Clan to soothe ruffled feathers or talk down an insulted Fire Clan general. But even the Mizu would not tolerate a demon walking freely through their territories, and though they were pacifists, they were also the second largest clan in the empire.

If they discovered my presence, or if they thought Hakaimono had crossed their borders and was threatening their people, having the whole of the Mizu family after us would make our quest nearly impossible.

So we traveled on foot and slept out in the open, or in caves or abandoned buildings where we could, though more often than not our campsite was a firepit beneath the boughs of trees in the forest, or a flat area beside a brook or stream. It was slow progress, avoiding the main towns and roads, and no one slept much, as suspicions of shinobi lurking in the trees and shadows made it difficult to relax. Once, the ronin suggested that we could perhaps "borrow" a few horses from any of the surrounding villages—it was for the good of the empire, after all—but neither the noble nor the shrine maiden would hear of us stealing what we needed. Besides, animals now had a violent reaction to my presence, something we discovered when we tried to obtain a ride with a sake merchant on the road, and his oxen nearly trampled us fleeing when they caught my scent.

So, riding to Umi Sabishi, either by horse or cart, was out of the question.

Finally, after days of travel, the grassy plains ended at the edge of a rocky coastline, jagged cliffs plunging into an iron gray sea. Gulls and seabirds wheeled overhead, their distant cries echoing on the wind, waves crashed and foamed against the rocks, and the air smelled of salt and the ocean.

"Sugoi," whispered Yumeko, her voice full of wonder. Standing at the edge of the cliff, the wind tossing her long hair and sleeves, she gazed with shining eyes at the endless expanse of water stretching away before her. "This is the ocean? I never imagined it would be so big." Her fox ears, swiveled all the way forward, fluttered in the wind as she glanced back. "How far does it go?"

"Farther than you could ever envision, Yumeko-san," the noble answered, smiling faintly. "There are stories about a land on the other side, but the journey takes many months, and most that set out don't make it back."

"Another land?" Yumeko's eyes sparkled. "What's it like?"

"No one really knows. Three hundred years ago, Emperor Taiyo no Yukimura forbade travel to that shore and closed off the empire to any outsiders. He feared that if foreign kingdoms discovered our lands, they would invade our shores, and the empire would be forced to defend itself. So we have remained hidden, isolated and unknown, from the rest of the world."

"I don't understand." Yumeko cocked her head, a slight frown crossing her features. "Why does the emperor fear outsiders so much?"

"Because apparently, the far country is full of barbarians who growl at each other and wear the fur of beasts," the ronin broke in, grinning at the shrine maiden, who wrinkled her nose. "Some of them even have hooves and tails because not only do they wear the fur of their beasts, they also—"

"You do not need to share that bit of information with certain people present," the miko said in a loud, firm voice. "And we have gotten rather far afield of our original goal. Umi Sabishi should not be far from here, is that right, Taiyo-san?"

The noble, his face carefully expressionless, nodded. "That is correct, Reika-san. If we continue south down this road, we should reach it before nightfall."

"Good." The shrine maiden shot the ronin a dark look before stalking away. "Then let us get there quickly," she muttered, her dog trotting along behind her. "Before certain uncouth individuals have a tragic accident along the cliff face and find themselves swept out to sea."

We continued following the road as it wound south along rugged cliffs and sweeping drops to the ocean. Overhead, the sky slowly turned a mottled gray, with distant rumbles of thunder over the sea. Eventually, the cliffs flattened out, becoming a rocky coastline with a few scattered trees twisted and bent with the wind.

"Here, Tatsumi," Yumeko announced as a sudden breeze tossed our hair and clothes. The air had grown heavy and warm, laced with the smell of brine and the approaching rain. The girl held a wide-brimmed straw hat, the kind farmers wore in the fields, and gave me a smile as she thrust it at me. "You might need this."

I shook my head. "Keep it. The rain doesn't bother me."

"It's not real, Tatsumi." Yumeko's smile turned faintly embarrassed as I frowned. "It's an illusion, so it won't stop the rain from hitting you. But since we'll be going into a town soon, I thought it would be better to hide your..." Her gaze flicked to my forehead, and the horns curling through my hair. "Just so people don't have the wrong idea. Okame said something about torches and angry mobs, and that sounds unpleasant."

One corner of my mouth curled. "I suppose we should try to prevent that."

I reached for the hat, surprised when I could curl my fingers around the brim, feeling the rough outline of the straw in my hand. It didn't feel like an illusion, though I knew kitsune magic would manipulate the person to see, hear, even feel what they expected. If I concentrated on the hat itself, knowing it wasn't real, I could suddenly feel the thin edge of a reed in my hand, the anchor that Yumeko had bound the magic to.

With a faint smile, I put the hat on, hiding my demonic marks from the rest of the world, and nodded at the kitsune. "Thank you."

She smiled back, causing an odd twisting sensation in the pit of my stomach, and we continued on.

As evening fell, so did the first drops of rain, growing in strength until it was a steady downpour, soaking our clothes and turning everything around us gray. As Yumeko had predicted, the hat did not keep my head dry; cold rainwater drenched my hair and ran down my back, though being able to see the brim of the hat as the rain hit my face was an odd sensation.

"I think I see the town," the ronin announced. He stood atop a large boulder on the side of the road, peering into the storm with the ocean behind him. "Or at least I see a bunch of blurry shapes that could be a town. I'm going to say it's a town, because I'm sick of this rain." He leaped off the boulder and landed on the muddy path, shaking his head like a dog. "I hope they have a halfway decent inn. I don't normally say this, but I think I could use a bath."

"How amusing," said the shrine maiden as we started down the road toward the cluster of dark shapes in the distance. "I think that all the time."

"I don't know why that is, Reika-san," the ronin shot back, grinning. "You smell quite pleasant most of the time."

She flicked a pebble at him. He dodged.

The path continued, becoming wider and muddier the closer we got to Umi Sabishi. A few isolated farms dotted the plains surrounding the village, but I couldn't see anyone outside or working the fields. Which might've been on account of the rain, but a feeling of disquiet began to creep up my spine the closer we got to the town.

"Interesting that there are no lights," the noble mused, his sharp eyes narrowed as he peered down the road. "Even through the rain, we should be able to see a few glimmers here and there. I know Umi Sabishi is surrounded by a wall. I would expect to see the lights of the gatehouse at the least."

A wooden gate flanked by a pair of watchtowers marked the entrance of the town. The gate stood open, creaking softly in the rain, and both towers were empty and dark.

The ronin gave a soft whistle, gazing up at them. "That's not a good sign."

As he spoke, the wind shifted, and a new scent brought me up short in the middle of the road. Yumeko turned at my sudden halt, eyes questioning as she glanced back. "Tatsumi? Is something wrong?"

"Blood," I muttered, causing the rest of them to stop, too. "I can smell it ahead." The air was drenched with it, heavy with the scent of death and decay. "Something has happened. The town has been compromised."

"Keep alert, everyone," the shrine maiden warned, pulling an ofuda from her sleeve. At her feet, her dog bristled and bared his teeth at the gate, the hackles on his spine standing straight up. "We don't know what's on the other side, but we can assume that it's not pleasant."

I glanced at Yumeko. "Stay close to me," I told her softly, and she nodded. I drew Kamigoroshi, bathing the gatehouse in purple light, and prodded the wooden door with the point of the blade. It groaned as it swung back, revealing the dark, empty town beyond.

Wooden buildings lined the street as we stepped through the gate into Umi Sabishi. Most were simple structures, standing on thick posts a few feet off the ground, weathered by decades of sea air and salt. Stones placed atop the roofs kept them from blowing away in a storm, and there were several buildings that leaned slightly to the left, as if wearied from the constant wind.

There were no people anywhere, living *or* dead. No bodies, dismembered limbs, even bloodstains, though the town itself bore signs of a terrible battle. Screens had been slashed open, walls had been torn down and items lay abandoned in the streets. An overturned cart, spilling its load of fish baskets into the mud, sat buzzing with flies in the middle of the road. A straw doll lay facedown in a puddle, as if the owner had dropped it and was unable to return. The streets, though saturated with water and churned to mud, had been gouged with the passing of dozens of panicked feet.

"What happened here?" the ronin muttered, gazing around

with an arrow nocked to his bow. "Where is everyone? They can't all be dead, we would've seen at least a few bodies."

"Perhaps there was some sort of catastrophe and they all fled the town," the noble mused, his hand resting on the hilt of his sword as he observed the empty streets.

"That doesn't explain the state of the buildings," I said, nodding to a pair of restaurant doors that had been ripped in half, the bamboo frames snapped and the rice paper shredded. "This place was attacked recently. And some of those attackers weren't human."

"Then where is everybody?" the ronin demanded again. "Was this place attacked by an army of oni that ate the townsfolk to a man? There's no blood, no bodies, nothing. You'd think we would see some sign of what happened."

The noble gazed around, and though his voice was calm, the hand resting on his sword hilt gave away his uneasiness. "Should we keep going forward or turn back?"

I looked at the others. "Forward," the shrine maiden said after a moment. "We'll still need a ship if we want to reach the Moon Clan islands. We certainly can't swim there. Let's head for the docks. Maybe there will be someone left who will be willing to let us sail with them."

"Um, Reika-san?" Yumeko's voice, wary and suddenly tense, drew our attention. "Chu is… I think he is trying to tell us something."

We glanced down at the shrine maiden's guardian, and my instincts bristled. The dog had gone rigid as he glared behind us, eyes hard and curly tail up. His hackles stood on end, his lips were curled back to reveal teeth, and harsh growling sounds emerged from his throat.

I looked up the street. A body, blurry and indistinct, was shuffling toward us through the rain. It moved with an awkward, staggering gait, weaving unsteadily on its feet, as if it was drunk. As it drew closer and the growling from Chu grew louder, it resolved itself into a woman dressed in a ragged shopkeeper's robe, a pair of scissors clutched in one hand. A smiling white mask covered her face, the kind used in Noh plays, and she stumbled barefoot through the mud, swaying erratically but still coming right for us.

It was then I noticed the broken haft of a spear shoved completely through her middle, staining one side of her robes dark red. An absolutely fatal wound, but it didn't appear to hurt or slow her down in the slightest.

Because she's not alive, I thought, just as the dead woman lifted her masked face…and suddenly put on a burst of speed, rushing us like a possessed marionette, scissors raised high.

Chu's growls erupted into snarls. The ronin let out a curse and released his arrow; it flew unerringly forward and struck the woman in the chest. She staggered a bit, slipped in the mud and kept moving, letting out an unearthly scream as she came.

The noble's sword rasped free, but I was already moving, Kamigoroshi in hand as the corpse lunged at me with a wail. I lashed out, dodging the scissors as they stabbed down, cutting through the woman's pale white neck. Her head toppled backward as her body kept moving forward several paces, driven by momentum, then collapsed into the mud.

A nose-burning stench rose from the twitching corpse, the smell of blood magic, rot and decay, but no fluids pumped from the hole where the woman's head used to sit. All the blood in her body had already been drained.

Yumeko put both hands to her mouth and nose, as if fighting the instinct to retch. Even the shrine maiden and the ronin looked a bit ill as they stared at the still-quivering body. Silence fell, but through the rain I could sense movement all around us, countless eyes turning in our direction.

"Don't stand there," I snapped, whirling on the group. "We have to keep moving! A blood mage wouldn't raise just one corpse. The whole town is probably—"

A clatter from the teahouse across the street interrupted me. Pale, smiling figures were emerging from the darkened interior, staggering through the doors and crawling from the holes in the walls. Even more stumbled out of the buildings we'd passed, or staggered from the alleys between structures, lurching into the road. The smell of death and blood magic rose into the damp air, as the horde of the smiling dead turned hollow, sightless eyes on us and began swarming into the street.

We fled, heading deeper into Umi Sabishi, the shrieks and wailing of the undead ringing all around us. Smiling, masked corpses shambled into the road, reaching for us with grasping fingers, or swinging at us with crude weapons. The noble and I led the way, the Taiyo slashing at the dead that got too close, severing arms and heads with deadly precision. Chu, transformed into his enormous guardian form, rampaged around us in a blur of red and gold, crushing the bodies in his path or flinging them aside. The ronin's arrows didn't help much; unless beheaded or their legs were taken off, the undead ignored normally fatal wounds and kept coming. But he kept shooting, knocking them back or making them stagger, giving the Taiyo and me more time to cut them down.

Yumeko's fox magic filled the air around us. She never attacked the corpses directly, but multiple copies of the four of us joined the fray, distracting and bewildering the undead, who didn't seem to know the difference. The illusions erupted with small pops of smoke when they were torn apart, but more would always appear, and their presence greatly kept the swarm at bay as we fought our way through the streets.

"Samurai! Over here!"

Through the chaos of battle and the groans of the dead, I thought I heard a voice. Glancing up, I caught a glimpse of a sake house on the corner of the street, wooden walls and barred windows seemingly untouched by the dead. A sugidama, a large ball made of cryptomeria needles, hung over the entrance, its withering brown color an indicator that the sake brewed within was ready to be consumed. A figure peered out of that doorway, one arm beckoning to us frantically. If we could get there, it might be a haven from the corpses swarming the town.

"Everyone!" The noble spared a quick glance at the rest of our party. "This way!" he called. "Head for the sake house!"

More dead crawled from empty doorways and windows, and behind us, a large swarm of smiling, masked corpses staggered into the street.

"Kuso!" swore the ronin, fitting another arrow to the string. "There's no end to these bastards." He started to raise his bow, but the shrine maiden snatched the arrow from the string, making him curse in surprise.

"What—?"

"Yumeko." The miko pointed back the way we'd come. "Block our path. Okame…" She pulled an ofuda from her sleeve, shoved the talisman halfway down the arrow shaft and handed the arrow back to the ronin. "Here. Aim for one in the center. Everyone else, look away."

Yumeko turned, sending a wall of blue-white foxfire roaring up to block the end of the street. At the same time, the ronin raised his bow, the ofuda fluttering along the length of the arrow. I saw the kanji for *light* written on the paper talisman, just as Okame released the string. It flew unerringly down the road and struck the chest of a corpse shambling toward us, a torn parasol clutched in one bloodless hand.

Brilliant light erupted from where the arrow hit the body, sending it and the ones around it stumbling back. "Go!" Reika cried, and we sprinted forward, dodging the reeling undead, until we reached the sake house on the corner. The human I had seen, a smaller man with a soft, rounded face and the finer clothes of a merchant, gaped at us as we came through the door.

"Samurai!" he gasped as I pushed the heavy wooden door shut and the ronin shoved a beam through the handles. "You…

you are not of the Mizu family! Have you come from Yamasura? Are there more of you on the...?"

His gaze suddenly fell on me, and he let out a little shriek, stumbling back a few steps. "Demon!"

"Quiet, fool!" The shrine maiden's voice cut like a whip. "Unless you want the dead outside to beat down the door."

He immediately fell silent, though his face was white as he backed away, clearly torn between fear of the dead outside and the demon in the room with him. I didn't have to look at myself to know the fight had brought out the claws, fangs and glowing red eyes, and that fiery runes were crawling up my arms and neck. And if that pathetic human kept staring at me, I was going to show him he had every right to be afraid.

I caught myself with a shiver. Savagery still pumped through my veins, the desire to rip apart everything that stood against me. Taking a furtive breath, I tried calming the rage inside, forcing it back below the surface. I felt the claws and fangs disappear, the glowing tattoos fade away, but the bloodlust remained, needing only a tiny push to erupt into violence again.

Yumeko stepped forward, hands raised in a soothing manner as the man's frightened gaze flicked to her. "It's all right," she told him. "We're not going to hurt you. We want to help."

"Who...who are you?" the merchant whispered. His gaze darted over all of us, wide and terrified. Chu had shrunk back into a normal dog, and Yumeko's kitsune features were invisible to most, but between the explosions of light from the shrine maiden's ofuda, Yumeko's foxfire and a mythical komainu rampaging around us, we hadn't been subtle. "Have you come to save us?" the man went on, a bewildered look crossing his face for a moment. "I thought...there were more of you."

A groan just outside the door caused us all to fall silent. The merchant turned a white face toward the entrance, then beckoned us farther inside. Swiftly but silently, we moved into the sake house, away from the door and the shuffling dead just beyond. Farther in, more people emerged, peering from corners and behind decorated fusuma panels. Several men and a few women and children, all staring at us with eyes that were both hopeful and fearful. I hung back, keeping to the shadows, as Reika and the others pressed forward. The last thing we needed was for someone to panic and alert the dead swarming just outside.

I felt a presence behind me, and Yumeko softly touched my elbow, sending a shiver up my arm. Silently, she pressed a straw hat into my fingers and continued into the room. Her hand trembled when it touched mine, whether from fear, adrenaline or something else, I wasn't sure, but it made my stomach curl in response. I slipped the hat on, covering the horns, and followed her into the room.

Reika stepped forward, facing the strangers that had edged into the open, and the presence of a shrine maiden seemed to calm them somewhat. "Don't be afraid," she announced, her calm, firm voice soothing the tension. "We're just simple travelers who came to find passage on a ship. Can you tell us what happened here?"

There was a moment of hesitation, and then a woman stepped forward, a small girl clinging to her kimono. "They came from the darkness," the woman whispered. "Last night, the dead swarmed the streets and started killing everyone. Those who fell rose again as corpses and joined in the massacre. We had no chance. The town was overrun in a night."

"Where were the samurai?" the noble asked. "Umi Sabishi is not defenseless. Surely there were guards, warriors, who could protect the town."

"We don't know," another man said. "Everything was chaos. But there are those who claim they have seen corpses with blades wandering the town, so we can only assume most of the samurai fell in the first attack."

"And there are no other survivors?"

"There were two men here earlier," said the woman. "But they left. They said they had to get to their ship at the end of the docks. But…" She trembled, her eyes wide and terrified. "That's where all the dead seem to be congregating. As if they're being drawn to the warehouse down by the harbor. If you go that way, they'll tear you to pieces."

"Oh, well, how lucky for us," the ronin sighed. "The docks are exactly where we need to go. It's as if someone knew we would come this way."

"Someone did," I said.

All eyes turned to me. I was suddenly grateful for the wide-brimmed hat concealing my demon marks, even if it was an illusion. "Do you think Genno is here, Tatsumi?" asked Yumeko.

I shook my head. "Not anymore. But he knows we survived the massacre at the temple. And he knows we're going to the Moon Clan islands to stop him. He's trying to slow us down, or keep us from following. This is the most likely place we would go to find a ship."

"So, this is because of us," Yumeko said quietly.

"No." The shrine maiden frowned, her voice firm. "This is because Genno is a madman with no respect for human life. All the more reason he must be stopped." She glared back at the entrance, dark gaze narrowed. "We need to get to the docks. Maybe there is still a ship that can take us to the Tsuki islands."

"You're leaving?" The woman with the child pressed forward, her voice and eyes desperate. "No, please, you can't leave us like this! We're not warriors. The dead will slaughter us all if they find us here. You must help us."

"I'm sorry." Reika shook her head, her voice sympathetic. "But we are only five, and there is no time. I will pray to the Kami for your safety, but we cannot offer any aid."

"We have to help them, Reika-san."

This, of course, was from Yumeko, who stepped toward the shrine maiden, her own expression pleading. "We're responsible for this mess," she argued. "Genno left these things here for us. We can't abandon these people to die."

"Yumeko." The miko's voice was not nearly as sympathetic as she glared at the kitsune. "We cannot fight an entire town of raised dead. Even if we could somehow slay them all, it would take far too long, and Genno already has a head start on us."

"What if we stopped the source?" Yumeko asked, and glanced at me. "This is blood magic, right? Is there a spell or a talisman that is causing the dead to rise? Could we end the curse that way?"

Once again, all eyes turned toward me. Uncomfortable with the scrutiny, I crossed my arms. "This is blood magic," I confirmed. "And typically, with a curse this strong, a coven or cabal of mages would have to be close by, maintaining the spell. Kill the cabal, and the spell fails. The dead will return to being dead."

"But we don't know where the mages would be," the shrine maiden said. "They could be anywhere in this town."

"Yes," I agreed, "but the greatest concentration of blood magic is where the dead will be drawn to. So, the area swarming with corpses is where we will find the cabal."

"The docks," the peasant woman gasped. "The warehouse. All the dead are coming from that direction. The coven must be there. Please…" She clasped her hands together, gazing at us hopefully. "Please, will you save us? Save us from this curse. I beg you."

"We have to go there anyway, Reika-san," Yumeko said, refusing to wilt as the shrine maiden glared at her. "We'll just take care of a coven of blood mages on the way."

Reika let out a long, exasperated sigh. "I suppose we have no choice now," she muttered, and looked at the rest of us. "If everyone else agrees…?"

"Of course," the noble said immediately. "These are not my lands, but what has been done here is blasphemous and an affront to the empire. Blood magic is punishable by death, and those who engage in such darkness forfeit their life. I will gladly rid the empire of such evil."

The ronin shrugged. "Well, I've got nowhere else to go," he said. "Fighting hordes of the dead seems a fun way to spend an evening. Unless we vote to stay here and make sure all the sake doesn't go to waste…? No? Fine, blood mages it is."

Yumeko glanced at me. "Tatsumi?"

"I'm with you, Yumeko," I answered simply. "Just point me at the cabal, and I'll make sure they die."

Reika shook her head, then turned to the gathered civilians. "Is there perhaps a back door we can sneak through?" she asked. "So we don't attract the attention of the dead outside?"

A few of them nodded. "This way," said the woman, and led us through the sake house to a singular door at the end of a storeroom. "This leads into the alley between the sake house and the restaurant next door," she told us in a hushed voice. "From here, the docks are due west, and the warehouse sits at the south end of the dock. Be careful."

"We'll try our best," Yumeko said.

The woman clutched Yumeko's sleeve. "Thank you," she whispered. "Thank you. Kami protect you all."

She hurried away, leaving us alone in the darkened room. Reika let out another sigh.

"Well," she said softly, glancing at us, "any ideas of how we're going to get past an army of raised dead?"

"Cut a path right through them?" I suggested.

"That's not very subtle, Kage-san." Reika frowned. "And we don't know how many we're dealing with. There could be hundreds of them out there, maybe thousands. We'd be letting the blood mages know exactly where we are."

"I fail to see another way." The miko's jaw tightened, and I shrugged. "Unless you want me to go alone. I can get past them unseen, head to the warehouse and deal with the mages, but I can't take all of you with me."

"No." Immediately, the noble shook his head. "No one goes alone, Kage-san. Not that I doubt your abilities, but we cannot lose you. This is our war. We fight it together."

"Right." The ronin rolled his shoulders back. "So, it's the old kick down the door and slaughter anything that moves approach, after all, is it? Seems to be our favorite. Not sure how many dead things I can kill with a handful of arrows, but at least I'll make a juicy target."

"Wait," came Yumeko's voice, and a ripple of fox magic went through the air. She turned and held something up to her face: a pale, smiling mask that seemed to glow in the darkness. "I have an idea."

5

Fooling the Dead

Yumeko

I opened the door cautiously, peeking through the crack. A quiet alley greeted me. At the moment, it was empty, and I took a furtive breath to calm my heart.

I hope this works.

"Kami, I can't believe we're doing this," Reika whispered at my back. "What makes you think this is going to work, kitsune?"

I glanced over my shoulder. The miko's face was hidden behind the white corpse mask, but I had no doubt she was frowning at me. The others pressed behind her, wearing the same white masks and looking quite dead. Their skin was a bloated gray, their clothes torn and bloody; Okame even had the illusion of an arrow jutting from his back, and one side of Daisuke's long white hair was stained red. A group of masked walking corpses was possibly the grimmest illusion I'd ever had to craft, and the strain of keeping so much fox magic active at once was starting to wear on me, but it was the best solution I could think of.

I gave the shrine maiden a weak smile, even though it was hidden by my mask. "Well, they didn't seem to know the difference between an illusion and the real thing when we first ran into them," I said. "I'm hoping they can't see through fox magic, and that we'll be able to walk right up to the warehouse."

"It's never that easy."

"Maybe it will be this time." I peered up and down the alley, making sure it was still vacant, and nodded. "All right, it looks clear. Just...act like you're dead, Reika-san. Shamble a little."

She glared daggers at me, but I ignored her and stepped into the alley.

Almost as soon as I did, there was a shuffle at the end of the street, and a body lurched into view, hitting the corner of the sake house. It gazed at me with flat gray eyes, and I froze, wondering if it could smell my breath and hear the pounding of my heart, sure indicators that I was not one of the raised dead. But after a long, chilling moment, the corpse turned and staggered away, and I breathed out slowly in relief.

"You are blessed by Tamafuku himself," Reika muttered behind me. "Let's hope that great luck of yours holds until we reach the warehouse."

Carefully, we headed toward the docks, trying to stay out of sight but not *look* like we were trying to stay out of sight. It was almost impossible. Living corpses filled the streets, shuffling aimlessly through the mud or just standing in place, staring at nothing. They didn't appear to notice us as we passed, however; it seemed the illusion, or the presence of the white masks hiding our faces, was working.

Through the cloying stench of blood and decay, I caught the faint, clean smell of the ocean and heard the lapping of waves against the stones. We passed through the space between two buildings, and the docks came into view, a series of long wooden walkways stretching over the water. A few smaller ships and fishing boats bobbed gently closer to shore, and a single large ship sat alone near the end of the docks.

There were a lot more raised dead here, ambling down the docks and even stumbling over the decks of the ships. But the greatest numbers swarmed around a long wooden warehouse at the far end of the docks. I could feel a darkness emanating from the building, a magic that felt like squirming maggots and buzzing flies, the unmistakable taint of blood magic.

I looked to the others, seeking their eyes behind the masks. "What now?" I asked.

Tatsumi met my gaze. "Keep going," he murmured, his voice very low. "The warehouse is our target."

I glanced at the swarms of bodies shambling between us and the distant warehouse, and my skin crawled. There was no way through without having to pass an arm's length from the crowds of dead. A cursory look was one thing, but would my illusions hold up if we got that close? Or if any of them actually touched us?

As we started walking, I reached into my obi and found one of the leaves I had hidden in the folds. I drew it out and released another tiny pulse of fox magic, then let the leaf flutter to the ground, just as the first group of corpses looked up and spotted us.

They didn't react to our presence, not at first. But as we continued on, hugging the edge of the street, more and more heads started to turn. Flat, dead gazes followed me down the road, and as we drew closer to the warehouse, several corpses broke away from the main swarm and stumbled in our direction. I could feel the tension in the bodies behind me, hands dropping to sword hilts, the soft but menacing growls from Chu, as the dead shuffled toward us.

"Looks like the farce is up," Okame muttered, and I saw him reach back for his bow. "So, now the question becomes, how quickly can we get to the warehouse before the entire town swarms us?"

"Wait, Okame-san," I whispered, holding out a hand. "Everyone. Don't do anything yet."

The ronin's eyes frowned at me behind the mask, but he dropped his hand from his weapon. "If you say so, Yumeko-chan," he murmured, and his gaze flicked to the crowds of dead shambling toward us. "But, uh, those dead are still coming. What exactly are we waiting—?"

A scream echoed over the docks. Immediately, all the dead in the area straightened and turned toward the sound. A figure stood at the end of the street, gazing in horror at the living corpses, her eyes wide with fear. She had my face, my clothes and my body, and she shrieked in my voice as she stumbled away from the dead, tripped over her robes and fell to the ground.

With chilling cries and groans, the horde lurched after her, rushing forward like ants descending on a locust body. The fake Yumeko scrambled to her feet, nearly falling again and screaming all the while, then fled with the mob at her heels. As she turned a corner and vanished from sight, I gave a mental command for the illusion to keep running as long as it could and turned to the others, who were watching the dead stream away from us in bemusement.

"Come on, minna! While they're distracted."

Okame gave a snort of laughter, shaking his head, as we started for the warehouse again. "That settles it," he muttered. "When this is over, you and I need to visit a gambling hall, Yumeko-chan. One night, and I'd earn more riches than the emperor."

We approached the warehouse, which was a long stone-and-wood building that appeared to be locked tight. We drew close, and I shivered as the dark magic radiating from within made my skin crawl and my stomach writhe. The double doors stood closed and unguarded, but Reika put out an arm, halting us.

"Wait." Drawing out an ofuda, she hurled it at the doors. When the strip of paper touched the wood, there was a pulse of magic that flared purple-black for a moment, and the ofuda sizzled to ashes. Reika gave a grim nod.

"There's a barrier around the warehouse," she told the rest of us. "Extremely strong blood magic that's either keeping something out, or something in. Either way, we don't want to touch it."

"How do we get in, then?" Okame wanted to know.

"Give me a few minutes," Reika said, pulling another ofuda and holding it between two fingers. "I might be able to dispel it..."

Tatsumi drew his sword. It screeched as it came into the light, causing the hairs on my arms to rise. Without a word, he walked to the warehouse doors and brought Kamigoroshi slicing down across the wood.

The second the glowing blade touched the barrier, there was a shriek, the sound of breaking porcelain and a pulse of energy exploding outward. I cringed, flattening my ears, as the sensation of being covered with writhing, wriggling things flowed over me before scattering to the winds. Reika blinked.

"Or, you could do that," she remarked.

Tatsumi raised a foot and kicked the doors, and they flew open with a crash, wrenching from their tracks and clattering to the floor. Without hesitation, he strode forward, blade pulsing against the darkness, and disappeared through the frame.

"Right," Okame sighed as the rest of us hurried after Tatsumi. "I guess the subtle approach is out."

Reika snorted. "When have we ever tried the subtle approach?"

The interior of the warehouse was dark and warm, the air stale. And as soon as I stepped through the doors, the heavy, cloying stench of rot and blood and decay hit me like a hammer. The reason for this was obvious; bodies were everywhere, stacked along the wall and in corners, some piled higher than my head. Swarms of flies crawled over the bloody mounds, their droning buzz filling the air, and several furry things scampered away from where they were chewing the exposed flesh. I put both hands to my nose and mouth, my insides twisting with horror, and lost my hold on the illusions covering us. With small pops of white smoke, the images of masks and corpses disappeared, and we were ourselves again.

"This is..." Daisuke shook his head, his normally cool, unruffled expression pale with shock "...blasphemy," he finally whispered. "Why would someone do such a thing?"

Tatsumi turned. His eyes glowed red in the dim light, and his horns and claws were fully exposed. Ominous tattoos had appeared on his arms and neck, flickering like they were made of fire. His mouth twisted in a chilling smile that was not in any way Kage Tatsumi. "This is blood magic," he told us. "The more blood, death and suffering, the more powerful the spell. Which means Genno's witches are very close."

"Indeed, Hakaimono," said a new voice overhead. I glanced up as a trio of figures appeared at the edge of the loft, gazing down at us. They were women, or perhaps they had been at one point. The one in front was tall and withered, with black claws curling from her fingers and a yellow glow to her eyes. The other two were more human-looking, though they both bore vivid red scars on their arms and legs, and one of them had a terrible gash down her face and a scarred hole where her eye used to be.

The head witch pointed a long talon at Tatsumi. "We knew you would come, First Oni," she rasped. "You and your companions will not leave this place alive. We will not allow you to interfere with Lord Genno's plans. He will summon the Dragon, and the empire will tremble with his return. But you will die here, as will everyone who stands against the Master of Demons."

She flung out a hand, and a ripple of dark power went through the air. Around us, the piles of corpses started to move. They shifted, roiling together, and then rose, enormous masses of flesh, limbs and bodies, dozens of corpses fused into grotesque, terrible monsters. They lurched and slithered from the piles, numerous hands reaching for us, numerous voices moaning as one.

"Okay, that is disgusting," Okame said, raising his bow. The mounds of corpses were converging on us, a slowly tightening circle. He fired an arrow into one monster's head with a *thunk*. The head slumped, the arrow sticking from its eye socket, but the rest of the groaning faces and reaching arms didn't seem to notice. "We might be in trouble, here."

"Yumeko, get back," Tatsumi said as Daisuke drew his blade and Chu erupted into his real form with a snarl. Stepping forward, the shrine guardian formed the points of a triangle with Tatsumi and Daisuke, with me, Reika and Okame in the center. Heart pounding, I opened my hands, and foxfire flickered to life in my palms, illuminating the horrible faces of the dead looming over us. Tatsumi gave a grim smile and raised his sword. "This is going to get messy."

The corpse mounds staggered forward with muffled groans. I yelped and threw up a wall of foxfire, causing a few of them to flinch back from the sudden light. As they lurched to a halt, Tatsumi and Daisuke lunged through the wall of kitsune-bi and into the midst of the dead.

The corpse mounds bellowed, reaching for them with dozens of hands, clawed fingers grasping. Daisuke spun and whirled around them, his sword a blur, and severed limbs fell twitching to the ground. Tatsumi snarled as he leaped into the air, bringing Kamigoroshi slicing through the middle of a corpse mound, cutting it in two. The bodies made disgusting squelching noises as they slid apart, and an eye-burning stench rose from the pile, making my stomach heave.

Flinging blood from his sword, Tatsumi spun toward another

mound, but the limbs of the severed corpse pile twitched, then rose again as two smaller, separate entities that reached for him once more. A few feet away, Daisuke was struggling to keep distance between himself and a pair of corpse mounds; no matter how many limbs he cut off, how many heads he dismembered, the piles kept coming.

"Yumeko!"

Reika's voice rang out, sharp and frightened. I turned just as a shadow fell over me from behind, a dozen hands clawing at me from every angle. I let out a yelp and sent a wave of foxfire into the monster's many faces, causing it to flinch, but not stop. A cold, clammy hand grabbed my wrist, dragging me forward, and I cried out in disgust and horror.

"Purify!"

An ofuda sped past my head, sticking to the putrid mass of the monster who'd grabbed me, and with a burst of spiritual light, part of the mound was flung apart. I stumbled back, the fingers of the severed arm still clinging to my wrist, as the corpse pile howled and reformed into a smaller mound of dead. It lurched forward again, but the enormous crimson bulk of Chu slammed into it with a roar, shoving it back.

"Ew, ew, ew." I shook my arm rapidly, dislodging the fingers still curled around my wrist. "This isn't working, Reika-san," I gasped. Behind me, I heard Tatsumi's furious snarl and the squelch of his blade tearing through the mounds of corpses, and I saw the flash of Daisuke's sword as it carved through limbs and bodies, but there were always more. "How do we kill things that are already dead?"

"The corpses are only puppets," Reika snapped, ducking as a pale hand clawed at her. "Kill the puppet masters, and you cut the strings."

"Oh!" Understanding dawned. I looked up at the witches, standing at the edge of the loft and smiling down at us, then to

Okame, who met my gaze through the lurching dead things. "Okame-san!"

"On it!" Without hesitation, the ronin raised his bow and fired three rapid shots at the trio of blood mages overhead. The arrows flew unerringly for their targets, but right before reaching them, they struck an invisible wall of force that sent them spinning away. For a moment, a barrier flickered into sight, surrounding the blood mages in a black-red dome, and the head witch let out a cackle.

"Fight and struggle all you want, pathetic mortals," she hissed. "No one will stop Lord Genno's glorious return."

"Reika-san!" I called, leaping back and blasting a corpse in the face with foxfire to little effect. "There's a barrier—"

"I saw." The miko cast a glare of pure annoyance at the witch trio before pulling an ofuda from her haori. "I just need a minute," she said, holding the slip in two fingers and bringing it to her face. "Keep them off me until then."

"Minna!" I called, as Chu lunged between his mistress and a pair of corpse mounds shuffling toward her. "Everyone! Protect Reika-san!"

Immediately, Tatsumi and Daisuke fell back to flank the shrine maiden, while Okame, Chu and I covered the front. Really, it was mostly Chu, who had become a roaring, raging whirlwind of teeth and claws, striking out at any dead thing that got too close. Snatching a pebble from the floor, I tossed it toward the corpse mounds, and a second komainu appeared, snarling and lashing out with enormous paws, adding to the confusion and chaos. Reika closed her eyes, murmuring words under her breath, and the paper in her hand started to glow.

"Enough of this foolishness." Above us, the head witch raised a bloody claw. "It is time for all of you to die. Destroy them," she called, and the corpse mounds seemed to swell and become even more grotesque, new arms and faces emerging through the putrid bodies. They lurched forward and one of them fell on

Chu, the komainu snarling as he was buried under a mountain of rotting flesh and grasping hands.

Okame swore, releasing an arrow that hit the corpse mound lying on Chu and sank halfway into the putrid flesh, but did nothing else. "Kuso!" he spat again, and pulled another arrow from his quiver, but Reika suddenly reached out and snatched the arrow from his hands.

"What—?"

"Not the corpses," she snapped. Raising the faintly glowing ofuda, she shoved the talisman halfway down the arrow shaft and tossed it back at him. "The witch, ronin. Shoot the witch!"

The corpse mounds closed in, hands flailing, stench overpowering. Okame leaped back, raised his bow and sent the arrow streaking toward the head witch gloating down at us. As before, the dart struck the barrier, but this time the arrowhead seemed to punch through the crimson dome, the ofuda glowing blindingly bright. With the sound of breaking porcelain, the barrier shattered, eliciting cries of alarm and fury from the witches as they flinched back, raising their arms.

"Curse you!" the head witch hissed and glared down at us, but Tatsumi sprang to the top of the ledge with a snarl, and the witch had just enough time to shriek in terror before she was split apart by Kamigoroshi. The other two gave cries of alarm and tried to flee, but the raging demonslayer struck them down before they took three steps, and their severed bodies thumped wetly to the wooden planks.

A shudder went through the air. Slowly, the corpse mounds stopped moving and began falling apart as the bodies went limp and slumped to the floor. Chu wriggled his way free from the motionless pile of corpses, shook himself violently and padded back to Reika, who was observing the now truly dead bodies with a look of disgusted triumph.

Okame took a deep breath. "You know, ever since I met you people, I've seen a lot of weird things," he announced, curling a lip as he gazed around. "Hungry ghosts, demons, giant centipedes that want to eat you. I thought it couldn't get any worse, that I had seen it all." He shook his head. "Apparently I was very, very wrong."

"Is everyone all right?" I asked as Tatsumi dropped from the platform, his eyes still shining a bloodthirsty red, his claws, horns and fangs fully visible. His gaze met mine, and I shivered at the cold fury glimmering within, but forced myself to face the demon staring back at me. "That should be the end of it, right? The curse should be lifted now that the coven is dead."

For a moment, the demonslayer watched me, an eerie, contemplative look on his face, as if he was considering springing forward and plunging his sword through my middle. But then he shook himself, and the demonic features faded as he turned away, gazing out the warehouse doors. I followed his gaze and saw that the street was strewn with bodies, lying motionless where they had fallen. A heavy silence hung in the air, and I felt my stomach churn as I stared at the piles of corpses. So much death and destruction, all because the Master of Demons didn't want us following him to reclaim the scroll.

"By the Harbinger's fickle whiskers, you did it!"

We turned. A man stood in a door on the opposite side of the warehouse, gazing at us and then the mounds of dead with wide eyes. He wasn't samurai, wearing rough but sturdy clothes, and his skin was leathery from the sun.

"My men and I were watching you," the stranger went on as another pair of rough, sun-blasted humans poked their heads inside and stared at us. "Saw you magic your way through the doors, then heard an awful commotion from inside. We've been stuck here for days, trying to figure out a way to get past the hordes of dead. I don't know who you are, strangers, or what sorcery you used to break the curse on this town, but I'm truly grateful."

"Who are you?" Tatsumi asked.

"Oh, my apologies." The man offered a quick bow, and the rest of his men did the same. "I am Tsuki Jotaro, first mate of the *Seadragon's Fortune*." He paused, his brow creasing with a painful memory. "Well, actually, now that Captain Fumio is dead, I suppose I am the new captain. We had stopped here to trade with Umi Sabishi when the town began swarming with the dead and we were unable to get to our ship. Now that you've dealt with the problem, we can finally return home."

"To Tsuki lands," Daisuke confirmed, as if he couldn't believe our good fortune.

Jotaro nodded. "As soon as I can find and gather the rest of my crew," he said. "We cannot leave this cursed place fast enough. But, whoever you are, you have my eternal gratitude, strangers. You saved this town, my crew and my ship. If I can be of any help, you have only to ask."

"Actually..." Reika stepped forward, smiling. "There is something you can help us with."

6

In the Crow's Nest

TATSUMI

I did not enjoy being on a ship.

Not because of the ocean, or the constant rocking of the ship itself. I was a strong swimmer and had been trained on all manner of unsteady platforms since I was young. Seasickness had never been a concern for me, unlike the ronin, who had been consistently and loudly miserable ever since we'd set sail from Umi Sabishi Mura.

It was the notion that I was, essentially, trapped on a small vessel with several other souls, and there was no escape—for anyone—should I get the sudden, bloodthirsty desire to slaughter them all. I could feel those urges now, that hunger for violence and carnage that never went away. I had spent the past day and most of the night in the crow's nest, far removed from the crew and the rest of my companions, so my demonic nature wouldn't be tempted to indulge in a killing spree.

Don't lie to yourself, Tatsumi, whispered a voice inside that wasn't entirely my own. *You're hiding...from* her.

I shut the voice out, closing my eyes, but I couldn't escape the truth of it. *Yumeko.* I *had* been thinking of her a lot lately. Ever since the terrible night when she had freed my soul from the demon possessing it, the fox girl was all I could think about. I worried for her in battle and felt hollow when we were apart. Even now, though I knew she was safely below on the ship, I ached to see her, to hear her laugh. I wished...

Wishing is for fools, Tatsumi. Ichiro's voice echoed in my head, cold and logical, repeating one of the many tenants of the Kage demonslayer. *Wishing for what cannot be only weakens your resolve. You are the Kage demonslayer. You must never waver, you must never question yourself, or you and everyone around you will be lost.*

"Tatsumi? Are you up here?"

My heart leaped as the familiar voice that had been haunting my thoughts for days on end sounded directly below. Across from me, four slender fingers curled over the edge of the crow's nest, just before a pair of black-tipped ears poked over the rim and Yumeko's face appeared, her hair streaming behind her in the strong wind. She spotted me, and her lips curved into a smile.

"There you are! I've been looking everywhere for you." She pulled herself up the side and half crawled, half fell into the basket, wincing as her forearms hit the floor of the crow's nest. "Ite. Well, that was exciting. I don't think I've ever been so terrified to look down. Even the old camphor tree in the forest near the Silent Winds temple wasn't this tall." Still on her knees and clutching one of the ropes with both hands, she peeked over the edge of the basket, and her ears flattened to her skull. "We are certainly very high up, aren't we? I hope Reika doesn't get too cross if I decide to stay here all night."

"What are you doing here, Yumeko?" I asked, not moving from my place against the side of the basket. Seeing her made my heart pound, but whether from excitement, fear or something else, I couldn't tell.

"I was worried." The girl scooted around the mast toward me, never letting go of the ropes or the edges of the crow's nest. "I haven't seen you in nearly two days, and no one else could find you, either. I thought you might have...decided to leave."

I frowned. "We're in the middle of the ocean," I pointed out, gesturing to the endless expanse of water surrounding us, glimmering in the moonlight. "Where would I go?"

"I'm not a shinobi." Still on her knees, she scooted closer, her knuckles white from gripping the ropes. "I didn't know if you had some secret Kage magic that let you become a fish or something. *Eee.*" A gust of wind tossed her sleeves and made the basket sway, and she closed her eyes, hugging the mast. "Well, that decides it. I'll be staying right here until we get to Moon Clan territory. It shouldn't be long until we reach the first island, right?"

It was now fairly crowded in the crow's nest, as the basket wasn't meant to hold more than one person. I sighed and got to my feet, gazing down at the girl still wrapped around the mast. "Give me your hand," I told her, holding out my own. She reached for me, stretching out her arm and grasping my palm, but kept one arm wrapped around the wooden post. "Let go of the mast, Yumeko," I told her, and her ears flattened again. "Trust me," I soothed, keeping a steady grip on her hand. "I won't let you fall."

She nodded and gingerly let go of the post. I drew her upright, but as she stood, a vicious blast of wind caused the sails to snap wildly. Yumeko winced, looking like she wanted to glue herself to the mast again, but I pulled her forward so that she was braced against me, one hand clutching my shoulder for balance while the other gripped my fingers like a vise.

"Get your feet under you," I told her softly. "Bend your knees and feel the rhythm of the waves as they move. Sway with the ship instead of letting it toss you around."

"This is certainly not like climbing the camphor tree," she muttered, staring fixedly at the fabric of my haori as she found her balance. "Even when the tree swayed, there were branches everywhere that you could grab if you slipped. Right now, there is nothing but air between me and a very long drop to the planks. Reika will probably lecture me if I break my neck falling from the mast."

"You're not going to fall," I said. "Relax, and feel the ship move. Once you're comfortable with the rhythm, it will be easy to climb back down."

She straightened, finally lifting her gaze. Atop her head, her fox ears pricked forward, and her posture relaxed against me. "Oh," she whispered, sounding awed. "You can see the whole ocean from up here." She gazed around at the glittering black expanse, the waves rippling silver beneath the moon, and drew in a slow breath. "It really does go on forever, doesn't it?"

Her fingers brushed my skin, trailing a line of heat across my arm, and my heart thumped in my ears. I was suddenly very aware that we were all alone up here, far removed from our companions and anyone who might see us. Not only that, our bodies were very close. I could feel Yumeko's slender form leaning slightly into me for balance, the softness of her under my fingers. In the past, having someone so near had made me highly uncomfortable and desperate to put distance between us; now I was filled with a terrifying, incomprehensible urge to pull her closer. "You should go back down," I said gruffly. "Ushima Island isn't far. We're scheduled to pull into the port of Heishi at dawn."

She nodded absently, still gazing over the water, the moonlight reflected in her eyes. "Everything is so big," she murmured, as if loath to speak any louder. "It feels like we're the only things out here. Just a tiny fleck between the ocean and the sky. It makes you realize how small and unimportant you really are. Like you're a bug who is trapped in a spiderweb, and you're fighting so hard, thinking that you're caught in this grand, life-or-death struggle, but really, you're just a bug." She paused, a faint smile crossing her face. "That was one of Denga's sayings. I never used to understand what he meant, but now… I think I get it."

With a sigh, she tilted her head back and looked up at the stars. "I feel like a bug right now, Tatsumi," she whispered. "How am I supposed to stop Genno, his army or the coming of the Dragon? I'm not that strong."

"I'll be your strength," I told her softly. "Let me be your weapon, the blade that cuts through your enemies. I can do that much, at least." She shivered against me, and my heartbeat picked up in response. "Strength isn't the only key to winning a battle," I said. "You told me that yourself, remember? You have other ways to fight, Yumeko."

"Fox magic," Yumeko murmured. "Illusions and tricks. I don't have real power like you or Reika. I'll try, Tatsumi. I'll fight as hard as I can, but Genno already knows what I am—how useful will my magic really be?"

"Enough to defeat an oni lord," I said, "the strongest demon Jigoku has ever known. Enough to keep the scroll hidden from the Kage demonslayer while traveling across half the country, and to stay alive when the immortal daimyo of the Shadow Clan wishes to kill you. And to make a Kage lord screech and dance like a marionette when an illusionary rodent scurries up his hakama." The last bit made her chuckle, and it made me smirk, as well. I'd heard about Lord Iesada's infamous tea ceremony from the ronin, and the disgraceful, hilarious way it had ended. I'd met the Kage lord only once, and though my human half was used to the casual arrogance and pomp of the nobles, my demon nature wanted to peel the haughty expression from his face and feed it back to him.

I sobered. "Enough to save a human soul from Jigoku, and an oni's from being trapped in a sword for eternity," I finished. Golden fox eyes met mine, and my heart gave a strange sideways lurch.

Chilled, I turned away, telling it to be still, to feel nothing. Gripping the edge of the crow's nest, I stared out over the water. What was I doing? Every time Yumeko was this close, my guard would drop and my emotions were in danger of being exposed, which was how I'd lost myself to Hakaimono the first time. I was even more dangerous now, with my demon side unrestrained and so close to the surface that I could feel the anger and bloodlust simmering inside.

"Though you might come to regret that decision, once Genno is dead," I told the kitsune at my back. "You might have saved Tatsumi, but you also saved a demon. Hakaimono is still here, don't ever forget that."

I felt her watching me, the wind tugging at our hair and making the platform sway. "Gomen, Tatsumi," she said at last, making me frown in confusion. "I didn't even ask if you wanted to become a demon. Do you wish I hadn't saved you?"

"No," I husked out. "I'm glad I'm here, that I have a chance to redeem myself by stopping the Wish and killing Genno. But… I can't trust myself not to turn on everyone, enemy or friend." Before, I could shut out Hakaimono's anger and bloodlust because they weren't mine. I had been trained to detach myself from all emotion, so I could control it. Now that viciousness was a part of me. Once I started killing, I might not be able to stop.

"I'm not afraid."

Fear and anger flickered. She still didn't understand what I was, what I could really do. *Enough of this, Tatsumi. If you truly care for the girl, you'll put a stop to this game right now. You're a demon; you have no business hoping for anything. And if this continues, the day will come when you turn on her and she won't see it coming. End this, once and for all.*

Turning around, I let the rage bubble to the surface, the fury and bloodlust that was always there now, burning through my veins. I felt my horns grow red and hot, casting Yumeko's face in a crimson glow. I felt fiery runes and symbols erupt along my arms and crawl up my neck, shining through my haori. As obsidian talons slid from my fingers, and curving fangs sliced up from my jaw, I stared at Yumeko and narrowed my eyes, which I knew were glowing a sullen red.

Yumkeo's eyes widened, and she shrank back. For a moment, she stared at me, at the demon that had appeared on the platform with her. I kept my glare hard, dangerous, letting her see the bloodlust kept barely in check, ignoring the weary despair gnawing my insides. I didn't want to do this to her. Yumeko was the first person who had ever seen me as something more than the Kage demonslayer, more than just the sword I carried. I hated that she would remember me like this: a demon. An oni lord, vicious and irredeemable. But it had to be done. Better to get this over with, that she learn to fear and hate me now, than wait for the day I inevitably betrayed her.

"This is what I am now," I said coldly, letting Hakaimono's harsh growl permeate my voice. "This is the merging of a demon and a human soul. I am grateful for what you did, Yumeko. Never think otherwise. But you should stay as far from me as you can. Otherwise this might be the last thing you ever see."

Yumeko blinked, and her ears flattened to her skull. A strange expression crossed her face, one of defiance and determination, as if she were gathering all her reserves of courage. Before I had realized what was happening, she strode one step forward, took my face in both hands and kissed me.

What—?

Stunned, I went rigid, instantly losing my hold on the searing anger and bloodlust. Claws and fangs retracted, and the glowing symbols on my arms faded, dissolving to embers on the wind.

My hands rose to grip her shoulders, feeling her body press close to mine, the rapid thudding of her heart against my chest.

It didn't last long, the brief, gentle touch of her lips on mine. Just enough to completely turn my world upside down and leave me reeling before she pulled back. Dazed, I stared down at the kitsune, whose piercing golden eyes, open, determined and still completely unafraid, peered up at me.

"I trust you." The words were a whisper into my soul. The tips of her thumbs brushed my cheek, unbearably tender, and I closed my eyes against the softness. "Oni or human, it doesn't matter how your appearance changes. Your soul is still the same. I'm not afraid, Tatsumi, I can't say it any clearer than that."

"Yumeko." Opening my eyes, I gazed down at the girl, gently curling my fingers around her wrist. She watched me, inhuman, naive, perfectly beautiful. She was going to be the death of us both, and I suddenly didn't care.

"Oiiiiiiii!" A shout came from below. "You in the crow's nest! Eyes to the ocean! Can you see anything strange?"

A growl rumbled in the back of my throat, but I released Yumeko and pulled away, then glared down at the bottom of the mast. One of the sailors stood there, pointing frantically at the side of the ship.

"Something is out there!" he yelled as Yumeko also peered down, fox ears swiveling and curious. "In the water! It might be circling the ship, but we can't make it out. Do you see anything up there?"

I looked over the black, glittering expanse of ocean, and a chill slid up my spine.

There *was* something in the water. Something huge. I could see a massive shadow gliding just below the waves, the rising bump of water as it approached the ship. Instinctively, I went through my list of large sea dwelling yokai and bakemono—ushi oni, koromodako and the enormous umibozu—and none of them were things I wanted to meet in the middle of the ocean.

"What is that?" Yumeko wondered, her voice barely above a whisper, as if she were afraid anything louder would draw the shadow's attention. I didn't reply, fearing I knew the answer, desperately hoping I was wrong.

The bump grew larger, rising into the air as it drew close. With an explosion of seawater and the roar of a tsunami, something dark and massive emerged from the depths and loomed to a terrifying height as it towered over us. A humanoid figure, but black as night, with no discerning features except two glowing eyes in its smooth, bald head. Those eyes fixed on us as the monster stared down at us in the crow's nest, its lanky form taller than even the ship's mast. Yumeko gasped, and I cursed under my breath as my suspicions were confirmed. This was *not* what we needed right now.

"Umibozu!" someone screamed from the deck, a frantic voice ringing into the night.

Instant panic swept the ship as every sailor's greatest fear—meeting the monstrous creature known as the umibozu in the middle of the ocean—was realized. Almost nothing was known of them—what they were, how they lived, if there were numerous umibozu deep in the ocean depths or if the huge, hulking form facing us now was the only one of its kind. It was unknown why the umibozu appeared when it did. It never spoke, made no demands nor gave any indication of what it wanted. But no ship survived an encounter with an umibozu; the giant creature, whatever it was, would rise out of the sea, smash a vessel to kindling and simply vanish into the depths once more.

Yumeko drew in a shaky breath as the umibozu stared at us, silent and unfathomable. Its huge head was nearly at eye level, though I couldn't see my reflection in that flat, pale gaze. I could feel the fox girl trembling against me, though she stood firm beneath the alien stare.

"Um...hello," Yumeko said softly, as the giant creature continued to observe us like insects. "We're sorry if we've trespassed where we don't belong. I don't suppose you're here to point us in the right direction, are you?"

Without a sound, the umibozu raised a giant, shadowy arm and smashed it toward us.

7
The Umibozu

Yumeko

Tatsumi grabbed me around the waist and leaped out of the crow's nest, making me yelp in surprise as we sprang into the air. Grabbing one of the dangling ropes, he swung toward the deck, as behind us, the snap of timber echoed at my back. Tatsumi dropped to the deck amid screaming, panicking sailors and immediately spun, drawing Kamigoroshi in a flare of purple light. Pieces of the mast crashed to the deck, rigging and wooden planks clattering around us, adding to the pandemonium.

"Find the others!" he snarled, as the monstrous bulk of the umibozu turned. "I'll keep it distracted for as long as I can."

"Tatsumi—"

"Don't worry about me—I'll meet you in Ushima. Go!"

With a howl, Tatsumi sprang for the shadowy monster, dodging humans as he raced across the deck. The umibozu raised an enormous arm and brought it crashing down, palm open like it was trying to squash a spider. At the last moment, Tatsumi threw himself to the side of the giant's hand, which struck the ship deck with the snapping of wood and splintering of planks. The ship rocked violently, nearly knocking me off my feet, and the screams of the humans grew louder.

Snarling, Tatsumi sprang for the shadowy arm as it was rising into the air again, and slashed Kamigoroshi across its wrist. A dark, watery substance sprayed from the umibozu's arm, and the monster jerked, still making no sound, though its eyes, fixed on the demonslayer, now held a shadow of anger.

"Yumeko!"

I heard the arrival of our companions and spared them all a quick glance as they joined me on the shattered deck. Daisuke had his sword drawn, Okame his bow and Reika was clutching an ofuda, their faces pale as they stared up at the looming umibozu.

"Kuso," the ronin breathed, sounding awed and horrified as he craned his neck back. "What the hell is that?"

"Umibozu." The shrine maiden's voice was resigned. "Great Kami, of all the creatures to meet on the way to the island..." She trembled, then shook herself and turned to the rest of us. "There's no beating that thing. The ship is doomed, and everyone knows it. We have to find the lifeboats and get out of here, now."

"What about Tatsumi?"

A shadow fell over the deck, as the umibozu raised one giant arm and brought it smashing down again. The boat bucked like a wild horse, and I collapsed to the deck. Its second arm swept down, hitting the mast, and the thick pole snapped like a twig and crashed to the deck, crushing two sailors beneath it.

"Abandon ship!" someone screeched in the swirling chaos. Wincing, I looked up to see the umibozu casually backhand a trio of sailors off the deck. They flew through the air, screaming, and plummeted into the dark waters below. I could no longer see Tatsumi through the scrambling mass of sailors around us, and worry for him twisted my stomach.

"Come on, Yumeko-chan!" A firm hand gripped my elbow,

pulling me upright. Okame's face was grim as he set me on my feet and held me steady as the ship bounced and shuddered. "This boat is going down—we need to get the hell out of here before it's too late."

I bit my lip, glanced once more at the enormous umibozu, and made a split-second decision.

"Keep going, I'll catch up!"

"Yumeko!" Reika cried as I broke away from Okame and ran toward the bow of the ship. Toward the huge umibozu looming at the front.

As I drew closer, dodging sailors and humans going the other way, I could see the glow of Kamigoroshi beneath the shadow of the umibozu. I saw Tatsumi, his face set and determined, plant his feet as the giant's hand descended toward him, palm open like it was going to squash him like a bug. As the limb came down, he braced himself and stabbed Kamigoroshi over his head, and the point of his blade impaled the umibozu's palm and tore through the back. The force of the blow still smashed the demonslayer to the deck, the wood breaking and splintering beneath him. A jet of what looked like ink sprayed from the umibozu's hand, but it didn't jerk back or pull away. As I watched, heart pounding, the long fingers curled around the demonslayer and raised him into the air.

Terror shot through me, and somewhere deep inside, an icy flame roared to life, igniting in the pit of my stomach. My hand opened, a sphere of kitsune-bi flaring to my fingers. It burned white-hot against my skin, warping the air around it, brighter than anything I had conjured before. With a cry, I threw it at the monstrous form of the umibozu.

The globe of foxfire struck the monster's elbow and exploded, and for the first time, a noise emerged from the previously silent umibozu. A wail like the howl of a typhoon or the screams of a hundred drowning men echoed into the night. It turned on me, dropping Tatsumi to the deck, the demonslayer forgotten.

Bloodied and torn, Tatsumi struggled to his feet, his eyes widening as they met my gaze.

Overhead, the umibozu raised both fists and brought them down with the force of a lightning strike. The ship lurched violently, and I was thrown off my feet, splinters and wood flying around me, stinging like hornets where they hit my skin. Twisting through the air, I saw deck rushing up at me and braced myself, covering my face with my arms.

I hit the shattered planks and rolled, the ground spinning wildly, before I came to a breathless, dizzy halt on the deck. Wincing, hoping the nausea would fade soon, I tried pushing myself to my elbows, but a searing pain ripped through my side, like someone had jabbed the point of a knife between my ribs. I gasped, my hand going to the spot where the pain originated, feeling the rough edges of a long piece of wood jutting from my skin. When I pulled my hand away, my fingers were smeared with something shiny and dark.

Not good, Yumeko. My mind whirled, confused, knowing I was hurt but refusing to accept that I could be dying. *Get up. Find...find Reika. She'll know what to do...*

"Yumeko!"

Tatsumi's voice rang across the deck, angry and almost desperate. I looked up...just in time to see the umibozu drive its fist through the top of the ship. The vessel bounced wildly as it was ripped apart, and the planks beneath me disappeared. I plummeted into the darkness, terror rising in my chest, before I struck the ocean and the icy waters closed over my head.

The currents dragged me under, and I couldn't find the strength to claw my way back to the air. I was sinking, cold and paralyzed, watching the surface get farther and farther away. Blackness crawled on the edges of my vision, a swarm of insects closing in, but looking up once more, I thought I could see a purple glow, coming steadily closer.

Then the darkness flooded in, and I knew nothing else.

PART II

8

Entering the Game

Suki

Suki had never known that the ocean could stretch on forever.

Her mother had spoken of it sometimes, in the years before she died. Originally, she had been from Kaigara Mura, a tiny coastal village in Water Clan territory. When she'd told stories of her childhood, they would be of a white beach full of seashells and the glittering expanse of water that stretched to the horizon. Having lived her whole life within the high walls and crowded streets of the Imperial City, Suki couldn't have imagined what that would be like.

Now, seeing nothing but water in every direction she looked, she concluded that it was terrifying.

"I love the ocean," Taka sighed. He sat in the open door of the flying carriage, his short legs dangling in open air, as they soared over the endless expanse of water. The interior of the gissha, the ox carriage, was boxy and windowless, with enough room to stand without hitting your head on the ceiling. The bamboo doors at the back were usually closed, but now hung open, revealing blue sky and floating clouds. Normally, these types of lacquered, two-wheeled carriages were pulled by a single ox and were reserved for the highest of nobility. Certainly, the ghost of a simple maid and a small talkative yokai did not qualify, but the owner of the carriage, Lord Seigetsu, did not seem to mind their presence, so she did not question it.

Taka took a deep breath, the corners of his mouth curling up. "I love the way it smells, too," he sighed. "Like fish and salt and rain." Glancing up at her, the little yokai with the clawed hands and single enormous eye grinned toothily, his fangs glimmering in the dim light of the carriage. "Aren't you glad you came back, Suki-chan? You would have missed all of this."

Suki managed a weak smile, and Taka returned to watching the waves. Turning from the open doors, she glanced back at the figure in the corner, seated cross-legged with his back to the wall and his eyes closed. Lord Seigetsu, the man she had followed from the Imperial City, across the Sun lands, to the tallest peaks of the Dragon Spine Mountains. Why she, a wandering spirit with no tie to the world, had chosen to travel across the empire with a beautiful, mysterious stranger and a one-eyed yokai, she still wasn't certain. Perhaps it was because she was still curious about Lord Seigetsu. With his long silver hair and strange powers, he remained just as enigmatic as the night she had met him. Perhaps it was because he could, with Taka's aid, see parts of the future. And even more disturbing, he had told Suki that she herself had a very important role to play in upcoming events.

This frightened Suki greatly. She was the ghost of a simple maid, insignificant and unimportant. At least, she thought she was; the memories of her previous life were becoming hazier with every passing day. She couldn't recall much of her old life now. If she thought hard about it, she remembered her father, the house they'd shared and her final days as a maid in the Imperial Palace. But those memories were painful, and Suki did not care to dwell on them. Perhaps that was why they were fading.

Though, there was one memory that continued to shine, no matter how much she tried to bury her past. One chance meeting with a noble, during her first day in the Imperial Palace. She had literally run into him with a tea tray while lost in the palace halls, and rather than punishing her for daring to touch him, he had smiled and responded with kindness, then pointed her in the right direction. She had never forgotten the way he'd spoken to her like she was a real person. Even with her death, his face remained as bright and clear in her memory as the day they had met.

Taiyo Daisuke of the Sun Clan. An Imperial noble, as far above her station as a prince to a farmer. He was the real reason she could not leave, why she couldn't seem to move on. Taiyo Daisuke was also part of Taka's prophecy, another key player in the game Lord Seigetsu kept referencing. A game with life-or-death consequences.

She had saved the noble from impending death once before, warning him and his companions of a demon attack that might've killed them all. Though she wouldn't have been able to do it—to find the courage to act—without Lord Seigetsu. He had shown her the way, encouraged her to save them. Now the game continued, and the lives of the Sun noble and his friends continued to hang in the balance.

In life, she had loved Daisuke-sama. She wasn't certain she could anymore, as a ghost; everything, even emotions, had become hazy. But she was invested now. For better or worse, she would see the game through to the end.

They came out of the clouds, and suddenly, an island as bright and green as a precious jewel appeared below them in the middle of the sea. Taka's eye lit up, a huge smile crossing his face as he scrambled to his feet.

"There's the island! Master, we're here. We've arrived."

"Silence."

Lord Seigetsu's tone was harsh. Chilled, Suki turned as the silver-haired man rose, moving slowly as if in a dream. His face caused a shiver to creep up her spine; she had never seen him look as shaken as he did now. He swayed on his feet, putting a hand against the carriage wall to steady himself, making Taka gasp.

"Are you all right, Master?"

Seigetsu didn't seem to hear him. "No," he murmured, but it was clear he was speaking to himself. "If she is gone now, the game is lost. I will not allow it."

His golden eyes shifted to Suki, and she shrank back at the emptiness behind them. In that stare, she saw a hunger that could swallow stars and drain the ocean. But then he blinked and returned to his normal, elegant self.

"Suki-chan." His voice was a caress, quiet and soothing. "I fear I must ask for your help. No, I… I must beg for your help." He stepped forward, holding out a long-fingered hand to her. "Please. The game is balanced on a razor's edge, and a single mistake could undo everything. If one piece disappears, the rest will follow. Including the Taiyo noble you still love."

Daisuke-sama. Suki trembled, remembering Taka's ominous words when he was in the throes of prophecy. *The white-haired prince seeks a battle he cannot win. He will break upon the demon's sword, and his dog will follow him unto death.*

"You can still save him," Seigetsu murmured. "His destiny is not yet decided. But we must act quickly, or they could all be lost. Will you help them?"

I have to be brave, Suki told herself, though she was still trembling. *If it means changing Daisuke-sama's fate, I will play Lord Seigetsu's game.*

Seigetsu-sama was still standing quietly, his golden eyes never leaving her. Suki hesitated a moment longer, gathering her courage, then raised her chin.

"What...what do you need me to do, Seigetsu-sama?" she whispered.

He smiled, and it was like the sun emerging from behind the clouds. "I need your eyes, Suki-chan," he told her. "I need to see what is happening on the island, and I don't dare set foot on it myself. Not yet. Though it has been a long time, it still recognizes me." That made her frown in confusion, but Seigetsu-sama didn't explain.

"I wish to see through your eyes, Suki-chan," Seigetsu went on. "You can go places I cannot, into the heart of the Tsuki itself. Genno's forces lurk just outside, like a shark circling a wounded seal, but they have not set foot on the island yet, either. The kami would sense them, but they will not notice another spirit wandering the land. Would you allow me this? To see through your eyes, and find those souls most important in the coming days?"

Suki considered. What Seigetsu-sama was asking didn't seem so bad, but it still made her very uncomfortable. Magic, in any form, frightened her. After all, it was Lady Satomi's blood magic that had summoned the oni that had killed her. "How would that work, Seigetsu-sama?" she asked. "Do I...need to do anything?"

"No, Suki-chan," Seigetsu said gently. "You needn't do anything. Only accept the fact that I will be with you, seeing through your eyes. When I meditate, the two of us will be connected, and I will be able to use you as a vessel for my consciousness. But only if you are willing. Are you?"

Suki was vaguely aware that Taka was standing beside them, gazing up at her with hooded eyes and a slight pout on his face. She didn't know why he was unhappy; perhaps he was upset that Seigetsu-sama had spoken to him coldly. If Suki was being honest, she wasn't certain she liked this idea, but Lord Seigetsu had always been truthful with her, even if he never told her everything. And if she was determined to save Daisuke-sama and see this game through to the end, there was only one answer she could give.

"Yes, Seigetsu-sama. I… I am willing."

He gave her that comforting smile. "Good," he whispered. "Time is short, Suki-chan. And the game marches on. Come." He held out an elegant hand to her. "Once we establish a connection, I will be able to go where you go, and see what you see."

"Will…it hurt?" Suki wanted to know as she drifted close. Lord Seigetsu shook his head.

"It will not," he assured her. "You won't even know I am there. Just close your eyes, Suki-chan, and empty your mind. This will not take long."

Suki did as he asked, and felt the lightest brush against her forehead, which shocked her for a moment and nearly caused her to open her eyes. She had long been unable to feel anything physical, her insubstantial form moving through everything she touched. She had almost forgotten what it felt like to interact with the world, and only her awe and trust in Seigetsu-sama kept her from flinching back.

"There," Lord Seigetsu murmured, and the sensation faded as quickly as it had come. "Now when I meditate, I will be able to find you, even if you are a great distance away. Thank you for this, Suki-chan. I am in your debt."

"It is nothing, Seigetsu-sama," Suki whispered. "I… I want to help. I don't know exactly what is going on, but I know that the fox girl is important. If I can aid them, I want to try. And I… I want Daisuke-sama to be happy." Maybe then she could finally move on.

Seigetsu nodded. "We will change the course of destiny together, Suki-chan," he said quietly, and motioned out the door with a billowy sleeve. To the great island floating beneath them in the sea. "These are the lands of the Moon Clan, the most spiritual of the great families. Long ago, they made a vow to the kami that they would remain distant from the politics of the empire and live in peace with the spirits of the island. That is their capital, Shinsei Yaju, the City of Sacred Beasts." He gestured, and Suki looked down to see a sprawling collection of buildings and roads surrounded by a massive forest. She had never seen a city from the air before, and marveled that something so huge could seem so tiny when viewed from the clouds.

"The daimyo of the Moon Clan resides there," Seigetsu went on, and for just a moment, Suki thought he sounded...wistful. "All decisions regarding the islands come from the Moon Clan Palace. That is where the seat of power dwells, and that is where our players will be heading. If they survived the last challenge.

"Suki-chan..." Seigetsu turned to her again. "You must be my eyes. I need you to go to the Moon Clan Palace and look for the fox girl and the others. Let no one in the palace see you, but return to me at once if you find them. Can you do this?"

"Yes, Seigetsu-sama," Suki whispered.

"Then, go," Seigetsu said. "And don't be afraid. I will be with you until you return."

A tiny thrill of fear went through her, but she pushed it aside. Ignoring Taka's dour glare, she shimmered into a ball of light, flew out of the carriage into open sky and soared in the direction of the island.

9

The Kodama's Favor

TATSUMI

Something cold and wet slapped my face, dragging me out of oblivion, and I opened my eyes.

Brilliant, searing light made me grimace. I lay on my stomach, my cheek pressed into cold pebbles, something sharp jutting uncomfortably into my ribs. Wincing, I raised my head and found myself on a stretch of rocky beach, black outcroppings jutting up between sand and pebbles. I lay half in, half out of the water, and though my clothes were drenched, I could feel the sun beating down on my back and shoulders.

A wave crawled over my body, hissing and smelling of brine, and my stomach roiled. I hunched my shoulders and retched up seawater, coughing and heaving until my stomach was empty. Panting, I pushed up, then sat back on my heels and gazed around, trying to get my bearings.

A rocky shoreline stretched away to either side of me, vanishing into a dense forest of pine and cedar. There were no docks, ships, buildings or any hint of civilization. I had no idea which island I was on, though I suspected this was Ushima, as we'd been closest to the Tsuki capital when we were attacked. The beach itself was scattered with broken boards, crates, barrels and other debris. Clearly the ship had not survived the encounter with the umibozu.

A flutter of white and red caught my eye, making my stomach turn over. Yumeko lay in a nearby tide pool, draped across a splintered plank that kept her face out of the water. Her body bobbed limply with the waves, her eyes were shut, and her skin was nearly as white as her robes. I remembered the terror I'd felt when the kitsune had gone overboard, thrown from the ship by the power of the umibozu's attacks. I remembered diving into the cold, inky waters without hesitation, reaching the girl, dragging her back to the surface. The umibozu had still been raging about, smashing what remained of the *Seadragon's Fortune* to splinters, and the water was filled with debris and bodies. Yumeko had slumped against me, her skin cold and her body limp in my arms. Gazing around, I'd spotted a blot against the horizon, a silhouette darker than the sky it was cast against. Ushima Island, or at least one of the Moon Clan islands; I wasn't going to be picky. Trying my best to keep the girl's head out of the water, I'd struck out for that tantalizing glimpse of land. That was the last thing I remembered.

I staggered to my feet and splashed through the pools to carefully gather Yumeko in my arms. She was alarmingly light, her small frame like a collection of twigs wrapped in silk, and my stomach twisted. Holding the girl close, I turned and carried her up the beach, my chest tightening with every step, my breath becoming ragged as I stumbled toward dry land.

Not dead, I told myself. *She's not dead. Not now.* I stared at her pale face, uncertain if I was trying to convince myself or screaming a challenge to the fortunes who dictated fate. *We've come this far, Yumeko; you can't leave us yet.*

Near the edge of the forest, I knelt and gently laid the girl on a patch of grass in the sun. With shaking fingers, I checked the pulse in her neck, bracing myself to find nothing, to accept that her spirit had fled, and that the cheerful, optimistic fox girl was gone. For a heartbeat, she lay still as death, her skin pallid and her body limp, and for one sickening moment, nothing in the world mattered at all.

Then there was a flutter beneath my fingers, and I could breathe again. Though the burst of relief was short-lived. Yumeko's heart still beat, but it was faint, frighteningly erratic, and a cold certainty crept over my thoughts. Yumeko was alive, but she was fading. Unless I could stop it, the fox girl wouldn't last the night.

Carefully, I eased aside the fabric of her robe to fully reveal what I was dealing with, and my blood chilled. A shard of wood jutted from her skin just below her ribs, the flesh around it oozing and swollen. Grimly, I checked my travel pouch, discovering what I had feared: I still had a roll of soggy bandages, but the powder to make medicine and numbing healing salves was gone, washed away in the sea. I would have to make do with what was left.

Yumeko remained unresponsive as I drew the piece of wood from her flesh, gritting my teeth as it came free, the jagged end soaked with blood. I cleaned and dressed the wound as best I could, the girl lying so still that twice I checked her pulse to make sure she was still alive. The silence throbbed in my ears, mocking me with its emptiness. Though it was probably best that she was unconscious for this, I wanted her to open her eyes, to yelp and jerk back, to tell me to be gentle. Yumeko was light and noise and cheerful, guileless wonder. Seeing her like this, pale and limp, knowing that she might never wake up again, made my stomach tighten and a knot form in my chest.

She's going to die, Tatsumi. You know that. The thought was both mine, the logical part of me that was used to blood and death, and also Hakaimono's. *She's lost too much blood, and you might be days away from any help. You won't be able to save her, and time is running out to stop Genno. Let her go.*

"Shut up," I growled to both sides of myself. They relented, but the terrible knowledge still remained. Yumeko was dying. And I had seen enough injury and death, in both my lifetimes, to know the terrible moment where her heart stopped forever was not far away.

But I would not let her go without a fight.

Reluctantly tearing myself from the girl, I stood, trying to get my bearings as I gazed around. Before me, the ocean stretched on to the horizon. To either side, a jagged, rocky shoreline continued until it curved and was lost from view. Behind me, the forest loomed, thick and tangled. From the position of the sun, I estimated we were on the northern side of the island, and Heishi, the port town to which the ship was originally headed, was somewhere along the west coast. I didn't know if there were any closer towns or villages, or how far away I really was, but Yumeko needed help, and that vague direction was all I had to go on.

Turning from the ocean, I bent and lifted the girl in my arms, feeling the lightness of her body, that ominous sensation of *wrongness* that came when death was not far behind. Closing my eyes, I bent my head until our foreheads touched, willing my strength into the fading body, praying my thoughts would reach her.

Stay with me, Yumeko. Don't die on me now. If you're gone, how will I find a reason to fight for anything?

The waves hissed over the rocky shoreline, and overhead, the sun slipped a little farther from the sky. Setting my jaw, holding the girl close, I walked into the forest.

The trees closed around us, huge and dense, blocking the wind and the sounds of the ocean. The farther I walked, the thicker the forest became, until there was nothing but trees and tangled undergrowth in every direction. Overhead, the canopy shut out the sky, only a few spots of sunlight poking through the leaves to mottle the floor. Moss grew everywhere, a thick spongy carpet that covered rocks and trees alike, muffling my footsteps and casting a green tinge over everything. The forest felt ancient, alive.

And it was watching us.

I could sense eyes on me from every angle, curious and intense. More than once, there was a ripple in the corner of my vision, a shimmer of movement through the trees, though nothing was there when I turned my head. Sometimes I was almost certain I saw faces, dark eyes peering between the branches, watching me through the leaves. Always gone when I focused on them, like shadows vanishing in the sun. Spirits and forest kami, I guessed, judging from how ancient and wild these woods felt. Like they had not seen the tread of human feet for centuries. Briefly, I wondered what the kami that called this place home thought about a demon marching through their territory, if they would take offense and try to do something about it, or simply wait until I was gone. I hoped they would not interfere; I wasn't afraid of what they would do to me, but if Yumeko was hurt or killed because of it, this forest would burn to ash before I was done.

Evening fell, and the forest continued, growing thicker and wilder the farther I walked. Ancient mossy trees towered over me, curtains of lichen trailing to the ground like silk streamers. Pale blue and white toadstools glowed with an eerie luminance on logs and fallen branches, brightening the forest floor as the daylight faded. Fireflies began drifting through the air, winking in and out of existence, and floating balls of ghostly fire—tsurubebi, onibi or other spirits—flew through the branches, trailing wisps of light behind them. The air was alive with kami and magic, and I continued to feel dozens of invisible eyes watching me as I walked through the undergrowth.

My legs shook, and I stumbled and fell to my knees with a

soft curse. The fight with the umibozu, being half drowned, my own wounds and the long march through the forest with no water or food were taking their toll. As I knelt there, gathering my strength to press on, my instincts pricked a warning, and I raised my head.

A kodama, one of the tiny tree kami of the forests, stood on a moss-covered log a few feet away, watching me with pupilless black eyes. My heart jumped, but as soon as our gazes met, it vanished, winking from sight before I could say a word. I could suddenly see more of the tiny green spirits in the branches around me, peering from behind leaves, but they, too, disappeared as soon as they realized I'd spotted them. Perhaps they were keeping an eye on the demon strolling through the forest, or maybe they were curious as to what he was carrying.

I looked down at Yumeko. She lay cradled in my arms with her head against my chest, eyes closed and face slack. Alarmed, I felt for a pulse again and found it, faint and erratic, in her wrist. Still fighting. Not gone yet.

Setting my jaw, I pushed myself to my feet to continue on.

As I started forward, there was the faintest stirring from the body in my arms, the softest intake of breath, and my heart jumped. I didn't stop, walking doggedly into the undergrowth, as Yumeko shifted against me and raised her head.

"Tatsumi?"

Her voice was weak, barely a whisper. It both caused my heart to leap and dread to blossom in my stomach at how faint it was.

"I'm here," I told her quietly.

"What...happened?" She turned her head a bit, trying to gaze around us. "Where are we?"

"The umibozu destroyed the ship," I went on. "We're on one of the Tsuki islands, hopefully Ushima."

"The others?"

"I don't know," I admitted. "I haven't seen them. If they're still alive, I can only assume they'll meet us in Heishi."

"I feel strange."

"You...were badly hurt, Yumeko." I swallowed the tightness in my throat. I had to keep her talking, keep her awake. If she fell asleep again, I knew for a certainty that she wasn't waking up again. "We're not far from Heishi," I lied. "Just hold on a little longer. What do you know about the Tsuki family?"

"The...Moon Clan? Not a lot."

"Tell me what you do know."

She paused, as if gathering her thoughts. I continued through the forest, seeing flashes of movement through the trees and undergrowth, spirits or kami keeping just out of sight.

"The Tsuki are the most reclusive of the great families," Yumeko went on, sounding like she was quoting something from a history class. Her voice slurred, as if she was battling exhaustion. "They used to live among the other clans, but two thousand years ago the entire Tsuki family moved to the islands off the western coast, and they've stayed there ever since. They don't like visitors, and they rarely get involved in the other clans' problems. No one knows much about them, but it's said that they're close to the kami. Although, the kami here...feel very sad." Raising her head, she peered up at the branches. "This forest...feels sad," she whispered. "Sad, but...but also angry. Like it's lost something, but it can't remember what it is." She slumped against me again as her strength failed her. "Gomen, I don't remember much else."

I stopped short, as with a rustle of leaves, a large stag stepped from the undergrowth a few yards away. It snorted when it saw me, but didn't seem overly troubled at the appearance of a half-demon, for it calmly turned and walked back into the forest, parting branches and undergrowth as it did. A few white moths, disturbed by the passing of the large creature, fluttered around us like bits of paper.

"I don't know," Yumeko whispered suddenly.

I glanced down at her. "What?"

"Master Isao," Yumeko said, causing an icy hand to clutch my heart. "He keeps…calling to me, trying to tell me something, but I can't quite hear him." She paused, as if realizing what she'd just said, then let out a quiet breath. "I'm…dying, aren't I?"

"Stay with me, Yumeko," I whispered, ducking my head. The tops of her ears brushed my jaw, and I closed my eyes. "Don't join him just yet, we need you here." *I…need you.*

"I'll try," Yumeko murmured, leaning her head against my chest again. "But…I don't think I have much longer, Tatsumi. When you hear Meido calling…you have to go." She let out a shaky breath, curling into me further. "You'll take care of the others, right?" she asked softly. "Reika, Daisuke, baka Okame… They'll need you if they're going to fight the Master of Demons. Reika will be quite cross that I didn't make it. Tell her… it's not your fault, and I'm sorry I died before we stopped the Summoning."

I couldn't answer that. I could barely keep myself walking. I just held her tighter, silently raging at the spirits, the Kami, the fortunes and myself most of all.

"I'm sorry," Yumeko said again. She shivered against me, one hand clutching my jacket. "I don't want to go," she whispered. "I want to stay here with you. There were so many things I wanted to do, to see…after we beat Genno." She paused, her breath coming in short, shallow gasps, as if talking now was an effort. "You'll have to see them for me, Tatsumi."

"Yumeko…" My voice came out choked, and there was a strange stinging sensation in the corner of my eyes. I had no future; once we defeated Genno and stopped the Summoning, there was no place for me in this world. The empire did not look kindly on half-demons, and the Shadow Clan would certainly want Hakaimono dead and Kamigoroshi returned. When this was over, I wasn't sure if I would continue Hakaimono's oath of vengeance against the Kage, or simply walk out to meet them all, knowing the result would be the same either way.

There was nothing but death waiting for me at the end of this road—I had always known that. But Yumeko deserved more than what fate had decided. She deserved to walk in the sun, to see the wonders she spoke of, to know years of peace without the threat of demons or dragons or darkness. "Don't give up on me yet," I told her in a husky voice. "I'm not going anywhere without you. If you want me to see those places, you'll have to come along and see them yourself."

There was no answer. I looked down and saw that Yumeko had fallen unconscious again, her head resting on my chest and her eyes closed. I could still feel her heartbeat, but just barely. Our time was nearly up.

The last of the light faded, plunging the woods into gloom and shadow, and a light rain began to drip through the canopy overhead, cold tendrils snaking into my hair and down my skin. As I stumbled again, managing to stay on my feet this time, I caught sight of something in the trees that made my blood run cold. An old oak, charred and blackened, its trunk split in two by lightning, stood a few yards away. I recognized it because I had seen it hours earlier, when I had first passed this way. There was no mistake. Seeing it again meant I'd been going in circles, though I knew I had been traveling west the whole time. Or, I thought I'd been going west. But a forest filled with kami and spirits was a fickle thing. Whether it was the creatures that lived here or the nature of the forest itself that had caused me to lose my way, the result was the same.

My legs gave out, and I collapsed to my knees in the grass, feeling the girl's limp body against mine. Bowing my head, I closed my eyes and held her tightly, as rage and despair began pulling me into the darkness. There was no time left. I had failed, and my world would soon lose the only bright spot it had ever known.

"I'm sorry," I whispered to the motionless girl in my arms.

She remained unresponsive, her skin cold against mine. "Forgive me, Yumeko. I..." My throat closed, and I gently brushed a strand of hair from her slack face. "I wanted to stay with you, too," I confessed in a whisper. "For however long I had left. You made me believe a demon could be worth saving."

There was the faintest of rustles in the grass in front of me, like a leaf skipping over the ground, and I raised my head.

A kodama, tiny and insubstantial, stood on a rock a few feet away, watching us as before. Briefly, I contemplated striking it down, then taking Kamigoroshi and carving a path through the forest until it let me go or until nothing was left standing. But the kodama didn't appear hostile or wary. Its huge black eyes, curious and concerned, were fixed on Yumeko.

Hope flickered, and I took a careful breath. "Please," I began, but as soon as I spoke, the tiny kami disappeared, twisting into the rain and vanishing from sight, snuffing that brief moment of hope as it did. I slumped back, anger and anguish like twin serpents coiling within. Even if they could help, the kodama wouldn't speak to a demon. Yumeko was the one they listened to, flocked around, allowed safe passage through their forest. Because she was kitsune, or because they could sense the pureness inside her, the light that drew everyone to her like moths to a flame. I remembered another night, another forest filled with kodama, their voices like hundreds of rustling leaves, and Yumeko sitting by the fire as the tree spirits approached and raised a single leaf that glowed with a soft inner light.

My heart stood still. The leaf. That night, the kodama had offered me a gift for slaying a savage demon bear that had been sucking the life out of the forest. I hadn't given any thought to the forest when I'd killed the monster; I had simply been trying to survive. But in the eyes of the kodama, I had done the land a favor, and the kami always repaid their debts.

That leaf signifies that you are a friend of the forest, I heard Yumeko saying. *If you are ever in need of the kami's help, whisper your request out loud and release it into the wind. It will carry your message to any nearby kodama, who will aid you in whatever way they can.*

Heart pounding, I gently laid Yumeko down, then yanked open my travel pouch, digging through the contents with trembling fingers. Much of it was gone, washed away in the sea. I pulled out empty medicine packets, soggy rice kernels, bandages, a roll of thread, my desperation growing as I searched in vain for the item I needed. Where had I put it? I remembered not giving it a second thought as I'd stuffed it into my pouch that night, thinking I would never need to call in a favor from the kami.

My fingertips brushed something fragile and papery, wedged into the seam of the pouch. With the utmost care, I freed it and pulled it out, my breath catching as it came to light. A leaf, tiny and green, the same color as the kodama that had presented it to me. Though weeks had passed since that night, it wasn't torn or brittle, pulsing with that soft inner light that cast my fingers in a faint glow.

With a sigh of both relief and fear, I closed my eyes and brought the leaf close to my face, praying the request would still be honored, that the kami would listen to the words of a demon.

"Spirits of the forest," I whispered, my voice coming out shaky, "help Yumeko. I care nothing for myself, do with me what you will, punish me for trespassing as you see fit. But please, if you can honor this one request, save her. She is desperately needed here."

A breeze gusted around me, tugging at my hair and rippling my clothes. Almost without thinking, I opened my hand and let the leaf swirl away on the wind, watching as it spiraled up into the branches and disappeared.

Silence fell, even the rain seeming to pause as the forest considered my request. As the seconds ticked by, I felt resignation and hopelessness settle heavy on my shoulders. I was an oni, a creature of Jigoku, the realm of evil. The kami would not listen to the tainted words of a demon.

Gathering up Yumeko, I sat back against a tree, drawing her into my lap. I didn't dare check for a pulse, afraid that I would feel nothing. Or worse, that I *would* feel it, fading slowly away, and could do nothing as the fox girl slipped from me forever.

My skin prickled, and the hairs on the back of my neck stood up. I lifted my gaze, and found the clearing filled with kami.

Kodama surrounded us, hundreds of them, peering down from branches and between leaves, their hollow black eyes fixed on me. They covered the forest floor like a softly glowing carpet, like dozens of pale green toadstools growing out of everything. Silently, they watched me, making no sound, and the forest itself seemed to hold its breath.

Something slipped through the trees, silent as a shadow, a brief glimmer in the darkness, and my pulse spiked. Beyond the ring of kami, a creature stepped out of the forest, halted at the edge of the clearing and stared at me. It was much larger than a kodama, with the legs and body of a small deer, yet somehow, it made even the most graceful deer seem boorish and clumsy. Tiny pearlescent scales covered its body, sometimes green, sometimes gold or silver, and a silken mane fell around its neck and shoulders. Its face was a cross between a stag and a dragon, and a single antlered horn, shining gold and black, crowned the top of its head.

Swishing a feathered, ox-like tail, it stepped into the open, cloven hooves barely touching the tops of the grass, and walked toward me.

I drew in a slow breath, as awe and a sudden, instinctive fear paralyzed my limbs. For the creature gliding toward me across the forest floor wasn't yokai or kami or any normal monster or spirit. In fact, it was the only one of its kind.

The sacred Kirin, a creature of legend, one of the four great holy beasts of Iwagoto. It was said that the Kirin was seen only during times of peace, and only when a great and wise ruler sat on the throne. I didn't know how much of the legend was true, because it was also said that the Kirin showed itself only to those with pure hearts and souls, and oni certainly did not qualify. I could feel the demon side of me recoiling from the sacred animal, filled with an innate loathing and fear. The immortal Kirin radiated holiness and purity, and an aura of sacred flame surrounded it, repelling evil. One blast of its holy fire would instantly char this body to dust and send its soul back to Jigoku, Kamigoroshi or whatever afterlife awaited.

The Kirin walked across the clearing, silent as a ripple of moonlight, seeming to step on the tops of the grass without bending them. The kodama made no effort to get out of the way and yet, somehow, the hooves of the Kirin always found an opening and never stepped on the multitude of kami spread throughout the grove.

When it was about a dozen yards away, the Kirin stopped. Depthless black eyes, as ancient as the forest itself, regarded me over the heads of the kodama. I didn't move, holding Yumeko close. If the Kirin was here to kill us, to purge the demon blood from its forest with one blast of sacred fire, so be it.

The Kirin slowly tilted its head, watching me. It didn't speak; there were no words, in my head or otherwise, but I could suddenly *feel* its unspoken question, the inquiry as clear as if it had shouted the words out loud.

Why do you come to my forest?

I bowed my head, feeling a sensation of utter tranquility emanating from the sacred beast, snuffing any thoughts of violence or desire to harm. Even if I'd had ill intent, raising a weapon against this creature would be nearly impossible. "Great Kirin," I replied, "forgive this intrusion into your domain. We are only passing through. My comrades and I came to these islands seeking a blood mage called Genno, who possesses the pieces of the Dragon's Prayer."

The night of the Wish approaches. The Kirin's "voice" was impassive. Around us, a noise rose up, like the rustle of a thousand dry leaves, as all the kodama began shaking and waving in the wind. The Kirin didn't seem to notice. *The Dragon is almost risen, and all the world trembles with the end of another age. But whether the Wish brings ruin or fortune is yet to be decided.*

The chatter from the kodama faded, and the Kirin's ancient black eyes fixed on me again. *Hakaimono,* it said flatly, and my stomach dropped. *And not Hakaimono. Your soul is fragmented, tangled with another's. I cannot tell where the human and the demon intersect.* It seemed to sigh, the ox tail swishing thoughtfully against its flanks. *Normally I do not speak with your kind, but the kodama called on me for aid, and I have come. The kami always honor their debts. Though make no mistake, it was for the kitsune that they responded tonight, not the demon.* Its elegant, deerlike ears swiveled forward, toward the girl in my arms. *She is nearly gone*, it said, making my heart clench. *Her spirit is ready to depart its body. It has perhaps a few breaths, a few heartbeats more.*

"Save her," I rasped, and the Kirin blinked. "Please. She can't…die now."

The sacred beast regarded me without expression. *Death is the natural order of things,* it stated calmly. *It comes for all mortals, human and yokai alike. To snatch a life from the jaws of death disrupts the balance of the world. Why should I change this fate?*

"Because, I…" I closed my eyes, trying to grasp the thought that could save Yumeko's life. A dozen responses sprang to mind: because she was the bearer of the Dragon scroll, because she could be important in stopping Genno and preventing the coming of the Harbinger. But those answers seemed trivial and inadequate, and I knew they would not satisfy the immortal creature before me.

"Because… I care for her," I whispered at last. A selfish reason, I knew, but it was the most honest one I could think of. Even as it shocked me just as much. I had lived a long time. I had seen countless mortals come and go. Their lives were insignificant dust motes on the wind. And yet, somehow, this slip of a half-fox had unassumingly bypassed all my defenses and wriggled her way into my soul.

"I can't lose her," I finished. "She's my light. If she disappears, the darkness will swallow me again."

The Kirin's expression didn't change. It took a step back, still managing to avoid the dozens of kodama behind it. *Come dawn, you will leave this place*, it told me. *The forest will not keep you here, and the spirits will not impede you any longer. When the night fades, a guide will appear to show you the way.*

I slumped in defeat, anger and despair rising once more, drowning that brief moment of hope. The Kirin wasn't going to help. It was a god, and the life of a single half human meant nothing to the fickle kami. A part of me considered leaping up, drawing Kamigoroshi and forcing the beast to help, but threatening the sacred Kirin would likely result in either a terrible curse or a swift death by holy fire. In either case, it wouldn't save her.

The Kirin swished its tail. *I will grant you this gift, human who is not*, it said, and turned away, though I could still sense its voice, resonating through the forest. *Sleep, and do not worry about enemies or creatures that mean you harm. Within this forest, nothing will touch you. Sleep now, and do not dream. Your burdens will be lighter with the dawn.*

I didn't want to sleep. I wanted to stay awake with Yumeko, to be there when her spirit left her body and she died in my arms. And when she was gone, I would depart this forest, find the Master of Demons and his army no matter where they were hiding, and tear every soul apart with my bare hands. The last thing I wanted to do now was fall unconscious.

Setting my jaw, I started to rise, intending to leave this clearing and the presence of a god who refused to help. But my body was suddenly sluggish, and my eyelids felt like they were made of stone. A feeling of deep peace swept through me, blissful and overwhelming, and then I knew nothing at all.

10

THE CITY OF SACRED BEASTS

Yumeko

Master Isao was waiting for me on the steps outside the temple.

"Hello, Yumeko-chan," he greeted, smiling. He held a piece of wood in one hand and a small knife in the other, whittling tiny flakes that drifted to the steps between his feet. The block in his hand had taken on the vague likeness of some four-legged beast, though it was still unrecognizable. He would spend months, sometimes years, on a particular piece, though I remembered he never kept the figurines that he finished, placing them in the woods outside the temple, returning them to nature.

"Hello, Master Isao," I said. "It's a nice morning."

"It is. Very peaceful." He nodded to the sun-warmed steps of the main hall. "Sit with me a moment, won't you, Yumeko-chan?"

Uh-oh, what had I done this time? I picked my way up the steps and sat next to my mentor, trying to remember if I had gotten into any trouble with Denga or Nitoru. I didn't think I had, though my memories of today seemed scattered and hazy. The sun was warm on my skin, and several birds sang in the branches of the nearby trees. It was quiet here, very peaceful, as Master Isao had said, but something nagged at me. A feeling I couldn't quite place.

"Where is everyone, Master Isao?" I asked, glancing up at him. I couldn't remember seeing Denga, Jin or Nitoru today.

"Around," Master Isao replied, continuing to whittle chips from the wood block in his hand. "I see them occasionally. From time to time, our paths will cross. But they have their own paths to walk now. Their own terms and conclusions to reach. I cannot guide them down these roads—they must find their own way to the beginning."

"I don't understand, Master Isao."

"Yumeko-chan." Master Isao's voice was firm. He lowered the items in his hands and stared at me, his dark eyes kind but intense. "You are not supposed to be here now," he said, making me frown in confusion. "Your mission is not complete. You still have an important task to fulfill. Do you remember?"

A chill went through me. I gazed around the peaceful garden, trying to recall how I got here, and couldn't. "I...don't remember," I stammered, feeling something hovering at the tip of my consciousness, just out of reach. "What do you mean, I'm not supposed to be here?"

Master Isao gave me another grave look, and pointed a long finger to something across the gardens.

I followed his hand, seeing the dark edges of a forest beyond the temple gate. Shadows cloaked the trees and undergrowth, and it seemed that where the temple grounds ended and the forest began, the sunlight simply stopped, as if it couldn't penetrate any farther.

At Master Isao's unspoken urging, I rose and walked halfway across the yard, peering into the darkness looming at the edge of the grounds. As I got closer, I could see a faint curtain of mist separating the temple from the forest, and for some reason, it caused goose bumps to scurry up my arms.

There was a figure sitting beneath a tree in the shadows of the forest, shoulders hunched, head bowed. He cradled a body in his lap, her skin as pale as rice paper, a bushy fox tail lying motionless on the ground.

The world seemed to pause, the air around me growing misty and surreal. In a daze, I turned back and found Master Isao sitting on the steps as before, his body hazy and transparent in the sunlight. He gave me a sad, gentle smile and shook his head.

"It is not time for you to cross the veil, Yumeko-chan," Master Isao told me, his voice softer than the breeze overhead. "Soon, perhaps, we will see each other again. But not now. The fate of the world is balanced on the thinnest of threads, and the Dragon casts the whole kingdom in his shadow. Your part in the story is not yet finished. You must see it through to the end." Master Isao gazed down at the wood in his hands and began carving again, splinters falling away into the dirt. "He is calling for you, Yumeko-chan," he murmured. "Can't you hear him? You don't want to keep him waiting too long, or his soul might fall into darkness again. He needs your light to guide him to the other side." Once more, his gaze rose to me, that faint, gentle smile crossing his face as he nodded. "Go now, little fox. You have people who need you in the living world. It is not your time."

And before my eyes, Master Isao shivered into a glowing sphere of light, drifted up the steps of the temple and vanished through the doors. Swallowing the lump in my throat, I glanced back at the forest and felt a shiver run all the way to my toes.

A magnificent creature stood at the edge of the fog, watching me. It had the body of a deer, the face of a dragon, and a beautiful, terrible horn arching back from its forehead. I remembered the stories of such a creature, how it would appear to wise and benevolent rulers, how its arrival was seen as a sign of great change. As it seemed to be waiting for me, I walked across the temple yard until I stood before the sacred Kirin.

It cocked its head, regarding me with a thoughtful, almost puzzled look on its ageless face. It wasn't much taller than me; we stood almost at eye level, but I felt I was gazing into the eyes of an ancient giant.

Daughter of the forest. There were no words, but I could feel the voice resonating inside me like the chime of a bell. *You return at last.*

I blinked, feeling that strange, surreal familiarity, as if this wasn't the first time we had met. Though I thought I would certainly remember if I had ever glimpsed the great Kirin of legend. "I'm sorry," I whispered, and it twitched its ears forward. "I don't understand."

No. The Kirin's "voice" was gentle. *You wouldn't. Not yet.* Its ox tail swished across its flanks, sending coils of mist writhing through the air. *Evil comes to these islands*, it went on, making me shiver. *The night of the Wish is almost upon us, and your allies are few. Go to Shinsei Yaju, the City of Sacred Beasts. Seek out Tsuki Kiyomi; you will need her aid in the days to come.*

"Tsuki Kiyomi," I repeated. "Will she help us?"

The Kirin didn't answer right away. It watched me a moment longer, then raised its head, ears swiveled, as if to catch a sound on the wind. *Can you feel it?* it whispered. *Below this forest, a curse holds the land hostage with sadness and fear. It has affected everything it touches, including the hearts of those who rule. Tread carefully, little fox. The faces here are not as they seem, and the one who appears the most familiar could be the origin of all that is corrupt.*

A chill traced my spine. I didn't understand completely, but I knew what the Kirin spoke of—the terrible sadness that had seeped into the ground and hung in the air. Like a shadow that hovered over everything, or a wound that could never heal. "What happened here?" I asked. "Why does the forest feel so sad and angry? What is this curse?"

The Kirin did not answer. Turning, it raised its head and blew out a breath that filled the air with the sound of whispers. The veil of mist before us parted and rolled away before the sacred creature, and I could see the other side clearly.

The path is open. Follow me back to the living world, little soul. You are still needed here.

I looked back at the temple, but could no longer see it. Only a landscape of drifting fog, with ghostly balls of light floating in and out of the haze. Chilled, I turned away from the land of mist and followed the Kirin into the looming forest, the fog curling around me.

I opened my eyes, and the world was dark. I lay on my side on a bed of soft grass, the tips brushing my cheek as I stirred. Wincing, I sat up slowly, gazing around to see where I was.

A moonlit grove, silver and black, greeted me, and whispers tickled my ears as I looked around in wonder. I caught glimpses of kodama in the surrounding branches, their tiny bodies glowing an ethereal green in the darkness, and blips of light flickered in and out of the trees. It was an odd sensation, like I was perhaps still caught in a dream. My body felt strange and light, as if not completely real.

I gazed down, and my heart skipped a beat.

Tatsumi lay on his side next to me, one arm curled beneath his head, his eyes closed. He breathed slowly, his expression unguarded and peaceful, and my stomach gave a weird little twist. It was the first time I'd ever seen him asleep, truly asleep, not dozing with his back against a wall and a sword in his lap. Without even realizing it, I reached down and softly touched his forehead, brushing a strand of hair from his face.

At that tiny bit of contact, his eyes snapped open and he surged upright, making me jump. His eyes, glowing and terrible, fixed on me, before he blinked and they were normal again.

"Yumeko."

"Gomen, Tatsumi," I said quickly, as the demonslayer stared at me, eyes wide and a little glassy. "I didn't mean to wake you. Well, I did, but not like this. Are you—"

I got no further. Tatsumi leaned forward, pressed a hand to the side of my face and kissed me. It was a hard, almost desperate kiss, filled with emotion and relief. I went rigid in shock, even as my entire soul leaped to meet him, bursting into blue-white flames that roared through every part of me.

Tatsumi pulled back, almost in surprise. Glancing at my face, his eyes clouded over, and he dropped his gaze. "Gomen," he muttered, starting to draw away. "I shouldn't have… Forgive me. I won't…"

I reached out and touched his cheek, stopping him and bringing his attention back. Our gazes met, and though crimson flames flickered in the depths of his eyes, his expression was dark with passion. This time, the kiss was gentle; Tatsumi let out a soft breath and pulled me close, sitting up and wrapping his arms around my waist. I closed my eyes and pressed myself into him, daring to slide my fingers through his thick hair, feeling the fires within settle into a bright, constant flame.

Tatsumi drew back, though only a breath separated us as he gazed up at me, his eyes shifting purple and red in turns. "I thought I lost you," he whispered. "When the Kirin walked away, I thought…" A shiver went through him, and his thumb brushed gently against my cheek. "You are here, aren't you, Yumeko?" he murmured, a faint shadow of uncertainty crossing his face. "This isn't a dream, is it?"

I covered his hand with my own. "If it is, then we're both dreaming."

He smiled and leaned forward to kiss me again, but there was a shimmer from the corner of my eye, and when I turned, I saw a red fox sitting on a log a few yards away, watching us with glowing amber eyes. An exceptionally bushy tail was curled around its legs, and when it saw that I'd noticed, it rose, still staring at us, and hopped off the log. As it did, its tail seemed to split apart, becoming two bushy, white-tipped tails brushing its hindquarters, and my heart leaped. The kitsune took three steps toward the trees, then turned back to gaze at us again, twitching its tails impatiently. Obviously waiting for us.

Tatsumi, following my gaze, gave a rueful smile. "I guess we're not welcome here anymore," he murmured.

"Hai." I nodded, reluctantly disentangling myself from the demonslayer. I wanted to stay in this peaceful, kami-filled forest awhile longer, to forget the outside world and the impossible odds stacked against us. But the dawn was waning, and time was running ever shorter. "I guess it's time to go."

We trailed the kitsune guide through the forest, following a path that only it knew, as the kodama watched us depart from the branches overhead. The kitsune moved swiftly, never pausing or looking back, its white-tipped tails bobbing through the darkness. Curiosity ate at me, a fire in my belly; I wanted to talk to the yokai, the first of my full-blooded kin I had seen, in the real world, anyway. And a kitsune with *two* tails, at that. I had so many questions, so many things about their world I wanted to know. But the kitsune didn't stop, always keeping the same distance between us, seeming uninterested and unconcerned with the half blood following it.

The skies overhead were brightening, and a faint pink tint had crept over the horizon, when Tatsumi and I followed the fox out of the trees to stand at the edge of a small valley. A few yards away, the land sloped down into a grassy bowl surrounded by forest and trees on one side and a soaring range of mountains on the other, the jagged tips brushing the clouds.

The kitsune looked back with glowing yellow eyes, twitched its tails once and disappeared. Disappointment blossomed in my chest, but only for a moment, as I saw what lay beyond the edge of the rise.

My eyes widened. A great city sprawled within the confines of the valley, glittering like a carpet of fireflies in the shadow of the mountains. A wall surrounded it, but it seemed as if the forest had crawled into the valley and now shared the space with the rest of the city. Large ancient trees towered over the narrow streets, and many of the houses had been built around the trunks rather than disturb the giants. Colorful pagoda roofs swept toward the sky, bright bridges spanned the web of rivers and streams that cut through the valley, and a magnificent castle with white walls and a red roof sat surrounded by moats in the very center. At each corner of the valley, four huge statues towered over the city like immortal guardians: Kirin, Phoenix, Tiger and the Great Dragon himself.

Tatsumi's gaze swept over the valley, taking everything in. "This must be Shinsei Yaju," he murmured. "The capital city of the Moon Clan. We'll have to be careful."

"Because outsiders aren't allowed to travel the island freely?" I guessed, and he nodded.

"They'll be even more suspicious around the capital." He nodded to the large red-and-white palace that sat in the center like a glistening jewel. "That's the home of Tsuki Kiyomi, the daimyo of the Moon Clan."

"Oh," I gasped. "Tsuki Kiyomi! That's who the Kirin told me to go see. It said Kiyomi-san could help us stop Genno."

"The Kirin," Tatsumi repeated. "It told you to speak to the Moon Clan daimyo?"

I nodded, and Tatsumi said nothing for a bit, observing the city and its people walking down the roads like ants. "I could sneak us in," he finally responded. "Though that might not inspire a lot of confidence in the daimyo, if two strangers suddenly appear inside her palace without warning. And if we're caught, they'll probably try to kill us. Especially since..."

He trailed off, but I knew what worried him. Since he looked like a half-demon, or at least, not entirely human. "I think," I began, "I'm going to have to go down there and ask to see the daimyo. The Kirin said we needed her aid. It wouldn't send us here without cause, right?"

Tatsumi didn't answer. I could feel his gaze on me, and reached for his hand. He hesitated, and then his fingers curled around mine. "I have to go," I went on, "but you don't need to come with me, Tatsumi. I'm sure you can use your shinobi magic and sneak into the city without being seen. We can meet up later when it's safe."

"No." Tatsumi shook his head. "If the Kirin sent you here, there's a reason for it. You need to speak to the daimyo, and I'm not leaving you alone."

"But what if they try to kill you?"

Unexpectedly, one corner of his mouth turned up. "They might…if they see a demon," he said, sounding strangely amused. "If only there was a way to disguise myself so that I looked like something else."

"Oh." Feeling foolish, I plucked a leaf from a nearby branch, then turned and scowled at the smirking demonslayer. "When did you learn sarcasm?" I asked. "Have you been listening to Okame-san? The Tatsumi I remember barely cracked a smile."

"I'm not sure." Abruptly serious, Tatsumi frowned, his eyes darkening. "I know I'm different now," he admitted in a soft voice. "I remember the person I was when we first met and… that Tatsumi seems like a stranger." He shook his head. "I don't know if it's Hakaimono's influence, or even his memories of the dozens of demonslayers that came before me, but… I know I'm not the same. I don't even know how much of the real Tatsumi is left."

My heart twisted. Stepping close, I placed a palm against his cheek, feeling warmth spread through my fingers as he closed his eyes. "I like this Tatsumi," I whispered.

A shiver went through him, and one hand rose, covering my own and sending tingles all the way down my arm. "I'm glad," he murmured. "Because I have no idea what is happening to me."

My heart raced. I wanted to kiss him, to run my fingers through his hair and feel his hands on my skin. I wanted to press myself close, burrow into him so that nothing separated us, and I was terrified that I felt this way.

Quickly, I pulled back and held the leaf up in two fingers. "Ready to go see the daimyo?"

"As long as you don't turn me into a goat." Tatsumi's voice was wry. "Or the ronin."

I bit my cheek at the thought of the demonslayer as a goat, then pressed the leaf to his forehead. Tatsumi didn't move, closing his eyes as I drew on my magic. There was a soundless explosion of smoke, and when it cleared, the demonslayer stared back at me, now draped in black robes with a metal staff clutched in one hand. A wide-brimmed straw hat sat on his head, and his horns were nowhere to be seen.

Tatsumi gazed down at himself, then back up at me, raising a brow. "A priest?"

"Nobody questions priests," I explained with a shrug. "Or shrine maidens. Have you ever noticed how Reika can go almost anywhere she wants, and no one gives her a second glance? Because she's obviously doing the work of the kami, and its bad luck to interfere in the way of the gods. That, and she gives them a terrible scolding if they question her."

"I see."

I cocked my head at him. "Do you not want to be a priest, Tatsumi-san? I could turn you into a shrine maiden instead."

He winced. "This is fine."

We found a path leading down the rise into the valley, and followed the narrow trail until the road widened and the gates of the city loomed before us. Unlike the Imperial capital of Kin Heigen Toshi, where lines formed outside the city gates to be allowed through, there was very little foot traffic on the road to and from the Tsuki capital; few travelers passed us, and the ones that did gave the barest of nods as they went by.

A pair of warriors in the black-and-silver colors of the Moon Clan guarded the gates of the city, their spears glinting in the evening light as they watched us approach. I had been hoping to blend in with other travelers going to the capital, but there were no crowds; Tatsumi and I were the only ones on the road.

"Halt."

I stifled a wince as one samurai left his post, stepping in front of me to block the gates. He didn't point his weapon at me, but his eyes were hard as they gave me a cursory glance before sweeping toward Tatsumi.

"More outsiders," he said flatly, making my heart leap to my throat. "State your business here. Are you with the group that came through earlier?"

"A-another group?" I repeated as Tatsumi straightened beside me. My heart pounded, and I leaned forward hopefully. "Was there a Taiyo noble, a shrine maiden and a yojimbo?"

The samurai relaxed, though he looked more annoyed than relieved. He turned back to answer, but suddenly froze, a look of disbelief crossing his face as he stared at me. I held my breath, wondering if he had somehow seen my true self and knew I was kitsune.

"H-hai," he finally whispered. "The group you described is already here, my lady. They are with the daimyo now." Stepping back, he gave a quick bow, his eyes on the ground. "We will take you to the palace, please follow us."

Relieved, but a bit confused, I followed the samurai through the gates into the streets of Shinsei Yaju.

Immediately, I could feel the presence of the kami.

It was like stepping into the heart of the sacred forest, only instead of trees, buildings, houses and shrines surrounded us. The city was full of kami. I saw kodama everywhere, in the branches of ancient trees growing along the road, skipping over the roofs of houses, even perched on the shoulders and heads of some humans, who were either used to the tiny kami's presence or oblivious. A bird with brilliant red plumage and long tail feathers wreathed in flame sat preening on the roof of a shrine, while below, a ghostly dog followed a boy through the streets, wagging its tail when the child turned to talk to it.

A giggle caught my attention. Glancing over, I saw a girl sitting on the steps of a simple house, a paper pinwheel in one small hand. She waved at me, and I caught the flash of yellow in her large eyes, saw the familiar black-tipped ears standing atop her head, and my breath caught. But when I stopped to call out to her, she turned and scurried up the steps to her house, bushy tail flowing behind her, and vanished through the doors of the house.

"So, yokai live here, too," Tatsumi murmured as we continued down the street. "Or, at least, they're not reviled and shunned. There was a bakeneko sitting on a fence earlier, and I'm sure I saw a kappa under one of the bridges. It's amazing they can live here without bloodshed."

"They have everything they need here," I realized, feeling an odd sense of longing tug at me. "The humans in this place accept them. They're not strange or monstrous or something to be feared—they're part of the natural world, just like the kami."

"I can see why the Moon Clan prefers to stay isolated," Tatsumi went on, watching as a glowing white moth drifted down, transparent wings beating erratically, to hover around him. "And why outsiders aren't allowed into their cities. Not all clans would take such a peaceful approach to the arrangement here."

I didn't answer. The kitsune girl had appeared again, leaping down the back steps of her home, only this time she was met by two children of similar age. They laughed together, bouncing around each other, and then all three of them scampered off, disappearing around a corner.

I took a shaky breath and turned away, a stinging sensation

in my eyes. "I'm glad," I whispered. "I'm glad they have somewhere they can be themselves. Where they can be safe."

Tatsumi didn't say anything to that, and we continued in silence through the city.

The Moon Clan Palace loomed above us as we crossed an arched bridge and made our way toward its gates. Fierce komainu statues, ten times larger than Chu, flanked the opening, their stone gazes proud and defiant. I wondered if, like Chu, they could also come alive to defend the palace if called upon. Past the gates was a serene, peaceful garden, raked white sand and bamboo glittering under the rising yellow moon. A few nobles were outside, clustered in small groups, their voices muted in the shadows.

As we passed a trio of noblewomen standing by a small pond, one of them glanced up, and her eyes went wide as she saw me. Quickly, she spun back, averting her gaze, but the frenzied whispers and furtive glances over their shoulders made my tail bristle. Tatsumi frowned. He, too, had seen the odd behavior, but there was nothing we could do but follow the guards up the steps and through the main entrance of the palace.

The hall beyond the enormous double doors glowed softly with lantern light, casting an orange light over the polished wood-and-tile floor. More nobles were scattered throughout the chamber, along with several samurai and guards. I saw more stares thrown my way as we crossed the room, caught the looks of confusion and disbelief in the eyes of the humans around me, and wondered, in this city full of kami, spirits and yokai, if they *all* could see through my disguise to the kitsune beneath.

And if they could see the fox striding so boldly through the palace, could they also see the demon beside her?

Near the back of the chamber, where the golden statues of a phoenix and a dragon loomed over the assembly, a voice rose into the air. Stern, female and instantly familiar. A small group of people clustered beneath the statues; I could see a ripple of long white hair, a small figure in red hakama, a lean form with a bow strapped over his back.

I gasped and rushed forward. "Minna!" I called, waving my arm. "Daisuke, Reika, Okame-san, you made it!"

They whirled, their faces registering disbelief and shock. "Yumeko," Reika cried, and hurried forward to throw her arms around me in a brief embrace. I returned it, but almost immediately, the shrine maiden pulled back to look me in the eye, her expression stern once more. "Are you all right?" she demanded, slender fingers digging into my arms. "What happened after the ship went down? Where…?" Her gaze flicked to Tatsumi, standing silently at my back, and a slender brow arched. "Kage-san?"

I didn't see Tatsumi, but he must've nodded, for she relaxed and turned back as Daisuke and Okame stepped forward, as well. "Yumeko-chan." Okame grinned, shaking his head. "So, you made it. I tried to tell these two not to worry, that you have the luck of Tamafuku himself. Even after we got separated, I knew you and Kage-san would turn up in the most unexpected place possible."

"Is that so?" Reika said flatly. "And who was drinking himself into a stupor that first night because he was sure they were both eaten by the umibozu?"

"That was because *I* nearly drowned." Okame raised a hand toward the ceiling. "And I'm not too proud to say that watching a fifty-foot shadow man rise out of the ocean and smash a ship to kindling is slightly traumatic. Frankly, I don't understand how you *don't* drink every night."

Daisuke smiled. "It is good to see you, Yumeko-san," he said, not bothering to hide the relief in his voice. "You and Kage-san both. I feared the sea had claimed you when the monster destroyed the ship. But you made it back to us, after all, thank the kami."

"What happened to the three of you?" I asked, gazing at

each of them. "After the ship was destroyed, how did you end up here?"

"We managed to float into Heishi harbor," Okame said. "After the locals fished us out of the water, we told them our reason for coming, and they sent us here to speak to the daimyo."

"We only just arrived," Reika added. She looked troubled now, watching me with shadowed eyes. Something in her gaze was a warning, though I didn't understand from what. "Kiyomi-sama was kind enough to grant us an audience, but..."

"But she was unaware that two others would also be coming to her city," said a voice behind Reika. "And that they were also looking to prevent the Summoning of the Dragon."

I looked up as Daisuke, Reika and Okame moved aside, revealing a woman standing between them. And suddenly, I couldn't move, feeling my shock rise to clash with the rest of the room's. I understood now the strange looks and glances of the nobles, the disbelief in the eyes of the court. Apparently, they weren't reacting to seeing a kitsune at all.

The daimyo of the Moon Clan stood before me, small and slender, with long, straight hair and a firm, no-nonsense mouth. Her billowing robes were silver gray with the silhouettes of bamboo and dragonflies staining the fabric like ink. Her dark eyes stared into mine, mirroring my own stunned expression. She was undoubtedly older—faint lines radiated from the corners of her eyes and mouth, and a few silvery strands were threaded in her hair, but the similarities were unmistakable.

Me. The woman staring wide-eyed, like she, too, had seen a ghost...was me.

11

Longings of Yurei

Suki

She's here.

Hovering invisible near the rafters of the main hall, Suki watched the fox girl enter the room and felt an immediate swell of relief. For two days, she had drifted around the Moon Clan Palace, watching nobles, servants and samurai go about their daily lives. She had been surprised to learn that she was not the only spirit hovering around the Tsuki palace; in the gardens, she had glimpsed a pale, glowing woman standing wistfully at the edge of the pond, and a child in a beautifully patterned kimono had laughed and waved to her in one of the halls before it turned and walked right through a shoji screen. They did not seem hostile, existing peacefully with the humans, the odd yokai and the hundreds of tiny green kami that were everywhere in and around the palace. The humans did not seem to begrudge sharing their home with ghosts and kami, leaving out offerings of food, sweets and sake, even asking a spirit's pardon before entering a room. If Suki could have chosen a place to haunt for the rest of eternity, there were certainly worse places in the empire than the palace of the Moon Clan.

But she had a job to do, and Seigetsu-sama was counting on her. She could sense him sometimes, another presence lurking behind her vision, not intrusive or frightening, but definitely there. Mostly, he was an impassive observer, one she could almost forget about. Only once, when she'd first seen the woman who she later learned was the daimyo of the Moon Clan, had she felt a glimmer of emotion that was not her own. Curiosity? Amusement? Regret? The emotion vanished before she could place it, and she suspected Lord Seigetsu would not explain his mysterious interest in the Moon Clan daimyo to her, so she watched the woman closely, knowing she was special.

Two days later, Suki had been in the main hall, observing the daimyo and the crowds from her place near the ceiling, when the doors opened and a pair of guards entered.

Escorting Daisuke-sama, the ronin and the shrine maiden.

Suki's hands had flown to her mouth, a relieved smile breaking over her face. The Sun Clan noble looked weary and disheveled, his robes torn and his long white hair a tangled mess, but he still looked beautiful to Suki's eyes. *Daisuke-sama*, she thought, watching as the guards led them to the daimyo. *You came. I'm so glad you're all right.*

There was a faint stirring from within, a ripple of something terrifying crossing her mind, and Suki had frozen, wondering what she had done wrong. Lord Seigetsu's voice echoed in her head, chilling and ominous. *The kitsune is not with them*, he observed. *Nor is the demonslayer. This was not supposed to happen. Why could I not predict this?*

His fury had been suffocating. Choking and terrible, even though, as a ghost, she didn't breathe. She huddled against the ceiling, wanting to flee but knowing she couldn't escape the presence inside her. *Taka*, she heard him muse in a cold voice that made her want to shiver into mist and disappear, *your visions did not account for this. Did I make a mistake, or has your usefulness come to an end?*

"Yumeko!"

Suki had jerked up as the shout echoed through the hall. Relief had filled her when the kitsune girl herself strode into the room, an old monk trailing after her. She was immediately surrounded by her friends, talking excitedly about what happened after they were separated, and Suki went numb as she observed their reunion.

She felt Seigetsu sigh, and the terrible fury evaporated like frost in the sun. *She is safe,* he breathed. *She and the demonslayer both. Her fortune continues to defy fate, and the game goes on. Suki-chan,* he said, making her start at the direct communication. *I thank you for this. You don't understand the significance, but all the pieces are now in place. The last maneuver is about to begin. Please return to me when you are ready. I have one final task for you.*

And just like that, he was gone, his consciousness fading from her mind completely. Startled by his abrupt departure and the sudden, eerie emptiness left behind, Suki looked back to where the fox girl and her companions were speaking to the daimyo. The Taiyo noble stood quietly beside the ronin, his beautiful face and relieved smile making her insides twist.

Daisuke-sama, she thought. *I'm afraid for you, for everyone. Something is about to begin, and only Lord Seigetsu knows what that is. I don't want you to die. I wish I could tell you what is happening.*

She hesitated. Perhaps she *could* find a way to speak to him, if only for a moment. Seigetsu-sama had asked her to return; he needed her for one final task, and she did not want to disappoint him. But this might be the last time she would see Taiyo Daisuke, her last chance to talk to the noble she had loved in life. Surely Seigetsu-sama would not begrudge her a few more minutes.

Suki struggled with herself a moment more, then gathered her courage and made a decision. Still invisible, she dropped from the ceiling and drifted silently toward the Taiyo noble.

12

The Moon Clan Daimyo

Yumeko

"*W*ho are you?" the daimyo whispered. Around us, the court, the samurai, and even Daisuke, Okame and Reika, disappeared, fading into a surreal background of blurred colors and muted sound. The woman standing before me was the only clear image in the room.

"I…my name is Yumeko," I answered. "I'm nobody, Kiyomi-sama, just a peasant from the Earth Clan mountains. I…" I trailed off, for the daimyo had stepped forward, her expression searching. I saw her gaze flit to the top of my head and knew, without a doubt, that she could see my true self. Briefly, I felt a stab of fear for Tatsumi: if the daimyo of the Moon Clan could see my fox nature, she would certainly notice the half-demon in the room, as well. But Tsuki-sama didn't even glance at Tatsumi. Shaking her head, she staggered back a pace, as if she could not believe her eyes.

"How?" she whispered, her voice barely audible. "How can

this be? I gave you up for lost. And now you return, on the eve of the Summoning, when the world teeters on the brink of change. I…" She paused, looking stricken, but then raised her chin and drew herself up. "Why have you come?" she asked in a hard voice.

I swallowed. "We've been chasing the Dragon scroll," I said, and her eyes widened once more. "A great evil has come to your lands, Kiyomi-sama. Genno, the Master of Demons, has all three pieces of the prayer, and intends to use the Wish to bring darkness to the empire."

"Your friends have told me this," the daimyo said. "But you must understand—the Moon Clan made a pact with the kami long ago not to interfere in the ways of men or gods. We are impartial observers, far removed from the strife and politics of the rest of the empire. These are the Dragon's lands. We thrive on the back of a sleeping god, and we have promised never to seek out the power of the Dragon's Prayer, nor attempt to stop those who wish to call upon the Harbinger. Change must come—it is the way of the kami."

"But your people are in danger," I insisted. "Genno is trying to overthrow the empire. He doesn't want to bring about change, he wants to bring about destruction. We came here to try to stop him, but the Master of Demons has an army, and we can't do this ourselves. We need your aid, Kiyomi-sama. The Kirin told me to find you. I can only assume it thought you could help."

"The Kirin spoke to you?" Kiyomi-sama looked taken aback. "In all my years as daimyo," she murmured, "I have seen the sacred beast only once, and it was from afar. It has never deigned to grace me with its wisdom. But it spoke to you." I nodded, and her brow furrowed. "One cannot ignore a sign from the kami," she whispered. "Though I shudder at what this means for the Moon Clan."

"Kiyomi-sama," Reika broke in, her voice carefully deferential, "I know you wish to protect your people. I know the

Moon Clan has declared themselves neutral from clan politics and the ways of the empire. And I know that your family has made a vow to live in peace with the kami, to not interfere in the ways of the gods. But if Genno gets his wish and summons the Dragon, the whole empire will be in danger, starting with these very islands. Together, we must stop him before he can call upon the Harbinger. The night of the Wish is almost here."

The Moon Clan daimyo was silent for several heartbeats, her expression clouded and far away. Finally, she stirred.

"I must...think on this," she announced. "Tonight, I will commune with the kami and seek their wisdom on these matters. I will give you my answer tomorrow, but until this conflict is resolved, please stay at the palace as honored guests. The servants will prepare your rooms. Girl..." She turned to me, a shadow of uncertainty, doubt and fear sliding through her eyes, before they hardened with resolve. "Yumeko-san... I would speak with you alone. You are in no danger, but I think there are questions we both need answers to. Please, follow me."

I glanced at the others who, aside from the stoic monk behind me, looked as dazed and confused by these revelations as I felt. My emotions seemed frozen, too stunned to comprehend the magnitude of what was happening. But Tatsumi gave me a somber nod as our gazes met, his dark eyes almost sympathetic. *We'll be fine*, he was telling me. *Go with the daimyo, Yumeko.* I smiled at him weakly, then took a deep breath and started after Kiyomi-sama.

I followed the Tsuki daimyo through the halls of the palace, passing servants, courtiers and samurai, who gave me curious glances while pretending not to see us. The palace was dim and cool, but unlike the dark, labyrinthine halls of the Shadow Clan castle, the Moon Clan Palace was airy and open, with many rooms and hallways offering access to the outside. Tiny gardens with bushes, stones lanterns and patches of bamboo were interspersed throughout the palace, meticulously planted and tended to, small havens of nature surrounded by railings and walkways. Fireflies drifted through the halls, blips of yellow and green in the shadows, floating around the heads of passersby or landing on their clothes. As we passed another miniature garden, I saw a single kodama sitting on a rock beside a goldfish pond. It waved as I passed by, and I smiled back.

Finally, Tsuki-sama led me down a series of verandas, across an arched bridge over a pond, to a small island in the very center of the water. A gazebo sat surrounded by bamboo, with twisted vines curled around its pillars and a hole in the roof open to the night sky. Delicate chimes dangling from the stalks swayed gently on the wind, filling the air with faint, shivering notes that mingled with the sound of the breeze and the water. All around us, the night was alive with the presence of the kami.

Kiyomi-sama didn't say anything at first. Walking to the edge of the gazebo, she gazed over the pond at the rising moon, whose pale light glimmered on the surface of the water. I waited silently, my emotions no longer frozen, but a writhing nest of nervousness, fear and disbelief. This woman…knew me. Tsuki Kiyomi, the daimyo of the entire Moon Clan, could be my…

"I come here sometimes," she said with her back still turned. "When the duties of court become too much, or when I need to commune with the kami. Their voices have always been soft, disjoined, fragmented, depending on how they feel and which ones choose to answer, but they have never led me astray. They can be fickle, but after listening to them for years, I have learned to discern their voices, to separate fact from emotion, to see the truth. But there has always been one question I have asked, time and time again, that they have never been able answer."

Kiyomi-sama finally turned, her dark eyes boring into me, as if seeking to see everything.

"I know you have questions," she said, and her voice was shaking now, the thin veneer of calm starting to fade. "And I will do my best to answer. But before I do, I must ask that you tell me your story first. Who are you? Where have you been these past sixteen years? Did your father tell you anything about your past, where you came from? Did you ever suspect that, perhaps, you did not belong?"

I blinked. "My…father?" I repeated in a whisper. "You knew him?"

"Of course I did." For a moment, Kiyomi-sama looked indignant and furious. "He was my husband. I loved him, gave him everything I had, only to have him betray me and everything I cared for." She paused, shoulders slumping, and suddenly looked decades older. "He never spoke of me? Even once?"

"I—I never knew him," I stammered. "I was found on the steps of a temple in the Earth Clan mountains and raised by the monks there. They taught me everything I know but…they never mentioned my family. I don't think they knew where I came from, either."

"I see," Kiyomi-sama whispered, and sat down on the wooden bench surrounding the gazebo edge. "Then it appears he betrayed us both."

Carefully, I perched on the edge of the bench across from her, watching as she seemed to gather herself. For a few moments, she stared blankly over the water, as if gathering memories long forgotten. Memories that she did not want to remember.

"Your father was yokai," Kiyomi-sama said at last. "Obviously, you know this. You are half-kitsune, so it should come as no surprise. My husband was a man named Tsuki Toshimoko, a noble from one of the major families of the Moon Clan. It was an arranged marriage, of course. As the heir of the Tsuki family, I was promised to Toshimoko from the time I was six, and married when I was fourteen."

"I'm sorry, Kiyomi-sama, but I'm confused. You said my father was yokai. Was Toshimoko-sama…?"

"No," said Kiyomi-sama. "At least, not at first. Of this I am certain." At my bewildered expression, she shook her head. "I know it sounds disjointed, Yumeko-san. It has taken me sixteen years to untangle what happened, and even now, I am uncertain as to when your father came into the picture. Nor do I know what happened to the real Toshimoko, though I fear the answer is obvious. Please bear with me as I try to explain."

I bit my lip and fell silent, though inside, my nervousness grew. I could feel the writhing of my stomach, and felt like I was standing on the edge of an abyss, waiting for the ground to give way beneath me. The Moon Clan daimyo paused, then turned to gaze over the water again.

"For the first few years," Kiyomi-sama went on, "everything was normal. My husband was a good man, honorable and fair. If he was distant, it was because his duties kept him very busy—his responsibility to the Moon Clan was his most pressing concern. Our marriage was one of convenience, though my failure to bear him an heir was always a point of contention between us. I believe he resented me for it, though he would never admit such a thing out loud.

"And then, one day, he simply...changed." Kiyomi-sama frowned, her lips pursing as if she was struggling with the words. "No, forgive me—I am making it sound as if he suddenly forgot who he was. I do not remember when I started to notice, but he was suddenly more attentive to me, kinder and sympathetic. Not that he had ever been cruel—we had always treated each other with courtesy, but there was a warmth to him that had not been there before. He seemed genuinely interested in me, in my thoughts and ideas, encouraging me to share both my dreams and my fears with him. For the first time, I felt seen, understood. And as the months passed, I began to fall in love with him.

"When I discovered I was pregnant, I concluded that it must have been a blessing from the gods. I thought, however foolishly, that our love had overcome my barren womb, for love conquers all and places even the impossible within reach." Kiyomi-sama gave a bitter smile. "Such notions are laughable now, but I was young and blissfully happy. Looking back, I lived those nine months as if in a dream." She took a deep breath, her face darkening. "And then, that dream shattered, and became the nightmare I still live with today."

A chill slid down my back. Kiyomi-sama continued to stare over the water, her expression growing haunted. "When the time came, my delivery had…complications," she said. "I lost a lot of blood, and became delirious near the end. Everything is hazy now, as if the entire event had been a dream. But… I remember being desperate not to lose the baby, and screaming at the midwives to save it, to not let it die. What happened next…"

The daimyo trembled, her voice beginning to shake. "I faded in and out of consciousness for a bit," she whispered, "but at one point, I remember looking up and thinking I saw my husband standing over me. That night, he…he seemed like a stranger, and his eyes…they were yellow, like the flicker of candle flames, and glowing in the darkness. He spoke to me, words that I can't recall now, but I remember being filled with fear and rage and despair. I thought it was a nightmare, but when I woke and asked for my child…" Kiyomi-sama's lip trembled; she had to pause and take a shaky breath before she could continue. "They told me that both the baby and my husband were gone. That they had vanished, sometime in the night, and that no one had seen them since."

I bit my cheek, as the ache that had been growing in my throat threatened to close it completely. "I… I'm sorry," I whispered, not knowing what to say.

"I looked for her," the daimyo murmured, as if she hadn't heard me. "I scoured the whole of the Moon Clan islands, every nook and hidden cranny, all the caves and deepest forests. I sent priests, warriors, even mercenaries to the mainland, searching for my stolen child and the husband who betrayed us all. No one could find a trace of them. It was as if they had vanished from this plane of existence.

"In the long years since that night," Kiyomi-sama continued, "I have tried my best to move on, to forget that I had a daughter, though I knew it would be impossible. One does not simply carry a life within them for so long without it becoming a part of them. I even had a name for her," Kiyomi-sama admitted shakily, "one that I shared only with my husband, and have not spoken since that night. Her name would be...Yumeko, because her existence, and the way she came into my life, had been like a dream."

The tears that had been threatening to burst forth finally did, spilling over and running hotly down my cheeks. Her grief echoed in her every word, every glance and gesture, a lifetime of sorrow and regret. I bowed my head and sobbed, for Kiyomi-sama and all she had lost, for the life that was stolen from her, and for the mother I had never known. For the first time, I found myself hating my father, the mysterious yokai who had planned this from the very beginning, who had made Kiyomi-sama fall in love with him and bear him a child, knowing he would tear her life apart in the end.

"I'm so sorry," I choked out, feeling the gaze of the daimyo on the top of my head. "I didn't... I would have come if I had known. Somehow, I would have found my way."

The daimyo was quiet a moment, watching me, before she rose. I heard the swish of her kimono as she walked to my side of the gazebo and gazed down at me. I didn't dare look up, suddenly terrified that I would see resentment in her eyes, anger and hate for the half-kitsune who had shown up on her doorstep, reminding her of everything she had lost. Then she bent down, her fingers softly brushing my elbows as she drew me to my feet. I raised my head and met her gaze, searching, apprising, but otherwise unreadable.

"He must have known," Kiyomi-sama whispered. "He must

have known, somehow, that you would find your way here. It is too much to believe that on the eve of the Dragon's Wish, you would appear before me by chance. And if the Kirin sent you to me, then there are forces at work beyond anyone's control or comprehension."

She sighed, and I imagined the mantle of leadership weighing heavily on her shoulders. I could practically see it bearing her down, though she raised her head and stood firm. "You will have your aid, Yumeko-san," the Tsuki daimyo said. "The Moon Clan will stand ready to help you and your companions. If that calls us to march on the sacred cliffs of Ryugake and confront an army of demons, so be it. I will gather my forces, and tomorrow we will travel to Tani Kaminari, the Valley of Lightning, that sits below the sacred mountains. There is only one path up the cliff face to the Summoning site. If Genno wishes to call on the Harbinger, he must get through us first."

I blinked rapidly. "Thank you, Kiyomi-sama."

Her eyes softened, and for just a moment, her hand rose to gently touch my cheek, a wistful shadow crossing her face. "You are a stranger to me," she murmured, her voice tinged with regret. "I would have liked to know you. Perhaps later, when this is all over, we can fill in the years we have lost."

"I'd like that."

She nodded. "Go, then," she said, gesturing back over the bridge. "Return to your friends if you wish. I will send word to my people and all parties involved, telling them of my decision. Sleep tonight, Yumeko-san. Rest while you are able, for tomorrow we march to war."

I bowed to the daimyo and started to turn away, but paused when I heard her voice again.

"And, Yumeko-san," Kiyomi-sama added, "that half-demon who followed you into the palace. He will not be a threat to my people, will he?"

My stomach twisted, and I shook my head. "No, Kiyomi-sama."

"Good." The daimyo gave a solemn nod. "As long as you vouch for him, I will not put him under guard. But his presence has made the kami very nervous, so please bear that in mind." She raised her sleeve in a gesture of farewell. "I will see you and your companions tomorrow, Yumeko-san, and we will prepare to confront the Master of Demons. Oyasuminasai."

"Good night," I repeated softly and gave a final bow before turning and walking back over the bridge. A servant waited on the other side, and I followed her into the palace, feeling the eyes of Kiyomi-sama on my back the entire way.

13

For Sake and Memories

Suki

Suki didn't particularly like spying, but as a ghost, there seemed to be little else she could do. She didn't want to reveal herself to everyone in the palace; even if yurei were tolerated here, there might be some that would react poorly to a strange spirit appearing out of nowhere. Regardless, it wasn't in Suki's nature to be seen. In life, attracting attention had been dangerous and something she'd avoided. She was used to fading into the background, becoming invisible and unimportant. It was even easier now that she was a ghost.

So she trailed Daisuke-sama invisibly through the hallways of the Moon Clan Palace, watching as various nobles stopped to talk to him, curious, she guessed, about a Taiyo in their midst. Or perhaps drawn to Daisuke-sama's beauty and kindness, as she had been, so long ago it seemed. As ever, the Taiyo noble was poised and gracious, though Suki thought he seemed a bit distracted tonight.

"There is a chill in the air surrounding you, Taiyo-san," one noble commented, peering over Daisuke's shoulder to where Suki hovered, unseen. "I think you might have attracted the attention of a yurei."

Suki jerked up, eyes widening, but Daisuke only smiled. "Oh? Is it something I should worry about?"

"Not necessarily." The other noble waved an airy hand. "There are always kami and spirits about, and from time to time, we do see ghosts drifting through the palace or in the city. They're not usually troublesome, but if you find yourself being haunted or harassed, there are many priests and shrine maidens here who can exorcise them. Kiyomi-sama herself is quite adept at convincing restless spirits to move on."

"Thank you," Daisuke said with a small bow. "I will remember that, but I fear I must retire. It has been a long journey."

"Of course, Taiyo-san." The other noble returned the bow, smiling. "Welcome to Tsuki lands. Oh, and do not be alarmed if you see kodama in your room, they are everywhere. Do not insult them, and they will leave on their own."

Daisuke murmured a reply and turned to the patiently waiting servant, indicating he was ready to continue. Suki followed, but at a greater distance than before, suddenly nervous that the Taiyo could sense her presence. But the noble walked steadily down the halls without pause, giving no indication that he thought anything was amiss. When the servant showed him to his guest quarters and departed, Suki floated through the wall and found Daisuke standing in a simple but elegant room, gazing around as if expecting to see someone.

"Are you here, Suki-san?" he asked quietly.

Suki was stunned for only a moment. Of course Daisuke-sama would guess that she was here. He might've even sensed her presence in the great hall. She hesitated, then shimmered into view, earning a raised brow and a sad smile from the noble.

"Still haunting me," he murmured. "Even here, on the islands of the Moon Clan, it seems I cannot escape my past."

Walking to the back of the room, he slid open a panel, revealing a veranda overlooking a small garden, flowered shrubs and stone lanterns surrounding a small pond. Suki drifted after him, watching as he leaned his elbows on the railing and gazed into the water, his face unreadable.

"It is almost time," he murmured, as if to himself. "I can feel it, Suki-san. The great battle draws near. The night of the Wish is almost upon us. I hope…" His smooth brow furrowed. "I will strive to fight well and die with honor, protecting what is most important to me. I will not fail those I care for, as I did with you."

Something twisted inside of her. The Taiyo blamed himself for her death? The confession would have brought tears to her eyes had she still been alive. "You…you didn't fail me, Daisuke-sama," Suki whispered, struggling to get the words out. It had been a while since she had last spoken to anyone but Lord Seigetsu, and remembering how again had become difficult. "My death wasn't caused by you, and I… I was nothing. Just a servant, worth no one's time."

The noble gave another sad smile. "If that is true, then why do you haunt me, Suki-san?" he asked in a quiet voice. "What keeps you here in the land of the living? Why can you not move on, if I am not at least somewhat accountable?"

Because, I…

Suki trembled. She could not get the words out. *I loved you. I want to save you from whatever is coming. I can't leave until I know…*

"Something is…happening, Daisuke-sama," she told him instead. "I don't know…what is coming, but it is very close. It feels…important. And…I get to see it, because of you."

The Taiyo noble still watched her, his expression unbearably soft. Suki trembled, the memory of burning cheeks and a pounding heart making her want to turn away, to vanish from sight, but she forced herself to remain still. "Whatever happens," she whispered, "I don't… I never blamed you for anything, Daisuke-sama. I just…want you to be happy."

The noble closed his eyes. "Arigatou, Suki-san," he murmured. "If these are truly the last days, I hope I greet them with honor. And I pray that you will find the peace to move on."

A tap came from the front door, followed by a gruff, familiar voice. "Taiyo-san? You in there?"

The ronin. Suki winked out of sight as Daisuke-sama straightened and turned toward the voice. A genuine smile crossed his face, one that made her shiver. It wasn't sad or wistful or full of shadows like before; in that moment, he seemed truly happy.

"Please, come in, Okame-san," Daisuke-sama called. "I was hoping you would stop by tonight."

"Oh?" The door slid back, revealing the ronin's smirking face on the other side. He held a pair of sake bottles in one hand, and continued to smile as he closed the door behind him. "How scandalous, Daisuke-san. What would the nobility think of you inviting a dirty ronin into your room late at night?"

"I am sure they would all be very offended," Daisuke replied. "Luckily, they are not here at the moment. And…" he paused, giving his head a tiny shake "…I find myself not caring what they would think anymore."

"Well, that's a good thing, I suppose." The ronin stepped into the room, placing the sake bottles on the small table in the center. "I always say it's better not to drink alone." He straightened, gesturing to the table with a smile. "What do you say, noble? Care to share a drink with me? Who knows, it might be our last one."

Daisuke smiled. "Of course."

He walked back into the room and seated himself cross-legged at the table. And for a moment that seemed timeless, the two men drank sake and spoke of their journey, what they had faced, who they had lost and what was still to come. Suki knew she should leave. This was a private conversation she had no part in. But, perhaps out of curiosity, perhaps longing, she couldn't quite bring herself to go. Besides, she was a ghost; no one cared if the dead were listening. So she hovered, invisible, in a corner of the room, watching as Daisuke and the ronin emptied the sake bottles and the moon rose higher into the sky.

"It appears we have reached the end," Daisuke murmured as the ronin poured sake into his cup and only a few drops came out. "Should we send for more, Okame-san?"

"No." The ronin set the bottle down, looking oddly serious. "I want to stay mostly sober tonight," he admitted. "Seems like a good idea, what with the final battle being so close. Nothing like tripping drunkenly over your own feet and falling on some demon's spear because you couldn't see straight."

"That would not be a glorious way to go," Daisuke agreed. "Though I once met a perpetually drunken master who might argue the point."

The ronin chuckled. "Ah, if only I'd known about the drunken masters when I was younger," he sighed. "I think I might've missed my calling. But there is another reason I'm embracing soberness tonight. I wanted to talk to you, Daisuke-san, and I didn't want it coming out as drunken ramblings. Because I…may not get another chance to say this…"

He paused, a flush creeping up his neck as he looked away. Daisuke straightened slowly, somberness chasing away his relaxed manner.

"I… That is…ah, kuso." The ronin rubbed the back of his neck. "Maybe I should've been drunk for this, after all," he muttered.

"There is no shame is talking to me, Okame-san," Daisuke said quietly. "We are alone here. I will promise that whatever you have to say will earn you no ridicule or scorn. I have always admired your honesty, even if it was hard to hear. Please, speak your mind. I will not judge, I swear it."

"Kuso," the ronin muttered again. "You know, from any other noble, that would come off as arrogant and condescending. But not you." He snorted, shaking his head, but it didn't seem angry or mocking, just resigned. "I've never met anyone like you, Taiyo-san. You are everything I thought I despised about the samurai, but the one exception is that you actually believe in the ideal of Bushido. The entire Code, not just the parts that are convenient. Not just the parts that will uphold your own personal honor."

"The Code of Bushido," Daisuke said in a serious voice, "is a contradiction, Okame-san. How can one be compassionate *and* obedient if one's lord demands cruelty? How can one have self-control if slaughtering his enemies brings him glory? If honor is everything, then why is it so easy to lose?"

"Daisuke-san." The ronin's voice was amused but weary. "Even if I wanted to, I've had way too much sake to debate the contradictive nature of Bushido and the samurai. That's not what I wanted to talk about."

"Then what *do* you wish to say, Okame-san?"

"Why me?"

Daisuke blinked. He appeared genuinely surprised by the question, though Suki didn't know what the ronin was talking about. "What do you mean, Okame-san?" Daisuke asked, echoing her own thoughts.

"I mean…" The other man raked a hand through his hair, his neck going red again. "You're a Taiyo. You could have your pick of literally anyone in the empire. And normally, I'm all for that. Hell, I've had a couple rowdy nights in a village just to blow off some steam. But you don't seem that type." The ronin paused, brow furrowed as he stared down at the polished table edge. Daisuke was motionless, hardly breathing, as if he feared any movement would shatter the world around them. Though he never took his gaze from the man across from him.

"So, why me?" the ronin said once more. "I'm a ronin dog,

you're the golden Taiyo. The status gulf between us couldn't be any wider. Am I just a passing fascination? Something you wanted to pursue because your family isn't here? Or have you gotten so bored and disillusioned of the court, you wanted to do something completely profane, just to spite it?"

"Is…is that what you believe, Okame-san?" Daisuke's voice actually trembled. "Truly?"

The ronin let out a long, frustrated sigh. "I don't know," he admitted with a hopeless gesture. "No. I don't believe that. It's just…" He gazed down at the table with shadowed eyes, as if he found the reflection staring back at him wanting. "I have never felt this way before," he murmured. "About anyone. Especially for a swaggering court peacock who should represent everything I hate about samurai. And you…you keep talking about a glorious death, Daisuke-san. Like it's a game, something you're racing toward, when personally, I have spent my entire life trying to survive one more day. Not to mention, I selfishly want to keep you around for as long as I can. But that's me—an honorless ronin dog." He sighed again, though this time it sounded sad, and glanced up at the still-motionless noble. "I'm not afraid of death, Daisuke-san," he said softly, "but…if I *am* going to die with someone… I want what we have to be real."

For a moment, the Taiyo noble didn't move. His beautiful face was expressionless, his eyes distant and unreadable. The ronin dropped his gaze again, looking down at his hands.

In one elegant motion, Daisuke rose, took two steps around the table and sank to his knees behind the ronin, slipping his arms around his neck. The other's breath caught, and he closed his eyes as Daisuke leaned in, his lips at the ronin's ear.

"I would not ask just anyone to die with me, Okame-san," he whispered. "You are more than ronin. You have loyalty, courage, compassion, everything a warrior should strive for, and your honesty about the world is something most samurai are blind to. It would be an honor to meet that glorious death at your side."

"Daisuke." The ronin's voice was a breath; his hands reached up to grip the noble's arms. In the corner, Suki couldn't move, her mind spinning like a child's top, unable to settle on any one thought or feeling. "Maybe we won't die," the ronin went on in a gruff whisper. "Maybe we'll win that battle, after all."

"I hope so," Daisuke murmured back. "And I will do everything in my power to ensure Yumeko-san emerges victorious. Genno *will* be defeated, and the Wish will not be used for evil in this era. But we are not the heroes of this story, Okame-san. It will be in the hands of a Shadow Clan demon and a half-kitsune peasant girl to save the empire and carry us to victory." A wry smile crossed his face. "Any other might hear those words and despair, but I have faith in our fox girl. After everything we have seen, everything thrown into our path, I believe she has the favor of the gods themselves. I am honored to have played even a small part in her story."

"Yeah," the ronin agreed, and gave his head a rueful shake. "It's been a pretty crazy journey," he muttered. "One I wouldn't trade for anything. But I think you're right, Daisuke-san. I think… I think we're coming to the end, whatever it may be. This fight for the Dragon scroll—it's that kind of battle where not all of us are going to make it." He sighed, leaning his head back. "I just hope the poets get my name right when they sing songs about us." He snorted. "Ah, hell, who am I kidding? I'll be happy if my name is mentioned in the story at all."

"It will be," Daisuke promised. "When they speak of us, Okame-san, it will be of the courageous ronin and the brave noble, standing against insurmountable odds, putting aside all differences in honor and status to protect the empire. Those will be the songs they will sing, Okame-san, the stories they will tell. Immortalized for all time. And in that way, we will always be together."

"The dog and the peacock," the ronin said, and chuckled. His arm rose, his fingers slipping into the noble's long white hair, pulling him close. "That sounds like a terrible poem. I hope someone writes it."

"I hope so, as well," Daisuke murmured. "But that battle is still on the horizon. It draws ever closer, but it is not here yet." He lowered his head, his lips brushing the ronin's shoulder, making the other draw in a slow breath. "Tonight is for the present. For sake and memories, and thinking back on all that has brought us here. For making sure that, should Meido call to us tomorrow, we will have no regrets tonight."

The ronin shivered. "No regrets, peacock?" he whispered.

"None."

"To our glorious death, then." At that, the ronin turned his head fully, meeting Daisuke's lips, and nothing more was said between them.

Suki fled their presence, flying through the ceiling, passing rafters and upper floors, until she went out through the roof. The night sky opened before her, scattered with a million stars, a pale moon veiled in the clouds like a silver coin. She paused, hovering over the peak of the tallest roof, the valley of the Moon Clan spread before her, and tried to sift through the emotions swirling through her insubstantial form.

I loved Daisuke-sama. Suki had always known that. From the moment she'd nearly bowled into him at the Golden Palace, she had been captivated by his beauty and his charm, but mostly by his kindness. Even to a humble maid. Some would scoff, claiming that one chance meeting between two people was not enough for a soul to fall in love. Suki would disagree. She had loved the Taiyo noble, knowing it would never be reciprocated, knowing he would never see her that way, not hoping for anything save a glimpse of his smile now and again. When she died, her soul had lingered on for one purpose only: to make certain Daisuke-sama was safe. Above all, she wanted him to be happy.

And now, it seemed he had found something, someone, who could do that.

I am...happy for you, Daisuke-sama, Suki thought, surprised to find that she really meant it. She was dead; jealousy and all the strife that came with it seemed silly and rather pointless. Perhaps, according to the ghost stories her mother used to tell, if she had died with such strong emotions in her heart, that anger would manifest itself onto the ronin. But she felt no malice toward the object of Daisuke's affection, no feelings of rage or ill will. Maybe she was incapable of it now.

I hope he brings you peace, Daisuke-sama. I am glad that you will have someone at your side in the final battle. May you both know happiness, for however long you have left.

A strange lightness filled her. For a moment, she could almost feel her bonds to the earth loosening, fading away. For a heartbeat, the world below did not seem quite so real anymore, and she sensed that if she simply stopped thinking, she would drift away into the unknown and whatever horizons lay beyond.

No. Suki shook herself, and a new resolve filled her ghostly body. *It isn't over. I can't leave yet. Not before I know how it ends.*

Overhead, the moon glimmered, and the distant halo of light seemed to beckon to her once more. Suki turned away from the sky and drifted back to the earth. Flying over the pond, leaving a trail of light behind her, she soared past the palace of the Moon Clan and disappeared into the forest.

14

Fox Magic in the Moonlight

Yumeko

It was a strangely surreal walk back to the palace. My mind felt like a swarm of moths, flitting crazily around a chochin lantern. I barely knew where I was going or what I was doing, until the servant paused in the hallway and informed me that we had reached my quarters. Inside was a small, simple room with thick tatami mats and an alcove with a tiny shrine dedicated to the kami. Through a pair of open shoji, I could see a veranda surrounding the room, and the lake beyond shimmering in the moonlight.

On the veranda, I leaned my elbows on the railing and gazed over the water, thinking back on everything that had happened tonight. All that had been revealed. It still felt like a dream. Maybe I'd imagined that whole conversation with Kiyomi-sama. All my life, I hadn't known who I was or where I came from. But now…

"What did the daimyo have to say?"

I jumped. "Tatsumi!" I exclaimed as a shadow melted silently off the wall behind me. Tatsumi, still disguised as an old monk in long robes and a straw hat, met my gaze with that calm stoicism he did so well.

"Did you find out what you needed? Will the Moon Clan help us?"

"Yes." I dissolved the illusion in a puff of smoke, letting the image of the monk fade into the breeze. If Kiyomi-sama already knew what he was, there was no point in trying to hide it. Though he might still need a hat so as not to terrify the rest of the court. "Kiyomi-sama agreed to aid us," I went on as Tatsumi pulled a leaf from his hair, gazed at it for a curious moment and let it flutter into the water. "The Moon Clan will be ready to defy the Master of Demons when the time comes. Kiyomi-sama knows where the Summoning will be. With any luck, she will have her forces in place before Genno ever gets there. If we can reach the valley before him, all we'll have to do is hold them off until the time for the Summoning has passed."

"Good." Tatsumi joined me at the railing, his eyes dark as he gazed over the water. "The army we fought at the Steel Feather temple wasn't Genno's full force," he added. "And he knows we're going to try to stop him. The daimyo's plan is sound, but the rest of us should head to the Summoning site because once the battle begins, Genno will be relentless. He will likely find a way through or around the army, and we need to be there when he arrives to summon the Dragon."

I nodded. "We'll stop him," I promised, lacing back my ears. "He's *not* going to summon the Dragon. Even if I have to stab him myself…though he *is* a ghost, so I suppose I'd have to use Kamigoroshi for that to work." I clenched my fists, then glanced at the demonslayer at my side. "Promise me you'll kill him, Tatsumi," I said. "No matter what it takes, we have to win. I don't care what you have to do—don't let him summon the Dragon and use the Wish. Promise me."

"I will, but..." Tatsumi cocked his head, a concerned frown crossing his face as he watched me. "We've always known the stakes, Yumeko. Nothing has changed. Are you all right?"

"I..." Pushing myself off the railing, I walked a few steps away, trying to put the fluttering thoughts in my head into words. "Kiyomi-sama... The daimyo..."

"She's your mother."

I whirled in surprise. Tatsumi offered a faint smile. "She looks just like you," he told me softly. "And from the conversation in the hall earlier, it wasn't that difficult to figure out." The smile widened a bit, though his voice stayed gentle. "So, you really are a kami princess."

"I can't lose now, Tatsumi," I whispered. "Before, I was alone. I thought I'd lost my only family to demons. But now..." I gazed back at the water, at the rest of the palace shining under the light of the moon. "I can't watch this disappear," I murmured. "I want to stay, to learn. To catch up on everything I missed. But if Genno destroys all of this..." I put a shaking hand on the railing, closing my eyes. "It doesn't seem fair," I said quietly, as Denga's stern face flashed before me, one brow raised and unimpressed. *Do you think life is fair, fox girl?* he'd asked on more than one occasion. *Do you think it cares about your petty desires?*

"I just...found her," I stammered out. "All those years at the temple, not knowing who I was, not really caring about my past. And now, I find out who I am, where I came from, on the eve when we could lose everything?" I sniffed, shaking my head. "The kami have a strange sense of humor."

Master Isao shimmered through my memory, his smile gentle as he met my gaze. *Life is not fair, Yumeko-chan,* he murmured. *Life is* balance. *Before spring, there must be winter. Before the sun, there must be darkness. What is, is what must be.*

There was a pause, and then a warm, calloused hand closed over my own. I looked up into Tatsumi's solemn eyes.

"I promise, Yumeko," he said in a quiet, intense voice. "Genno *will* die. I won't let him destroy what you've found here. I'll fight to protect you and all you care for. You have my word."

My vision blurred. Stepping forward, I leaned into him and he pulled me close, wrapping his arms around me. For a moment, we stayed like that, our breaths mingling and the moonlight blazing down on us. Tatsumi's fingers slipped into my hair, sliding it through his palm in an almost reverent manner, as if he were amazed by something so simple. Closing my eyes, I relaxed into him and listened to his heartbeat, remembering the first time I'd seen the cold, purple-eyed killer in the woods outside my burning home. He had changed so much since that terrible night. I wondered if my old self would even recognize the beautiful half-demon holding me in his arms now.

I wondered if I would recognize myself.

"Arigatou," I whispered. "For everything, Tatsumi. I wouldn't have made it this far… I wouldn't have found *her*, if it wasn't for you."

He gazed down at me, his eyes softer than I'd ever seen before. "My life is yours," he said simply, his voice barely above a murmur. One palm framed the side of my face, long fingers and calloused skin pressing against my cheek. "You gave me purpose again, Yumeko. On my honor, I'll make sure you have a home to go back to."

Leaning in, he kissed me. I closed my eyes and wrapped my arms around his neck, feeling his own tighten around my waist, almost lifting me off my feet. My heart pounded as ribbons of light and heat began coiling through my stomach, spreading through my chest and every part of my body.

The snap of a shoji screen pulled me out of the emotions beginning to swirl around us. Drawing back, I frowned as a noble stepped onto the veranda several doors down, pausing to admire the lake and moonlight, before she turned in our direction. Tatsumi and I didn't move, but the noble stiffened, and though it was too far to see her face clearly, I thought I saw her turn rather red. Smoothly, she pivoted, pretending to admire the lake once more, then walked swiftly down the veranda and disappeared around a bend.

Tatsumi didn't seem concerned or affected by our sudden visitor, but I felt my cheeks flush. Drawing out of his embrace, I took his hands and started backing toward my room. Tatsumi followed without question or hesitation, though his eyes were faintly puzzled, his head tilted at a curious angle. When we had crossed the threshold, I released him, went to the doors and closed them with faint snaps, shutting out the sky and the enormous silver moon. The room dimmed, plunged into darkness and shadow, and I turned around with a deep breath.

Closing my eyes, I drew on my magic, feeling it rise from that ball of power somewhere deep within. With an outward push, I released it into the room, feeling it wash over the walls, floor and ceiling, engulfing the entire chamber in a cocoon of fox magic.

I opened my eyes and smiled at my handiwork. Tatsumi and I now stood in the center of a small moonlit grove, bamboo and sakura trees surrounding us. Fireflies danced through the air, pink sakura blossoms drifted around us like snow, and purple ayame-irises swayed gently in the wind. The grass beneath our feet was soft and thick, and overhead, the same enormous moon shone through the branches, spilling silver light over the grove.

I looked at Tatsumi. He stood in the center of the meadow, gazing around with an awed look on his face. "This is..." He gave his head a disbelieving shake and glanced at me, his eyes still bright with amazement. "Incredible. I've never seen fox magic this strong."

"I've learned a lot." Smiling, I stepped toward him, feeling long grass brush my ankles, hearing the hiss of the wind in the bamboo. "No one will disturb us here, Tatsumi. This is our last night, before we have to face Genno. Before the night of the Wish. I thought I could show you someplace beautiful."

His eyes went a little glassy, and the look on his face caused a lump to rise to my throat. As I stepped forward, he held out a hand. I placed my palm in his and he drew me close, one arm sliding around my waist as he kissed me gently.

"Arigatou," he whispered when we drew back. His forehead touched mine, our faces just a breath apart. "You are constantly surprising me." He raised his head and gazed around in wonder, his voice barely a murmur in the darkness. "Ichiro-sensei always told me wishing is for fools, but… I wish we had more time."

"Me, too." I ran my fingers down his chest, feeling him shiver as they passed. "But tonight is for us, Tatsumi. No one will bother us here. No one will see a demon or a fox or a peasant or a shinobi. This is our place. One last night, before we face Genno in the morning."

We kissed again, the moonlight blazing down on us, the wind ruffling our hair as it whispered through the bamboo. That strange feeling of warmth and light ignited in my stomach again, flickering under my skin like blue-white foxfire as it spread to every part of me. Tatsumi picked me up, carried me to a spot beneath the sakura trees and knelt, laying me gently in the grass. The breeze was cool, the ground soft and the cherry blossoms were like feathers drifting from the sky, as we leaned back and lost ourselves in fox magic.

15
The Hidden Path

Suki

Suki found Lord Seigetsu on a cliff overlooking the valley. The moon hung low in the sky and the stars were beginning to fade, but they still cast a pale glow around him, shining off his silver hair. Below, the valley was cloaked in shadow, but the city glowed with a soft orange light, like a chochin lantern pulsing cheerfully against the darkness. For a moment, she wondered if Seigetsu-sama would be angry at her for lingering in the Moon Clan Palace instead of returning straightaway, but he only gave her a knowing smile and turned back toward the edge of the cliff.

Suki looked around, feeling that something was wrong. Missing. After a moment, she realized what it was. "Where is Taka?" she whispered.

"Taka." Seigetsu's voice was flat, and he didn't look at her. "He is with the carriage. His sulkiness was beginning to wear on me. But it is of no matter. The board is set. The pieces are nearly in place. There is only one maneuver left."

He turned, holding out a hand to her. "We are near the end, Suki-chan," he said softly. "Very close to changing fate. I need you to do one more thing. If not for me, then for your Taiyo prince, the fox girl and the entire empire. I promise, Suki-chan, this will be the last thing I ask of you. Will you help them, and me, one final time?"

"I..." Suki looked down at the city, at the palace glowing with light in the very center. Where she had left Daisuke-sama in the arms of his ronin. He was happy, but not safe. Not yet. "Yes, Seigetsu-sama," she whispered. One more time, and maybe it would be enough. Maybe Daisuke-sama, the fox girl and all the people she had come to care for would survive, and then she could finally move on.

"Good," Seigetsu murmured, and stepped forward, raising two fingers to her forehead. "This will not hurt," he assured her, and as before, she felt the faintest brush against her skin as Seigetsu closed his eyes. "Just relax, and let the memories come to you."

There was a flare of light across her vision, and suddenly, she was at the bottom of a cliff, the waves crashing against the rocks below and sending up sprays of white foam. Before her, she could see the imposing wall of the cliff, a sheer rise of jagged rock that soared into the air. As she watched, a section of the wall seemed to dissolve into mist, revealing a narrow gap in the rock face.

Of its own accord, her body moved forward, flying across the rocks, and the black hole filled her vision. Then she was through the gap and into a series of winding, narrow tunnels and caverns. She couldn't stop or even slow, flying through the caves with no control over where she was going. Boulders and stalactites zipped past, barely missing her, and once she soared right through an enormous column and continued down the tunnel without slowing down.

The passageway twisted around, and she entered an immense cavern, the ceiling so high that she could barely see it. As she soared through, the stone floor flashing beneath her, she caught a glow from the corner of her eye, a hazy, box-shaped structure that flickered with an ominous nonlight. It was gone before she could see it clearly, but Suki was suddenly filled with dread. She knew, without a doubt, that she was not alone in these caves. That something terrible lurked in the narrow passageways, something ancient and terrifying. Stomach twisting, she willed her body to go faster, wanting only to find the way out.

At last, a tiny oval of light appeared ahead of her, growing larger and brighter with every passing moment. Relieved, Suki focused on that light, not daring to look behind her, until she flew through the gap and into open sky.

Once more, her body moved of its own accord. Squinting, she looked up to see a jagged mountain peak rising into the air, the point seeming to scrape the sky. Overhead, clouds swirled and lightning flashed, and for just a moment, she thought she glimpsed the silhouette of something massive within the storm.

Suki blinked, and abruptly, she was floating before Lord Seigetsu once more, feeling dazed as he lowered his arm. "What—what was that, Seigetsu-sama?" she whispered, not certain of what she had seen. She did remember the cave system, the ominous presence lurking within and the massive, terrifying form in the clouds.

The silver-haired man offered a faint smile and turned away, walking back to the edge of the cliff. "A path," he said, to her further confusion. "And you will be the guide to light their way. Do not worry on it overmuch, Suki-chan," he continued as she floated beside him, feeling lost. "When the time comes, you will know what to do. But now, we must watch and wait. The final play has begun."

Movement stirred the valley below. From the trees surrounding the city, tiny pinpricks of light emerged, blinking yellow and red in the shadows. With a start, Suki realized they were eyes. Hundreds, maybe thousands, of glowing eyes flowing out of the woods toward the city in the center of the valley.

"Genno is making his move," Seigetsu said quietly. "The end has finally started. The demons will overtake Shinsei Yaju by dawn."

16

Demons at the Gate

TATSUMI

You knew this couldn't last forever, Tatsumi.

I opened my eyes and found myself sitting in a dark, ordinary room. Sometime during the night, Yumeko had either lost her hold on the illusion or had simply released it. The moonlit grove was gone, the bamboo and sakura trees replaced with four simple walls, a raftered ceiling shutting out the night sky. I found that I missed it, and the feeling of peace it had brought. For the first time, I had been able to forget everything that had brought me here, my past, my training, the missions of death and pain and destruction. Under her touch, all of that had faded away. For the first time in both my lives, I had been content.

A soft sigh rippled across my senses. Yumeko lay beside me, curled into her kimono, eyes closed and face peaceful. Her fox ears twitched in her sleep, and her bushy tail was draped across her legs, the white tip standing out in the shadows. A faint smile crossed my face as I watched her. Kitsune. Peasant. Daughter of a daimyo. She was all these things and more, but to me, she was just Yumeko.

Reaching down, I gently brushed a dark strand of hair from her cheek and felt a stirring of amused dismay from somewhere deep within. *Kuso. I'm in love with her.*

Yumeko slept on, oblivious to the world and my realization. Pulling my hand back, I waited for the flicker of demonic rage to follow, the anger toward both Yumeko and myself for succumbing to such a weakness. Oni did not love. Oni were incapable of weak human emotions. But even my demon half could not muster any hostile feelings toward the sleeping kitsune, just a somewhat wry resignation. I had slaughtered armies and laid waste to cities, but the thought of harming one slip of a fox girl was unimaginable. She was my reason to fight now. I didn't expect to survive this final battle, and even if I did, there was no world where a half-oni demonslayer could exist. The Kage would come for me; they would want Kamigoroshi returned, but more than that, they would want Hakaimono destroyed. Running wasn't an option; they would always follow. Hanshou would never let me go. I had betrayed my clan and, by continuing to exist, I was the enemy of the empire, but I would see this battle through. Whatever happened, I would make sure Yumeko's newfound home and family were safe.

Beside me, Yumeko shivered, curling tighter into herself as if cold. I reached down and pulled the kimono up farther, covering her shoulders, but she trembled again, her brow furrowing in distress.

"N-no." The soft whisper cut through the quiet. Yumeko stirred under the coverings, her hands clenching into fists. "No," she whispered again, jerking as if to ward something away. "Stop it. Please…"

"Yumeko." I reached down and put a hand on her shoulder. She flinched at my touch, pinning her ears back, and I shook her gently. "You're dreaming, Yumeko. Wake up."

"No," she said again, and then jerked upright with a gasp. Golden eyes flared in the shadows of the room, glazed and terrified as they stared at me, before they blinked and recognition emerged once more.

"I'm here," I told her quietly. "It was just a dream. Are you all right?"

"Tatsumi." Rather than calming, Yumeko reached out and grabbed my sleeve, her face pale. "Something is wrong," she whispered. "The kami…the kami are terrified. I can feel them, crying out in fear." Her frightened gaze swept the room before settling on me again. "Something is happening, something terrible. We have to find Kiyomi-sama and—"

"Yumeko-chan!"

The voice rang outside the door, a moment before it was flung open with a snap, revealing the shrine maiden in the frame, Chu at her heels.

"Yumeko-chan, get up! We have to— Oh, Kage-san. You're here, too." Reika blinked at me, and her cheeks flared red as she realized what was happening. But, even then, the shrine maiden refused to let a small thing like embarrassment distract her. "Jinkei's mercy," she groaned, "I suppose I shouldn't be surprised. If you two are quite ready, we do have a madman to stop and an empire to save. And the risks just got a lot higher."

"What's happening?" I growled, rising swiftly and stepping in front of Yumeko, shielding her from the miko's gaze. Yumeko's cheeks were tinged pink, and she had drawn her robe tightly around herself, but she seemed more concerned about Reika's warning than the unexpected interruption. The shrine maiden gave me a grim look.

"Kiyomi-sama has called for us. An army of demons and yokai have been spotted coming toward the city. They'll be at the eastern gates before dawn." Yumeko gasped, and the miko's eyes hardened. "It seems the Master of Demons has been one step ahead of us."

"We'll be right there!" Yumeko leaped to her feet, and Reika quickly averted her gaze. I silently stepped into the hall, closing the door behind me, while the kitsune prepared herself for what was likely our last battle. After only a few seconds, she shoved the doors open and stepped out, golden eyes hard and determined.

"All right," she said, and took a deep breath. "I'm ready."

This is it, then. I nodded and shoved Kamigoroshi through my sash, resolve settling in my gut like a stone. "Let's go."

We hurried into the corridors, where confusion and panic were already spreading throughout the palace. Servants and nobles alike rushed through the halls or hovered in doorways, looking lost. Samurai in suits of black-and-gray lacquered armor hurried past us, ornate helms perched atop their heads. They looked like noble warriors, but their presence only added to the tension and fear sweeping through the halls. Samurai dressed in full battle gear only when they were going to war.

"Yumeko! Kage-san!"

The call echoed behind us. We turned as the ronin stepped through a door into the hall, hurriedly tying his obi around his waist. The Taiyo noble followed on his heels, as poised and unruffled as always, though his hair seemed a bit more unkempt than normal.

"We heard the commotion," the ronin announced as they joined us. "Is it true that an army of demons is marching on the city right now?"

"Yes," the shrine maiden confirmed as we rushed down the hallway. "Thankfully, Kiyomi-sama was already gathering her forces, so the city won't be caught unprepared. But the army is very close. We'll need to help with the defenses as quickly as we can."

The corridor opened into the main hall, where a familiar woman in silver and black stood in the center of the room, a cluster of robed figures around her. The figures' robes were black, their faces white but for a single, moon-shaped crescent painted onto their foreheads. The majutsushi of the Moon Clan, I realized.

"Kiyomi-sama," Yumeko cried, rushing forward. The Moon Clan daimyo glanced up, and for just a moment, the similarities between the two women were unmistakable.

"Yumeko-san." The daimyo stepped toward us, her expression grave. "I am sorry," she told all of us. "But I will not be able to send my forces to Tani Kaminari to engage the Master of Demons. It seems he has sent his army to my doorstep, and I must defend my people."

"Of course, Kiyomi-sama," Yumeko said immediately. "What can we do to help?"

"Hang on, Yumeko-chan," interrupted the ronin. "You don't see what's happening, do you? This is exactly what Genno wants. To keep us distracted with his army while he makes his way to the Summoning site. If we ignore him, he'll get there without opposition."

"I'm afraid your friend is right, Yumeko-san," the Moon Clan daimyo said. "Unfortunately, I see little that you could do to stop that. The cliffs of Ryugake lie beyond the Valley of Lightning, which is where the army is coming from. There is no way to sneak around the demons."

I narrowed my eyes and gripped the hilt of Kamigoroshi. "Then we'll carve a path straight through."

"Kiyomi-sama!"

An armored samurai raced across the floor and fell to his knees before the daimyo. "My lady, the demons are massing at the eastern wall," he said in a rush. "We are holding them back, but we fear the gates will soon be breached."

"Hold them," the Moon daimyo said in a hard voice. "Send every warrior we can spare to the eastern wall. The gates cannot fall. Those monsters cannot be allowed into the city. The people will be slaughtered."

I caught Yumeko's gaze as she looked at me, pleading and terrified. Not for herself, but for the rest of the city. For Kiyomi-sama and the lands she now called home.

"We'll stop them," I told the Moon Clan daimyo, who glanced at me warily. "Send us there. We'll hold them back."

Kiyomi-sama's jaw tightened, and she gave a short nod. "Go," she said, and I immediately turned and began jogging toward the doors, hearing the others do the same.

"Yumeko-san!" the daimyo called before we had crossed the room. Yumeko stopped and turned to gaze back at the Moon Clan daimyo, who watched her with a dark, conflicted expression.

"Come back to me," the daimyo ordered softly. She said nothing else, but her voice seemed to resonate through the chamber, shivering off the walls.

Yumeko nodded once. "I will," the girl promised, then continued on to join me near the doors. The look on her face sent a chill up my spine. Her eyes glowed an angry yellow, a mask of grim determination set firmly in place. Yumeko the peasant girl had disappeared; this was a kitsune prepared to fight tooth and nail for what she considered hers.

We sprinted out of the palace and into a panicked, terrified city. Civilians rushed down the streets, heading toward the palace and away from the gates, while samurai hurried past, going in the opposite direction. A tinge of smoke hung in the air, mingling with fear and desperation, and in the distance, I could see a few trees and roof corners flickering with orange flames. Grimly, I realized it hadn't been long from the time the first alarm was sounded at the palace; if the city was already in flames, the situation was dire indeed.

As we neared the eastern wall, a scream rang out ahead of us. As I drew my sword, we rounded a building and came upon a scene of horror. Bodies were scattered in the road, mostly citizens, but a few samurai, as well. Most were burned, charred to blackened husks, and several were missing a limb or two.

Yumeko gasped, her hands going to her mouth, and the ronin let out an emphatic curse.

"What the hell? What happened? Have the gates been breached?" He gazed toward the wall, squinting to peer through the smoke from the flames and charred bodies. "How did these bastards get into the city?"

"They're demons, Okame-san," the shrine maiden snapped, yanking an ofuda from her sleeve. "Some of them can fly."

The smoke billowed around us like a black curtain, and as the light dimmed, something flew toward me through the cloud—a spinning wheel wreathed in flame. I twisted aside to avoid it and saw a face, grinning madly as it passed me, in the very center of the spokes.

"Wanyudo!" cried Reika, just as another flaming wheel came at Yumeko from behind. I lunged forward, managing to push her out of the way, and felt the burning edge of the wheel strike me in the ribs, sending me crashing into a pile of crates. Grimacing, I shoved my way free to find two wanyudo—demons with human faces trapped in the hub of a burning wheel—circling us like grinning sharks. One of them held a dismembered arm in its jaws, and it crunched down and swallowed the limb even as I watched.

"Tatsumi!" Yumeko rushed to my side. Her eyes flickered yellow in the dancing flames and smoke. "Are you all right?"

"Get back, Yumeko," I growled, raising my sword. Wanyudo were not minor demons. They were creatures of pure rage, hate, madness and pain, and were extremely nasty. A few feet away, Chu erupted into his real form with a howl, and Reika flung her ofuda at a circling demon, but the flaming wheel pulsed with a gout of fire, and the paper strip dissolved to cinders on the wind.

With a maniacal laugh, one wanyudo rose higher, the heat from the hellish flames washing over us. The ronin raised his bow and sent an arrow streaking at its face, but the demon spun like a top, knocking the dart aside, and lunged at him with a shriek. I didn't have time to respond as the second tilted on its side and flew at me like an enormous shuriken. I stepped forward and slashed at the demon, but Kamigoroshi was knocked aside by the velocity of the wheel's edge, and the wanyudo slammed into me like a battering ram. Pain erupted through my ribs as I was hurled back again, tumbling to the ground with the stench of blood and burned flesh in my nostrils.

Kuso! Rage flickered, and I dug my fingers into the dirt to control the surge of bloodlust, feeling claws extend and slice through the hard-packed ground like paper. I could not lose control now. Raising my head, I saw Chu lunge at a demon with a roar, saw the wanyudo veer out of the way, spin around and slam into the komainu's side. The shrine guardian let out a yelp as it tumbled away while the Taiyo noble drew his sword and sliced at the second demon swooping in. Like Kamigoroshi, his blade clanged off the spinning wood, and the demon slammed into the noble, knocking him into the side of a building. The Taiyo crumpled to the ground, the edge of his sleeve on fire, as both demons swooped around and flew toward him with gaping mouths and twin howls of triumph.

I pushed myself upright, knowing I would never get there in time, but with a roar, a wall of blue-white fire erupted from the ground in front of the noble. It flared in the darkness, almost blinding in its suddenness, and the wanyudo veered away with snarls of alarm.

Yumeko and Reika stood in the center of the chaos, the shrine maiden beside the kitsune, their hair and sleeves whipping about in the wind. Yumeko's eyes were narrowed, her jaw set in anger and determination as she held out a hand wreathed in foxfire. Reika held up an ofuda, the strip of paper beginning to glow with power.

"Everyone cover your eyes!" the shrine maiden called, as with enraged howls, both wanyudo shot toward the two women, gaping jaws showing jagged teeth. Yumeko and Reika didn't move, but as the demons came in, a circle of foxfire flared around them, lighting up the darkness once more. The wanyudo flinched but didn't stop, careening through the flames to slam into the kitsune and miko in the center—

Only to have them disappear in a puff of smoke. As they winked from existence, I caught a split-second glance of the ofuda, still glowing with power as the demons came in, and quickly turned away as the talisman exploded in a brilliant flare of holy magic. I felt the light even through my closed eyelids, heard the stunned shrieks of the demons and hoped that the rest of my companions had heeded the miko's warning.

"Now, everyone!" Yumeko's voice echoed from somewhere I couldn't see. I looked back as Chu lunged through the shadows and slammed his clawed forepaws into a dazed wanyudo, crushing it to the earth, while Reika's voice rose above the cacophony. "Aim for the center!"

The wanyudo in the air howled. I glanced over and met the eyes of Taiyo Daisuke, on his feet with his sword in hand. He nodded, and we flew at the demon as one, slashing our blades through the snarling face and out the other side. It screamed, a piercing wail of rage and hate, before the burning wheel split in two and vanished into tendrils of smoke. I whirled to see Okame leap onto the komainu's broad shoulders, raise his bow and send an arrow directly between the eyes of the second demon. It shrieked and disappeared, curling into black smoke and flames that drifted away on the wind.

Panting, I lowered my sword, gazing around for Yumeko. She appeared from the shadows of a building, stepping into the light with Reika beside her. Relieved, I nodded at her, and she gave me a fierce smile, the remnants of fox magic still flickering between her fingers.

"Is everyone all right?" the miko asked as Chu impatiently shook the ronin off and trotted back to her. I glanced at the noble, trying to judge his injuries. One sleeve was charred, and he was standing a bit more stiffly than normal, but he didn't seem seriously hurt. Unless something was broken on the inside. I could feel my own ribs twinge, protesting if I moved too quickly. It would be annoying, but it would not slow me down that much.

The ronin muttered a curse as he got to his feet. "A little worse for wear, but I think we're fine," he gruffed. "Though, if this is the scouting party, I'd hate to see the main force."

The noble stepped forward with a decisive nod. "We must get to the gates as quickly as we can," he said, and I did notice a flash of pain that he did his best to hide. "The people here will not stand a chance if more demons like this break through."

We hurried on through the smoking city, now eerily empty of people. Briefly, I wondered where Genno was at this very moment, how close he was to the Summoning site, and how we were doing exactly what he wanted right now. Which was defending a city from demons and not going after the man responsible.

But leaving an entire people to be slaughtered was not an option, either.

"Tatsumi," Yumeko said in a breathless voice, and pointed a finger toward the sky. "Look!"

I followed her gesture above the trees and the rooftops interspersed between them, past the city walls, to the statue of the Great Dragon towering far overhead.

A figure stood on the Dragon's skull, tiny and indistinct, though I could just make out the billow of sleeves and a faint crimson glow surrounding it. On a hunch, I looked at the statue across from it, the majestic Phoenix with outstretched wings, and saw a second figure atop that statue, as well. The line of trees and buildings blocked my view of the other two, but I didn't need to look at them—the mighty Tiger and sacred Kirin—to guess that they, too, would be occupied.

"Blood magic," the shrine maiden said darkly. "Genno must be performing some sort of ritual."

"Targeting the entire city?" Yumeko asked, sounding horrified. "He can't do that, can he? Do you think Kiyomi-sama is in danger?"

"We don't know what he's doing," I told her. "But we can't get up there now. The eastern gate is just ahead."

As if in answer, a thunderous boom echoed over the rooftops, shaking the tree branches. Another followed, making the air vibrate with the distinct, chilling sound of something big and heavy smashing against wood. We rounded the corner of a building and reached the main road, and the eastern gate loomed tall and elegant before us. The heavy wooden doors were barred from the inside, but they looked dangerously cracked and weakened. Samurai stood atop the walls, firing arrows and hurling spears down on whatever clustered below, and bodies of both human and yokai were scattered over the ground and along the parapets. Beyond the gate, the shriek and howl of a massive army was deafening.

And then, I saw an enormous tetsubo—a giant, iron studded club—rise into the air beyond the gate, and I realized what kind of demon was assaulting the wall.

"Everyone get back!" I roared, knowing it was too late. "The gate won't hold—"

With a splintering crash that shook the ground, the gates flew inward. Samurai were flung away, shredded and torn apart with the explosion or knocked into trees or buildings with sickening cracks, as something massive appeared in the destroyed frame. Bigger than Yaburama, his skin was the blue of a drowned infant, and a tangled black mane fell down his back and shoulders. Four huge tusks curled from his jaws, glowing horns crowned his forehead, and his eyes burned with malevolent fire as they peered down at us. He held two giant tetsubo, one in each of his clawed hands, and he dragged the spiked clubs through the earth as he lumbered forward, raking deep gouges behind him. Our gazes met, and a slow smile spread across his brutish face. He recognized me. I knew him, as well.

Akumu, Nightmare of Jigoku, the third oni general of O-Hakumon himself.

Behind Akumu, the flood of demons, yokai and tainted kami let out deafening roars of bloodlust and surged into the city.

17

Protecting the Daimyo

Yumeko

I stared at the massive oni in fear and horror. It was huge, about twenty feet tall, with fiery obsidian horns, a tangled black mane and an enormous spiked club held in each of its claws. With the exception of Hakaimono in his true form, it was the biggest demon I'd ever seen. Worse, behind him came Genno's army, swarming through the splintered gates and setting upon the warriors who had been defending it. They would wreak havoc throughout the city, and a lot of people were going to die, but that oni was the biggest problem now.

The oni stepped through the gates, ignoring the smaller demons and yokai that swarmed around its feet, and casually smashed its club into a group of archers firing at it from atop the wall. Its cruel red gaze fell on Tatsumi, standing in the center of the road, and its brutish mouth curved in a smile.

"Hakaimono." The oni's voice made the air tremble, and another swipe of its club sent a pair of charging samurai flying into a wall. "So, the rumors are true. The great general has been reduced to sharing a body with a weakling mortal."

Tatsumi drew Kamigoroshi in a flash of purple light. "When did Genno summon you, Akumu?" The words sent chills up my back; it was Tatsumi's voice, low and controlled, but it was also Hakaimono's, an eager bloodlust pulsing just below the surface. "Yaburama I could understand—of the four of us, he was the weakest and stupidest. What did Genno promise to get you to help him and not laugh in his arrogant mortal face the second you arrived in Ningen-kai?"

The huge oni, Akumu, snorted. "I follow Lord O-Hakumon's commands," he stated. "The mortal is a tool to carry out the ruler of Jigoku's will. Lord O-Hakumon agreed to allow Genno's soul to return to Ningen-kai, if the blood mage would do him a service in return."

"What?" Tatsumi actually took a step back, sounding stunned and furious. "The Lord of Jigoku knows better than to bargain with the souls of the damned," he snarled. "He knows the consequences could unravel the stability of all the realms, from Jigoku to Ningen-kai to Meido. What kind of game is O-Hakumon playing?"

Akumu chuckled. "You would know, if you hadn't been stuck in Kamigoroshi all these centuries, Hakaimono. The Lord of Jigoku is eternally patient, but even he could not wait for you any longer." He bared his fangs in a sneer and raised his twin clubs. "Perhaps when you die with the rest of these mortals, your soul will be reborn in Jigoku this time and not sucked back into Kamigoroshi. Then you can ask O-Hakumon what you've been missing."

He lifted a club skyward, raised his head and let out a roar that shook the ground and made the air shiver. "Demons!" he boomed. "Yokai! Take the city! Tear it apart! Reach the heart of this sanctuary and leave no one alive."

"No!" I whispered, but my voice was lost in the howl of

the army as they swarmed into the streets, scaling roofs and swooping overhead. The oni took two enormous strides forward, momentarily blocking out the sun, and brought one tetsubo sweeping down with a snarl.

Tatsumi leaped back, the tetsubo crushing a massive hole in the center of the road. With his other arm, Akumu lashed out and swept the second club into a trio of samurai, smearing them across the stones.

"Tatsumi!" I cried as the oni threw back his head with a triumphant bellow. "The army is heading for the palace!"

He shot me a split-second glance, concern flashing in his eyes for just a moment. "Go!" he told me, sweeping his hand out. "All of you! Get to the palace, protect the daimyo and the people. I'll deal with the oni."

"Tatsumi..." I wavered a moment, my heart twisting around my ribs before I made my decision. "I trust you," I whispered, backing away, though the ache in my heart made it difficult to breathe. "Be careful."

He couldn't have heard me, but his gaze flicked to mine all the same, solemn and grim, and he nodded. *He'll be all right*, I told myself. *No demon will ever beat him. I have to trust he'll come back.*

"Reika!" I cried, whirling to find the shrine maiden. "Let's go! We have to get to the palace before the demons do!"

"Chu!" called the miko, and the komainu bounded to her side in a blur of red and gold. Reika threw herself onto his back and turned to me, holding out a hand. Heart pounding, I grabbed her arm, and she hauled me up behind her. The komainu's coat was smooth, his mane silky and light, and he radiated heat, as if a fire pulsed just below muscles and fur.

"Hang on!" Okame jogged forward and threw himself onto the shrine guardian's back behind me. "I can't do much against that big bastard," he muttered as we stared back at him. "But I can pick off a whole lot of ankle-biters before they can reach the palace. Taiyo-san!" he called, and pointed a finger at the noble a few yards away. "It is not time for that glorious death, peacock," he warned as, with a jolt, I realized Daisuke was staying to fight the oni lord with Tatsumi. "I can't stop you," the ronin went on, his voice shaking a little, "but you're not allowed to die without me. Cut this thing down and then find me again. I expect one final drink before we meet on the other side."

Daisuke met Okame's gaze and gave a solemn bow. Then with a sharp word from the miko, Chu sprang into the air, powerful muscles carrying him onto the roof of a building. With another leap, he soared over a burning fallen tree, landed on the roof beyond and bounded in the direction of the palace.

Demons and yokai swarmed below us, a shrieking, chaotic mass. They skittered down the roads, setting things on fire, attacking any living creature they came across. I saw kami fleeing in terror from the approaching demons, kodama scurrying through the tree branches and leaping onto roofs, frantically trying to escape. My heart twisted as I saw a trio of amanjaku chasing a girl with fox ears and a tail through the streets, the light gleaming off their curved blades and spears as they drew closer.

"Reika!" I cried as the ronin raised his bow and put an arrow through the skull of the nearest demon, sending it crashing to the road with a shriek. The remaining two glanced up with angry snarls and drew their spears back to hurl them at us.

"Banish!" the miko cried, and flung an ofuda at the remaining amanjaku. The holy talisman streaked toward the demons and exploded in a flash of brilliant light, causing the amanjaku to scream and flinch away, before writhing into clouds of reddish-black smoke and fading on the wind.

I looked up, but the kitsune girl was gone, vanished into the chaos and confusion. I hoped she was all right, that she possessed her own bit of fox trickery to keep her safe, but there was no time to look for her. Something swooped by us—the head of an old woman wreathed in flame, heading for the palace—and Chu lunged at it with a snarl. One clawed forepaw swatted the yokai from the air, causing it to crash headfirst into a stone wall and crumple lifelessly to the ground. With a triumphant snort, the komainu spun and bounded for the palace again.

The fighting was thick as we approached the center of the city. Soldiers and samurai clashed with demons, bakemono and monstrous yokai, desperately trying to hold them back. Smaller fires had started, orange flames flickering across rooftops and catching trees alight. Winged demons and yokai swooped overhead, breathing fire or snatching warriors from the ground, and arrows and spears flew through the air, trying to bring them down. Chu bowled his way through a group of yokai in the road, crushing several or knocking them aside. Okame shot another pair charging at us, and Reika hurled an ofuda into the road with a cry of "Light!" In the brilliant flash that followed, we raced through the gap in the mob of demons, leaped over the line of samurai holding the courtyard and galloped up the steps to the palace.

"Kiyomi-sama!" I cried, as Chu skidded to a halt at the top of the steps. A covered veranda stretched away to either side, surrounding the front of the palace, with thick red pillars holding up the roof. Archers and samurai clustered at the railings, protecting the palace entrance, and glared at us as we bounded past. "Kiyomi-sama, where are you?"

I spotted the Moon Clan daimyo near the palace wall, surrounded by a ring of female majutsushi, their hands glowing with light and their voices rising in a unified chant. Kiyomi-sama knelt in the center of the circle, palms raised and eyes closed, as power pulsed and flickered around her.

"Kiyomi-sama." I halted outside the circle of mages, who eyed me warily but did not stop chanting. "The demons have broken through and are coming for the palace. You should escape, hide—"

"No." The daimyo's voice was calm. "This is my city and my people. It is my duty to protect them. I will call on the Kami for aid. Hopefully they will hear my plea and respond." Her eyes opened, dark and determined, gazing up at me. "You must keep the demons away from the palace, Yumeko-san. Give me the time I need to call for help. Do not let them through."

"We can do that," Reika said, appearing beside me. Reaching into her haori, she withdrew a handful of ofuda and spun, striding to the top of the steps. Below, in the courtyard, the hoard of demons and yokai were beginning to push through, the samurai falling back as they gave ground.

"Reika!" I sprinted toward her as the shrine maiden slapped an ofuda onto one of the pillars at the top of the steps. She whirled, thrusting a pair of ofuda into my hands, and then Okame's as he joined us.

"Put those on the pillars," she snapped, pointing to the columns at each corner of the covered veranda where we stood. "Hurry!"

I did as she asked, jogging to the red pillar and pressing the ofuda strip onto the wood, where it adhered itself to the column like the back was covered with sticky rice.

As I started for the second pillar, a noise echoed overhead, raising the hair on the back of my neck and making my stomach drop in terror. A booming, screaming wail that seemed to come from the throats of a dozen monsters at once. I looked up as something huge and terrible dropped from the sky, landing with a crash in the center of the courtyard.

My bones melted into mochi as I stared up at the monstrous form of an enormous serpent dragon, towering over the army of samurai. It had eight terrible, snakelike heads that writhed and coiled about like they had minds of their own. Horns grew from each head, spines bristled down its back, and its tail was split into eight writhing limbs that whipped and thrashed around its scaly body. It raised all its heads and wailed again, making the air tremble and causing a few samurai to clutch at their skulls.

"The Orochi," I heard Reika breathe, the horror in her voice palpable. Snapping out of her daze, she glared at me and Okame as Chu roared his defiance to the massive creature looming in the courtyard. "Okame-san, Yumeko-chan, we have to hold this position. We can't let that monster get close to Kiyomi-sama!"

She raised two fingers to her face, closed her eyes and whispered a few words in the language of the kami. The ofuda on the columns glowed, then flared to life. A shimmering barrier expanded outward, surrounding us, the majutsushi and the Moon Clan daimyo in the center.

As I turned back to the dragon creature, two smaller figures leaped off its back and landed in front of its clawed legs. My blood chilled as I recognized the pair of slender bodies and their matching dark braids that nearly touched the ground. The duo stepped forward, identical grins stretching their almost childlike faces. It was the scorpion twins, the yokai sisters who had attacked the Steel Feather temple with Genno. The ones who had killed the daitengu for the temple's piece of the scroll.

"Please excuse us!" one called as she and her sister loosened the deadly spiked chains at their waists and began to spin them in glittering circles. "Apologies for dropping in so suddenly."

Her sister grinned. "We're just here to slaughter you all and kill your daimyo. We hope you don't mind."

With a yowl that shook the ground, the Orochi whipped its tails at the samurai rushing to surround them, smashing men aside like sake bottles. Its heads snaked down to seize and crush warriors in its jaws, then hurl them away. The scorpion twins leaped forward, spiked chains swinging in lethal arcs, scything through men and armor like they were made of straw. Demons and yokai swarmed around them, flinging themselves at the rapidly diminishing human ranks, tearing into them with fang and claw and blade. As the samurai fell, the Orochi gave a booming roar and lunged, barreling through the ranks of warriors, coming right for us.

18
THE NIGHTMARE

TATSUMI

I remembered Akumu.

Akumu the Nightmare. The third demon general of Jigoku. Of the four of us, he wasn't the strongest, or the most savage, but he was the one oni I had to watch my back around. Akumu was cunning, more intelligent than he let on, and far too ambitious for my liking. In Jigoku, he had followed me because he respected strength, and I was smart enough not to let his schemes get out of hand. Yaburama had always been a savage, mindless brute, strong but easy to control, and my second general, Rasetsu, had been powerful enough to pose a threat, but he'd lacked the ambition to challenge me. Akumu had always been pushing, testing. He'd never challenged openly, but he had always resented the fact that I had been First Oni, and if there had ever come an opportunity to get rid of me, he would've taken it in a heartbeat.

And now there was no question. I would either kill him, here and now, or he would smash me into pulp for all the years he'd wanted to in Jigoku. Only one of us would walk away from these gates tonight.

I glanced at the noble, who walked up calmly beside me, his own blade unsheathed. "Are you certain you want to do this, Taiyo? Akumu is a lot tougher than Yaburama was. One mistake and we're both dead."

The Taiyo gave a half smile. "I have learned much since I last fought an oni lord," he stated quietly. "And it is not yet my time to die. I have a vow to keep, a promise that I will not break. So, come, Kage-san." He raised his sword so that the light gleamed down the razor edge. "Let us fell this foul demon and return to those who need us."

Akumu chuckled and took one thunderous step forward, raising his twin tetsubo. "That easy, is it?" He smiled.

And lunged.

Daisuke and I split, dodging aside, as the oni's clubs came smashing down in an explosion of dust, shattering rock and stone where they landed. Immediately, I circled around, targeting the thick calves and ankles. Even a monster like Akumu couldn't fight if he couldn't walk. But Akumu pivoted with surprising grace, taking his legs out of harm's way, and brought both tetsubo down like he was playing a drum. I dodged and spun as the clubs beat the earth around me, coming within inches of leaving a bloody smear over the ground.

"Isn't this fun, Hakaimono?" Akumu laughed, as we continued our ridiculous dance over the battlefield. Anger and frustration flared; I needed to get close if I was going to stab anything vital, but the oni wasn't stupid, using his greater reach to his full advantage. Though the tight quarters and narrow streets were slowing him down a bit. The shops and houses lining either side of the road offered some cover from a rampaging oni, provided he didn't decide to smash right through them.

"I must admit, Hakaimono," Akumu went on, "I feel almost

bad for you. It's disgusting being so small and human, isn't it? I don't know how Rasetsu agreed to such a thing. Oh, and don't worry, I haven't forgotten about your little human friend. He can die, too, right about now!"

Akumu half turned, smashing one club down at the figure darting behind him. Daisuke threw himself aside, and the tetsubo struck deep into the earth, missing the noble by inches. He rolled to his feet and quickly sprang back, and we retreated a few paces as Akumu watched us, grinning.

"All the oni lords knew about this," I growled. "Rasetsu, as well. It's part of whatever bargain Genno made with O-Hakumon. What is he planning, Akumu? Tell me!"

The oni snorted. "I don't answer to you any longer, Hakaimono," he stated, swinging one club to a meaty shoulder. "But since you're going to die in a moment anyway, here's something to think about when you're sucked back into Kamigoroshi. Jigoku is eternal, but it is always hungry, and it never forgets. Long has O-Hakumon wished for Jigoku to grow, for his children, the oni, to walk freely in the mortal realm. When the damned soul known as Genno arrived in Jigoku, O-Hakumon saw an opportunity. The Master of Demons was the most powerful blood mage in the history of the human empire; he could affect the mortal world in a way the ruler of Jigoku could not. So Lord O-Hakumon offered Genno a deal. He would allow the mage's soul to return to Ningen-kai, if Genno promised to do him a service while he was there."

"And what service was that?" I asked, almost dreading the answer. But Akumu only chuckled.

"Oh, no, Hakaimono," he crooned. "I won't give it away so easily. But it is soon. It's almost here, in fact." His gaze flickered to something in the distance, above the city, and I felt a chill as I remembered the figures on the four guardian statues. "This city will burn, and all its souls will be sacrificed to fuel what's coming. You can't stop it."

I growled, curling my talons around the hilt of Kamigoroshi as beside me, Taiyo Daisuke straightened and raised his sword.

"I believe I have heard enough. Shall we show him how wrong he is, Kage-san?"

"My thoughts exactly."

We lunged at the oni, who laughed and twirled his clubs as we came in, then smashed them down in vicious arcs. Dirt and rock shards flew as the tetsubo crushed the earth around us, leaving huge craters in the road, but we managed to avoid the deadly pounding clubs. Still, this was a dangerous game. One misstep and we'd be nothing but red smears in the dirt.

Dammit, I have to get higher. I can't do anything stabbing at his ankles.

"Distract him!" I snapped at the noble, and ducked away, putting the corner of a burning house between us. Akumu casually swiped his club through the building, sending the roof and parts of the wall flying, and rubble rained down around me. Dodging wood and falling stones, I sprang to what was left of the roof, ran along a burning beam and launched myself at the oni with a snarl. Kamigoroshi flashed, cutting deep into his chest, slicing through his ribs in a spray of dark blood, and Akumu howled. As I fell, I saw the noble dart under the reeling oni, leap up and slash through the back of the monster's knee.

With a bellow of pain, Akumu staggered back and fell, crashing into a storefront and splintering the building under his weight. As clouds of dust rose into the air, Daisuke joined me, watching wood and roof tiles settle over the body of the oni.

"I don't suppose that's the end of it," he remarked calmly. I shook my head.

"No, it's just made him mad. Now the real fun begins."

With a roar and an explosion of roof tiles, Akumu surged upright. Eyes blazing red, he turned on us, raising both tetsubo, and lunged. Daisuke and I scrambled back, dodging and ducking behind walls to avoid the pounding clubs, knowing the oni's size wouldn't let him follow.

Snarling, Akumu swept his tetsubo through the buildings themselves, smashing walls and crushing roofs with furious abandon. I slipped through an alley to escape and found the buildings crumbling around me. Immediately, I lunged for the open street, wood, thatch and stone raining down, but something hit the back of my skull and I stumbled as the wall collapsed on me with a roar.

Gritting my teeth, I pushed splintered wood and stones off my chest, feeling the ground shake as Akumu rounded a corner, his crimson gaze sweeping the ground. Spotting me half-buried in the rubble pile, he gave a slow grin and raised his clubs.

Something tiny flew through the air and exploded with a burst of fire in the oni's face. Roaring, Akumu staggered back, wincing and shaking his head as if blinded, and I stared in amazement.

"Get up, demonslayer. I taught you better than this."

Stunned, I looked up as a figure dropped onto the rocks out of nowhere, glowering down at me. A man dressed all in black, with graying hair and an easily forgettable face. But I recognized him immediately and had to stifle a surge of rage toward this human, for he was the one who taught the Kage demonslayers to control the oni inside them.

"Ichiro-sensei." I shoved off the last of the rocks and rose, glaring at the master shinobi. I knew my horns, claws and tattoos were fully visible, but the older human didn't appear distressed or surprised by them. "What are you doing here?"

"That is not what you should be worried about now."

Akumu stepped forward with an enraged bellow, baring his fangs. And then, from the roofs of the buildings surrounding us, dozens of figures in black appeared. Silent and swift, they loosed arrows, flung kunai and hurled smoke bombs at the hulking oni before darting away again. Akumu howled in fury, smashing his clubs into the roofs and buildings, and I saw several shinobi fall or be crushed under rock, but most had already disappeared.

I looked back at Ichiro in amazement. "Is the whole school here?"

"Not all of us," the master shinobi replied. "Only those who agreed to walk the Path. But we're wasting time. Go, demon-slayer." He pointed a crooked finger at the oni overhead. "Do your job. There'll be time for answers later."

A part of me sneered, tempted to tell the old human he wasn't my master any longer. But I gripped Kamigoroshi, turned and sprinted toward the raging oni and the dozens of humans swarming in and out of cover, striking and harrying where they could.

"Kill the monster!"

Footsteps echoed down a street, and a squad of Moon Clan samurai appeared, huge greatbows in hand as they came to a halt at the edge of the road and prepared to fire. Akumu turned and struck a rubble pile with a club, sending several large rocks flying toward the archers. They stood their ground, though several would be killed by the oncoming projectiles, and drew their bows back to fire.

And then, the shadows around them came to life. Dark tendrils erupted from the ground, writhing and thrashing like some huge sea creature. They struck the boulders from the air, batting them aside or smashing them to pebbles. At the same time, the bowmen loosed their strings, and two dozen arrows arced through the air to pepper the oni.

Beset from all sides, Akumu flew into a rage. Roaring, he turned and smashed his tetsubo into everything around him, crushing buildings, snapping trees and sending rubble flying. As I raced toward the oni, I caught sight of Daisuke, huddled beneath an overhang as debris fell around him. Our eyes met across the road, and he gave a single nod.

Darting from cover, the Taiyo sprinted behind the raging oni.

His blade flashed twice, cutting through thick calf tendons in a spray of blood. Akumu stumbled, falling to his knees, his tetsubo smashing to the ground. I leaped from a crumbling wall onto a roof and sprang into the air, Kamigoroshi raised over my head. For just a moment, I was above Akumu as the oni bellowed in fury and started to rise. With a roar, I landed on his shoulders and drove Kamigoroshi into the back of his neck, shoving the point of the blade through his throat.

Akumu let out a garbled cry and staggered, the tetsubo dropping from his claws. Yanking Kamigoroshi back, I gripped the hilt in both hands and slashed the blade across the thick neck. The oni's head toppled forward, rolled down his chest and hit the ground with a wet thud that seemed to echo through the city. The headless body stayed upright for a few seconds, seeming to defy the laws of gravity, before it, too, collapsed with the rumble of an avalanche. I leaped off before it struck the ground and rolled upright, panting, as the third demon general of Jigoku twitched several times and was finally still.

I took a deep breath, though I knew we couldn't relax yet. With the gate breached, the demons would be swarming the city. I had to return to the palace to help Yumeko and the others, but there was one small matter here that required attention.

"Well done, demonslayer. Or, should I say Hakaimono now?"

"Why is the Shadow Clan here?" I growled, turning as Kage Ichiro appeared on a section of wall behind me. Around us, I could sense movement, flashes and blurs in the darkness, and I knew I was surrounded by shinobi. "Did Hanshou order this? How did you even get here—the Path of Shadows can be walked by only a few at a time."

"For a normal Shadow mage, yes," said a soft, instantly recognizable voice. I bristled, and my vision flooded with red. "But for one who has been practicing this art for a few centuries, we have uncovered a few secrets over the years. It's been a long time… Hakaimono."

I looked across the corpse of the dead Akumu, and Lady Hanshou herself smiled at me over the battlefield.

19

The Barrier Falls

Yumeko

The courtyard was turning into a bloodbath.

The Orochi roared as it stomped toward us, crushing samurai under its claws, flinging them aside with its multiple heads. On either side of the monster, the scorpion twins slashed and whirled in a deadly, graceful dance, beheading samurai or cutting them apart with their spinning chains. Demons and yokai flung themselves at the humans, tearing into them even as their own numbers were cut apart with swords, spears or arrows. Everything was pure pandemonium, but despite the valiant efforts of the samurai, the Orochi and the scorpion twins drew ever closer to the palace, the miko standing at the top of the steps and the daimyo within her circle of majutsushi.

"Okame!" I cried, but the ronin was already striding forward, raising his bow, and the first arrow slammed into the chest of a minor oni, toppling it backward. The second pierced the throat of an amanjaku, while the third struck the forehead of a dog-like yokai with the face of an old man. As they shrieked and collapsed, three of the Orochi's heads turned toward the steps, eyes narrowing as they spotted us.

I reached behind me, grabbed a handful of chrysanthemum leaves from the bushes growing beside the door and hurried to join Okame at the top of the steps. He glanced over, met my gaze with a smile and a nod and turned toward the enemy as I released a surge of fox magic into the courtyard.

Dozens more samurai appeared, exploding into existence with small puffs of smoke, and rushed the demon army with unified battle cries. Startled, the hoard turned to face this new threat, giving the real warriors time to regroup. The Orochi snarled in rage, sending its heads down to bite at the newcomers, shredding illusions and slicing through them with its tails. But for each illusion the monsters destroyed, I added two more to the battle, tossing leaves into the air and filling the courtyard with fox magic.

As Okame continued to rain down arrows and I continued to bolster the samurai army with illusions, one of the scorpion twins looked up and met my gaze over the carnage. Her eyes narrowed, and she leaped onto the Orochi's back, then stood up and swept her arm over the mass of demons.

"We're fighting illusions!" she cried, and pointed at me with a long black fingernail. "It's the kitsune! Kill the fox, and the shadows will vanish. Orochi, destroy her!"

With a roar, the Orochi reared up, four of its jaws opening and breathing a wave of fire at the top of the steps. I cringed back as the inferno howled toward me, but before the flames could get close, they slammed into a wall of magic that flared blue-white between us. The fire sputtered out, and a few steps away, Reika winced, her brow furrowed in concentration. The few demons that made it past the samurai and Okame's arrows hurled themselves up the steps but they, too, hit the barrier of holy magic and were flung back, though each time they did, Reika would shudder as she fought to maintain her hold on the wall.

I flung out a hand, and a trio of Yumekos appeared to surround me. "Okame!" I cried, tossing a pair of illusionary ronin into the fray, as well. "We have to take down the Orochi! If it gets up here, Reika won't be able to hold it back."

"Don't ask for much, do you?" the ronin gritted out, but he turned his bow on the massive creature still making its way across the courtyard, snapping and crushing the samurai around it. He loosed an arrow that hit the Orochi right in the chest, but the monster didn't even notice it.

"The heads, Okame," I gasped at the ronin. "It's too big to hurt directly, but cut off the heads, and maybe the body will die."

The Orochi was very close now, a writhing, unstoppable force just a few yards away. As it reached the first step, an arrow sped through the air, and a head that had been rearing back to breathe flame spasmed as the dart slammed between its jaws and pierced its throat.

As the neck fell limply to the monster's side, a shout of triumph arose from the remaining samurai in the courtyard. Perhaps seeing that the creature could be hurt, after all, they surged forward with renewed effort, blades rising and falling through the demon ranks. One warrior, standing his ground as a head snaked down at him, slashed at it viciously and managed to strike the Orochi's neck. The head reared up with a scream, half-severed from its body, spilling bright red blood over the stones as it thrashed.

Another gout of flame came at me, again sputtering out against Reika's barrier, and a demon snarled as it bounced off and tumbled down the steps. Reika gasped, and I spared a split-second glance at Tsuki-sama and the mages, desperately hoping they were almost done. We couldn't keep this up much longer.

A chill slithered up my spine, and the hairs on my neck rose.

I turned, just as the scorpion twin on the Orochi's back raised her arm, dark metal glinting between her fingers, and hurled it at Okame. The black, razor-edged throwing dagger, the kind I'd sometimes seen Tatsumi use, flashed through the barrier and struck the ronin in the chest. He staggered back with a strangled gasp, dropped his bow and exploded into a cloud of white smoke as the yokai's slitted eyes met mine through the barrier. Her lips curled into a cruel smile as she raised her arm once more.

I flinched as that arm came down, the dagger blinking from her fingers in a dark blur. I felt the wind from its passing as it missed my head by inches, zipping past me, and struck the shrine maiden in the chest.

Reika jerked with a gasp, sleeves billowing around her, and staggered back. One hand clutched at her heart, but the other still remained before her face, maintaining concentration even as the barrier flickered and sputtered like a candle in a wind. She swayed, clenching her jaw, and dropped to one knee, as crimson spread over her spotless white haori and spattered the stones beneath.

Reika-san!

Something inside me snapped. The ball of light that had been a low, continuous flicker in the pit of my stomach exploded, flaring up and out, expanding through my veins, my skin, erupting all around me. I screamed my rage at the demons swarming up the steps and sent a column of foxfire roaring through their ranks.

The blue-white flames howled, flaring hungrily as they engulfed the demons, and screams began rising into the air as the kitsune-bi consumed them. The ones that the flames touched first had just enough time to shriek before twisting into smoke and vanishing on the wind. Baring my teeth, I walked to the edge of the steps, foxfire blazing and snapping around me, and sent tendrils of fire cutting through my enemies like a kama through rice. Yokai wailed in pain, demons shrieked as they were sent back to Jigoku, and euphoric rage rushed through my veins as I seared through everything in my path.

At the bottom of the steps, the huge Orochi snorted, pausing in surprise as a flaming kitsune glared up at it, but then its remaining heads gave angry hisses and reared back to strike. The scorpion yokai on its back narrowed her eyes as our gazes met once more, and raised an arm, the lethal dagger ready to fly at me.

An arrow streaked from nowhere, striking her in the chest. Her yellow eyes widened in shock as from the corner of my eye, I saw Okame, jaw clenched and teeth bared, put another arrow to his string, before the second dart struck the yokai in the throat and punched out the other side.

Somewhere in the courtyard, there was a scream of fury and anguish from the second scorpion twin, and the Orochi howled in response. I flung my arm at the monster towering overhead, scoring it with flame, and the creature turned its heads away with a snarl. But its eight long tails whipped around, faster than thought, and something struck me in the side. I was lifted off my feet and smashed into the courtyard, the impact jolting the breath from my lungs as I rolled to a painful stop on the hard stones. The foxfire flared once and sputtered out.

Dazed, gasping through the searing pain down one side of my body, I raised my head. Demons and yokai surrounded me, and the monstrous Orochi was still attacking at the foot of the steps, only now there was no barrier and no foxfire to keep it back. For just a moment, I saw Chu on the top stair, snarling his defiance to the demons and towering Orochi, and Okame grimly raising his bow for a last stand. Then the enemies surrounding me rushed forward with shrieks and snarls, blocking my view, and I saw nothing but my own death closing in.

And then, the area around me exploded in brilliant golden light.

Warmth blazed down on me, like the eruption of the sun

through the clouds. The demons and yokai that had been surging forward to kill me jerked back with shrieks of alarm, flinching in the intense light. Wincing, I pushed myself up a little farther, and something stepped in front of me, an elegant creature with shifting scales, cloven hooves and a single horn curling back on its brow. The Kirin, blazing with holy fire, raised its head, its dragon-like face terrifyingly blank as it gazed over the battlefield, and let out a cry that send chills racing up my back. The demons closest to us burst into golden flames and vanished, twisting away on the wind, leaving nothing behind but smoke. With a swish of its tail, the Kirin leaped skyward, soaring like a phoenix toward the huge monster near the front of the palace. Where it landed, there was another burst of light, and more demons howled as they erupted into flames and disappeared.

The Orochi turned, its six remaining heads whipping around to face the holy beast blazing like a sun as it strode forward across the stones. With a hiss, four of the heads reared up and spat fire, which engulfed the Kirin and caused it to disappear in the flames.

I gasped, but the inferno surrounding the Kirin flared, the tongues of fire turning a brilliant white gold and then exploding in a flash of heat and light. The Kirin continued to stride forward, the flames engulfing it almost too bright to look at. I could feel the intense heat from where I lay across the courtyard, though for me, it was akin to lying in a beam of very warm sunlight, pure and soothing. I was certain it didn't feel like that to the demons.

With a snarl, the Orochi backpedaled, retreating from the Kirin and the dazzling radiance shining from its body. The army, too, was retreating, fleeing blindly, while the remaining samurai struck down the demons or yokai that were too slow. I saw the surviving scorpion twin on the Orochi's back, her sister's body cradled in her arms, one hand stroking her twin's pale forehead. She shot a final, lethal glare at the palace, at the ronin who still guarded the top of the steps, before calling something up to the monster.

With a last, defiant hiss, the Orochi turned and fled, abandoning the demon army to its fate. With shocking speed given its bulk, the monster sprinted across the courtyard, slithered up the wall and vanished over the edge. Its eight tails whipped and thrashed behind it, and then it was gone.

It took me a few tries to get up. My body ached, my shoulder crushed from where I had landed when the Orochi hurled me aside. I felt empty and drained, the searing, white-hot ball of power within now a tiny flickering ember. Setting my jaw, I finally pushed myself to my feet, clutching my throbbing shoulder, and gazed around at the aftermath.

It was a scene of carnage. Bodies, both human and yokai, lay everywhere, bleeding, smoldering, some twitching weakly in their death throes or too hurt to move. The air was filled with the stench of blood and smoke, and the moans of the wounded and dying drifted over the wind. Swallowing the nausea in my stomach, I began walking toward the palace, trying to ignore the gaping wounds, the bodies that had been burned, cut open or torn apart.

In the center of it all, holy fires faded but still glowed with ethereal light, the Kirin stood motionless, its great noble head turned toward the palace. Toward the figure of the daimyo approaching it. Kiyomi-sama had come down the steps, moving slowly but steadily across the bloody courtyard, toward the Kirin waiting for her in the center. When she stood in front of the great beast, she lowered her head and bowed deeply at the waist, while the Kirin watched her with impassive dark eyes.

Lady of the moon islands. As before in the forest, there were no words, but I could feel the Kirin's voice inside me. *Ruler of the Tsuki. The kami have heard your request. You have called on me, and I have come.*

"Thank you, lord of the forest," Kiyomi-sama murmured, still bowing low. "I am in their debt, and in yours. What would the kami ask of me?"

The Kirin swished its tail, raising its magnificent head. *Only that you keep these islands safe, as your line has promised since the day they made their pact with the kami. Let it be a haven for the spirit world. Let the shadow of man's greed never touch this place, and may it be a place of peace for all living creatures.*

Kiyomi-sama straightened slowly. "I swear it will be so."

The Kirin tossed its head. *You will not see me again in your lifetime*, it said simply. *Rule well, lady of the moon.* For just a moment, its dark gaze flickered to me. *And may those who follow rule as wisely as you.*

The Moon Clan daimyo bowed again, and the Kirin turned away. There was a glimmer of light through the courtyard, like a ray of sun piercing the branches of the trees, making me wince. When I looked up, the Kirin was gone.

When she raised her head, Kiyomi-sama's gaze found mine over the courtyard, and something in that grim, sorrowful expression made my stomach clench and everything inside turn to ice. Without speaking, I hurried across the yard and up the steps, searching frantically for a figure in white and red, unwilling to believe what I had seen.

You're okay, Reika-san. You're too strong to die. Any second now, you're going to march up, swat my ears and scold me for being so reckless…

My thoughts trailed off, and the breath froze in my throat. Okame knelt beside the palace wall, Chu's hulking, furry form across from him, both flanking a figure in red and white, leaning against a pillar. The shrine maiden's face was pale, her hands fallen into her lap, her head resting back against the wood. The once spotless white of her haori was stained crimson.

"Reika-san?"

Numbly, I approached the miko, ignoring Okame and the

grim, anguished look in his eyes. Chu's soft, hopeless moans. As I knelt at her side, Reika's eyes opened, dark and glazed over with pain, fixing on me. One hand, pale and stained with red, rose toward my face.

"Yumeko-chan." Her voice was barely a murmur. I had to lean close to hear her, taking the offered hand. "You're all right. Is…the daimyo safe?"

I nodded, unable to speak, and she smiled. "Good," she breathed. "I was afraid you would do some…foolish kitsune thing, and then how would I explain to Master Jiro…that I let you die?"

I choked on a sob, and the flood of tears lurking behind my eyes finally burst forth, running down my cheeks in a hot stream. "You can't go, Reika-san," I whispered, barely able to get the words out. "We need you here. How…how will we defeat Genno without you?"

"Baka." Reika's fingers gently squeezed my hand. "You don't need me," she whispered. "You have…everyone else. Okame, Daisuke and Kage-san…they'll fight for you. You're not alone, Yumeko-chan. Besides…" She smiled, serene and completely at peace. "Death isn't goodbye forever. I'll be keeping an eye on all of you from the other side, don't think I won't. And if you ever visit the shrines and hear the kami whispering in the trees, know that I'll be there, watching over you always."

I could no longer speak. I bent over our clasped hands and sobbed, hearing Okame sniff loudly, wiping his eyes. Chu leaned forward, not whining or making any sound, and pressed his blocky muzzle gently into Reika's side. She looked over at him with a sad smile, placing a hand on his forehead.

"You miss Ko, don't you?" she whispered, stroking the guardian's silky mane. "Don't worry, we'll see her soon. Master Jiro, too. Yumeko-chan," she breathed, and I raised my eyes to hers, tears still pouring down my cheeks. "Thank you," Reika murmured. "For letting me be a part of this. For all the adventure and frustration and nearly dying more times than I can count. I don't regret any of it." One last smile, as the light behind her eyes started to dim. "You…you did good, kitsune. I am proud… to call you a friend."

Her eyes closed, and her chin dropped to her chest, her hand going limp in mine.

Wordlessly, I lowered her arm and lay it gently in her lap, folding her hands so it looked like she was just sleeping. "Goodbye, Reika-san," I whispered, drawing back. "Thank you for everything. And don't worry. We'll beat Genno, and I'll make sure the Dragon isn't called into this world. I swear it."

There was no answer. The shrine maiden lay against the pillar, eyes closed, a faint smile still on her face. Against her side, Chu's body flickered, glowed red, and then shimmered into a million tiny lights. They floated around us for a moment, warm and soft, like tiny embers on the breeze, before they spiraled up and vanished into the wind.

20

Departure of the Kami

TATSUMI

The ring of shinobi surrounded us, a silent black swarm, blades glittering in the flickering lights of the fire. Kage Ichiro hovered at my back, and from the rubble, Taiyo Daisuke emerged, nodding to me in grim triumph, but it was the woman a few yards away who drew all my attention.

Lady Hanshou smiled at me over the bloody corpse of Akumu, Kage Masao at her side. She stood straight and unbowed, her pale skin smooth and unwrinkled, her raven hair long and thick. With a shock, I realized this wasn't an illusion; that somehow, the Kage daimyo had restored her health, her beauty and her lost youth.

But then I saw the black veins crawling up her arms, the dark spiderweb spread across her temple and jawline, and I realized how she had accomplished such a feat. Hanshou had always been a talented majutsushi, one of the strongest Shadow mages in Iwagoto. But those lines down her arms and face were the marks of a much darker, forbidden magic. Blood magic.

Not that it was surprising. She had used blood magic before. Long ago, a thousand years past, Lady Hanshou had summoned the greatest oni of Jigoku to fetch the scroll from her champion, Kage Hirotaka, because she feared Hirotaka would betray her and take the power of the Wish for himself.

Searing rage flooded my veins. Those were Hakaimono's memories, his sudden, ancient hatred for the Kage daimyo stirring to life. For a moment, I had visions of springing forward and driving my claws through the woman across from me. But that would prompt the Shadow Clan to attack, and though wiping out the Kage had always been the goal, there were other, larger enemies to deal with tonight. A whole army of yokai. And the Master of Demons himself.

"Hello, First Oni," Hanshou greeted, watching me calmly over the field of carnage and death. "Or, is it Tatsumi-san? From here, it is rather hard to tell."

I smiled, showing fangs, and raised Kamigoroshi to the sickly light. "Lady Hanshou. It's been a while. I'll come closer and let you get a good look before I tear out your heart."

"Ah. So, it is Hakaimono, after all." The Shadow Clan daimyo did not sound alarmed, though her face turned grim. "Striking me down here would not be advisable, First Oni," she warned, raising a billowy sleeve. "I come with an offer of help."

I barked a laugh, causing the shinobi surrounding me to jump. "You have never helped anyone without it directly benefiting you," I said. "What is the catch? Why are you really here?"

"Do you not feel it, Hakaimono?" The words were a whisper, but I still heard them over the roar of the fires and the sound of distant battle. The ancient Kage daimyo stepped forward, crossing the road and walking by the smoking corpse of Akumu to stand in front of me. Kage Masao came with her, though he hovered at her back, watching me with dark, wary eyes. "We are at the end of an era," Lady Hanshou said gravely. "The night of the Wish is upon us, and Genno still holds the scroll. If he summons the Harbinger, nothing that you or I have done in the past will matter. The world as we know it will end. Look."

She raised her eyes over the rooftops, to the edge of the city and the four great statues that loomed over at the corners: Phoenix, Tiger, Kirin and Dragon. I followed her gaze and saw the figures still on each of the statue heads, arms raised and sleeves billowing in the wind. Only now, they seemed to be drawing in some kind of malevolent, sullen energy, for an aura of darkness hovered around each of them. A black-red cloud of swirling energy.

"Blood magic," Hanshou said. "An extremely complex, powerful ritual. I have not felt anything so strong in…centuries. They are using the lives lost, the blood spilled and the slaughter here to power whatever it is they are doing. An entire city's worth of carnage and death. I shudder to imagine what Genno is planning."

At my side, the noble blew out a horrified breath. "Kage-san, we must return to the palace," he said, turning to me in alarm. "Kiyomi-sama must know about this. Yumeko-san, as well."

"An excellent idea," said Lady Hanshou, smiling faintly at the Taiyo noble. "Let us *all* return to the palace. I imagine Kiyomi-sama will want to know why a contingent of Kage warriors suddenly appeared in her city out of nowhere. Hakaimono," she went on, her voice growing softer as she turned to me. "You and I go back a long way, First Oni. I know you wish to take your vengeance, and perhaps you will one day." Her eyes narrowed. "But on *this* day, we have the same enemy. And he is close to achieving victory. The Shadow Clan is here, and we will offer whatever aid we can. I suggest you take it."

"On one condition," I told her, making the ancient daimyo raise a perfectly inked eyebrow. "Stop calling me Hakaimono. My name is Kage Tatsumi, and I am no longer yours to command."

Lady Hanshou blinked at that, and a faint smile curled one corner of her lips, but she only nodded. "Then let us go, before Genno completes whatever ritual he is casting."

★★★

The journey back to the palace was swift. Demons and yokai still roamed the streets, but they appeared to be fleeing the city instead of attacking. We killed the stragglers we came across without slowing down, and soon reached the outer walls of the palace.

When we entered the courtyard, we came upon a scene of slaughter. Bodies of both humans and yokai, samurai and monsters alike, were scattered across the stones. It was clear that a horrific battle had taken place here, and worry for Yumeko twisted my stomach. Hanshou's expression was grim as she gazed around at the massacre and I remembered her words about death powering the ritual. If that was truly the case, then Genno would have all the blood and butchery he needed.

I saw the Moon Clan daimyo in the courtyard, directing samurai and servants as she dealt with the aftermath of the brutal battle. Spotting us, her eyes widened, and she straightened quickly, her attention not on me or the Taiyo noble, but on the Kage daimyo striding toward her over the carnage. Lady Hanshou's demeanor was calm as she and Masao walked easily across the yard, but by Kiyomi-sama's expression, the Tsuki daimyo wasn't entirely certain that having the Shadow Clan appear in her city was a good thing.

"Daisuke!"

The ronin came hurrying across the courtyard, dodging or leaping over bodies, his gaze only for the Taiyo. The noble didn't move, only held out an arm, and before samurai, daimyos and servants alike, pulled Okame close as the ronin crashed into him.

"Yokatta," muttered Okame, his voice muffled against the noble's haori. "You're alive." His brow furrowed, and he pulled back to glare at the Taiyo, shaking his head. "*Baka* noble. Why do you always have to fling yourself at the biggest thing on the battlefield?"

"Forgive me." Daisuke's lips curved faintly, and one hand rose to touch the ronin's face. "But I was in no danger. I promised I would not meet that glorious death without you, Okame-san. And I have yet to break a promise." His fingers traced the stubbly jaw, and the other shivered. "We are here, and we are victorious. It is not yet our time."

The ronin sighed, his face darkening as a flicker of grief went through his eyes. "We lost Reika."

I straightened, and Daisuke's eyes widened. Shoulders slumping, Okame turned, observing the massacre spread through the open yard.

"It was crazy," he muttered. "Demons and yokai everywhere, all trying to get to the daimyo and slaughter the rest of us on the way. And that was before they brought out this huge, eight-headed monster that started killing everything in its path."

"The Orochi?" I asked in disbelief. My worry for Yumeko spiked, and I glanced toward the palace, hoping to see the flash of ears and a bushy tail. The eight-headed serpent of legend had popped up a few times in the history of the empire, and though heroes had fought and slain the monster each time, powerful blood mages were quite fond of summoning the dreaded Orochi simply because it was so nasty.

"Yeah." The ronin bobbed his head once. "Orochi. That's what they called the bastard. Kiyomi-sama managed to call on the Kirin for aid, but Reika-san held the barrier against the demons and the Orochi and gave her time to complete the ritual. We would've all been eaten had she not been there."

"She died with honor," Daisuke said solemnly. "That is all any of us can hope for in the end. Protecting the land and those we care about from the greater evil. I can only hope to follow her example." He exhaled, closing his eyes as he bowed his head. "Though the world is a little less bright today. She will be missed."

The ronin glanced at me. "Yumeko is taking it pretty hard, Kage-san," he said, making my pulse jump at her name. "She was there, when Reika..."

I nodded. "Where is she?"

He gestured across the courtyard. I glanced at Kiyomi-sama and Lady Hanshou, still deep in conversation, and made my way toward the palace.

I found Yumeko sitting on the railing of the veranda, her legs and fox tail dangling over the side as she gazed out over the courtyard. Though her face was dry, her eyes were red, her expression haunted and far away. Wordlessly, I joined her, vaulting up to sit beside her on the railing. One of her ears twitched in my direction, and she raised her head.

"Tatsumi." Her voice was soft with relief, and a glimmer of emotion pierced the darkness that had gathered in her eyes. "You're here. I guess you killed the oni, then."

"Yes." It was strange, seeing her like this; stranger still that I wanted to say something, to ease the sadness in her voice, but I didn't know how.

"I heard about Reika," I said quietly.

She sniffed, the sheen in her eyes growing bright again. "She was *right there*, Tatsumi," Yumeko whispered. "Right there, holding up the barrier against everything. And then I look back… and she's gone." Her bottom lip trembled, and she took a shaky breath to compose herself. "It doesn't seem real," she went on. "I keep expecting her to walk up and scold me for wasting time while Genno is still out there."

Mention of Genno caused a shiver of warning to race up my spine. I glanced toward the sky, to the distant statues that could be seen even over the roof of the palace, and could just make out the figure atop the head of the Great Tiger, a faint glow of magic around it.

Yumeko followed my gaze, and her expression darkened even more. "Something is going to happen, isn't it?" she asked in a small voice. "I can feel it. There's a terrible dark energy swirling around the city. Genno is about to do something even more unforgivable."

Her voice shook. I reached out and placed a hand on her arm, picturing all my strength flowing into her, everything I felt: my anger, determination...and this strange, terrible emotion that could only be love. "We'll stop him," I told the kitsune next to me. "This fight will not be in vain, Yumeko. There is still time. And I will be at your side until the very end, I promise."

Yumeko gazed at me, golden fox eyes meeting my own, and the depth of emotion staring back made my stomach twist wildly. A small part of me wanted to flee, to turn away and put distance between myself and an obvious weakness, to slam the door on these emotions and become an empty shell, as I had in the days before I met her. I stayed where I was, meeting her eyes, though my heart and stomach refused to calm. I was still stumbling in the dark, letting these strange feelings take me where they would, but with her, I knew I was safe. I trusted she would not put a knife in my back and push me into the void, that she would at least catch me if I fell.

Who are you trying to fool, Tatsumi? You've already fallen.

"Tatsumi," Yumeko whispered, and even the sound of my name on her lips made my pulse spike. One slender hand rose, trailing soft fingers down my cheek, and I closed my eyes. "I..."

A shudder went through the air. It rippled across the ground, seeming to originate from the center of the city and expand outward, a pulse of darkness fed from blood and death and human souls.

"It's happening," Yumeko whispered, just as the pulse of magic reached us. I had the brief sensation of being swarmed, of millions of spiders, centipedes, worms and crawling things scuttling over my body and under my clothes, wriggling into my flesh. I saw Yumeko cringe, her ears flattening against her skull in loathing, before the feeling passed and all felt normal again. Silence descended over the palace, every human frozen in fear and confusion, hands on the hilts of weapons as we waited for what was to come.

And then, the kami started to scream.

It wasn't a physical sound. There were no high-pitched shrieks carried over the wind, no cries or wails or anything you could hear. It was more a sensation of utter terror, of thousands of voices rising in one unified cry of pain and horror. It came from the earth, the sky, the forest surrounding the city, a bombardment of emotion and fear that pierced right through you, shredding your soul from the inside.

Yumeko gasped, flinching and clapping her hands to her ears, as if the screams of the kami were physically painful. I leaped off the railing, gazing around for the others, for Lady Hanshou and the Tsuki daimyo, knowing that whatever Genno had planned, it had started. The final play had begun, and we needed to move now.

"Kage-san! Yumeko-chan!"

The ronin leaped up the steps, bow in hand, followed closely by the Taiyo. "What the hell is going on?" Okame asked, his face pale as he strode toward us. "Does anyone else hear that? I feel like my ears are going to start bleeding."

"It's the kami," Yumeko said, her voice shaking as she slid off the railing. She gazed at the sky, at the forest looming beyond the city, her eyes huge with fear. "I've never...heard them scream like this. Something terrible is happening. We need to find Kiyomi-sama."

"I am here." The Moon Clan daimyo strode up the steps, her face as pale and grim as Yumeko's. Behind her, like a poised, elegant shadow, came Lady Hanshou, though her lips were also set in a tight line, her expression dark. Yumeko drew in a sharp breath as she caught sight of the Kage ruler, her back straightening in alarm.

"It's all right," I said in a voice only for her. "The Kage are here, but they've come to help us stop Genno."

She shot me a brief worried glance. I could see the questions in her eyes, the concern for me, knowing that if the Kage were here, they would have also come for Hakaimono and the sword. I had no doubt that Hanshou had plans for me once this was over, if any of us survived. But right now, stopping Genno and preventing the Summoning was the only issue that mattered.

"Yumeko-san." The Moon Clan daimyo's voice was grave. She paused in front of her daughter, and the similarities between the two women were remarkable and obvious. "I must gather my remaining forces for the final march," the daimyo stated. "Whatever the Master of Demons has set in motion, we cannot let it stop us. Whatever Genno has brought about, no matter the cost, we must reach the cliffs of Ryugake and halt the Summoning of the Dragon." She sighed, and for a moment, seemed decades older. "The kami are fleeing the island," she whispered. "I can feel their presence leaving the land, and soon they will be gone completely. I am not certain what the day will bring. My forces have been decimated, and even with the Kage's help, we will be at a terrible disadvantage. You have seen Genno's army, what he is capable of, and you have lost someone dear. We might not survive this battle, Yumeko-san, but our time is nearly up, and our choices are gone. Are you and your friends still with us?"

"Yes," Yumeko answered, and there was no hesitation or fear in her voice. "This is why we came, Kiyomi-sama. We're not giving up now."

The Moon Clan ruler nodded. "Then make ready," she told her daughter. "Gather what you need, pray to the kami and say your goodbyes. Whatever horror the dawn brings, we will face it with honor, and we will either stop a madman from summoning a god, or we will meet our ancestors in the next life."

PART III

21

Valley of Demons

Yumeko

My soul felt sick.

That was the only way I could describe what I was feeling; the terrible sensation of *wrongness* that lingered over the entire island. The very air seemed lifeless, the once lush forests felt barren and dead. Where the land once teemed with life, it felt hollow now. Empty. And it wasn't hard to figure out why.

The kami were gone. Whatever Genno had done, whatever dark magic he had performed, it had caused the mass evacuation of every spirit on the island. And with them, the heart of the land had vanished, as well.

I rode beside Kiyomi-sama at the head of a procession of Moon Clan warriors, the last of the army that had survived the attack. Mounted, armored samurai rode behind contingents of ashigaru, spear-carrying foot soldiers who, according to Okame, were made up of farmers and peasants that had been "volunteered" to serve in the army. Unlike the heavy black-and-silver armor of the samurai, the ashigaru wore little more than cuirasses and bracers, with conical metal hats perched on their heads. They also looked rather scared, like they didn't really want to be marching to their deaths alongside the warriors and samurai. I couldn't blame them. I didn't know anything about armies or warfare, but to my eyes, our forces looked frighteningly small. How would we stand up to Genno's army of demons, monstrous yokai, blood mages and whatever other surprises he had planned?

However, outside the city walls, a second force of mounted samurai greeted us, all in the black-and-silver colors of the Moon Clan. I blinked in amazement, wondering where they had all come from, before realizing the Moon Clan capital was not the only city in Tsuki lands. Kiyomi-sama must have put out the call to the rest of her islands, who had answered their daimyo's command and sent forces of their own.

"Kiyomi-sama," one of the lead samurai greeted, bowing to her in the saddle. "You have called us. We have come."

The Moon Clan daimyo cast an appraising glance at the assembled samurai and ashigaru soldiers behind him. "How many have answered?"

"So far, forces from Miho, Izena and Yugawa are here, my lady," the samurai answered. "There are likely more, but they have farther to travel and will not be here soon. With such short notice, we came as fast as we could."

Kiyomi-sama gave a solemn nod. "Then we will continue with whom we have. And we will pray that it will be enough."

Now a much larger force, we left the city outskirts and entered a gently rolling grassland dotted with copses of trees, the blades of grass so long they brushed the bellies of the horses. As the light broke over the horizon, it illuminated a mottled gray sky, bleak and dark and sullen, or perhaps those were just my feelings coming to the surface. I hoped it was not an omen of what was to come.

On Kiyomi-sama's other side, Lady Hanshou rode a horse as

dark as shadow, her black-and-purple armor seeming to absorb the shifting light. The Shadow Clan daimyo spoke to no one, not even Masao, riding quietly at her flank. I had not seen a single Kage samurai since we had left the city, but occasionally, I thought I would catch movement in the grasslands around us, a ripple of darkness or a blur that didn't quite belong. Hanshou's shinobi trailed us, following alongside like deadly shadows. Behind me, Okame and Daisuke were mounted as well, but Tatsumi had opted not to ride with us, as it seemed horses still had a strong aversion to having a demon on their backs and refused to calm down when he was present. I couldn't see Tatsumi, but I knew, like the shinobi, he was close, following in the shadows, and would appear when we needed him. I could also feel something in the air, a growing dread and darkness, getting stronger and more terrible the closer we came, like walking toward a violent storm.

Ahead of us, the land sloped upward in a gentle rise, the top empty of trees and showing a clear view of the sullen gray sky. Thunder growled overhead, and my heartbeat picked up in response. Something was out there, waiting for us. We started toward the rise, but at the bottom of the hill my horse suddenly gave a violent squeal and half reared, nearly throwing me from the saddle. I yelped and grabbed for the reins, clutching them tightly, as the animal snorted and danced in place, throwing back its head. From the corner of my eye, I saw Okame and Daisuke struggling with their mounts, though they were faring far better than me, and heard the snorts and squeals of the horses behind us.

A hand grabbed my horse's bridle, bringing the animal to a snorting halt, though its eyes were still white with fear, its ears pinned flat against its skull. I blinked and looked up into Kiyomi-sama's grim face.

"The horses will take us no farther," she told me. "The

amount of corruption and fear in the air is too much for them. The rest of the way must be traveled on foot."

That sounded good to me. I nodded and quickly slid from the saddle, grateful when my feet touched solid ground again. Kiyomi-sama released the horse, which immediately cantered back the way we'd come, tossing its head. She turned to the army behind her.

"Dismount!" she called to the closest ranks of samurai. "From here, we go on foot!"

It took a few minutes for the army to release the rest of the horses, who were all too eager to be gone. In the organized chaos of dismounting and setting horses free, I realized Tatsumi had appeared again, standing beside me as we watched the army of horses gallop away over the plains. I also noticed that a pair of black-clad shinobi had appeared before Hanshou-sama, their heads bowed as they knelt before her. It was impossible to see their faces, but both were trembling violently through their dark haori.

"Over that rise is Tani Kaminari, the Valley of Lightning," Tsuki-sama told us, gesturing up the slope to the clouds crawling above it. "Beyond the valley is the ascent to the sacred cliffs of Ryugake, where the Dragon will be summoned. Whatever is waiting for us, whatever lies between the valley and the cliffs, we must reach the Summoning site if we want any hope of stopping the Master of Demons."

"Then let us stop talking about it," Lady Hanshou said quietly. "There is no time left. My scouts have reported demons in the valley, apparently pouring from a hole in the very earth. They could not tell me where this hole came from or why it appeared, but both were nearly out of their minds with terror. There is no doubt that Genno is close." She lifted her chin, giving the Moon Clan daimyo an almost challenging look. "The Shadow Clan stands ready to die defying the Master of Demons, Lady Moon. Is your clan prepared to do the same?"

Kiyomi-sama's jaw tightened. But instead of answering the Kage ruler, she deliberately turned away from her, her gaze seeking me. "Yumeko-san," she said in a soft voice, making my stomach tighten at the hidden emotion in her words. "Fate, it appears, has been cruel to us both. Were these any other circumstances, I would thank the Kami for guiding you here, for giving me another chance to rediscover something I lost so long ago. But I realize destiny has another path for you, and that you were brought here for a specific purpose, one that my selfish desires cannot stand in the way of." Kiyomi-sama briefly closed her eyes, a flash of pain crossing her face, before she opened them again, hard and determined. "And so, I will release you with these words. Do not worry about me, do not think of my clan—this night, we are but tools to help you achieve your purpose. When this is over, and we both yet live, perhaps there will be time to mourn the years lost, and to celebrate the ones that remain. But not tonight." Her gaze lifted, staring at something on the horizon, her voice going distant. "There will be loss this day, Yumeko-san," she told me. "Loss, and grief, and sacrifice. And there may come a time where you will have to make a choice. But you know what you must do."

I swallowed the tightness in my throat, trying not to let the tears pressing against my eyes spill forth as I nodded. "I know."

"Then may the Kami guide your steps," Kiyomi-sama whispered. "And may you not falter on your path. I will pray for our victory, and your safe return. Now let us see what Genno has prepared for us."

We turned, and with Tatsumi, Okame and Daisuke at my side, and the two daimyos leading the way, we walked the rest of the way up the rise and gazed down toward the valley.

Into hell itself.

The valley floor was a writhing, squirming mass of demons. Demons, amanjaku and monsters I didn't even have a name for crawled, leaped or slithered over the ground. Terrible oni stomped their way through the crowds, ignoring the lesser demons or swatting them out of the way. Wanyudo and other flying horrors wheeled through the sky, leaving trails of flame behind them.

But even more chilling than the demons were the hundreds of wailing, tormented spirits that swarmed through the ranks of monsters. All once human, surrounded by a sullen red glow, they drifted over the ground, their voices a cacophony of madness, rage and grief. Some were dressed in armor, some trailed long white funeral robes behind them and some had only a few rags clinging to their ghostly bodies. Amanjaku tormented them, chasing or stabbing at a passing spirit, laughing as the soul writhed in terror and pain. Sometimes even the oni would take a swat at one of them, though the spirits seemed to instinctively flee from the monstrous demons.

And yet, even that was nothing compared to the true horror that lay below us. In the center of the valley, lit by a baleful purple glow, a gaping pit like the maw of an enormous beast seemed to descend straight into the underworld. Oni, demons and tortured spirits crawled from the fissure in waves, fighting each other as they clawed their way into the living world. My breath came in short gasps, as a fear unlike anything I'd ever felt crawled up to burrow into my heart.

"Merciful Kami," Kiyomi-sama whispered behind me, her voice faint. "What has Genno done?"

"He's opened the gates to Jigoku." Though Tatsumi sounded horrified, there was something in his voice that made me shiver. Something almost contemplative. *Hakaimono.* I wondered what the First Oni thought of this, of a gate opening directly to his home world. "That's what Akumu was talking about," Tatsumi went on, staring into the valley. "Why O-Hakumon allowed Genno's soul to be summoned to the mortal world. It was to open the way for Jigoku." He paused, a wry look crossing his face as his voice turned almost gleeful. "I didn't think the old bastard had it in him."

"How are we going to get through that?" I whispered, watching even more demons and spirits crawl out of the pit, some being yanked back down by larger demons or even other souls trying to escape. I looked beyond the valley, to a line of jagged cliffs that marked the end of the island. I also saw, with a chill that went through my whole body, a faint, sickly glow that announced the arrival of the dawn. The last full day before the night of the Wish had begun.

"We're not," Okame muttered, sounding grave. "There's no way we'll be able to cut our way through that. The whole damn army will be pulled down before we're halfway across."

"We must." Kiyomi-sama stepped forward, gazing down on the mass of demons below. "I will make ready my forces. We will march on the valley, and we will meet the enemy today with honor."

"Kiyomi-sama." Hanshou spoke, her low voice a warning. "The gate of Jigoku lies open. There is no end to the demons and tortured spirits coming from the pit, and no way to close it. Even if your forces destroy the first wave, more will come, and they will keep coming until every one of us lies dead."

"The demons are moving," the Moon daimyo replied far too calmly. "If we do not stop them here, they will reach the city and slaughter everyone still living. But first, they will sweep through the villages, the farmlands, the communities on the outskirts with no walls and no soldiers to protect them. If I must sacrifice my entire army to see my people safe, I will do so."

"We cannot win this..." Hanshou began.

"I know that, Hanshou-sama," the Moon daimyo said quietly. "But what would you have me do? Ignore the danger? If your land was threatened with annihilation, would you not give everything to try to stop it?" The Kage ruler fell silent at this, her eyes darkening, her lips pressed into a thin line.

"Very well, Lady Moon," the Shadow ruler said. "If this is your decision, the Kage will fight at your side. The shadows will defend this land for as long as we are able. Kage Tatsumi," she continued, and I blinked as her dark gaze fastened on the demonslayer. "You know what you must do. There is still time to make up for past failures." Her lip curled at the edge. "Do not disappoint me."

Tatsumi didn't answer his daimyo, just nodded once, and Lady Hanshou turned away, sauntering back down the hill with Masao at her side. Kiyomi-sama paused a moment, then turned to me again.

"Yumeko-san." Her voice was bleak, but resolved. "I must dispatch messengers to every town and village in Tsuki lands, with orders to evacuate the islands," she told me. "The people here must flee, or the demons will slaughter us all. The warriors will stay, defend these lands for as long as they are able to fight, but this has become a losing battle. If you decide to leave the island with the rest of my people, I will not fault you."

"No." I swallowed hard. "We're not going to flee. But shouldn't...shouldn't you leave with your people, Kiyomi-sama? You're the daimyo, the leader of the Moon Clan."

"Yes," the daimyo replied, and she sounded tired now. "And it is my responsibility to stay. If the gate to Jigoku is not closed, in a few days there will be nothing left of us. My duty as ruler of these lands is to protect my people and every spirit that calls this place their home. Even if those odds are impossible."

For a moment, her eyes softened, a shadow of regret or longing crossing her face as she gazed at me. "I am sorry that I will never truly know the child I lost," she whispered, her voice barely audible. "But I am grateful I had the chance to see her, if only for a moment." One slender hand rose, the ends of her fingers barely touching my cheek, as the daimyo gave a sad smile. "Fight well, daughter," she murmured. "If Fate is kind, perhaps we will meet again in the next life."

Then the daimyo of the Moon Clan turned and walked away, toward the army waiting for her at the bottom of the rise. I watched her, hardly able to see through my blurry vision, then wrenched my gaze away and turned back to my friends.

Daisuke, watching the demons swarm the valley below, let out a long breath, his pale hair rippling behind him in the wind. "So, we come to the end," he murmured, one hand resting easily on his sword hilt. The faintest of smiles crossed his face. "It is a good day to die."

"Better than most, I suppose." Okame sighed, joining him at the top of the bluff, resting an elbow against Daisuke's shoulder. "Just don't go off without me, peacock. We want this to be a good poem, after all."

Tatsumi met my gaze, his eyes soft and his expression solemn in the growing light. He wasn't looking at Kiyomi-sama, our friends, or the army of demons and tortured souls swarming the valley behind him. His gaze was only for me. I moved beside him, staring down the rise, at the open maw that continued to spew forth demons, spirits and other horrors. The ground was rocky and broken; there was no grass, trees, bushes or anything that could hide us or provide cover, even if we could sneak through unseen. Surrounding the valley were the stark, jagged cliffs that either rose straight up or plunged down into the ocean. So going around was impossible. Not if we wanted to make it in time.

"Is there…*any* way we could get through without having to fight?" I wondered, trying not to sound terrified and desperate. "A spell or some kind of Shadow magic that would hide us?"

"I can't maintain a spell that long," Tatsumi said grimly. "Even if I could, all it would take was one touch or glance from a demon, and they would see us."

"What about the Path of Shadows?"

His expression went so grave I instantly disregarded that idea. "Only a powerful majutsushi can open the Path," he said. "And right now, with the gates to Jigoku open, the veil between the spirit world and the mortal world has been torn apart. Using the Path of Shadows to get through Jigoku..." He shook his head. "We could bring even more spirits into this world, or worse, the demons here could infiltrate Meido itself."

My stomach twisted. Well, that was a bad, *bad* idea. And I was out of options. Taking one step forward, I stared at the distant peaks, clenching my fists at my side. Genno was so close, just on the far side of the valley, preparing to summon the Dragon, unopposed. I had promised I would stop him. I had sworn to never let the Wish be used for evil. So many were counting on us to reach this madman, halt the Summoning and save the empire. There was still time. All we had to do was fight our way through the literal plane of hell.

I took a deep breath. "Then, I suppose there's no other way... except straight through." An icy fist grabbed my insides and squeezed, making me sick with fear, but I fought down the nausea and forced a smile. "It doesn't look that bad, really. Maybe we'll get lucky."

Tatsumi stepped close, his voice only for me. "I'll be right beside you," he murmured. "If I fall, don't look back. Keep going, get to Genno, stop the Summoning. I...promise to do the same, if I can."

Silently, I turned into him, clutching his haori as I pressed my face into the fabric, trying to control my shaking. His arms came up, one slipping around my waist, the other resting against my head as he slid his fingers into my hair. He didn't say anything, but I heard his heartbeat pounding against my ear, felt the slightest of tremors in his arms, and closed my eyes, letting myself disappear into him for just a moment. One more time, before we went out to meet Jigoku and the army that awaited us.

Fox girl. This way.

I opened my eyes as the faintest of whispers drifted over the wind, tickling my ears. Like the voice of the Kirin, it wasn't a physical sound so much as a sensation, prodding at my attention. Raising my head from Tatsumi's chest, I looked around, trying to see who had called to me.

A harsh wind blew along the top of the rise, shaking the grass and causing silver-black shadows to glide over the ground. About a hundred yards away, I could see a lone tree, barren of leaves, the trunk almost white against the darkness.

A figure stood under that tree, her translucent form as pale as the branches and the streams of light through the clouds. Her eyes met mine over the waving grass, and I felt a shiver of recognition run down my spine.

"Suki-san," I whispered, and felt Tatsumi turn to look as well, stiffening as he caught sight of her. Ghostly and almost invisible in the harsh light, the yurei raised an insubstantial arm and beckoned to us, before turning into a glowing sphere of light and drifting away. But it went only a few feet before it paused, hovering over the grass and casting a silvery circle of light in the air around it.

"She wants us to follow." This from Daisuke, as he and Okame had also noticed our sudden visitor. "Perhaps we should heed her calling and see what she wants."

"Yeah, but..." Okame jerked a thumb down the rise, toward the valley and the surging throng at the bottom. "She's moving *away* from the giant portal to hell. Which, don't get me wrong, I'm all for not getting dragged down and ripped apart by demons, but it kind of defeats the purpose of why we're here." The ronin gave a shrug and one of his defiant smirks. "I'd hate to have gotten all dressed up and ready to die for nothing."

"Yumeko-san," Daisuke said softly. "While I wish for nothing more than to greet my enemies with honor, a visit from Suki-san in the past has always turned the tide in some way. She has never led us wrong before. We should not ignore her presence now."

I swallowed. "But what about Kiyomi-sama?" I asked. "We

can't leave now. She'll think we're abandoning the mission. I don't want her to think I'm running away."

"Go," said a new voice. I looked up, and there was Kage Masao, standing a few feet away with his hands clasped in front of him. I hadn't heard or seen him approach; he had been with Lady Hanshou the last time I'd checked. But like Tatsumi, it seemed Lady Hanshou's adviser had the Kage talent for moving unseen. He looked tired, I thought. His fine robes were rumpled, dark circles crouched under his eyes, and a few strands of hair had come loose of his topknot to frame his narrow face. But he still looked poised and elegant as he stood there, smiling faintly as he watched us.

"Go, Yumeko-san," he urged again. "Do not worry about your daimyo." His sharp black gaze flicked to Tatsumi standing beside me. "Do not worry about *our* daimyo. Our fate is sealed. The forces of Shadow and Moon will meet the hordes of Jigoku in battle today, and what comes next has yet to be written. But they know you have a different part to play in this tale. So, do what you must, Yumeko-san. I will inform the daimyos of your decision, but whatever you decide, both Kiyomi-sama and Lady Hanshou trust you will do everything in your power to stop the Summoning. Tatsumi-kun..." He gave Tatsumi one of his knowing, mysterious smiles. "She is quite special, isn't she?" he said. "I saw it the first time I met her. It seems even Hakaimono cannot help to be drawn to that light."

Tatsumi went rigid beside me, and Masao chuckled. "Keep her safe, demonslayer," he said, drawing back. "I do not think I will see you again, so good luck to you both. Yumeko-san, whatever this day brings, it has been an honor knowing you. May the Kami's favor find you, and may they guide your steps to your final destination."

"Yours as well, Masao-san," I replied. "Thank you for all your help."

He bowed to us both, then turned and walked away, moving gracefully back down the slope toward the army waiting at the bottom. I spotted Kiyomi-sama among the samurai, and quickly turned away so I wouldn't see her look up at me. The hitodama that was Suki still hovered in the same place, waiting patiently, and I took a deep breath.

"Okay," I told my remaining companions, "let's go."

We walked along the top of the slope, away from Kiyomi-sama, Lady Hanshou and the forces of Shadow and Moon about to engage the army of Jigoku. With every step, I felt my heart twist a little in my chest, hoping Kiyomi-sama didn't think I was abandoning the mission or her. I thought I could feel the gazes of the samurai as we walked away, the four of us silhouetted clearly against the stormy sky, and didn't dare glance down, keeping my gaze on the glowing ball of light floating beneath the tree.

The hitodama didn't wait for us to catch up. As soon as we started walking, it drifted away, over the grass and gently rising hills, heading north toward the edge of the island. We followed it for a goodly while, walking through grass that sometimes brushed against my thighs, making *shushing* sounds as we passed. With the mottled clouds and shifting spots of light over the grasslands, it should have been pretty, in a somber sort of way. But the land felt dead, lifeless, without the presence of the kami, and it made my stomach squirm.

Finally, we could go no farther. The grasslands ended at the base of the cliffs, which dropped away into the ocean far, far below. As we approached the edge of the island, I realized I could no longer see the hitodama. Until this moment, it had kept its distance but had always been clearly visible, a distinctive white sphere drifting steadily away. But now, as I looked over the sullen gray ocean, the wind whipping and tugging at my hair, I saw no trace of the glowing ball of light, and my pulse fluttered wildly in alarm.

Where did she go? She wouldn't lead us here and then abandon us, would she? That's not like her at all.

"There," said Tatsumi, before I could truly start panicking. I followed his gaze...down. Straight down, past mossy walls and small bushes growing out of the rock, to where the glowing sphere of light hovered over a narrow ledge only a few feet from the crashing waves. Still waiting.

"Ugh, you gotta be kidding," Okame groaned, peering over my shoulder. "I guess we're going to have to climb, then. Anyone got a rope? Yumeko-chan?" He looked at me. I stared back at him.

"Um, I don't have a rope, Okame-san."

"I know, but can't you magic one into existence?"

Daisuke gave a quiet chuckle. "Regardless of our kitsune's talents, I am unsure if we can trust an illusionary rope to climb down the side of a cliff, Okame-san."

Tatsumi sighed. "Baka," I heard him mutter. Reaching into the pouch at his waist, he withdrew a long, thin rope with a metal claw at the end and tossed it at the ronin. "Here. Tie that around yourself if you want. It should hold you both, just don't jerk or yank on it too hard."

"Oho." Okame grinned as he caught it, looking at the noble. "Don't you feel honored, Daisuke-san? We get the secret shinobi rope used for scaling castle walls to assassinate daimyo in their sleep." He waggled the coil of rope at Tatsumi, still smirking. "Are you sure you want us to use this, Kage-san? Doesn't it break some sort of Shadow Clan code?

Tatsumi snorted. "I'm not carrying you down there," he said, and turned to me. I blinked as he stepped close, his expression suddenly uncertain.

"Gomen," he murmured. "I don't mean to presume. But we don't have a lot of time, and I figure this is the fastest way."

"The...fastest way?" I repeated, and he picked me up as easily as lifting a fish basket. My heart leaped, sending flutters of warmth through my insides, as Tatsumi turned and stepped to the edge of the cliff. A blast of damp, icy wind hit us, whipping at my hair and clothes, and I made the mistake of looking down.

Oh, kami. My heart sped up for a completely different reason, and I clutched at the front of Tatsumi's haori. He shifted me in his arms, freeing one limb but holding me tight with the other. I felt his own heartbeat thudding beneath his shirt as he bent his head close to mine.

"Put your arms around my neck," he told me. I did, pressing myself as close to him as I could, and felt his breath against my ear as he murmured, "Hold on, and don't look down. I won't let you fall."

"I know," I whispered, and Tatsumi dropped off the edge of the cliff, plummeting straight down. A shriek lodged in my throat, and I fought the compulsion to squeeze my eyes shut as we dropped like a stone for the bottom. Tatsumi's free hand lashed out, catching a shard of rock jutting from the cliff wall, and our downward plunge was halted as he clung to the side of the ledge. I peeked up and saw his eyes flickering crimson, curved talons digging into the rock wall as we dangled there.

"Still all right?" he murmured.

"Ask me again when we get to the bottom."

He shoved off the cliff face, falling another dozen or so feet before landing on a narrow ledge, somehow balancing us both on the tiny strip of stone. I caught sight of the bottom of the cliff, white waves crashing against the rock, and gave in to the compulsion to shut my eyes, turning my face into Tatsumi's haori. We continued this way for several short but panic-inducing moments, leaping from rock to rock, sliding down the jagged wall and dropping through the air, until after one heart-pounding, terrifying drop, we finally stopped moving.

"Yumeko," Tatsumi said after a few moments had passed. He sounded amused and concerned at the same time. "We're here. You can let me go now."

"I could," I agreed. "As soon as my heart starts back up."

I let out a relieved sigh as Tatsumi gently set me down, grateful to have the earth under my own feet again. Glancing up, I saw Daisuke and Okame descending the cliff wall, much more slowly than our terrifying plunge to the bottom. Still, it wouldn't take them long to reach us. Stepping back from Tatsumi, I gazed around, searching for what had brought us here.

The ghostly figure of a girl hovered several yards away, transparent and nearly invisible against the steel-gray sky. When our gazes met, she quickly dropped her eyes.

"Suki-san?" Carefully, I stepped forward, flinching as a wave crashed against the rocks several feet below us, sending a huge spray of water into the air. Beside us, the wall of the cliff soared overhead, but behind the ghostly figure, I could see a jagged, narrow crack in the rock wall, a hole stretching back into darkness.

I drew in a breath, and beside me, Tatsumi straightened.

"A cave. Is this what you were trying to show us, Suki-san?" I asked, as the yurei eyed Tatsumi with large pale eyes. She shivered, losing form for a moment, winking in and out of existence as she hovered there. The demon obviously frightened her, but she was trying hard to be brave, fighting her instincts to go invisible. With a final shudder, she turned back to me.

"Yes," she whispered. "This...this will lead you under the Valley of Lightning, past the demons and the gates of Jigoku... and will take you close to the cliffs of Ryugake, where Genno is. If we hurry...you'll be able to reach it in time to stop the Summoning. I... I will lead you there, if you will follow me."

"Suki-san." I let out a breath in a rush, as relief and hope bloomed in my chest, dispelling some of the darkness. "Thank you!" I whispered. I didn't even care how the ghost knew of this passage, this miraculous hidden detour under the valley, and I didn't want to question it. It couldn't be coincidence, I knew that. I was aware that something about this situation was very wrong. But I was desperate to stop Genno and save Kiyomi-sama; I would take any help I could, even if it was a trap.

Tatsumi, however, was not as accepting of our sudden good fortune.

"How did you know of this?" he growled, glancing at the mouth of the cave, then back at the hitodama with narrowed eyes. "Not even the daimyo of the Moon Clan knows about this route, otherwise she would have sent us here. Who told you of this passage?"

Suki paled, becoming a bit more transparent in the face of the wary demonslayer. "I… I was bid to help you," she said in a breathy, trembling voice. "Lord Sei—" She paused, catching herself, before continuing. "The person I follow… He showed me this passage…and told me to lead you here. He wants you to stop Genno. Stop the Summoning. That is…all I know."

"Yumeko-san." Daisuke's voice echoed behind us, as the noble carefully made his way along the ledge. The ronin walked close behind him, but as far from the edge of the cliff as he could, nearly pressing his body into the rock wall. The yurei half turned, and a strange expression crossed her face as she saw the noble: one of happiness, contentment and relief, but tinged with sorrow. Daisuke smiled as he joined us, gazing at the dark mouth of the cave with a surprised, hopeful expression. Unlike Tatsumi, he didn't appear suspicious at all.

"Suki-san," he murmured, glancing at the hitodama, who instantly dropped her gaze, looking at the ground. Daisuke's voice was faintly awed as he continued. "You appear once again to show us the way. Perhaps you are not a hitodama at all, but a guardian spirit sent by the Kami themselves?"

Suki closed her eyes. If she had been living, I was sure she would have blushed. "I… I am just a ghost, Daisuke-sama," she whispered. "I am not worthy of anyone's attention. I will guide you and your friends to the Summoning site…and Genno. If that is what you wish.

"But," she added, quickly looking up, "I must warn you all. The path ahead…is dangerous. There is something in these caves, a presence that is…very powerful. Powerful enough to keep the kami themselves away." She shivered, casting a fearful glance at the jagged tear in the rock face. "And it…is…angry. If whatever is in the caves finds us…you could all die."

I bit my lip, trembling. I could still see Reika smiling at me as she faded away, proud that she had given her life to save the daimyo. I could see Master Isao, his determination and serene calm, as he strode out to meet the oni that would kill him. For them, death wasn't something to be feared, but a duty that they had accepted. If my time came, I could only hope to do so well, facing it proudly on my feet. Ready to give my life to protect those I loved.

"If this is the only way to Genno, we have to keep going," I said. "I'll face whatever I must if we can get to the Summoning site and stop the Wish."

"I was afraid you would say that." The ronin sighed, raking a hand through his hair, and gazed defiantly at the mouth of the cave. "Well, the day isn't getting any shorter. Let's go meet that glorious death."

"Lead on, Suki-san," Daisuke said, sounding as close to elated as I had ever heard from him. "We have a demon master to confront, a Summoning to prevent, and as Okame-san pointed out, the day is not getting any younger."

22

The Cave of Sorrows

TATSUMI

I didn't like this.

The ghost was right. There was something lurking in these caves. Something…powerful. I could feel it in the walls, in the air itself, a dark, pulsing energy that seemed to grow the deeper we went into the tunnels. It made my demon instincts bristle, prodding at them like an open wound, making me tense. Whatever was down here was not a lone kami or even a wandering yokai. It was darker than that, old and powerful. Though the question of whether or not we would run into it was unknown. The cave system was enormous; we had been walking for a couple hours, following the hitodama through caverns and narrow passages, ducking stalactites and low-hanging ceilings, the glow of the floating sphere our only light in the utter blackness.

"How do you know where you're going, Suki-san?" Yumeko asked at one point, her voice echoing in the cavern overhead. "Have you been here before?"

The sphere shimmered into the figure of a girl, who then shook her head. "Not exactly," she whispered. "I came through these caves once…in a vision. But the path is clear. The person who sent me to fetch you showed me the way. I…know where we're going."

"Pretty convenient, this passage," came the ronin's gruff voice. "I find it hard to believe no one knows about it. Especially if it goes right to the place we're trying to get to."

"It was…hidden," replied the hitodama. "Only recently has the way been opened. No one, not even the daimyo…knew of this passage." She shivered, losing form for a moment, before flickering into sight again, gazing around nervously. "This is…a dead place. The kami avoid this mountain. They fear…what lives in the tunnels."

"Oh, good. And here we are, marching right into the jaws of…whatever it is. Sure sounds like us."

"Did anyone hear that?" Yumeko suddenly whispered.

We stopped, and silence descended, closing around us like the stillness of a tomb. Overhead, the ghost girl floated nervously back and forth, making the shadows on the walls sway. The quiet throbbed in my ears, broken only by the faint thump of my own heart.

And then, I heard it, drifting through the tunnels: a low, shuddering noise, like something gasping for breath. It raised the hairs on the back of my neck and caused the hitodama to lose form, shivering once more into a ball of light.

"What is that?" Yumeko whispered. She cocked her head, ears twitching, and a frown crossed her face. "It almost sounds like…someone crying."

"Right, because that's not alarming at all," the ronin muttered. "I can think of several things that live in dark, lonely, horribly depressing caves, and all of them are things I'd rather not meet, crying or not."

The sound faded away, and there was only silence again.

Yumeko shivered and looked up at the hitodama. "Suki-san, do you know what could be down here?"

The ball of light floated toward her, rippling into the image of the girl again before shaking her head. "No," she whispered. "I just know…that it is dangerous, and we should try to avoid it if we can. But…this is the only way…through the valley. If we want to reach the Summoning site, we must keep going."

"Do not worry about us, Suki-san," the noble said. "Whatever is down here, we will meet it with honor. And we will not let it stop us from completing our mission. So please…lead on."

We continued, following the glow of the hitodama as it drifted silently through dark, narrow passages. For a time, all was quiet, but then the sound of sobbing arose once more, chilling and faint, echoing all around us. It didn't seem to be coming from any one direction, and the sound rose and fell in waves, growing in volume before fading to barely audible whispers. As if the entire cavern and cave system was suffused with some terrible grief that pulsed from the very walls.

The deeper we went, the louder the sobbing became. Eventually, it was impossible not to hear the shuddering gasps of pain, the low, continuous moans of sorrow. Whatever was down here, we were getting steadily closer.

Yumeko suddenly paused, twitching her ears forward as if something had caught her attention. She blinked, then stepped off the path and crouched down, her gaze on the ground in front of her. Curious and wary, I stepped forward as well, and saw something small and fragile-looking in the shadow of a stone. A moment later, I realized it was a flower. An iris, the petals so dark a purple they were almost black.

"How is this growing here?" Yumeko wondered softly. Her hand hovered over it, glowing softly with foxfire, casting the tiny plant in a hazy, flickering light. "It looks…almost sad."

"I don't know, but maybe you shouldn't touch the weird flower in the creepy moaning cave," Okame suggested. "It probably drinks blood and spits out poison spores or centipedes. Something nasty like that. I say we leave it alone."

"Whatever it is," I muttered as Yumeko rose, and the foxfire in her hand winked out, "it means we're close to whatever is living down here. If it's living at all."

"You just had to add that last part, didn't you, Kage-san?" The ronin groaned and unshouldered his bow. "Not sure how much help I'm going to be if we meet a sobbing ghost with a penchant for man-eating flowers, but I'll do my best. Anyone bring any exorcism slips?"

He caught himself at the last moment, wincing, but it was already too late. Yumeko sniffed, her eyes going glassy for a moment. "I wish Reika was here."

"Yeah." Okame sighed and put a hand on her shoulder, making a small part of me bristle. "Me, too, Yumeko-chan. But we can't dishonor her memory by forgetting what she did. As Taiyo-san would say, she died in the noblest way possible, protecting the ones she loved. We have to follow her example and do the same. So..." He squeezed her shoulder and lifted a hand, pointing down the tunnel. "Onward! To victory, or our most glorious death."

The shout echoed through the cave, cheerfully insolent and defiant. As if he was challenging whatever entity lurked in the darkness to do its worst. The rest of us winced or, in Yumeko's case, flattened her ears, and continued.

As soon as the ronin stepped away, I caught up to Yumeko, touching her arm as we moved into the tunnels. "Yumeko?"

"It's all right, Tatsumi." She took a deep breath, swiping at her eyes. "Okame is right. Reika-san knew what she was doing. She'd accepted that she could die protecting Kiyomi-sama, and she never faltered." She blinked, and a tear traced its way down her cheek. "I can't falter, either. No matter what happens and no matter what it takes, I can't let Genno summon the Dragon. I won't let her sacrifice be for nothing."

As the hitodama led us deeper, the darkness ahead was broken by the orange flicker of torch or candle flame. As we continued, the sobbing, which had been growing steadily louder, both in noise and intensity, now came from a clear direction: straight ahead toward the light.

The passage opened into a vast cavern surrounded by flickering torches, the ceiling soaring so high that the torchlight couldn't penetrate the darkness overhead. The floor of the cavern was carpeted in flowers, the same black irises Yumeko had found earlier. A terrible, sickly smell wafted from them: blood and rot and dying flowers, even though the plants looked healthy. The air was cold, damp and tasted wrong. Almost like…tears.

Looking up, a chill went through me. I drew my sword, and the purple light of Kamigoroshi joined the hazy luminescence of the hitodama.

Something massive crouched in the shadows of the far wall, an enormous hulking shape that was a good twelve feet tall, even bent over as it was. Its back was to us, huge shoulders shaking with sobs, the low, anguished cries emanating from its hulking form. It wore what might once have been an elegant, many-layered kimono, but that was now torn and filthy, with a wide obi sash tied into a bow at its waist. Long, jet-black hair fell down its back and shoulders, pooling over the floor; unlike the wild, tangled manes of the oni, it was straight and fine and looked almost human, which seemed even more disturbing on the huge creature it was attached to.

"Gone."

Its voice echoed through the cavern, deep and throaty, and shockingly female. It raised the hairs on the back of my neck, confirming what I already knew. What we had stumbled onto.

A kijo. A female counterpoint to the oni. But, unlike oni, who mainly originated in Jigoku and tormented the souls of the damned, kijo were solely human women whose rage, jealousy, hate or grief was so great it had turned them into demons. Also unlike oni, they could not be summoned by blood magic, did not work with other demons and were beholden to no one. They lived alone, in caves or deep wildernesses, retreating from the world to nurse their suffering or plans of revenge in isolation. Sometimes you could call upon their services, as most kijo could work powerful hexes or curses, but usually they were so consumed by their own torment it was difficult to reason with them.

The massive creature against the wall drew in a raspy, shuddering breath. "Why?" it moaned, followed by a low sob. "Gone. Gone, both of them gone. How could he betray me? I am alone. Always alone."

As we stepped into the room, the aroma of the flowers filled my senses, cloying and bitter, clogging the back of my throat. I tasted salt and tears, and it was suddenly difficult to breathe, as if I had been sobbing nonstop for hours and could no longer catch my breath. It was an alarming, alien sensation, and I fought the urge to gasp out loud.

But Yumeko drew in a faint, ragged breath, barely a whisper in the vastness of the cave, and the sound of crying ceased.

The kijo turned and faced us across the carpet of flowers. Her face was covered by a white Noh mask sculpted in the throes of terrible grief. The eyes were closed, the mouth open in a sob, and painted tears streaked one side of the porcelain cheek. A pair of black horns curled from her brow above the mask rim, and her nails, painted bright red, were nearly a foot long. She stood there, towering over us, and I saw what she had been hunched over.

Flanked by torches, a small wooden shrine sat against the far wall. Through the open doors, a scattering of items flickered in the torchlight: a folded obi sash, a hina doll with its tiny miniature kimono and painted face, an omamori talisman for luck and protection. The shrine itself, though faded and gray, pulsed with an aura of menace and despair, warping the air around it. The black iris flowers were thickest near the base of the shrine, and they rustled softly as the huge kijo stared at us.

"Who are you?" Her deep voice rippled through the air, and the flowers beneath us trembled. "Why are you here? Have you come to take what is mine?" She stepped forward, placing herself between us and the altar, hiding it with her bulk, and her voice became menacing. "No, you cannot. It is mine! It was always mine!"

"We're sorry to have intruded." Yumeko eased forward a step, holding up her hands in a soothing gesture. Her voice was strained, as if she were struggling not to burst into tears. "Please excuse us. We're not here to take anything. We're just trying to find the path through the mountains."

"Thieves!" the kijo roared, seeming to swell with fury, flaring her claws as she rose to her full terrible height. "Traitors! I won't let you take it! It is mine! It is all I have left!"

I muttered a curse and raised Kamigoroshi before me. The monster was lost in her own world of grief and rage and wouldn't hear anything we had to say.

"Yumeko, get back," I warned, stepping in front of the girl. "You can't reason with it. It's going to attack—"

With a chilling howl that shook the walls and made the flowers writhe madly, the kijo raised her talons and barreled toward us like an avalanche.

23

The Kijo's Curse

Yumeko

*M*y fear spiked, driving away the relentless despair clawing at my insides. The monster—the oni or demoness or whatever she was—wailed as she came at us, a maelstrom of fury and anguish that battered me like a hurricane. I staggered back, but Tatsumi and Daisuke leaped forward, blades drawn, and Okame swiftly raised his bow, firing two shots as the demon charged. One hit her forehead and deflected with the sound of cracking porcelain, but the other struck the monster square in the chest, sinking deep into her billowing robes. She screamed but didn't seem slowed by what should have been a fatal shot, turning her attention to the warriors in her path.

Tatsumi and Daisuke dove to either side as the demoness reached them, avoiding the long, bright red talons scything down at them. Their swords flashed in unison, cutting across her sides, parting the fabric of the many-layered kimono and slashing deep into her flesh.

The demoness howled, rearing back in pain. What erupted from beneath her robes wasn't blood but dark ash shooting into the air like a swarm of flies. It misted into the air and settled over the flowers in a choking fog, clogging the back of my throat as I breathed it in. I coughed violently, tears burning my eyes, the taste of salt thick on my tongue. Tatsumi and Daisuke staggered back, wincing and covering their faces with their sleeves, as the demon's howl turned into a piercing wail.

"It hurts!" she sobbed, tearing at her own robes with her talons, ripping through the cloth like it was made of parchment. "The pain, it never goes away! I cannot bear it!" She gave another sob and turned on Daisuke and Tatsumi again, raising her claws. I swiftly knelt and plucked one of the flowers from the cave floor, hoping that a few more Daisukes and Tatsumis would confuse the monster long enough for the real ones to kill her. But as soon as it left the ground, the flower turned to ashes in my hand, dissolving into black dust.

With a shriek, the demoness lashed out at Daisuke, and the noble barely ducked and twisted aside to avoid it. Her claws caught the ends of his hair, and a few pale strands drifted to the ground, sliced neatly in two. "Villain!" she screamed at him as he swiftly backed away. "Monster! I loved you! I gave you everything!" She lunged at the noble, reaching for him with her talons, but an arrow flew through the air, striking the side of her neck, making her flinch and stagger.

The demoness wailed, frantically swiping at Daisuke with one claw, and this time, the noble didn't leap back. His sword flashed, cutting into the demon's sleeve, severing the hand at the wrist. More darkness rushed from the stump left behind, swirling into the air as the demoness stumbled back, her shrieks reaching a crescendo. And then, a streak of darkness from the side, as Tatsumi rushed in, ducked beneath a flailing talon and stabbed up with Kamigoroshi. The point of the blade struck the demon in the throat, right below the mask, and exploded out the top of her head. Grabbing the sword hilt with both hands, Tatsumi yanked the blade out through the skull, splitting the demon's face in two and sending the mask flying into the flowers.

With an agonized howl that shook the ground, the demoness frayed apart, her huge body exploding into ashes. I put a sleeve to my mouth and nose as the black dust cloud settled over everything like a softly falling rain, coating the flowers and making my eyes burn. With the passing of the demon, silence descended, broken only by the roar of my heart in my ears.

Tatsumi and Daisuke sheathed their blades, giving the other a respectful nod as the dust settled around them. Forgotten, Suki drifted down from where she had been hovering overhead, her intangible form wide-eyed and frightened as she gazed where the massive demon had disappeared in a cloud of ash. "Is…is it gone?" she whispered.

Cautiously, I dropped my sleeve from my face. "I think so," I murmured back. My eyes watered, and I swiped at a final tear that had crawled down my cheek. "That must have been what the Kirin warned me about," I whispered. "The lingering spirit of grief and rage that haunts this island. What could have caused it to stay here? Tatsumi-san?"

Tatsumi and the others had joined us, looking tired. Ash streaked their faces, and Okame's jaw was set, as if he was trying not to let his emotions get the better of him. Even Daisuke looked strained, his posture stiff and his mouth pressed into a grim line.

Tatsumi rubbed a hand over his eyes. "I don't know," he admitted. "It wasn't like anything I've seen before. Normally, women who become kijo are still flesh and blood. But that was clearly some sort of spirit. Perhaps it was a reiki—a demon who has died but is so consumed with revenge that it cannot return to Jigoku to be reborn."

"Well, whatever it was," Okame broke in, "it's gone now. Though, it *really* didn't seem to like you, peacock," he added, gazing at Daisuke. "You didn't piss off a demon in a previous life, did you?"

"Not that I am aware of," Daisuke said, and his normally tranquil voice shook a bit at the end. Wincing, he put a hand over his eyes, as Okame gazed at him in concern. "Forgive me," he murmured, "but the scent of these flowers is making it difficult to concentrate. I fear I might dishonor myself and start weeping if we stay here much longer. Now that the spirit has been put to rest, perhaps we can move on."

"But..." Suki hesitated, gazing around with fearful eyes. "I can still...hear it crying."

We fell silent, a chill going through the air, as the echoes of sobbing rose from the flowers surrounding us. Against the far wall, the wooden shrine glowed, flaring with an ominous purple light. Blackened flakes of ash and soot began rising from the petals in front of it, floating up to swirl through the air, growing thicker and darker with every passing second. The white Noh mask, threaded with cracks but still in one piece, drifted up and flew silently across the room until it hovered in front of the black cloud.

The sobbing grew louder, now coming from the swirling mass near the shrine, and my heart sank. With a final, ear-piercing wail, the ash cloud reintegrated, as the huge demoness, unhurt and very much alive, threw back her head and howled.

"Kuso!" Okame scrambled back, raising his bow again. "Well, this could get tiring. How many times are we going to have to kill the thing?"

"The shrine." Tatsumi drew Kamigoroshi in a flare of light as the demoness lowered her arms and turned toward us. "The shrine is the anchor," he growled, his narrowed gaze on the tiny wooden structure behind the monster. "We can't kill the kijo itself. Something is keeping its spirit tied to this world. Destroy the shrine, and its anchor might disappear."

"Nooooooooo!"

The frantic, terrible scream made me wince—I clapped my hands over my ears—and caused the flowers to sway wildly. The demoness whirled, covering the shrine with her huge body, wrapping her arms around it. "No, you cannot!" she sobbed, glaring back at us. "It is mine! You cannot take it! The memories are all I have left of her!"

All I have left of her.

I jerked up, eyes widening in disbelief. *Could it be...?*

Raising their blades, Tatsumi and Daisuke started grimly forward, while beside me, Okame fit an arrow to his string. The demoness was still crying, arms curled protectively around the shrine, her huge body trembling with sobs. "Forgive us," I heard Daisuke murmur, as he and the demonslayer drew closer to the sobbing monster. "No one should have to live so mired in despair. Whoever you were, we'll set you free."

The demon's sobbing ceased. She raised her head, though she didn't turn to face the warriors approaching her from behind. "A curse on you," she whispered, and around us, the very air stilled. I felt the power of her words, tinged with hate and grief, ripple out from where she stood, twisting my stomach into a knot. "May you know the same pain. May it burrow so deep into your soul your memories become poison and you drown in a river of tears. May it lodge itself like a broken mirror in your heart, cutting and slicing with every breath, every heartbeat tearing it wider." She turned, holding out a bright, foot-long talon, her voice rising in volume and intensity. "May it rack your bodies and consume your minds, until you are a husk of what you were! Until nothing is left but poison, tears and agony, and you wish to die, but even death will elude you!"

Tatsumi let out a savage, unearthly snarl and lunged, Kamigoroshi flaring purple in the dim light. He was moving before the demoness finished her curse, but she rose even higher, eyes glowing red behind the Noh mask, and screamed.

This time, the wail was a physical force, slamming into me

and knocking me back. The flowers danced wildly, many of them dissolving into black soot and swirling through the air. For a moment, I couldn't breathe, the taste of salt, ash and grief clogging the back of my throat, as something dark and terrible burrowed under my skin.

Beside me, Okame let out a strangled noise and collapsed, falling to his knees in the flowers, his bow dropping from his hands. Farther ahead, Tatsumi and Daisuke also went down, though Tatsumi stayed on his feet a few seconds longer, shoulders hunched and sword gripped in one hand, before a gasp escaped him and he fell, disappearing into the flowers.

"Tatsumi!"

The demoness slumped back, sagging into the flowers, head bowed and hair covering her face. For the moment, she didn't seem to be moving. I rushed forward, though a sudden cry of pain from Okame made my stomach twist. Reaching the spot where Tatsumi fell, I saw him lying in the black petals, arms curled around himself and knees drawn to his chest. He was shaking, jaw clenched, and his eyes were glassy. He didn't seem to notice me as I knelt beside him. I put a hand on his arm, and a chill shot through me. His muscles were like steel cords, locked into unyielding bars around him. I could suddenly see fiery bands racking his body, stabbing into his chest.

"Tatsumi," I whispered, seeing no response, no flicker of recognition in his eyes. A few yards away, there was a howl of pain that made my heart clench. I had never heard Daisuke cry out before, in pain, anger, grief or fear. "What's happening? What can I do?"

Tatsumi's expression contorted. He tried to move, uncurling his arms to push himself upright, but the fiery bands around his body flared and he cried out, collapsing back into the flowers. "The…curse," he gritted out. "Can't…m-move." He grimaced, clenching his jaw to keep a gasp from escaping. "Destroy… demon. Only way…to break— Agh!"

"Tatsumi." I clutched at his sleeve, feeling helpless, as he curled in on himself. In front of the shrine, the demoness stirred, slowly raising her head. Our gazes met, and behind the sobbing Noh mask, I saw her eyes.

For just a moment, they were clear, almost regretful, as we stared at each other. But then a curtain fell over her expression, and her eyes glazed over, slipping into the madness of grief and rage once more.

"You." The demoness straightened, her shadow creeping toward me across the blanket of flowers. I flattened my ears but moved in front of Tatsumi, trying to shield him from her as best I could. Unfortunately, this small action seemed to incense her further. Her eyes glowed, and tears began leaking from beneath her mask as her voice turned chilling.

"You would protect him? The thief? The one who would steal away what is mine? You would shield him from *me*?" She flexed her claws, seeming to grow in size, even as I shrank back in fear. "Do you seek what is mine, as well?"

"No," I said, holding up my hands. "Please, listen to me. We're not thieves! We don't want to take anything from you, we just want to help you move on."

"Thief!" the demoness snarled, gliding forward. "Traitors! I will kill them all! They will not take what is mine! I have lost too much already!"

Terror shot through me. I raised my hands, and a wave of foxfire erupted from my palms, flaring a brilliant blue-white in the darkness. As before, I could sense the tiny ball of power glowing in my chest, and felt the searing heat from the kitsune-bi warp the air around it. The demoness screamed as the fire struck her, catching her robes and igniting her hair. But she didn't stop, plowing through the wall of flames until she was directly above me. Her burning, grotesque face filled my vision, and I gave a yelp of fear, throwing up foxfire-shrouded hands to ward her away.

With a shriek, the demoness lashed out, and something struck me in the side with the force of a mallet. I was hurled through the air and landed several yards away, rolling through the flowers in a black cloud, the ground spinning wildly before I came to a hard, dizzying stop. Blinking back tears of pain, I clenched my jaw and pushed myself upright, searching wildly for Tatsumi and the demon.

Tatsumi tried to stand, his snarl of pain and defiance filling the air as he shoved himself to his feet, clutching his blade. Planting his feet, agony written on every part of his clenched muscles, he faced the demoness towering over him, and for a moment, the monster paused, stunned to see him upright and facing her.

Then the bands coiled around Tatsumi flared, and the demonslayer staggered. With a scream, the demoness stabbed down, slamming Tatsumi into the ground, her claws sinking deep into the earth to pin him in place. As Tatsumi cried out, she raised her other arm, bright red talons gleaming in the darkness, to strip the life from him.

"Kiyomi-sama, stop!"

My voice rang over the flowers, frantic and terrified, echoing around the cavern. And the huge demoness froze.

Slowly, she lowered her arm. Slowly, her masked, terrible face swung around to stare at me. I trembled as her blank, hollow eyes met mine, and dug my fingers into the earth as the demoness pulled her claws from Tatsumi and began walking toward me.

Cautiously, I stood, being careful not to jerk or move too quickly, though my limbs were shaking and my heart was fluttering around my chest like a moth. As I rose, a shadow fell over me, the scent of tears and ash burning my throat. I swallowed and looked up into the dark, glassy gaze of the demon.

"That name." The demoness's voice was flat. Curious, but wary. "I know that name."

Slowly, I nodded. "Kiyomi-sama is the ruler of the Tsuki islands," I whispered. "Long ago, she was betrayed by the man she loved, and her daughter was stolen from her. She spent years living with her anger and grief, and I think that, over time, those emotions took on a life of their own. They seeped into the land and, for whatever reason, became trapped here."

"Daughter," repeated the spirit of Kiyomi-sama. Her voice was low, hollow, as if trying to remember something painful. "Yes, I had a daughter. Once, a long time ago. She was…she was taken from me." She began to shake, tendrils of black soot rising up to swirl around her. Her claws flexed, and the eyes behind the mask flickered red. "Stolen," she whispered, the tenor of her voice beginning to slip into madness again. "Gone. All I have left are memories…memories and…" She glanced back toward the shrine, glowing black and purple against the cavern wall. "You will not take them."

"Your daughter is alive!" I said, wincing as the demoness spun back, raising her claw. "She returned to the island and…" I trailed off, heart pounding, as those bright red talons hovered right over my head. "She's…right here," I whispered. "My… my name is Yumeko, Kiyomi-sama. I…was the child you lost. The daughter that was stolen."

The demoness stared at me. "Yumeko," she whispered. A tremor went through her, and the raised talon slowly dropped. "That…that was her name," she whispered, as if in a daze. "The name I wanted to give her, the name I had chosen for my baby. Yumeko. Child of dreams." She swayed, talons opening and closing, as if unsure of what to do. Behind the mask, her gaze shifted to me, eyes narrowing. "Why?" she asked, the faintest thread of anger nestled deep in her voice. "You were gone so long. I mourned you for so long. Why did you never come back?"

"I'm sorry," I whispered. The reasons rose to my tongue—I didn't know my past, I had been raised in isolation for years—but I bit them down. Excuses wouldn't placate a spirit, not one so consumed with rage and despair. "I'm here now," I told her, meeting the terrible gaze under the mask. "If it will bring you peace, take your vengeance on me, Kiyomi-sama, and release the curse on my friends. They're not responsible for your pain."

"Vengeance." Slowly, one arm rose, crimson talons flaring wide a few inches from my head. I flinched, but the tips of the claws very gently touched my face, tracing my cheek and jaw. "I never wanted retribution," the spirit of Kiyomi-sama murmured. "I only wanted to see her, to watch her grow, to share in all the blessings and trials life would give her." Her other arm rose, both sets of talons framing my face, curling through my hair. "But she has grown up strong, beautiful. It is all a mother could hope for."

My throat closed up. And even though my heart still pounded and my hands shook, I slowly reached out and touched the edges of the Noh mask covering the demon's face. The porcelain was cold against my fingers as I met the stark gaze underneath.

"You've been in pain for too long, Kiyomi-sama," I said softly. "It's time to let go."

Very gently, I pulled. The Noh mask came away easily in my hands, brittle and lifeless. The face beneath was Kiyomi-sama's, human except for the horns still curling from her forehead, but ravaged with a lifetime of grief and despair. Her pupils were streaked with red, her gaunt cheekbones standing sharply against her skin, all her beauty worn away. But she gazed at me with eyes that, though they still held an eternity of sorrow, were clear.

"Home," she whispered, and one talon rose to gently catch a strand of my hair. "You've come home."

I swallowed hard as the spirit of Kiyomi-sama began to fray apart at the edges, black soot spiraling into the air and drifting away into the dark. The talon holding up the strand of my hair dissolved, as did the hand, and then the arm a moment later. From the corner of my eyes, I could see the carpet of flowers doing the same, black petals turning to dust and rising into the air until they vanished into the blackness overhead.

"Yumeko-chan." The spirit was almost gone now. Just her face and a bit of her robes remained, though they, too, were dissolving rapidly. "Do not be deceived," she murmured. "The tainted one, the soul who opened the gates of Jigoku, he is but a pawn. Everything that has happened, all the trials you have faced, the failures and victories you have claimed, it all has come together by *his* design. We are all pawns in his game, and he will be the one you must face at the very end."

"Who, Kiyomi-sama?" I whispered, feeling as if a hole had opened up beneath me. The thought that Genno, the Master of Demons, was only a pawn, that there was yet another, even more powerful enemy I had to face…it made me a bit sick inside. I was still playing all of this by ear, using fortune and blind chance to get where I needed. I trusted my friends with my life, but I knew determination and luck could take us only so far. "If he is even stronger than Genno, how will I be able to beat him?"

The spirit of Kiyomi-sama smiled. "Be brave, daughter," she said. "He is powerful, but do not underestimate yourself. He is part of you, after all."

Blinking, I watched as the final bits of ash that had been Kiyomi-sama swirled around me for a moment, then scattered to the winds. Of the spirit, nothing remained; even her robes had faded into dust and vanished. The only item left behind was the cold porcelain mask I still held.

As the demoness vanished, the lights in the cavern flared once, then faded to darkness, the torches snuffed, the glow of the altar winking out. Shadows crept over the room, now eerily silent and empty. Only the faint, ethereal glow from a hovering hitodama kept the cavern from being plunged into utter blackness.

Someone groaned in the darkness, and my heart leaped. Tossing a ball of kitsune-bi into the air, I hurried back to where I had left my companions.

In the flickering foxfire, I could easily make out a dark form lying against the bare rock of the cavern floor. As I approached, it stirred, and Tatsumi slowly pushed himself to his knees, breathing hard. His shoulders were hunched, his muscles stiff, as if he was bracing himself for a sudden onslaught of agony. From somewhere in the darkness, I heard a rough, muttered curse, likely from Okame, followed by sounds of someone struggling to their feet.

"Tatsumi-san." I knelt in front of the demonslayer, peering into his face. "Are you all right? Are you in any pain?"

He hesitated a moment, then slowly relaxed, muscles unclenching one by one. "I don't think so," he muttered. "The hex appears to have been broken…or lifted." His gaze rose to mine, then to the cavern around us. "The kijo?"

"Gone," I whispered. "I don't think she's coming back."

He gave a painful nod. "Was it really the daimyo?"

I shook my head. "No," I mused, trying to make sense of it all. "I don't think so. I think this was a manifestation of Kiyomi-sama's negative emotions. All her anger, all her grief and shock and despair when she realized her daughter was stolen away. For some reason, it was drawn down here and trapped, and has been festering ever since." I took a deep breath, driving away the lingering heaviness around my heart, the last shreds of despair clinging stubbornly to my mind. "That's what the Kirin warned me about," I said. "The darkness haunting this island. The sadness infecting the Moon Clan. Why, even after all this time, Kiyomi-sama has been unable to move on. It was all because of that spirit."

"You freed it, though," Tatsumi said.

I blinked at the fresh, untainted stinging in my eyes. "It was so angry," I whispered. "So much in pain. All it knew was betrayal and despair, grieving over what it had lost. Maybe now Kiyomi-sama will finally find peace."

"Yes," said a new voice, echoing through the cavern. We jerked up as silvery light flared overhead, illuminating the entire room. "I believe she will."

A figure stepped from the shadows, coming to stand before

the shrine against the far wall. My heart leaped to my throat as I recognized him. I'd only seen him once, in the narrow back alleys of Chochin Machi, but he was impossible to forget.

"Well done, Yumeko," greeted Seigetsu-sama. He smiled at me, still stunning, breathtaking, even this time around. His yellow eyes glowed in the shadows, and his long silver hair glimmered like a waterfall in the moonlight. "I should not be surprised, given your bloodline. But you have done better than even I could have hoped."

24

Ninetail

Suki

Seigetsu-sama?

In a daze, Suki watched Seigetsu emerge from the darkness. He was smiling, his silver hair and white robes seeming to glow as he stepped from the shadows. Taka was not with him, and for some reason, this made Suki very nervous. Like something terrible was about to happen.

The demonslayer leaped to his feet, drawing his blade in a flash of purple light. From the shadows behind him, the ronin and Daisuke-sama appeared, coming forward to flank the Kage warrior.

No, Daisuke-sama! Suki threw out a hand, wanting to fly down and grab the noble before he could step forward and challenge the silver-haired man. The Taiyo was a fierce warrior and amazing swordsman, but she had seen a little of Lord Seigetsu's power, and knew that he was capable of so much more. She didn't know if Daisuke-sama could win a battle with the mysterious man she had been following all this time, and she did not want to find out.

"Who are you?" The Kage's voice was hard, chilling. He took one step forward, placing himself between the fox girl and the stranger who had appeared out of nowhere. "What do you want here?"

"Peace, Hakaimono." Lord Seigetsu held up a hand. His words were as low and soothing as a mountain spring. "I am not your enemy. I did not come for a confrontation, merely to claim an item I left here long ago. Yumeko..." His golden eyes shifted, fixing on the fox girl, who stiffened. "Child of dreams." He chuckled, and Suki was shocked to hear genuine affection in his tone. "You have done well. Only you could have freed the spirit of grief and rage who had dwelled here for so long. You have played your part admirably, as I knew you would. For that, you have my gratitude. But now, if you would kindly hand over the item I left behind..."

He raised a hand, and the mask that had been clutched in the kitsune's fingers somehow left her grip and floated across the cavern. As it came to rest in Seigetsu's palm, a terrible smile crossed his face, eyes gleaming. In that moment, he looked like a stranger.

"The mask." At that moment, the fox girl sounded as Suki felt, on the verge of a terrible realization. The pieces were coming together, not enough to form a whole picture, but very close. "You...left that here."

"Sixteen years ago," Lord Seigetsu agreed. "Along with the shrine, and a few special items that were tied to the birth of a particular infant. The shrine would serve as the anchor, or perhaps a beacon, for Kiyomi's feelings of grief and loss. Those emotions were drawn here, grew and festered by the day, and eventually became the spirit you just encountered. The kami could do nothing against it because it was a manifestation of Kiyomi herself, her rage and sorrow that, over the years, became a powerful curse that shadowed the whole island. Even the real Kiyomi, though time has dulled the pain and the memories of that night, could not forget or find solace. Only one thing could placate the spirit and convince it to move on. The source of its obsession and grief." He smiled, his gaze lingering on the fox girl. "Child of dreams. The monks raised you well. I could not have hoped for a better outcome."

"Then...you..." Yumeko's face had gone the color of the porcelain mask; her legs trembled, and she sank to her knees on the stones, staring at Lord Seigetsu. The others, too, seemed dazed or stunned into silence. "*You* were Kiyomi-sama's husband."

Suki felt numb, as if everything she had known had been ripped away from her. She had followed Lord Seigetsu, obeyed him, watched as he moved his pieces around the board—pieces that were the lives of everyone around her. She thought she had been helping the fox girl and Daisuke-sama, keeping them alive, but it seemed Lord Seigetsu's plans went far deeper than she could have ever imagined.

"Why?" Yumeko whispered after several moments. "Why did you do all this? Everything we've gone through, everything we've faced...coming to this island, running into Kiyomi-sama...have you been watching us the whole time? Has this been a game to you?"

"A game, she says." Seigetsu-sama chuckled softly, shaking his head with a wry half smile. "It has been a *very* long game, Yumeko," he told her. "One that was started many years ago, before you were even a glimmer in your mother's thoughts. And now the game is almost finished. The final play is in sight. And the last piece is finally ready."

He raised a hand, and the mask floated up, outlined in soft blue-white flames. "Sixteen years is the blink of an eye," he murmured, gazing at the porcelain image in contemplation. "And yet, it can be a lifetime. A lifetime of grief, rage, hate and despair can corrupt even the purest heart and drive anyone, or anything, to madness. Even those who are immortal. All it takes is a tiny splinter, a crack in their armor, and they can be consumed."

The flames surrounding the mask flared, becoming almost too bright to look at. Suki flinched, turning away for a moment, and when she looked back, the porcelain mask was gone.

An arrow floated in the air before Seigetsu-sama, flickering with soft blue flames. The pointed arrowhead was white, streaked with lines of crimson, and the wooden shaft was the purple-black of the flowers that had once carpeted the chamber. A cloud of ash and darkness clung to the arrow, tendrils of dust swirling through the air before drifting to the ground. It sent a chill through Suki just looking at it, but Lord Seigetsu smiled, his eyes glowing yellow in the flickering light.

"Did you know that all living things can be corrupted?" His voice was triumphant, a murmur in the darkness. "Nothing is immune. Not even the Kami themselves."

"I've heard enough."

Raising his sword, the demon lunged at Lord Seigetsu with a snarl, his blade flaring with purple fire. Suki covered her mouth, a spear of alarm coursing through her, not knowing who she was more frightened for, the half-demon or Seigetsu-sama.

"No, Hakaimono." Lord Seigetsu raised his head, and fire erupted before him, a wall of blue-white flames that filled the cavern with light. Even though she was transparent and had no body, Suki could actually *feel* the heat, a searing, terrible brightness that threatened to burn her from existence. She cringed, darting behind a stalactite, as below her, the fox girl cried out and even the demon flinched back, shielding his eyes.

When Suki dared peek out from behind the stone, the world fell away, and she was suddenly frozen with terror.

Lord Seigetsu stood in the same place, surrounded by ghostly flames that cast a terrible shadow over the walls and floors around him. His eyes glowed, his robes and silver hair glowed, billowing in an unnatural wind, the eerie firelight dancing over them.

A long, bushy tail rose behind his shoulders, swaying slowly, as if it had a mind of its own. It was silvery white, the same color as Seigetsu's hair, and pulsed with dancing blue flames at the tip. Another followed, and another, rising like serpents to sway and coil about, until there were nine of them altogether, framing Seigetsu-sama in a halo of light.

Nine tails.

A chill unlike anything Suki had ever known settled over her. She knew the stories. The legends of the ninetailed fox. Of how, when a kitsune grew old enough to acquire its ninth tail, its fur would turn gold or silver, and it would become one of the most powerful yokai in existence. A ninetailed fox was an ancient, mysterious, dangerous creature, possessing the knowledge of a thousand lifetimes and the magic to rival the Kami themselves. Some myths claimed they could create their own kingdoms of illusion and shadow, destroy whole cities with fire, even call down the moon. In one of the most famous, frightening stories, a ninetailed fox had been responsible for the near destruction of the country by becoming the emperor's favorite wife and driving him to madness. The stories of ninetailed foxes were many, but that was all Suki had thought they were…stories.

Until now.

Lord Seigetsu flickered with pale fire, his tails swaying hypnotically as he observed the small party before him, his gaze lingering on the kitsune girl and the demon. "I am not your enemy," he said in a low, compelling voice. "And you are running out of time. Genno has begun the ritual to summon the Dragon. Even now he prepares to recite the incantation on the Scroll of a Thousand Prayers. It will not take him long to complete it."

His inhuman gaze lifted then, finding Suki near the ceiling, hovering behind the stones, and he smiled. "Suki-chan," he said quietly, sincerely, "thank you for doing your part. For leading them to where they needed to go, for keeping them alive when I could not be there. It has been an honor traveling with you, but I fear our time together has come to an end. I have no more need of you." His billowy sleeve lifted, one hand gesturing toward the sky through the ceiling. "Move on, Suki-chan. This was never your fight. You have no part to play anymore, and I am certain Meido has been calling you for a while now. This world is no place for the pure of heart."

"Seigetsu-sama," Suki whispered, but it went unheard in the vastness of the cavern. Seigetsu returned his attention to the others and nodded at the kitsune, who still knelt a few feet away, her eyes wide as she stared at him.

"He awakens," he whispered, and though his words were for the fox girl, they sent a chill racing up Suki's back. "He stirs, and the world trembles with the movement. Can't you hear him coming? Hurry, Yumeko. It is almost time."

With a wave of his tails, Lord Seigetsu erupted in a flare of brilliant luminance, the ghostly flames surging up with a roar, turning the entire cavern white. When the light faded, plunging the chamber into blackness once more, the ninetailed kitsune was gone.

"Kuso!" An emphatic curse rang out in the darkness, followed by the shuffling of feet. "What *the hell* was that? First we have demons and curses and ghosts and an oni that might be Yumeko's mother, oh, and by the way, the gates of Jigoku have been opened and Genno is about to summon the Dragon and make a wish that will doom the world. I thought that was quite enough to deal with without some crazy ninetailed fox popping in and hinting that he planned all this from the beginning!" One hand rose to the side of the ronin's skull, clutching at his hair. "This is crazy. Does anyone else feel like the world has been turned on its head, or is it just my brain that's about to explode?"

Suki peered farther out from behind the stone, seeing, in the hazy light, the noble stride across the floor and slip his arms around the ronin from the side. The other relaxed, slumping in the embrace, as Daisuke murmured something only the ronin could hear. Suki didn't know what it was, but it made the other chuckle and ruefully shake his head. As the echoes of the ronin's outburst died away and silence fell over the cavern again, Suki drifted down to where the fox girl still knelt on the stones. She was shaking, her eyes wide as she gazed blankly at the spot where Lord Seigetsu had disappeared. Even through the numbness of being a ghost, Suki ached for her. In the span of a few heartbeats, she had discovered something about herself and her past that was absolutely terrifying. Her world, and everything she knew, had been torn apart. In her place, had she been alive, Suki wouldn't know what to do, either.

"Yumeko." The demon boy sheathed his blade and knelt in front of her, close enough that their knees were touching. His hand rose, hesitated, then gently brushed the hair from her cheek, sliding his knuckles along her skin. "Stay with me," he urged, his voice a low murmur in the darkness. "This doesn't change anything."

"Tatsumi." The kitsune's voice was numb. "Seigetsu is… And he…" She closed her eyes, her ears flattening to her skull. "I don't know who I am anymore," she whispered. "Have I just been a pawn all this time? Something that just blindly followed the path set out for her?" She opened her eyes, gazing around the cavern, at the shrine, dark and lifeless, against the wall. "He meant for me to come here. He meant for me to see all of this, to find Kiyomi-sama and discover this place. Have I been the catalyst for everything? If I…if I was never born, would Genno still be threatening to destroy the empire? Or would the scroll still be safely in the Silent Winds temple? So many people have died because of me. Reika. Master Jiro. Master Isao." On her knees, her hands curled into fists. "What am I?" she whispered. "Have *any* of my choices been my own?"

"Yumeko." The demon shifted closer, lowering his voice. He seemed hesitant to speak, though the sight of the distraught kitsune clearly concerned him. "I don't know who or what you are, exactly," he told her in a quiet voice. "But I do know what you've done. You protected the Dragon scroll as best you could. You risked your life to keep it safe, even though it would've been easier to give it up, to let someone else take that burden."

The fox girl sniffed, hunching her shoulders. The demon eased closer still and gently cupped her chin with his fingers, peering into her face. "You confronted the most dangerous demon alive," he murmured, "risked your own soul to face him, to free the human he had possessed. You gave up the Dragon's Prayer to save your friends, but then you followed Genno to this island to stop him from summoning the Harbinger, even though he has an army of demons at his call and the odds of survival are nearly nonexistent. All of these choices, every decision and branching point along the way, they were made because you… are you. Because the kitsune I followed from the Silent Winds temple, the girl who talks to ghosts and charms emperors and made the most powerful oni Jigoku has ever spawned fall in love with her, wouldn't do anything else."

The fox girl blinked, then stared at the demon with wide eyes. He gave a faint, rueful smile, as if he couldn't quite believe he had said that. "Your choices," he went on, "your decisions—that's why I'm here, Yumeko. Why we're all here. And it is why we'll continue to follow you, to the brink of Jigoku and back." He paused once more, then leaned in, his voice becoming nearly inaudible. "I have the soul of the First Oni inside me," he whispered. "And if you say the word, he would give his life for you in a heartbeat. Not even the most powerful ninetailed fox in Iwagoto can claim that."

Suki's throat felt curiously tight, and there was a pull in the pit of her stomach as she hovered there, watching the demon and the fox girl. Odd sensations, because she had no body, not even the ghostly image of one at the moment, but the emotions that came from observing the pair were real. The kitsune sniffed, leaning forward until their foreheads touched, one hand on the back of his head. The demon didn't move, closing his eyes, and they stayed like that for a long moment, before the fox girl took a deep breath and leaned back, her eyes clear.

"Gomen," she whispered. "Gomen, Tatsumi. I'm ready now." She rose to her feet, her expression hard and determined as she lifted her head. "I have to stay focused," she said. "Stop Genno, prevent the Summoning—that's the only thing that matters. Okame-san, Daisuke-san? Are you still with us?"

"Until the end, Yumeko-san." Daisuke's voice echoed calmly in the stillness. He stood quietly against the wall, his arms around the ronin's waist, neither embarrassed nor in a hurry to move them. And the ronin, leaning back into the noble, seemed content not to move, either.

"Suki-san?" The fox girl turned, finding Suki hovering overhead. For a moment, Suki tensed, wondering what the kitsune thought of the part she had to play for Seigetsu-sama. But there was no condemnation in the eyes of the fox girl, only sympathy and understanding. "If you are still willing, would you be able to lead us out?"

Move on, Suki-chan, Lord Seigetsu had told her. *This was never your fight. You have no part to play anymore.*

She glanced at Daisuke-sama, his face calm and his eyes peaceful, standing quietly beside the ronin who had captured his heart. At the fox girl and the demon standing behind her, his fierce, protective gaze only for the kitsune.

This world is no place for the pure of heart.

No, Suki thought, as a tiny spark of anger flickered to life within. *You're wrong, Seigetsu-sama. I might be dead, but there are hearts and souls in this world that are worth saving. I won't let them be lost. This has become my fight, as well.*

She floated down until she hovered a few feet before the kitsune girl, who watched her calmly, the hazy light flickering over her face. *I'm sorry*, Suki wanted to tell her. *I didn't know who Seigetsu-sama was, what he wanted with you. I'm sorry he deceived us both.*

The kitsune smiled faintly, as if reading her thoughts. Suki rose into the air, circled her and the demon once, then flew across the room until she found the tunnel that led outside. *I will see this through*, Suki thought, hearing the footsteps of the four who followed behind. Kitsune, demon, ronin and the noble she'd once loved. *To the end.*

The sky was nearly black when they emerged from the caves, roiling clouds blotting out any hint of moon or stars. A gust of wind howled through the crags, tossing the hair and clothes of the living bodies as they stepped onto a narrow rocky ledge overlooking the valley.

Far below, the plains were cloaked in shadow, but the gaping hole to the center of Jigoku pulsed with hellish light, like a terrible wound in the earth. Demons and damned souls still crawled from the pit, their shrieks and wails rising into the air.

In the ghastly hell-light, the valley was a writhing mass of bodies, as demons, spirits and oni clashed with the armies of Moon and Shadow. The number of demons seemed endless, a constant wave surging against the wall of humans trying to force them back. Suki could see the row of torches where the armies held the line, a barrier between the horde flooding up from the pit and the rest of the island. For now, the dam held, but night was falling and the demons kept coming. Eventually, the human forces would be overrun.

"Kiyomi-sama," Suki heard the kitsune whisper behind her, voice choked and horrified. "I'm so sorry."

Overhead, a streak of lightning cut across the sky, slicing through the clouds like a knife, and a peal of thunder made the ground tremble. Below the ledge, a slim winding staircase snaked up the mountain, rising toward a peak where the clouds were gathering in a swirling maelstrom overhead.

"There's the Summoning site," the demon pointed out. His gaze followed the staircase, eyes glowing red as he stared up the mountain. "We're almost there."

"Well, look at that." The ronin turned to grin at Daisuke, his voice awed and triumphant. "We actually made it. One step closer to Genno—I hope you're thinking up a good poem, peacock."

As he spoke, a flash of lightning turned the world a blinding white. For a split second, between one pulse and the next, Suki thought she caught a glimpse of a shadow above them, a thin, dark figure with hate-filled eyes and a long swinging braid. It raised its arm, something glinting between its fingers, and Suki opened her mouth to cry out as lightning flashed and everything disappeared.

The ronin grunted. He staggered, a strange look crossing his face as everyone stared at him in alarm. "Ah, kuso," he whispered, and collapsed to the stones, his bow dropping from his fingers.

"Okame-san!" the kitsune cried, as Daisuke immediately knelt beside him, catching the ronin before he could fall the rest of the way to the ground. The noble's expression was anxious, his smooth brow furrowed in alarm. Chilled, Suki looked down to see the hilt of a black kunai sunk between Okame's shoulder blades, the knife glimmering darkly against his haori, the edges starting to well with blood.

"Okame," he whispered, as the fox girl caught sight of the blade as well and gasped, her hands going to her mouth. Suki, floating helplessly above them, could only watch the scene unfold, seeing the devastation on Daisuke's face as the ronin slumped against him. The noble raised a trembling hand, hesitated and curled his long fingers around the hilt of the knife.

"Forgive me," he whispered, and yanked the blade free.

The ronin immediately gave a howl of pain that seemed to cut through Daisuke like an arrow; the noble winced, pressing his forehead to the ronin's, as if trying to take the hurt onto himself.

"Kuso," the other gritted out, his voice tight with pain. "I wasn't paying attention." One hand clutched the front of Daisuke's robes as the noble gazed down at him, stricken. "Don't...focus on me, peacock," the ronin gasped. "That demon bitch is still out there—"

Daisuke's gaze shot up, his eyes hard and lethal. In a blinding motion, he drew his sword and slashed it through the air over Okame. There was a clang of metal on metal, and another black knife went hurling end over end to clatter against the rocks.

The demonslayer drew his blade in a flare of purple fire, as low, mocking laughter echoed behind them. Suki turned as another streak of lightning threaded the sky, outlining the monstrous figure that appeared on a jutting wedge of rock, grinning down at them.

"Predictable," the demon announced. His wild crimson hair snapped in the wind, horns curled from his brow, a curved obsidian blade clutched in one claw. "Predictable, and foolish. Did you really think Genno would leave this pass unguarded?"

"Rasetsu." The demonslayer stepped forward, his blade flickering in his hand. "So you're the final obstacle, are you?" He gave a humorless smile, eyes glowing red, and raised his weapon. "I'm not trapped in a binding circle this time—you won't be able to run me through so easily. Come on, then," he challenged, baring his fangs. "If Genno is on the other side, I guess I'll have to carve a path right through you."

"No."

Daisuke raised his head, his voice and eyes hard. Gently, he lay the ronin against the rock wall and stood, his hair billowing around him, to face the half-oni.

"There is no time, Kage-san," he said. "We have come to

the end of the road, and the objective is mere steps away. Take Yumeko-san and continue. I will stay and deal with the demon."

"Taiyo." The demonslayer glanced at him, his voice was full of warning. "This isn't a normal demon. His name is Rasetsu, the second oni general of Jigoku. I don't know the type of bargain he's made with Genno, or why he's suddenly sharing a body with a human, but Rasetsu is on the same level as Akumu and Yaburama. You won't be able to beat him."

Suki trembled, but Daisuke only gave a faint smile. "Then the duel I have longed for is finally here," he stated calmly.

"Daisuke-san..." The fox girl stepped forward, eyes pleading. "Please. We've come so far, and Genno is so close. We can't stop now."

"That is exactly why I must stay, Yumeko-san," the noble replied. "It was never my fate to face the Master of Demons and stop the Wish. That destiny is yours. Okame and I have brought you as far as we could. Now let us protect you and Kage-san one last time."

"He's right, Yumeko-chan," added the ronin, his voice tight with pain. He tried shifting to another position against the rock but slumped back, clenching his teeth. The stone behind him was smeared with red. "Kuso. My fight is done, and there's no time left. You two go on, stop Genno. That's all that matters now."

"Okame-san." Yumeko's voice shook, on the verge of tears. "What if we never see you again?"

"Hey." The ronin gave a tired smile. "Don't think like that, Yumeko-chan. We'll see each other again. Just make sure you beat Genno so we can all drink to our victory tonight. And if I'm not there, pour out a bottle for me."

"Arigatou, Yumeko-san," Daisuke said. Looking from her to the demonslayer, a beautiful smile crossed his face. "For letting me be a part of your journey. For helping me to push beyond what I thought I could do. Kage-san, my only regret is that we never completed our duel, but I was proud to fight at your side.

I count our time as friends a far greater accomplishment than all my victories as Oni no Mikoto." He lifted his sword before him in a final salute. "Good luck to you both. It has been an honor."

"All right, I'm bored with this." The Second Oni leaped into the air and came down with a crash a few paces away, brandishing his sword as he rose. "I don't know why you mortals have to talk so much before you die!"

With a roar that made the ground shake, he lunged at the kitsune.

Both demonslayer and noble leaped forward, intercepting the monstrous demon as it came in. The oni's black sword flashed up, screeching off and deflecting both blades as the monster spun with shocking grace and kicked the demonslayer in the head with a heel, knocking him aside. The demonslayer tumbled over the rocks and bounced upright with a snarl, tensing to leap in again, but Daisuke's voice rang out, halting him.

"Leave us!" The noble's voice was hard, even as he desperately parried a blow from the red-haired demon that sent him stumbling back. "This isn't your fight any longer, Kage-san! Stop Genno, stop the Summoning, that is all that matters now."

"Go, Yumeko-chan!" added the ronin leaning against the stones, his voice rough. "Get out of here. We'll be fine."

The demonslayer hesitated, clearly torn between leaving and springing into the fray again. But then he set his jaw and turned, holding out a hand to the fox girl.

"Yumeko, hurry."

The kitsune sobbed, clenching her fists. But she turned and sprinted to where the demonslayer waited, and together they started up the narrow path. Toward the distant peak and the clouds swirling overhead.

But as they turned away, a dark figure appeared on the rocks overhead, braid swinging behind her, and raised an arm, a glittering knife between her fingers. Suki started to cry out a warning, but with a streak of darkness, an arrow flew out of nowhere, striking the demon in the back. She screamed and toppled off the stones, and Suki whirled to see the ronin, bow in hand, smiling grimly as he lowered the weapon.

"Don't count me out just yet," Suki heard him mutter. Nearby, Daisuke's sword flashed, sparking off the oni's blade as the two circled each other in their lethal dance. The oni didn't notice or seem to care about the two bodies vanishing up the mountain, so Suki watched as the kitsune and the demonslayer drew farther and farther away and trembled, feeling as if her ghostly body were being ripped in two. Genno was up that trail. The fate of the empire hung on whether the kitsune and her demonslayer could reach him in time.

And yet…

Daisuke-sama. Suki turned, her gaze falling on the noble in his desperate battle, knowing she could not leave him. She watched as he nimbly avoided the oni's savage blows, the obsidian blade barely missing him as he whirled and parried, his own sword a blur. But the oni, too, deftly avoided or parried Daisuke's weapon, and the screech of steel against steel echoed off the rocks. The monster appeared to be enjoying himself, grinning viciously as he battered and cut at the swordsman, using not only his blade, but his claws, horns and feet to strike blow after blow, barely giving the other a chance to breathe. But…and Suki felt a flutter of amazement…Daisuke-sama was smiling, too, his eyes bright and intense as he danced around his enemy.

Daisuke-sama…he's enjoying this, Suki realized, just as the first of the demon's blows got through, the curved talons ripping a savage tear across the noble's shoulder and chest. Suki cried out, but Daisuke didn't flinch. Instead, he spun with the blow, hair swirling around him, and brought his weapon toward the oni's unprotected back. At the last second, the demon twisted away, but not fast enough, and the blade sheared across his arm, cutting deeply into muscle in a spray of dark blood.

Both combatants staggered back a few paces, panting. The

front of Daisuke's robe was torn open, and blood soaked the fabric from the terrible wounds across his chest. His face and hair were streaked with red, blood running down his sword arm and spattering the rock with crimson.

The oni smiled, seemingly unconcerned with the darkness dripping from his elbow and pooling at his feet. "You're fast, human," he said, nodding. "I'll give you that. But you're not better than me." He raised the obsidian blade, dripping with Daisuke's blood. "You're going to die here, and your friends won't make it in time to stop the Summoning. The new age of demons has begun."

Daisuke gave a grim smile. "The first part might be true," he said, panting. "But I'm afraid you've underestimated the rest of us. I have no doubt that Yumeko and Kage-san will reach Genno and emerge victorious. Our kitsune does not know how to fail."

The oni chuckled. "Too bad you won't get to see it," he said, and lunged.

The clang of swords filled the air, echoing above the shrieking wind, as the demon and master swordsman continued their lethal dance. Suki watched, terrified but unable to look away, as Daisuke and the oni clashed at the edge of the cliff, mere feet from a heart-stopping plunge into the valley below. Overhead, the clouds swirled, and the wind ripped at their hair and clothes, as the demon and Taiyo swordsman fought on, their blades moving so fast Suki could barely follow them.

Once again, they drew back, swords raised as they faced each other across the stone. The oni was breathing hard, but he was smirking as he watched the Taiyo a few yards away. For a moment, Daisuke stood tall and proud, the wind tugging at his long hair, a look of stoic calm on his face.

Then he grimaced, and dropped to his knees on the stones, one hand going to his side. Blood gushed from somewhere beneath his robes, spreading across the fabric and staining it crimson. The demon's smirk turned into a grin.

"You can't beat me, human." The oni's voice held the certainty of death. "Even in Jigoku, I was Hakaimono's equal when it came to battle. He had the stronger personality, and I had no desire to lead, but in a one-on-one fight I might have killed him, and we both knew it. You have no chance against me." He took a step forward, causing the Taiyo to glance up, his face tight. "But you were a challenge for a human, and that's not something I can usually say. I'll do you a favor and end this quickly."

He raised his sword, but jerked back as an arrow streaked toward his head, missing him by inches. "Oy, ugly. Did you forget I'm here, too?" called the ronin's harsh voice. Though he still slumped painfully against the rocks, his bow was raised and his quiver lay beside him on the ground. "Just because I can't stand doesn't mean I won't shove arrows through your ugly face."

"No, Okame-san!" Clenching his jaw, Daisuke pushed himself to his feet. Blood soaked one side of his robes, pooling on the rocks beneath him, but he still raised his sword and faced the demon proudly. "This is my fight," he said calmly. "Please, do not interfere. I am not defeated yet."

"Dammit, peacock." The ronin gritted his teeth, but reluctantly lowered the bow. "I said I'd chase that glorious death with you," he almost whispered. "I never thought...I would be the one watching you die."

The oni chuckled, low and ominous. "Oh, don't worry, human," he said, glancing at the ronin with an evil smile. "Neither of you are leaving this mountain alive. Have you forgotten there are two enemies here?" His grin widened, and his eyes glimmered red. "We haven't."

Daisuke paled, and at that moment, a shadow slid from a crevice above the ronin, black eyes narrowed with hate. The scorpion woman, somehow alive, pulled her lips back from her teeth as she glared at the ronin below her and raised her kunai, the throwing dagger glimmering black in the moonlight.

"For my sister," she hissed, and brought her hand down.

Without thinking, Suki flew at her with a shriek, and the world seemed to slow.

The female demon jerked back, eyes going wide, as Suki appeared in front of her with a ghostly wail. The knife, however, still left her fingers as below them, the ronin twisted, somehow bringing up his weapon. The bow in his hand thrummed as he fired one blind, desperate shot, an instant before the black knife slammed into his chest. At the same time, Suki felt something foreign and cold zip through her body, fraying it like mist as it passed through, and the arrow struck the demon through one shiny black eye. The demon jerked, then toppled backward, her body spasming against the rocks as she finally died.

"No, Okame!"

The noble's shout echoed behind her. Numb, Suki looked back as Daisuke strode toward the oni with his sword at his side. The look on his face chilled her; it wasn't one of rage, anger or grief, but a focused, icy resignation. Halfway to his enemy, he lunged, moving blindingly quick, cutting savagely at the demon's head. The oni took a step back, letting the point of the sword barely graze him, and plunged his sword through Daisuke's stomach, the obsidian point exploding out his back.

Someone screamed. A moment later, Suki realized the high-pitched, keening wail was her. Impaled on the demon's sword, Daisuke staggered, blood pouring down his clothes and staining his entire front red, but he didn't fall. Before the oni could yank the blade free, one hand reached up and gripped the demon's wrist, holding it in place. As the oni blinked in surprise, the noble raised his head, a defiant smile crossing his features, before he took one step forward, pulling himself along the blade, and drove his sword through the demon's chest, sinking it nearly to the hilt.

The oni's eyes bulged, mouth gaping, but nothing came out. Still with that faint smile on his face, Daisuke twisted the hilt of his sword around and yanked it up, through the demon's collarbone, and brought the weapon slicing down through the monster's neck. The oni's head, still wearing a stunned, incredulous expression, toppled backwards, bounced over the rocks, and dropped off the edge of the cliff, vanishing into the waves far below.

Taiyo Daisuke staggered back, tearing himself from the oni's sword, as the monster's headless body fell to its knees then collapsed to the rocky ground. The noble's entire front, from the chest down, was covered in red, and streams of crimson pooled in the stones beneath him.

For a moment, he stayed upright, the wind ruffling his hair and the bloody remains of his robe and sleeves. His face, lifted to the sky, was serene, and for just a moment, Suki dared to hope. To believe that the noble Taiyo, the beautiful swordsman who had smiled at a lowly maid in the halls of the Golden Palace, would be fine.

Then his blade dropped from his fingers, hitting the rocks with a clink that sent a chill through Suki's entire insubstantial body. Taiyo Daisuke swayed, then fell to his knees on the stones, bowing his head. Suki sobbed his name, screamed his name, her voice tossed by the wind howling up from the sea, but he didn't move.

"Oy. Don't you dare die yet, peacock."

Suki jerked up. The ronin was crawling over the rocks toward the noble, pulling himself painfully along the ground. He left a trail of red behind him, but his jaw was set, his eyes glassy with determination as he dragged himself, inch by agonizing inch, toward the body slumped on its knees a few yards away. Suki dropped lower, wanting to encourage him, desperately wishing she could do something to help him reach his goal. When the ronin paused, collapsing to the dirt and panting through gritted teeth, Suki drifted down until she hovered directly over Daisuke-sama, letting her light spill over the motionless body.

"Don't stop," she whispered. "You're almost there. Don't let him die alone."

The ronin raised his head. With a surge of determination, he pushed himself upright and half staggered, half fell over the rocks until he reached the kneeling body. Gasping, he lay there a moment, his features twisted with pain, as lightning flickered and the clouds swirled overhead.

"Okame."

The word was barely a breath, a whisper on the wind. Daisuke turned his head, gazing at the ronin lying beside him, and one bloody hand twitched. "You're here. For-forgive me."

"Dammit, peacock," the ronin gritted out. Clenching his jaw, he struggled to a sitting position, then gently reached out and eased the other back until both of them were braced against a rock, the noble leaning against his chest. Daisuke slumped, relaxing in the ronin's arms, and Suki drifted higher, giving them a little privacy. Silently, she hovered overhead, casting them in a faint light—the ronin, and the noble they both loved—as the wind howled and night fell over Taiyo Daisuke's final moments.

"Well." The ronin's quiet, weary voice was the first to break the silence. "Looks like you got your wish, peacock. That was one hell of a glorious death."

Daisuke raised a trembling hand, clasping the ronin's palm resting against his chest. "I am glad you're here, Okame," he breathed with his eyes still closed. "And I am...pleased that you will survive this. If one of us made it... I was hoping it would be you."

But the ronin shook his head. "No," he murmured in a resigned voice. "I've lost too much blood. And I'm pretty sure those knives were poisoned. Don't worry, peacock." A faint, rueful smirk tugged at one corner of his lip as he bowed his head. "I'm not about to break my promise. I'll be following you soon enough."

"Together then, after all," Daisuke murmured, as the ronin's free hand brushed a strand of bloody hair from his cheek. "No... regrets, Okame?"

"Regrets." The ronin gave a soft chuckle. "Peacock, before I met you, Yumeko-chan and everyone else, I was a bandit and a ronin with no purpose in the world. I didn't care about anything, because I thought there was nothing in this life worth caring for. Not honor, family, friends or empire." The hint of a smile crossed his face, and he shook his head. "Then this impudent little fox girl gave me a second chance, and everything changed. I've been to places few mortals have ever seen. I've fought things straight out of the legend scrolls. And I've been a part of something far greater than anyone, especially an honorless ronin dog, could ever hope for."

He paused, a shadow of pain going through his eyes for a moment, before it smoothed out again. "So no, peacock," he sighed. "I have no regrets. If I never joined Yumeko that day, I would still be a worthless, wandering ronin with no goals, no friends and nothing redeemable about him. And I never would have seen Oni no Mikoto on the bridge that night and, for the first time, wished I could be something more."

Daisuke's arm lifted, and he pressed a palm against the ronin's jaw. "You were...always something more to me," he whispered, and Okame closed his eyes. "Do you think...they'll tell stories of us, Okame?"

"I hope so," the ronin choked out, pressing his own hand over Daisuke's. "Or at least a tragic poem that will make everyone cry when they hear it."

"I would like that," Daisuke whispered. His eyes opened, peaceful and calm, gazing up at the sky. "I feel...warm," he murmured. "Light. I think... I think it's time, Okame."

The ronin blinked, and a streak of moisture ran down his cheek as he lowered his head, pressing his lips to Daisuke's. "Go on, then," he whispered, smiling through the tears on his face.

"You've earned it. And don't worry about me. I'll be right behind you."

"Okame." Suki could barely hear him now. The noble's voice was a breath that the wind tore away and scattered over the sea. His eyes closed, and he sank further into the ronin's arms. "I'll… wait for you," he whispered. "Don't be…too long."

His body slumped, and the hand still pressed against the ronin's cheek slid away, dropping into his lap. The ronin let out a quiet breath and leaned back, gazing up at the sky. His dark eyes fell on Suki hovering overhead, and a faint smile crossed his face.

"Still hanging around, yurei?" he murmured, though it was mostly to himself. "I guess if we get lost on our way to Meido, we'll at least have a guide. Oy, Suki-chan, wasn't it?" the ronin went on, his eyes focusing on her. "If you see Yumeko again, tell her…thank you. For taking in a stray dog. She's going to cry, but…we'll see each other again. I don't regret a thing. It was one hell of an adventure."

He drew in a shuddering breath and sighed, as his eyes flickered shut. "Kuso," he muttered, his voice growing fainter. "I wish… I could've seen the end. I hope you and Kage-san make it, Yumeko-chan. If not… I guess I'll see you both soon enough."

Painfully, the ronin straightened, bowing his head so that his lips brushed the noble's cheek. "All right, peacock," Suki heard, though his voice was nearly gone, and growing fainter with every word. "Meet you on the other side. I hope it has good sake, or…I'm going to be…disappointed."

His head dropped the final few inches, resting on Daisuke's shoulder, and he didn't move again. Numb, Suki hovered there a moment, as the clouds opened and rain began falling over the two bodies slumped together in the flickering light of a hitodama.

A pair of glowing spheres rose from each of the bodies on the ground, pulsing softly as they drifted into the air. As Suki watched, the two globes of light climbed steadily into the sky, circling each other in a graceful, almost excited dance, and floated away toward the clouds.

25

The Summoning Site

TATSUMI

Nearly there.

I was expecting trouble. The last stretch up the mountain was narrow and rocky, with soaring cliffs and jagged crags to one side. Perfect for an ambush, or to trap us between a wall of stone and a sheer drop down the cliff face. But there were no demons waiting for us, no monsters, yokai, bakemono or blood mages lurking in the cracks between rocks. No ambushes or traps of any kind. Either Genno was overconfident in Rasetsu's ability to guard the path—not to mention the oni's loyalty—or there was something we didn't know about.

I could see the top of the peak overhead, a flat surface of stone rising over the sea, with nothing but air between the cliff and the drop to the waves below. Directly above it, clouds swirled frantically in the sky, a whirlpool of darkness and flickering strands of lightning. Rain and wind beat the sides of the cliff, ripping at our hair and clothes and slashing at us with icy talons.

As lightning flashed, it lit up the valley far below the mountain, showing a split-second glimpse of the desperate, futile battle between men and demons still raging in the dark. Neither the fall of night nor the vicious storm halted the march of demons on their way to slaughter every living thing, and the armies of Shadow and Moon continued to fight a losing battle in the rain and darkness.

Yumeko stumbled on the rough path, falling to her knees with a small exclamation of pain. I turned and took her hand, pulling her upright, and she raised her head, fox ears twitching in the wind.

"Do you hear that?" she gasped.

I did. A voice echoing over the storm, rising over the wind and rain, coming from the top of the peak. The individual words were lost in the howl of the gale, but there was no question as to who it was, or what was happening.

"Genno," I growled. "Summoning the Dragon. He's not finished with the prayer, though. We can still make it."

Yumeko nodded, a steely glint in her yellow eyes. Together we began sprinting up the path, as the booming, droning chant from the Master of Demons grew louder, and the clouds swirled even faster.

The path curved around a cliff, and suddenly ended at a steep flight of stone stairs going up the mountain. A weathered gray torii gate stood over the first step, marking the entrance to the territory of the gods, and I heard Yumeko gasp when she saw it. This was it, the final staircase. At the top was the Summoning site, and the Master of Demons.

But as we started for the steps, there was a blinding flash, and a wall of blue flames erupted at the base of the staircase. Snarling, I flinched back from the light and sudden heat, then squinted up at the fire.

He stood atop the torii gate, silver hair and robes billowing in the wind, golden eyes shining in the dark; the ninetail from the demoness cave. His multiple tails swayed and fluttered behind him, the ends glowing with foxfire, casting his shadow over the ground before us.

"Not yet." His voice was a warning, almost a command, and I felt rage surge up within. Drawing Kamigoroshi, I leaped into the air toward the kitsune standing in our way, bringing the sword down in a vicious arc.

The ninetail didn't move, though a small smile played over his face as I fell toward him, Kamigoroshi blazing purple as it sliced toward his head. There was a blur of motion, and a ringing screech that sent vibrations up my arm, as Kamigoroshi met the blade of another sword that appeared in front of the ninetail. I blinked in shock as we faced each other on the torii gate, staring at him over our crossed blades. At the ninetail's fingers curled around the hilt of his own weapon, blocking my sword, and me, one-handed.

The kitsune smiled at me over the crossed blades. "Save your strength, Hakaimono," he said calmly. "Your greatest battle is yet to come."

His tails moved, a blur of silver and blue-white foxfire, and two of them struck me in the chest. It felt like Yaburama had punched me; I was hurled away, hitting the path and tumbling a good hundred feet down the mountain until I came to a bruised stop at the base of a cliff. Growling, I pushed myself to my feet, Kamigoroshi blazing in my hand, to see Yumeko at the base of the stairs, facing the ninetail overhead.

"What is it you want, Seigetsu-sama?" she asked, bathed in the ghostly light of the foxfire. "You've aided us before—why are you trying to stop us now? You said you had no interest in the Dragon's Wish."

"I don't."

"Then...why are you helping the Master of Demons?"

Gripping my sword, I started up the path again as the nine-tailed fox tilted his head, regarding Yumeko with impassive golden eyes. "I am not aiding the Master of Demons, little fox," he told her. "Genno is simply another piece in this game. An important piece, yes, but his part in the story is about to end. Yokai, demons and kami cannot make a wish to the Harbinger of Change. Only a mortal soul can call the Great Kami from the sea, and Genno, though his soul has been tainted by hate and revenge, fits that description. I simply needed him to summon the Dragon."

Yumeko's ears flattened. "You *want* Genno to summon the Dragon?" she whispered, sounding horrified and stunned. "Why?"

The other kitsune offered that faint, knowing smile and shook his head. "Not yet," he said, his voice a low murmur. "It is not time to reveal that part of the game. Soon, though. Soon, you will understand everything."

A howl echoed over the storm, and the air itself seemed to tremble. A massive streak of lightning split the sky overhead, turning everything a blinding white, and in the flash, the nine-tail's expression was almost mad with glee. "Hurry, little fox," he told Yumeko, as a chill unlike any I had felt before slid through my veins. "He comes."

I leaped at the ninetailed fox with a snarl, springing over the wall of kitsune-bi and slashing down with Kamigoroshi. This time, the silver-haired figure didn't move, but his golden eyes rose to me, his smile never wavering. The snapping purple blade cut into his collarbone and passed out the other side, splitting him in two. As I dropped from the torii gate, there was an explosion of white smoke, and the halves of the kitsune's body disappeared. A red maple leaf, sliced in two, fluttered to the ground and danced away over the wind.

The wall of kitsune-bi sputtered and went out. I landed on the steps and glanced back at Yumeko, whose face was pale in the dying light of the foxfire.

"An illusion," she whispered in horrified disbelief. She shook herself and hurried forward, joining me on the steps, though her eyes were shadowed with fear and alarm. "Kami, how strong is he? What is his game? And how are we going to stop a nine-tailed fox with that much power?"

"No time for that now," I told her as we raced up the stairs. "We take care of Genno first, and worry about the ninetail after we send the Master of Demons back to Jigoku."

The steps curved up the mountain, growing steeper and rougher by the second, until they finally ended at the very top of the cliffs. A flat circle of rock surrounded by torches and crumbling stone pillars stretched before us, overlooking the ocean.

In the center of the circle, with his hands raised and his ghostly robes billowing around him, a translucent figure in white stood before a stone altar. A long scroll, one end weighed down by a rock, lay on the altar, the other end flapping in the wind. The Dragon's Prayer, the pieces brought together and made whole once again. A bleached human skull sat in the center, the eye sockets glowing with crimson light. Around the figure, lining the edges of the circle, nearly a dozen bodies knelt motionless on the rocks, glimmering daggers lying forgotten at their sides. Their chins rested on their chests, and streams of blood ran from their recently slit throats, dripping to the ground.

"You're too late." The ghostly specter lowered his arms and turned, smiling at us over the circle of rock. Genno, his transparent form a pale blur against the rain and darkness, met my gaze with triumph in his eyes. "You cannot stop me now, Hakaimono," he said, raising one translucent arm toward the sea. "The prayer has been completed. The Harbinger comes!"

A massive bolt of lightning streaked from the clouds, hitting the surface of the ocean. I felt a rumble from deep below travel all the way up the mountain, shaking the stones at my feet. Yumeko staggered, and above us, the tempest swirled like a whirlpool in the sky.

"All will be darkness." Genno's droning voice rose over the

wind. The yurei turned his back on us, gazing toward the ocean with his arms lifted to welcome the Dragon. "All will be pain, fear and death. I will strike down the empire and rebuild this land in my image. There will be no more samurai, no emperor, no noble class. There will be only men and demons, and as Jigoku and Ningen-kai merge, all human souls will bow to me, as O-Hakumon promised."

I gripped Kamigoroshi as rage and bloodlust swelled, a maelstrom of demonic fury rising to the surface. "Not if I send you back to O-Hakumon first," I snarled, and lunged at the Master of Demons.

The second my feet touched the stone circle, there was a flash, and pain erupted through my body. Glowing, red-hot chains appeared, wrapped around my limbs, anchoring me to the rock. I looked down to see symbols and kanji appear on the stones, written in blood, covering the entirety of the flat surface.

"Did you not think I would be ready for you, Hakaimono?" Genno turned back, a cruelly amused look on his narrow face. "Did you really believe I would allow you to make it this far without consequence?" He gestured to the bodies surrounding us. "My blood mages, they gave their lives to create this binding circle for the express purpose of stopping the First Oni. You will not interfere, not when my moment of triumph is at hand."

A glowing ball of foxfire flew past my head toward the yurei in the center of the circle. For a split second, a look of shock crossed his pale face before he dodged nimbly aside. The sphere of kitsune-bi arced over the ocean, leaving a trail of light behind it, and Genno's eyes snapped to the girl who had stepped into the circle beside me.

Yumeko opened her hands, and foxfire flared, engulfing not only her palms, but her entire body. It raced up her arms, her back, spreading over her robes, until she was wreathed in blue-white flames. Her tail swayed and whipped behind her, snapping with foxfire, and her golden eyes shone with fury as she faced the Master of Demons across the stone.

"No more, Genno," she said, a virtual torch blazing blue-white at the edge of the circle. "This ends tonight."

"Annoying fox." The Master of Demons drifted back, a faint red glow surrounding him as he gestured almost contemptuously. "Begone."

Three sickles of darkness, deadly spinning crescents, flew at Yumeko, trailing black fire as they sped toward her. She dodged, throwing herself to the ground as she dove aside, though one of them caught her sleeve as it passed, slicing through the fabric like it wasn't there.

"Yumeko!" I lunged toward her, straining against the chains, feeling several of them snap as I pressed forward. I was free only for a moment, as several more instantly rose to take their place, coiling around my legs, arms and chest, burning and searing where they touched, and I snarled in frustration.

"Rise." Genno raised both arms, red light shining from his fingers, and I felt the chilling ripple of blood magic wash across the stones. "Crush them, my faithful minions," he ordered. "Obey me in death as you did in life. Rise, and serve your master."

The corpses lining the edges of the circle stirred, lifting their heads to reveal their sliced throats, then seemed to float upright, hovering a few inches from the ground. Clutching knives in pale, bloody hands, they glided forward.

Yumeko pushed herself upright, ears laced back and eyes wide with alarm. Blood soaked the fabric of one sleeve, dripping to the ground from her arm, but she raised her hands, foxfire pulsing at her fingers, and unleashed a roaring line of kitsune-bi. Not at the ghostly Master of Demons, or even the corpses floating toward her with their knives raised, but at the binding circle at her feet.

For a moment, the words of power flared red, shining like

fresh blood as the foxfire struck the surface. Then, with a roar, the entire circle seemed to catch fire, kitsune-bi racing along the runes and symbols, until with one final flare-up, the foxfire sputtered and died, taking the circle with it.

The chains holding me down vanished. Genno spun, eyes widening, as I sprang to the center of the circle, Kamigoroshi ripping the first blood mage's corpse in two. The others turned on me, jerking forward like marionettes, eyes blank as they slashed down with their weapons. Unhindered, I lunged into the center of the swarm, cutting through limbs and dead flesh, fighting my way forward. I lost Yumeko in the press of bodies, though I did catch glimpses of Genno through the slashing arms and flapping sleeves, the blood mage drifting farther away, a grim, triumphant smile on his face. With a snarl, I lunged after him, but the corpses pressed closer, relentless and unfeeling, forcing me back.

"WHO SUMMONS ME?"

Everything froze. Even the floating corpses shivered in place, paralyzed by the deep, inhuman rumble coming from the heart of the storm. I glanced up, and my stomach dropped as a massive head emerged from the clouds, trailing a long, endless body behind it. It defied belief, bigger than any living creature I had seen, a mountain of horns and fangs and scales the color of the ocean.

The Great Dragon god, the Lord of Tides and the Harbinger of Change, coiled his huge body around the mountain peak and gazed down on us insignificant mortals far below.

Genno spun, raising his arms to the huge Kami, his face alight with savage triumph. Desperately, I slashed at the corpses surrounding me, lunging for the Master of Demons even as I knew we had failed. The Dragon had come, and Genno was too far away; all he had to do was speak his wish, and everything would be over.

"Ryuujin-sama!" Genno cried, using the Harbinger's formal

name. The yurei's voice rang over the storm, triumphant, but he spoke quickly, knowing time was of the essence. "I, Genno, Master of Demons, am the soul who summoned you tonight! By my right as scroll bearer, I ask that you grant me my heart's desire!" He didn't pause to accept the Dragon's acknowledgment, but hurried on, and the world seemed to hold its breath. "Great Dragon, I wish—"

A sharp crack rang out, echoing over the chaos. It wasn't loud or booming, just a split-second noise that was almost lost in the madness, but amazingly, Genno jerked as if he had been shot. His body flickered, like a candle flame in the wind, and he turned huge pale eyes from the Dragon to something behind him. Tearing through the last of the corpses, I looked up, and my heart stuttered.

Yumeko stood in front of the altar, the opened scroll flapping wildly in the gale, but she wasn't looking at the prayer. The naked skull sat in front of her, glowing faintly with power, though the top of the skull was cracked and broken, as if it had been struck with something heavy.

Yumeko, her jaw set in determination, held a large stone in both hands, and slowly raised it over her head.

"Nooo!"

Genno's shriek echoed over the wind, high-pitched and desperate. His face was no longer triumphant as he lunged forward, throwing out a ghostly hand. "Fox, do not dare!"

Yumeko gave a savage smile. "For Master Isao," she whispered, and brought the stone down hard.

The skull shattered. Tendrils of black and purple light rose from the pieces, spiraling into the air as the power was released, and Genno wailed. His body seemed to dissipate, fraying apart like mist even as he clutched at it, desperately trying to hold himself together. But he grew fainter and fainter, until he was only the vaguest outline of a man hovering before the Dragon.

Genno.

The voice wasn't the Dragon's, but it seemed to echo in the clouds, in the rolling thunder all around us. I recognized it; even after a thousand years, it was impossible to mistake that voice for anyone else.

O-Hakumon, the ruler of Jigoku.

Master of Demons, the voice droned, a terrible rumble in the clouds. The fading yurei cringed, eyes wide with terror as he looked toward the ocean. *You have failed, and by our contract, your soul is once again forfeit to me.*

With a final scream, the ghost of the Master of Demons became a crimson ball of light that rose swiftly into the air and streaked toward the horizon as if demons were chasing it.

It hadn't gone far, however, when there was a blast of heat, and a pair of flaming wheels with grinning faces soared overhead. Cackling, the wanyudo demons sped after the fleeing soul, which darted and flew like a terrified dragonfly, trying to escape them. But the demons were faster, and as one wanyudo caught up to the frantic soul, its huge mouth opened, gaping wide, as it clamped its jaws around the ball of light. A tiny scream emerged from the tainted soul as it was dragged from the air in the grip of the demon, who sped toward the ocean without slowing down. I tensed as they approached, but the wanyudo dropped past us in twin balls of fire, plunged into the waves and jagged rocks far below, and vanished from sight.

26
THE HARBINGER

Yumeko

We…we did it.

I held my breath as the screams from the flaming wheel demons faded into the wind. For a moment, I stood motionless before the altar, my heart pounding in my chest, waiting for something to happen. For Genno's furious spirit to rise back into the air with a maniacal laugh, mocking us for being so foolish to think we had beaten him. But Genno did not appear. The storm continued to rage, and overhead, the terrifying visage of the Great Dragon still hovered in the clouds, his eyes shining like moons as they watched us.

My legs shook, and I sank to my knees on the rough stone. The rain beat down on me, and there was a prickling sensation where a jagged piece of skull pierced my calf, but I hardly felt it. It was hard to believe, after everything we'd been through, the hardships we'd endured and the sacrifices that had been made, but it seemed that we had won.

"Yumeko." Tatsumi knelt in front of me, and I collapsed into him, pressing my face to his haori as he pulled me close.

"We did it." My voice came out choked, and I closed my eyes. Beneath my hands, Tatsumi was shaking, too. "Genno is gone, Tatsumi. It's really over."

I felt him take a deep, steadying breath. "What about the Wish?" he mused. "What will happen to it, now that the summoner is dead? Will the Dragon disappear, or will he give it to someone else?"

"I don't know." I swallowed and peeked up at the huge Dragon god, still coiled around the mountaintop, uncaring of mortals and their short existences. "Maybe we should ask him."

"That won't be necessary."

The low, familiar voice echoed behind us. I peered up to see Seigetsu standing at the edge of the circle, his hair and tails whipping behind him in the gale. He wasn't looking at us, however, but at the Great Dragon looming overhead, endless coils flowing in and out of the clouds.

"There will be no more wishes," the ninetail intoned, and raised a great yumi longbow, aiming it at the God of Tides overhead. The arrowhead pointed at the Great Dragon was white, streaked with veins of crimson, and flickered with a malevolent darkness that seemed to corrupt the very air around it. I could suddenly smell salt and tears on the wind, and the taste of ash clogged the back of my throat, as Seigetsu gave a triumphant smile. "Not tonight, or ever again. *This* is the final play."

With a scream from the arrow that turned my blood to ice, it flew through the air in a streak of light and darkness and struck the Great Dragon between the eyes.

A terrible roar rang out, causing the rain to spiral and the clouds to swirl even faster as the Harbinger convulsed like a snake that had been jabbed with a spear. It thrashed, huge coils slamming against the mountainside, causing the peaks to shake and huge rocks to tumble into the ocean. Rain beat painfully against my skin, stinging like needles, and the wind shrieked like an enraged yurei in my ear.

I whirled on the other kitsune, clenching my fists, my heart hammering a panicked rhythm in my ears. "What did you do to the Dragon?"

Seigetsu raised a hand. "As I said before, all living things can be corrupted. Even Kami. The Great Dragon is no longer the God of Tides and the impassive Harbinger of Change. Kiyomi-sama's madness is now his own—the arrow has twisted his mind and corrupted his spirit and he is a force of rage, sorrow and destruction. He will flatten this island, and everything on it, if he is not destroyed."

Another roar rang out, the sound bordering on madness, and the Dragon appeared through the clouds. My breath caught, my stomach twisting in horror and fear. The Harbinger's moonlike eyes now glowed purple-black, his huge jaws gaping in an animalistic snarl. A baleful crimson glow surrounded him as the massive creature coiled and thrashed in mindless fury, lashing out at invisible enemies. The ground under our feet shook, and I stumbled, nearly falling into Tatsumi, as the whole mountain trembled with the rage of a god.

Throwing back its head, the Dragon screamed, and threads of lightning, hundreds of them, streaked from the clouds, raining over the entire island. Tatsumi grabbed my wrist and yanked me to him, shielding me with his body, as a sizzling bolt of energy slammed into the circle mere yards from us, sending stone shards flying. Rocks pelted us, and as the brightness faded, we looked up to see the Dragon's huge body uncoil from around the mountaintop and fly away. Back toward the valley and the armies of Shadow and Moon, still at its edge.

"He will destroy them all." Seigetsu's voice held a terrible ring of finality. "Every living soul on this island will be consumed by the Dragon's fury and sorrow. And when he is done, he will sink the other islands, and then move on to the empire itself. Nothing will be able to stand against him, unless he is stopped here, tonight."

"You say that like you expect *us* to kill him." I shook my head wildly, my heart fluttering around my chest like a panicked bird. "Even if we wanted to, it's the Great Dragon! A Kami. A *god*."

"And you carry a sword named *Godslayer*." Those cold yellow eyes slid to Tatsumi, and a chill went up my spine at the realization. "Even the Harbinger is not exempt from his own rules," the ninetail said gravely. "You are the only one that can stop him, Hakaimono. The only one with the power to slay a god. You and the fox of dreams. It is time to fulfill your destiny and bring the game to its conclusion."

He raised a hand, sleeves billowing in the wind, and a polished horseless carriage floated up to perch at the edge of the circle. It was a simple but elegant vehicle, a box made of dark wood, the entire back consisting of two doors that opened outward. I could see the faint outline of foxfire engulfing the entire carriage, and something in the pit of my stomach surged up, as if drawn to that light.

"Take the carriage," Seigetsu ordered, as if he were sending us on a simple errand. A task to deliver a letter, not to kill an enormous ancient Kami who was now mad with grief and rage. "Use it to reach the Dragon. You have the means to control the carriage, just as I do. It will respond to your magic as it does to mine." His smile was ghastly in the flickering light. "Go now, and slay the Harbinger, little fox. If you cannot, he will tear this island apart and destroy everything that you've come to care for."

Kiyomi-sama.

I didn't want to. I couldn't kill an ancient Kami, even one driven mad. But if I didn't do *something*, the Dragon would turn his wrath on Kiyomi-sama, the Moon Clan, the Shadow Clan, everything. Everyone on this island would be destroyed in the wake of the Kami's rampage, and I couldn't let that happen. I could not lose the family and the home I had just found.

"Tatsumi..." In desperation, I glanced at the demonslayer, wondering what he was thinking. I didn't know what I could do if he refused to help me stop the Dragon, but I knew I couldn't do it alone.

Tatsumi's violet gaze met mine, and he gave a single solemn nod. "Go, Yumeko. I'm right behind you."

Grateful tears rose to my eyes. Sprinting to the carriage, I braced myself as I leaped inside, half expecting the wooden floor to either burn the soles of my feet or for the entire vehicle to lose whatever magic held it up and plummet down the side of the mountain. But the carriage, though it bobbed a little when I entered, continued to hover in the air. Despite the elegant outward appearance, the interior was plain, the floor polished wood with no seats or cushions to sit on. Except for the nimbus of foxfire flickering through the open doors, everything was cloaked in darkness.

I had no idea how I would make it work.

Tatsumi leaped up beside me, one hand against the frame, and gazed around cautiously, as if he'd expected the carriage to be filled with demons. "There's a body here," he said quietly. I jumped and spun around, and he nodded to a shadowy corner. "Yokai. It's dead."

I gazed past him to where a small form lay crumpled against the wall, a single enormous eye staring up at nothing. The front of its shirt was dark with blood, as if it had been stabbed through the back. The final expression on the round little face seemed to be one of confusion. For some reason, I felt a twinge of sadness as I stared at the body; I had certainly never seen this yokai before, but he was obviously another pawn in Seigetsu's endless game, one that had been used and thrown away.

Swallowing, I turned from the body and gazed out the front of the carriage, at the wheels outlined in foxfire, floating several paces above the ground. *It responds to your magic, same as mine*, Seigetsu had said. So, how did I control this thing? I glanced to where I had last seen the ninetail at the edge of the circle, only to find he was gone. No help from him, then.

The flicker in the pit of my stomach intensified. On impulse, I opened my palms, igniting a flame of kitsune-bi within each of them, and felt the carriage under my feet respond.

Okay, I think I'm onto something. With Tatsumi watching, I shrugged and lifted a flame-shrouded hand toward the ceiling. "Rise?"

The carriage shot upward, like it was being yanked by invisible ropes. I yelped, nearly toppling out the open doors, and felt Tatsumi grab my arm and yank me back. I fell into him, and the carriage pitched to the left, rocking sideways and slamming us against one wall. Tatsumi grunted with the impact, somehow keeping both of us on our feet, as I desperately tried to find my balance to stop the carriage from bucking like a wild horse.

The carriage stopped pitching, though it still swayed and trembled wildly in the sudden gale, the doors banging loudly against the walls. Through the frame, the clouds swirled in frantic, terrifying patterns, rain and hail pummeled the carriage walls, and the roar of the wind sounded like a hurricane. Lightning seared the air, close enough that I felt the hairs on my arms rise, right before the clap of thunder made the walls vibrate. The Dragon was nowhere to be seen.

I shivered, realizing we were going to have to fly headfirst into that shrieking maelstrom, and felt Tatsumi's arms wrap a little tighter around my waist. "Don't be afraid," he murmured, his lips close to my ear. "You can do this. Just get us as close to the Dragon as you can. I won't let you fall."

I leaned on him gratefully, drawing strength from his touch, and closed my eyes. "How...how can we do this, Tatsumi," I whispered, my voice coming out shaky and choked. "This is the Great Dragon, the Harbinger of Change, who appears only once every thousand years. What will happen if he's suddenly gone?"

Tatsumi sighed, pressing his forehead to the back of my neck.

"I don't know," he murmured darkly. "I can't imagine the bad fortune that will come with killing a god. This...might be the end of the Shadow Clan. After all the darkness we've brought to the empire, killing the Dragon might be the final push for the gods to be done with us forever."

"Seigetsu planned this," I went on. "All of this. From tricking Kiyomi-sama to leaving the arrow in the cave to letting Genno summon the Harbinger. Why? What does he gain from the death of a Kami?"

"Who can say?" Tatsumi shook his head. "He's old, Yumeko. Kitsune who live to be ninetails are at least a thousand years old. Who knows what he wants? Vengeance, perhaps? Or maybe he got tired of mortals changing the course of history every millennium and decided to put an end to it once and for all."

"Maybe we can talk to him," I suggested. "The Dragon. Maybe if we get close enough, we can reason with him. It worked in the cave with the spirit of Kiyomi-sama."

"We can try." Tatsumi sounded uncertain, though he nodded slowly. "After everything I've seen you do, I've learned nothing is impossible." His voice became lower, almost a growl. "But the ninetail is right about one thing. The land cannot bear a corrupted Great Kami. If he has truly gone mad, he has the power to tear the world apart before he's done."

Lightning flashed, backlighting the clouds, and within the swirling mass, the coil of a huge silhouette flickered against the darkness. The Dragon. Enraged, corrupted, driven to madness by fury and grief. He would destroy this island and everyone on it, kami, yokai and human alike. Somehow, no matter what it took, we had to stop him.

Kami forgive us. I extended my arm and felt the carriage respond, rising up and flying toward the clouds. I bit my lip as the huge, roiling mass of darkness and lightning loomed above us, and then we were in the heart of the storm.

Wind buffeted us, yanking at the carriage and causing it

to plummet every few feet. I clenched my jaw and fought to maintain control as we were tossed and jerked about like a leaf. Through the doors, I couldn't see anything but rain, roiling clouds and streaks of lightning, some of which came close to hitting the carriage. Tatsumi kept one arm around my waist and the other braced against the wall, talons dug into the wood, keeping us both upright.

Where is the Dragon? I wondered, just as a huge, black-scaled coil slithered through the clouds ahead of us, appearing in a blink and vanishing the next.

"There," Tatsumi growled as the glimmer of the Dragon's enormous body appeared again. I sent the carriage after it, but a blast of wind pushed us off course, and the Kami disappeared once more.

Setting my jaw, I chased after the god, plunging into the storm. It was all I could do to keep the carriage steady while pushing through wind, rain and swirling clouds, searching for a dragon the size of a mountain. It shouldn't have been difficult, but the Dragon moved through the storm like an eel through water, effortlessly sliding in and out of the storm. We were in his territory now, and he was the undisputed lord of the skies. I gritted my teeth against the shrieking of the gale against the carriage and kept flying, feeling like a sparrow trapped in a hurricane.

And then, the curtain of clouds and slashing wind gave way, and we were flying alongside the massive head of the Dragon.

My breath caught at how truly enormous the Great Kami was up close, and how terrifying he looked, his eyes blazing red and his teeth fully bared. His mane and whiskers fluttered behind him, snapping in the wind, and lightning strands seemed to follow him through the clouds, lighting up the sky.

Raising my head, I gazed into the maddened eye of the Harbinger of Change.

"Great Kami!" My voice sounded tiny, nearly lost in the storm and howling wind. "Ryuujin-sama, please listen to me!"

The Harbinger's eye rolled back, fixing us with a burning glare, and my heart stuttered in terror. There was no sanity in that gaze, no sentience or empathy or reason. Just raw, mindless fury, and a madness that chilled my soul.

Still, I had to try to reach him for the sake of Kiyomi-sama and everyone below. "Ryuujin-sama," I called again. "Please, stop! This isn't what you want! I know you're angry, that you're in pain, but destroying everything isn't the answer! Think of all the lives you're ending, all the souls you're snuffing out. The people who live here are innocent. They don't deserve your wrath—"

The Dragon whipped his head around with a roar, jaws gaping. I saw the black hole of his maw, the edges lined with spear-like fangs, and jerked the carriage to the side as those jaws closed with the sound of grinding boulders. As I wheeled away, the Harbinger's gaze followed me, and he lunged forward with a scream.

Heart in my throat, I turned the carriage and fled through the storm, hearing the thunderous roar of the Dragon behind us. Lightning flashed, missing us by inches and causing the fur on my tail to stand straight up.

Dodging lightning strands, we flew out of a cloud bank, and the island appeared below us, dark and sprawling. I could see the terrible scar in the earth where the entrance to Jigoku gaped open, the demons and tortured spirits still climbing free. Against the storm and flashes of light, I could see the line where the demons met the armies of the Shadow and Moon Clans, and the terrible battle taking place below. Bodies were scattered across the plain, men and monster alike, though the human army looked frighteningly small compared to the floods coming up from the pit. Still, the line held, the human forces seeming unwilling to give ground until every one of them were slaughtered.

An eerie silence seemed to fall over the battlefield as we soared overhead, the fighting paused as, one by one, human, demon and spirit alike wrenched their gazes upward. Cries of alarm rang out, mouths fell open as the huge Dragon emerged from the storm, baleful crimson eyes glowing against the night as he observed the tiny creatures far below.

With a roar, the Dragon snaked from the clouds, plunging toward the battle, making my stomach drop. As it swooped overhead, a massive cluster of lightning followed it, falling from the sky like rain and searing into both armies. Screams replaced battle cries, shrieks and wails rising over the chaos, as the threads of lightning cut through bodies like they were made of paper. Demons exploded into dark clouds and writhed away on the wind. Humans were flung away, burned and ruined. Even the spirits cringed back, wailing, and fled from the lightning storm, though it didn't seem to harm them. The stench of smoke, ozone and charred flesh swirled into the carriage, and my stomach churned.

"Yumeko." Tatsumi's voice was a growl; one arm was still around my waist, the other had sunk its claws so deep into the frame that the wood had cracked beneath it.

"I know," I choked out, swallowing the sob in my throat. This had gone too far. The Dragon was beyond saving and had turned his madness on everyone we were trying to protect. "I'll take us in," I told the demonslayer, raising my hands to direct the carriage. "I'll get us as close as I can, and then you can... take him down."

But as we started toward the Harbinger, the huge Kami paused, hovering overhead as it watched the armies scurry below it. A chilling look went through its glowing eyes, before it coiled around and flew straight up into the clouds, vanishing from sight.

Pinning back my ears, I sent the carriage after it, rising through wind and slashing rain, ignoring the lightning that streaked around us. We broke through the clouds, and the night sky stretched overhead, a giant moon casting silvery light over everything. Directly below us, the storm raged and swirled, a tempest of fury that covered the whole island. Around us, the sea, black and glimmering, stretched in every direction until it hit the horizon.

"Where's the Dragon?" muttered Tatsumi, purple eyes scanning the sea of flickering clouds.

I swallowed hard, gazing around the suddenly peaceful landscape. "Perhaps he left, after all," I whispered, knowing it was a foolish hope. "Maybe he got tired of wreaking havoc and went home."

A ripple went through the surface, and the Dragon rose out of the pale sea, his massive head casting us in his shadow as he spiraled into the air, momentarily blotting out the moon. Hovering over the clouds, the Harbinger raised his head and let out a roar that the emperor in his Golden Palace across the sea must've heard. The terrible sound vibrated through my skull and brought tears to my eyes, and I clapped my hands over my ears to drown it out. It didn't stop, but went on and on for several heartbeats, until I wanted to tear out my eardrums.

Finally, after my head started to throb like it was in a vise, the awful bellow stopped. I slumped against Tatsumi, my ears ringing, feeling his heart pounding in his chest. "What…was that?" I muttered.

Tatsumi went perfectly, terrifyingly still. "Yumeko," he whispered, and his voice was strangled. Chilled, I looked through the open door frame at the sea of clouds and the ocean below, the moonlight letting me see all the way to the horizon.

The horizon looked strange. Almost like it was moving, rippling. Getting closer even as I stared.

My legs shook, and I would've collapsed to the floor if Tatsumi hadn't been holding me up. The horizon wasn't moving, but the huge wall of water against it was. I couldn't tell how far away it was, but it seemed that the ocean itself had risen up and was crawling toward us, getting larger and higher with every second that passed.

"Tsunami," Tatsumi murmured. "The God of Tides has just doomed the entire island."

No. Panic and terror crushed me from within. I couldn't catch my breath, thinking of everyone below us, the kami, yokai and humans, battling the demons who still spilled from the gates of Jigoku. Of Kiyomi-sama, the Tsuki and the family I had never known.

Tatsumi's hold on me tightened, and he drew in a breath, as if bracing himself for the inevitable. "Take us in, Yumeko," he murmured close to my ear, and I nodded. "We have to kill him. Now."

I felt sick, but I set my jaw, steeled myself and sent the carriage into the clouds.

Instantly, a blast of wind slammed into the carriage, yanking it sideways and nearly tossing me out the door. Only Tatsumi's grip around my waist kept me from plummeting to my death. Though it didn't seem possible, the storm had grown even wilder, perhaps reflecting the chaotic mind of the Harbinger as the Dragon twisted through the clouds.

"Get closer," Tatsumi muttered in my ear. "Toward its head."

"I'm trying," I gritted out, raising my arm to send the carriage after a disappearing coil. For something so big, the Dragon was incredibly fast. And visibility within the swirling clouds was dim at best. "If you can see its head, tell me which direction to—"

There was a blinding flash, and something struck the top of the carriage in an explosion of wood and fire. I shrieked as splinters and flaming bits of wood fell all around us, flickering where they landed. Wind rushed into the space from the gaping hole in the roof, and the walls themselves seemed ready to split apart.

I swallowed my panic, fighting to bring the carriage under control, knowing we couldn't survive another hit like that. "Where is the Dragon?" I panted, gazing into the roiling clouds, flinching as lightning flashed close. A coil swept across my view and was gone in the next blink. "Dammit, he's so fast. If he would just stop moving for a second..."

"Harbinger!"

The shout echoed over the storm, faint and tiny, but perfectly clear. A figure rose out of the clouds, seeming uncaring of the lightning that flashed and seared the air around it. At first, I thought the pale, skeletal figure was a demon—despite its elegant kimono, which flapped and billowed in the wind, the claws, horns and shadowy, bat-like wings certainly indicated a demonic nature.

Behind me, Tatsumi drew in a quiet breath. "Hanshou," he muttered, sounding both stunned and oddly resigned. "She's finally given in to the darkness."

I blinked in shock. It *was* Lady Hanshou, but not the beautiful, elegant daimyo who met me in Hakumei castle. This was the ancient, withered crone I'd seen beneath the illusion, only now it seemed she had abandoned any pretense of humanity. She was more skeleton than human, shriveled and bent, nearly swallowed by her kimono. The tattered, sweeping wings seemed made of shadow, and her eyes flickered red as she rose through the storm, twisting her head from side to side, searching wildly.

"She's nearly gone," Tatsumi muttered at my shoulder. "Almost swallowed by Jigoku's taint. This is a desperate act, even for her."

"What is she doing?" I asked, wincing as a spear of lightning slashed down, barely missing the Kage daimyo. But the ruler of the Shadow Clan flew on, oblivious to the storm, the danger flashing all around her. Her eyes were wild, her hands withered claws as she continued to rise, until she was in the very center of the maelstrom.

"Harbinger!" Lady Hanshou cried again, beating her wings to hover in the gale. "Dragon! I know you're here! Face me! Come, behold the creature you created!"

For a moment, nothing happened. The storm raged around

us, impassive. Then, the Dragon's enormous head rose out of the clouds below, eyes blazing as he loomed above the pale, once-human creature glaring up at him. Hanshou's lip curled in an expression of pure hate, and she flung out her arms.

"Look!" she snarled at the huge Kami. "Look at me! Was this what you intended all those years ago, Great Dragon? When you granted me immortal life, did you intend to make me a monster?"

The Dragon said nothing, gazing down with a blank, impassive stare, its long whiskers streaming behind it. At Tatsumi's whispered encouragement, I raised my hands and sent the battered carriage forward, coming at the Harbinger from the side. Wind howled through the cracks in the timber walls, rattling the whole structure, and I bit my lip, praying a stray lightning bolt wouldn't hit us again. If we suffered another direct strike, the carriage probably wouldn't survive.

"Two thousand years!" Lady Hanshou was still raging at the Dragon, her voice echoing above the wind and rain. "For two thousand years, I have been this way! Aging, decaying, growing weak and withered. Watching my youth and my health slip away bit by bit, year after year, but never dying. I had to turn to blood magic to protect myself, to save my sanity and my life. *You* did this!" She pointed a black talon at the Kami, her voice starting to shake. "You said you would grant my heart's desire, but your Wish was nothing but a curse. And now, you will take it back."

I had nearly reached the Dragon, coming close enough that I had to avoid one of its long whiskers fluttering in the wind. I ducked under the flapping tendril and gave the carriage a final push, sending it over the Dragon's horns to soar above its broad head. I felt Tatsumi's arms release my waist as he moved to the edge of the frame, his jaw set with determination, as Lady Hanshou rose higher in the air to stare the Great Kami in the face.

"You will take it back," she said again. "Take back your curse and return to me all the years I have lost because of it. A thousand years ago, I tried to summon you again and failed because of Hirotaka's treachery. But that wish should have been mine."

The Dragon's eyes narrowed, as Hanshou raised both arms once more, her voice becoming desperate and shrill. "I will not spend another thousand years in this living hell!" she cried. "Grant me the Wish I should have had, or free me from this curse once and for all!"

The Dragon roared. The bellow made the rain dance and sent the wind into a mad swirl, tossing the carriage like a leaf. From above, below and all around us, lightning flashed, streaked from the clouds and converged on the figure hovering before the Dragon. Lady Hanshou threw back her head and screamed, convulsing like a bug in the center of the lightning web. I bit my lip, unable to look away or cover my eyes, and could only watch as the energy strands tore into the Kage daimyo again and again, making her body jerk erratically in the flashes.

Finally, the lightning storm ceased. For a moment, I saw Lady Hanshou floating there, her withered form now a charred, blackened husk, wings torn away, eyes blank and unseeing, before she dropped from the sky like a bundle of old twigs and rags, vanished into the swirling clouds below, and was gone.

I swallowed the sickness in my throat, and Tatsumi leaped from the carriage. Kamigoroshi blazing in his hand, he fell toward the Dragon, hair and clothes flapping in the wind, the deadly sword raised over his head. Eyes narrowed, he landed between the Kami's sweeping, antlered horns and plunged Kamigoroshi point down into the Dragon's skull.

The Dragon screamed. Its great body convulsed, thrashing and writhing in the air like it had been stuck with one of its own lightning bolts. The agonized wail tore through me like a hundred arrows, and in the echo of the storm, I could hear millions of voices raised in answering cries, the kami of the island, of perhaps the whole empire, reacting to the death of the great Dragon, the Lord of Tides and the Harbinger of Change.

A sob rose to my throat. But as the voices continued to scream, a shadow fell over me from behind, and the hairs on the back of my neck stood up. I spun and saw silver hair, golden eyes and multiple tails as Seigetsu stared down at me, his gaze terrible and cold in the flickering light of the storm.

My heart stood still. "Seigetsu! How—?"

With lightning speed, the ninetail grabbed my wrist and lifted me off my feet. I gasped at the sudden pain, dangling in his grip, as Seigetsu regarded me with a smile.

"You have something of mine."

I snarled at him, foxfire springing to my fingers, but he raised his other hand, and my stomach gave a violent lurch as if trying to expel an awful sickness. I gagged, mouth gaping open, as something forced its way up my throat, leaving a trail of cold fire behind it. A small globe the color of the moon slid between my jaws and into Seigetsu's open palm. The ninetail gave a grim nod, and the ball vanished into his robes. I suddenly felt hollow and cold, like the flames that had been smoldering in the pit of my stomach had been snuffed out. Seigetsu gave me a sympathetic look, as if he knew what I was feeling.

"Thank you, daughter," he told me. "Truly, I could not have done any of this without you. You have played your role admirably, but I'm afraid your part in this game is done. Say hello to Kiyomi when you reach the other side."

And he hurled me out of the carriage.

A shriek lodged in my throat, terror flooding my body, as I flew into open air and started to plummet. I twisted, grasping desperately at nothing as tears streamed from my eyes and the wind tore at my hair and clothes, but only the roiling sky rose to embrace me.

Then there was a ripple of darkness, the glint of blue-black scales, and I struck something solid and unyielding that crushed my arm and drove the breath from me. Before I could comprehend what had happened, the thing I had landed on—*the Dragon!*—twisted sharply, sending me rolling. I gave a yelp and lashed out wildly, but my fingers slipped on the Harbinger's smooth, hard scales and I slid steadily toward the edge of what could only be the Dragon's skull.

As my feet slid over the Kami's head into open air, my fingers closed on a handful of the Dragon's long rippling mane, finally stopping my plunge into oblivion. Gasping, paralyzed with fear, I clung to the lifeline with both hands, seeing nothing beyond my sandals but swirling clouds.

"Yumeko!"

At Tatsumi's frantic voice, I finally wrenched my wide-eyed stare from the drop past my feet and looked at the top of the Dragon's head. Painfully, I pulled myself up the mane and saw a figure in the center of the Kami's skull, still clutching the hilt of a sword as the Dragon's body twisted and writhed beneath him in agony. Tatsumi met my gaze over the pitching of the Harbinger, his expression tortured, as if he was torn between slaying the Dragon and going to me.

As I took a breath to call to him, a pale shadow fell from the sky overhead. The demonslayer glanced up, and Seigetsu dropped onto the Dragon's head and slashed his sword across Tatsumi's chest. Blood arced from the demonslayer in a vivid stream, misting into the air, and Tatsumi fell backward, losing his hold on Kamigoroshi. I screamed his name in horror.

Seigetsu's gaze flickered to me for the briefest of moments, before he turned away. Grasping the hilt of Kamigoroshi, still plunged halfway into the Dragon's head, he paused, eyes narrowed and contemplative, and I wondered if he was going to pull it free.

The ninetail gave a terrible smile…and shoved the Godslayer the rest of the way into the Dragon's head, sinking it past the hilt.

The Dragon jerked, jaws gaping, though no sound escaped it

this time. But I saw its eye roll back, saw the moment the light faded from the Kami's gaze and felt a sickness I'd never known spread from my heart to the rest of my soul.

Numb, I looked at Seigetsu, who straightened, hair and tails whipping around him, to stare at the Dragon's head. Slowly, his hand rose, palm down and fingers spread, still gazing down at the Kami he had slain. Something flared in the Dragon's forehead, glimmering like a fallen star. It floated steadily into the air, a tiny pearl, iridescent and beautiful, shining brighter than the moon itself. Seigetsu tilted his palm, and the jewel drifted into it, illuminating the kitsune's face and the terrible, terrible triumph in his golden eyes.

"At last," he whispered, his voice actually trembling as his fingers closed around the pearl. Tangling my fingers in the Dragon's mane, I choked out an apology and pulled, yanking a few long, silky strands free, as Seigetsu's voice continued overhead.

"One thousand years," he murmured. "A millennia of planning, scheming, nudging the waters of fate, changing the destiny of countless lives, moving the pieces on the board without a single mistake. The game is finally over. The Fushi no Tama is mine." He brought his fist to his face, the light from the jewel shining through his fingers. "I will be a god."

"Seigetsu!" I pulled myself up the Dragon's mane, using the last of my strength as I crawled onto the Harbinger's skull. The ninetail lowered his arm and gazed at me as I opened my palms, calling my foxfire to life. One elegant eyebrow rose, and the kitsune smiled.

"What are you doing, daughter?" he asked, shaking his head as if I were an impertinent child. Below us, the Dragon's body seemed to defy nature as it hovered motionless in the air, as if it were a feather floating on the surface of a pond. Seigetsu's hair streamed around him as he tucked his hands into his sleeves, and the jewel vanished from sight. "It is over. The game is done, and the winner takes the prize."

"That's what you were after this whole time?" I panted. "A jewel? Why...?"

The words caught in my throat. A memory came to me then, from a lifetime ago. Sitting in a tiny room with Master Isao, listening to a story of an arrogant mortal and the jewel in the Dragon's head.

"The Fushi no Tama grants immortality to anyone who possesses it." Seigetsu's voice echoed over the wind, and the eyes of the ninetail glowed yellow in the darkness. "The Harbinger's wishes have brought nothing but ruin to this world. It is time for a new god to rise, one who is unconcerned with the desires of mortal men. I will shape this world anew and purge the greed of humans from the land once and for all. The Dragon is gone. A new Harbinger of Change has come!"

A shudder went through the Dragon. I felt the shiver ripple through the huge body, as whatever force was holding the mighty creature aloft departed. For a heartbeat, the Kami hung in the clouds, and in the second before it started to fall, Tatsumi lunged forward, yanked Kamigoroshi from the Dragon's head and slashed it at the ninetail.

Seigetsu whirled, moving his head just enough so that the sword missed his face by a hairbreadth. A few strands of silver hair tumbled free and danced away on the wind. Tatsumi, the front of his haori drenched with blood, blinked as Seigetsu smiled.

"Not this time, Hakaimono. Now you face a god."

He flicked a tail, and blue-white flames erupted from Tatsumi's body, engulfing him completely. The demonslayer screamed as he was consumed by foxfire, dropping his weapon and falling to his knees.

Just as the real Tatsumi lunged through the blazing illusion and slashed Kamigoroshi into the ninetail.

Blood and smoke erupted as the illusionary Tatsumi vanished in a cloud of smoke, a single strand of Dragon whisker fluttering away on the wind. Seigetsu stumbled backward, the front of his white haori exploding in a spray of crimson, a look of shock and rage on his face. His gaze flickered to me, a chilling understanding in his eyes, and I felt a shiver of fear as I saw the promise of retribution in the stare of the ninetail. He dropped from the Dragon's head, hair and tails streaming behind him, and fell into the roiling clouds.

"Tatsumi!" I crawled toward the demonslayer on my knees, clutching at whiskers and mane and whatever I could, for the Dragon was falling now, its serpentine form spiraling almost lazily through the air. Tendrils of blue and green light rose from its body as it plummeted, fragments of spirit swirling into the clouds and vanishing in the dark. My hair and sleeves had turned into sails, the wind yanking at them savagely, trying to hurl me into open sky.

Fingers closed around my wrist, and Tatsumi pulled me to him, wrapping an arm tightly around my waist as we knelt on the spiraling head of the Dragon. Even in death, the Great Kami seemed to defy the laws of nature as its massive body fell like a paper streamer toward the earth. I clung to his haori, my stomach twisting at the gaping wound across his chest, the blood warm beneath my fingers. The ribbons of light from the Dragon's body swirled around us, soaring like schools of fish toward the sky, beautiful and terrible at the same time. For a moment, I closed my eyes and leaned into Tatsumi, numb from the tragedy of the night, the failures upon failures, all the death, pain and destruction we hadn't been able to prevent.

"I'm sorry," Tatsumi whispered in my ear, his own voice coming out choked. "I tried to stop it."

I swallowed hard, wanting to tell him it wasn't his fault, that we couldn't have known what Seigetsu was going to do. That the ninetail had been the cause of everything. Not Genno or Hanshou or even the Lord of Jigoku himself. Everyone had been a pawn in the kitsune's game, which had finally come to its conclusion. And we had lost.

The Dragon's body broke through the clouds, and the island was suddenly spread out below us, growing larger with every passing second. The gaping wound leading to the center of Jigoku still glowed against the dark, sullen and ominous, and we seemed to be falling directly toward it.

I shivered, weary and soul-sick, and pressed closer to Tatsumi. "I guess it doesn't matter now," I whispered, feeling cold inside and out. "If the fall doesn't kill us, the demons will. No flying carriage will carry us away at the last second."

"No," Tatsumi agreed, and one hand slipped into his obi. "But we do have this."

He held up his arm, a tiny green leaf pinned between two fingers. As I blinked in shock, he gave a faint, weary smile. "After meeting you, I always have a few on me now. Just in case."

I stared at the leaf, hopeful, grateful, but also terrified. "Tatsumi, I...I don't know if I can do anything now," I told him. I could feel the gaping hollowness in my stomach where the hoshi no tama, the star ball, had once resided. "Seigetsu took his magic back. I don't know if I'm strong enough to do anything but simple illusions."

"You are," Tatsumi said. "You don't need his magic. You're his blood, Yumeko. You're the daughter of Tsuki Kiyomi, and the protector of the Dragon scroll. You have all the strength you need."

Swallowing the lump in my throat, I reached for the leaf, curling my fingers around his own. My hand shook, and Tatsumi bent his head to mine. "You can do this," he murmured, as I took the leaf from him and closed my eyes. "You're stronger than you know."

I nodded, took a deep breath and searched within for my magic, hoping this idea would work.

For a moment, nothing happened. I could feel the hollowness

inside me, like a hunger that would never go away. But then, something flickered to life, an ember caught in a sudden breeze. It pulsed, then expanded outward, searing and familiar: my own fox magic, the magic that had been suppressed by the power of the ninetail. It flared, bright and joyful, suffusing my whole body, eager to be used again. I held the image of what I wanted in my mind, then sent the magic into the leaf at my fingertips.

The tiny leaf shivered, and then began to grow. It swelled to twice its size, then five times, then ten. I set it down as it continued to grow, until the once tiny leaf was the size of a tatami mat, just big enough for two people to sit on.

Below us, the Dragon shuddered, continuing to tumble lazily from the sky. The ground and the gash to Jigoku were frighteningly close. I glanced at Tatsumi and gave a sickly, hopeful smile. "Let's hope this works."

We knelt on the now giant leaf, Tatsumi wrapping his arms tightly around my waist, as I raised my hands and foxfire flared to life in my palms. It spread to the leaf below us, outlining the whole platform with flickering blue fire. Swallowing my nerves, I lifted my arms as I had while controlling Seigetsu's floating carriage, willing the same to happen here.

Instantly, the leaf floated upward, leaving the Harbinger's skull. I bit my lip, feeling Tatsumi's hold on me tighten as I maneuvered the leaf away from the dead Dragon into open air. My heart pounded, my hands shook and beads of sweat trickled down my neck as I pointed us toward a mountain peak. The leaf began to sway slightly, as if it were a real leaf caught in the wind, drifting closer and closer to the edge of a rocky shelf. I thought I heard Tatsumi whispering words of encouragement, but the magic roared in my ears, and I couldn't discern what he was saying.

This is real. I didn't know fox magic could do this. But…this is *real. I think?* I shook myself. *No, don't think, Yumeko. Just keep going. Think later.*

I held on to the magic until we were at least a couple dozen yards above the ledge. Then I lost control, and the illusion popped in a cloud of white smoke. We plummeted to the rocky peak, but Tatsumi managed to sweep me into his arms and land on his feet with a soft but pained grunt that made my stomach clench. Gently, he set me down and waited as I got my feet under me, adjusting to solid ground again and not the pitching, rolling platform of a dead Kami.

I looked up, over Tatsumi's shoulder, and everything inside me went cold.

The Dragon tumbled from the sky in a slow, almost lazy fashion, like it weighed no more than cloth. Tendrils of colored light still streamed from the huge Kami, spiraling back into the clouds, giving the impression that the Dragon was on fire. I lost sight of it as it dropped below the ledge, and then the whole world trembled as the Harbinger struck the earth.

Numb, I staggered to the edge of the peak and looked down, my stomach nearly crawling up my throat in despair. The Great Dragon, the Lord of Tides and the Harbinger of Change, lay dead in the center of the valley, his huge body coiled around the gaping scar to Jigoku. The hellish light reflected off the Dragon's scales, and hordes of demons and spirits—those his great body hadn't crushed—clustered around him, dancing and cavorting in apparent glee.

My legs shook, and I stumbled back from the edge, too dazed even for tears. "We…we have to get down there," I whispered, turning from the devastation below. "Maybe there's something we can do, some way to…bring the Dragon back. We have to try, don't we?"

"Yumeko." Tatsumi's voice was bleak. I heard the impossibility in it and sank to my knees on the rock, trapped in a nightmare I couldn't wake up from. How had we failed so spectacularly? The Dragon was dead, the gate to Jigoku lay open and all my closest friends were gone. We had stopped Genno from using the Wish, but even that seemed trivial to the passing of a Great Kami and the loss of what Seigetsu had wanted all along. Not the Wish, but the jewel that would grant him the power and immortality of a god.

Tatsumi knelt and drew me to him, bowing his head as he pulled me close. "I'm sorry," he murmured again, his voice sounding broken. One hand rose and cupped the back of my head, his fingers burrowing in my hair. "I wanted to give you a home to go back to."

I took a shaky breath, feeling my eyes burn and hot tears start down my face. "What do we do now, Tatsumi?" I whispered. "The gate to Jigoku is open. The demons and spirits will keep coming out until they overrun everything. How do we close it?"

"I…don't know." Tatsumi himself seemed on the verge of breaking down. He trembled against me, then took a breath to compose himself. "Blood magic, perhaps. But a spell that powerful would need a lot of sacrifice, and that's something neither of us are willing to do even if we could."

"What will happen if it's not closed?" I asked in a small voice. Knowing, dreading, that I already knew the answer. Tatsumi was quiet a moment before answering.

"The demons and spirits will continue to pour out," he said slowly. "The island won't be able to contain them. After they kill everything here, they'll move on to the mainland of the empire. As long as that gate is open, not only will the demons keep emerging, Jigoku's taint will corrupt this entire land. The kami will die, living things will become twisted and the humans that aren't killed will turn into demons themselves. Eventually, Ningen-kai will become another Jigoku, and O-Hakumon will likely rule them both."

"No, Hakaimono. That is incorrect."

A blast of frigid wind tugged at my sleeves and hair, as the voice echoed all around us, tangled with the storm itself. A cold, familiar voice that chilled my blood and made all the hairs on my arms stand up.

"If O-Hakumon tries to rule this realm," the voice continued, *"he will find that it has already been claimed. This is my empire now. I will purge this land of human strife and weakness, and all will bow before their new god!"*

An enormous streak of blue-white lightning descended from the clouds, smashing into the top of the mountain overhead. I gasped, and Tatsumi pulled me close again, hunching his body over mine, as the ground shook and stones fell all around us. When the rumbles ceased, I blinked dust from my eyes and looked up, and my heart froze in terror.

Something massive sat atop the mountain, shining against the night with an eerie glow all around it. An enormous fox, a thousand times larger than a normal kitsune, with pale fur and blazing yellow eyes. Nine huge, sweeping tails framed its lithe body, the ends tipped with crackling foxfire, swaying and writhing against the night.

"This world," the Great Ninetail said, his voice echoing all around us, *"is corrupted. Even before the gates of Jigoku opened, humankind infested the land that once belonged to us. I have seen nothing but war, greed, bloodshed, death. Time and time again, season after season. An endless cycle. Four thousand years ago, the Harbinger granted mortals the power to change their world, and what did they wish for? Immortality. Destruction. Vengeance."* The huge Ninetail raised his face to the sky. *"No longer. There will be no more wishes, no more Dragon scroll, no more humans claiming the power of a god. I will be their Harbinger. Let the new age begin."*

"Seigetsu-sama!" I rose on trembling legs and took two steps toward the ancient kitsune, who didn't turn his head or even twitch an ear in my direction. "Please," I called, wondering if he would hear me, if the tiny, impassioned words of a mere fox would even register, "I'm begging you—close the gates of

Jigoku. Don't let everyone here die. Why would you want to rule a land overrun with demons?"

His muzzle lowered, and I was suddenly pinned in the terrible gaze of a god, who stared at me a moment before throwing back his head with a laugh. The terrible sound made the clouds swirl overhead and caused lightning to flicker all around us, as the Ninetail's voice shivered through the storm.

"Even if I could," he said at last, giving me a hard stare. *"I would not. Do you think I am the Dragon, who will grant whatever you wish if called upon?"* His lip curled, showing a flash of shining fangs. *"Mortals brought this catastrophe upon themselves. Let them reap the consequences of their greed. I am a god—demons and the spawn of Jigoku are of no importance to me now. Except for one."*

His eyes shifted, the burning golden gaze landing on Tatsumi, who had leaped to his feet beside me. "It is time, Hakaimono," he growled. "Time for you to return to the sword for eternity. I will not allow the Godslayer to claim one more life. If I must bury it in the deepest ocean or in the center of the earth, Kamigoroshi's shadow will never darken this realm again!"

The Ninetail's expression changed, becoming savage and terrifying. A lethal madness entered his eyes as his muzzle curled back from his fangs, and the inside of his mouth began to glow a brilliant blue-white.

A huge fireball shot toward us, streaking like a comet from the Ninetail's jaws, searing the air and growing larger with every second. Tatsumi grabbed me and leaped off the ledge as the flaming sphere struck the ground behind us and exploded with a roar of kitsune-bi. We plummeted down the mountain, Tatsumi springing off ledges and jutting rocks, until we landed atop a lower cliff overlooking the valley. Around us, the land was flat and rocky, a large semicircle of open ground seemingly carved out of the mountain, with clusters of pine and bramble growing along the edge of the walls, forming a ring of shadows and vegetation. The center area seemed frighteningly open, not a lot of cover to fight an enormous, fire-breathing fox god. But if we hid in the shelter of the trees, would he just set the whole forest ablaze?

Tatsumi released me and drew Kamigoroshi, gazing up at the rising cliffs behind us. "Hide," he told me, eyes narrowed to glowing slits. "Get out of sight, Yumeko. He's coming."

I glanced desperately around and spotted the nearest cluster of pine in the shadow of the mountain, the branches thick and cloaked in darkness. "I'm not leaving," I told him, taking a step back. "I'm fighting, too. But..."

"I know." Tatsumi nodded. "Work your fox magic. I'll keep him distracted for as long as I can. Maybe it will be enough to fool a kitsune who thinks he's a god."

Fear knotted my insides, but I refused to think on it. "Be careful, Tatsumi," I whispered.

I started to draw away, but Tatsumi pulled me close and kissed me, quick and fierce, making my senses stand straight up. "In case I meet Daisuke's glorious death," he murmured as we pulled back. And though he still wore a faint smile, his eyes were shadowed. Resigned. "Thank you, Yumeko. For everything."

I swallowed the sob in my throat. "We'll win this," I whispered. "We have to beat him, Tatsumi. For Kiyomi-sama. For the Dragon, the kami and all our friends who brought us this far. This ends tonight."

"One way or another," Tatsumi agreed.

A chilling howl echoed over the storm, and dozens of lightning strands seared the sky, flickering over the valley. I broke from Tatsumi and sprinted toward the trees, darting behind a trunk as with a roar, an enormous ninetailed fox landed at the edge of the cliff and turned toward us, cold triumph in its golden eyes.

27

THE FOX WHO WOULD BE A GOD

TATSUMI

I drew Kamigoroshi and faced the creature looming over me. A ninetailed fox, the most dangerous of yokai, imbued with the power of a god. Its tails writhed behind it, snapping with foxfire, and its yellow gaze was fixed on me as it took one terrifying step forward, jaws open to reveal a maw of shining fangs.

My blood surged, and I raised Kamigoroshi, backing away from the huge creature. I knew why it wanted me dead. The reason lay curled around the pit to Jigoku: the immortal Kami that had been slain. If Kamigoroshi could kill the Great Dragon, it could also slay a ninetail, even one who was immortal.

It had already killed one god tonight. I would just have to kill another.

The Ninetail didn't bother with words. There was no mocking laughter or announcements that I was doomed. The kitsune's open jaws released a blast of blistering foxfire that scorched the air as it surged toward me. I dodged the first wave, dove away from the second and ducked behind a rock as fire seared the boulder and caused the nearby trees to crumble to ash. I felt the intense heat in the rock behind me, saw tongues of blue flame curl around the edges of the boulder and gripped my sword as the Ninetail came forward, its steps making the earth tremble.

I felt a presence beside me and glanced back into the face of a second Tatsumi, who gave a grim smile and raised his weapon. For just a moment I was startled, until I realized Yumeko was working her magic. I nodded, and the false Tatsumi darted from cover, dodging the blast of fire that ignited the trees behind him.

I paused a heartbeat, then did the same, seeing the illusion disappear in a blast of foxfire. In that split second of distraction, I leaped at the monstrous Ninetail with a snarl, blade sweeping toward its neck, figuring even a god would die if Kamigoroshi severed its head from its body.

One of the kitsune's tails lashed out, slamming me from the air. Pain seared half my body as white-hot foxfire scorched my skin. My demon half was used to the fires of Jigoku, and even in human form I tolerated heat better than most mortals, but the flames of the Ninetail defied belief. I struck the ground, and as I did, my body seemed to fracture into dozens of Tatsumis, tumbling through the dirt to either side.

Yumeko. Though there was no time to marvel at the kitsune's distractions, or what her ultimate plan was. If she even had one. I pushed myself to my feet, gripping my sword and seeing the small army of myself do the same. I didn't know where Yumeko was or how she was doing this, but there had to be at least a few dozen duplicates of myself that had suddenly joined the battle. Raising multiple Kamigoroshis, they began to surround the huge Ninetail, who watched them without concern.

"Daughter," it said, sounding unimpressed, "I have lived a thousand lifetimes. I have watched clans rise and crumble. I have seen the birth of forests and the death of stars. I have created my own kingdoms and filled them with servants, lovers and enemies. Do you really think you can defeat me with simple tricks?"

It waved a single tail, and half of the duplicates surrounding it burst into flame, consumed in an instant. But the other half sprang forward, rushing the Ninetail with Kamigoroshi blazing a sickly purple as they swarmed their enemy.

I lunged forward as well, hoping the images would do their job and distract the Ninetail long enough for me to get close. The kitsune snorted, shaking its head in contempt, and casually swiped a tail toward the illusions. Another half of the crowd went up in flames, fraying apart and turning into smoke as kitsune-bi consumed them. I gritted my teeth and charged the monster, seeing the few duplicates left do the same, as the huge Ninetail chuckled.

"You insult me, little fox," it said, leaping gracefully back. "Sending these false demonslayers to distract and confuse. As if I have not used such tactics a thousand times before. As if I do not know the difference between what is real and what is not."

Turning from the illusions, it looked right at me with blazing yellow eyes. I had a split second to realize it knew I was real before the kitsune lunged, a blur of silver against the dark, and a huge paw slammed into me, pinning me to the ground. I felt the breath leave my lungs in a gasp, and curved black claws dug into my chest as the monster fox loomed over me, tails writhing madly behind it.

"Sayonara, Hakaimono," the Ninetail said, and its mouth began to glow blindingly bright. I braced myself for the blast of foxfire that would char me to ash, when one of the duplicate Tatsumis leaped into the air and brought Kamigoroshi slashing across the monster's neck.

Blood, bright and vivid, erupted from the white fur, and the Ninetail screamed. Jerking back, it stared wildly at the illusion, golden eyes wide with disbelief and shock. I blinked in shock as well, watching a stain of crimson spread through the pale fur, dripping to the ground. Real blood. Not an illusion.

Utterly bewildered, I glanced at the other Tatsumi, who gave the equally stunned Ninetail a grim smile.

"You may be a god," he said, and rippled into Yumeko with a swirl of white smoke, making my heart stutter. A bloody tanto was clutched in her hand, and she glared up at the monster in defiance. "But you can still bleed."

With a snarl, the Ninetail lunged, covering the space between them in a blink. Before I could move, its deadly jaws opened, snatched the girl up and shook her like a rabbit in the teeth of a hound. Yumeko screamed as her body was torn apart, before she exploded into a cloud of smoke that writhed from the monster's fangs and vanished on the wind.

My heart lurched into motion again. The monster fox straightened, tails writhing menacingly behind it as it gazed around. "You cannot hide forever, daughter."

"I learned a lot from you." Yumeko's voice still echoed around us, from the tongues of foxfire crawling over the ground, from the trees and the rocks and the very mountain overhead. "Never be where your enemy expects. Let them chase shadows, like reflections in a pond. Make it so they don't know what is real and what is not. But there was one trick you didn't tell me, something you always kept back. It's all right, though. I figured it out."

The branches rustled, and dozens of Tatsumis strode from the trees, a small army of demonslayers with glowing eyes and swords. As one, they came forward, not speaking, their faces grim as they converged on the massive fox. Melting into the throng, I felt a chill slide up my back as dozens of versions of myself surrounded me. I had seen Yumeko's magic many times before. Her illusions were always lifelike, a perfect image of reality, but these seemed different somehow.

"Your illusions." The voice of the Ninetail sounded reluctantly impressed and…could it be…afraid? "They are…real."

With unified battle cries, the swarm of Tatsumis around me attacked. Instantly, the giant fox reared up, multiple tails waving, and howled. Its powerful voice rose into the air, swirling the clouds overhead, and lightning fell from the sky like rain. Flickering white strands seared into the ground, and dozens of Tatsumis frayed apart, becoming tendrils of smoke on the wind. One of the bolts hit a pine next to me, and the trunk exploded in splinters and flames, sending me tumbling to the ground.

Wincing, I pushed myself upright, intending to rejoin the battle, when a soft whistle made me stop. I glanced over to see another Tatsumi shake his head, putting a finger to his lips as he drew back into the trees. Setting my jaw, I stepped back and crouched behind a boulder, reluctant to hide but knowing Yumeko had a plan. The kitsune knew what she was doing, and I would trust her.

With a roar, the huge Ninetail landed in the midst of the remaining Tatsumis, tails and claws flashing as it scythed through them like paper. Leaves scattered to the wind, wisps of smoke dissolving around them, as the fox destroyed the army of demonslayers in an instant. But even as they were incinerated, the branches rustled, and even more emerged from the trees on the far side of the battlefield, filling the air with fox magic.

"Enough."

The Ninetail shook its head, rising to its full impressive height. "I weary of these games," it announced, glancing at the new mob of demonslayers walking toward it. "I wished only to kill the demonslayer and bury Kamigoroshi where none would ever find it. These tricks are amusing, but I have seen them before. And I know better than to continuously chase shadows." It looked at the trees beyond the army of demonslayers, narrowing its eyes. "I can feel you, little fox," it said quietly. "If one wants to destroy the hornet's nest, one does not waste time with drones. You take out the queen."

Its tails writhed madly, igniting with kitsune-bi at the tips, before it sent a storm of foxfire into the trees. Flames roared as ancient pines were consumed, turning to ash. Trunks snapped, trees curled and blackened in the heat, and embers swirled into the air, as an entire swath of forest became an inferno of blue-white flames. The army of Tatsumis jerked up, shuddering, and seemed to lose form, crumpling to the ground before dissolving into mist. I tensed, ready to spring from cover and charge the Ninetail, but a rock struck the trunk by my head, startling me. The other Tatsumi, crouched a few feet away, shook his head emphatically and mouthed a firm command. *Not yet.*

A scream drifted over the roar of the fire, making my stomach clench. Heart in my throat, I looked back to see a figure stagger from the flames, coughing and hunched over. Her long hair was scorched away, smoke curled from her body, and I could see the skin of one arm blackened and charred. Heart in my throat, I watched Yumeko stagger, then fall to her knees, gasping and surrounded by her fading army, as the Ninetail loomed over her. The monster fox was no longer smiling.

"I win," it said quietly, and waved a tail. Immediately, Yumeko burst into flames, blue-white foxfire consuming her body. She screamed, jerking up as she vanished in the conflagration, and shriveled into a blackened husk before crumbling to ash.

I dug my fingers into the tree, reminding myself that wasn't her. It couldn't be the real her. If it was, there was no way the other Tatsumi could still be here, a few feet from me. I glanced back at the image, saw him wink, and my heart unclenched a little.

"All right," he began, "while he's distracted…"

I rose, but abruptly the other Tatsumi jerked up as a fireball streaked from the air and slammed into his chest. Ignited instantly, he fell back with a cry, writhing on the stones as foxfire roared around him, and my blood froze as *her* familiar voice tore through me.

"No!"

Forgetting everything else, I rushed to her side, falling to my knees in the dirt. Yumeko lay curled on the ground, the illusion faded, tongues of foxfire still flickering over her robes. I smothered the flames and gently pulled her to me, turning her face to the light.

My blood chilled. One side of her face was seared, the flesh blackened and weeping, her long hair burned away. She drew in a shuddering breath, as everything inside me contracted in helpless agony and rage.

"Yumeko..."

"Gomen... Tatsumi," Yumeko whispered, clutching at my sleeve. "I'm sorry. I...I don't think I can help you anymore. I tried..."

The ground trembled, and a shadow fell over us, the heat of foxfire making the air shimmer. I gritted my teeth and held Yumeko close as the pale form of the Ninetail loomed over us, yellow eyes shining through the darkness and smoke.

"Goodbye, little fox." Its voice echoed with the finality of death. "I will admit, your talents are admirable. Few kitsune ever learn how to make their creations real, if but for a moment. In another life, I might have considered keeping you. But you were only a piece in a game, and I have no need for you anymore. Take solace in that, when your soul is reborn, it will be a far different world than the one you know now. Sayonara."

"Wait!" I threw out a hand.

The kitsune flicked a tail, and Yumeko burst into flames in my arms.

Heat seared my arms, my chest, my face, but I barely felt anything as the fox girl instantly shriveled against me and turned to ash, her small body vanishing into the flames. She didn't even make a sound. I choked, unable to move or even think, watching numbly as the kitsune-bi sputtered and died and I was left holding nothing. Nothing, except…

I blinked. A leaf, tiny and miraculously unsinged, lay in my palm, a curl of white smoke fading into the breeze. My breath caught, my heart stuttering into motion again, as behind me, the Ninetail let out a sigh that almost sounded sad.

"Now, Hakaimono," it said, crouching down to peer at me with blazing yellow eyes. "Let us continue, with no distractions. If you wish, I will make your death as painless as I did hers." His jaws gaped open, glowing with blue-white light. "One brief flash, and then nothing. It will be faster than the edge of a blade. The gods must be merciful, after all—"

I rose, turning to face the huge yokai. As, like a streak of lightning from above, another Tatsumi dropped from the sky and drove his sword into the Ninetail's back.

The fox god roared, rearing up in shock, its multiple tails lashing out wildly. The demonslayer on its back burst into flames and disappeared, but I felt a ripple of fox magic from every direction, as dozens of Tatsumis and Yumekos emerged from the flames. Smiling grimly, the closest Yumeko stepped forward, chin high as she faced the monster fox.

"You are not the Harbinger," she called. "Power and immortality does not make you a god. The Kami exist because humans worship and revere them. And as long as there is hope, we will keep fighting. The game isn't over yet."

She raised an arm, and the demonslayers around her charged. The Ninetail howled, sweeping fire and lightning through their ranks, incinerating demonslayers by the handful. But those that got close lashed out with Kamigoroshi, and blood streaked the monster's fur as the blades struck home. Screaming, the Ninetail leaped into the air and came down in an explosion of foxfire that might've wiped out the whole army. But the Yumekos raised their hands, kitsune-bi flaring in their palms, directing the deadly flames away, sending them harmlessly into the air.

"Go, Tatsumi," whispered a voice behind me. *Her* voice. Strained and exhausted, but unmistakable. "While he doesn't know what is real and what isn't. End this once and for all."

I smiled. Drawing Kamigoroshi, I turned and sprinted into the madness, weaving through flames and duplicates of myself, toward the fox who thought he could become a god. In a desperate attempt to protect himself, the Ninetail covered his whole body in flames. Kitsune-bi roared, strands of lightning crawled over his fur, and the demonslayers closest to him frayed apart, charred in an instant.

"Seigetsu!"

The shout came from the trees, from the spot I had left moments ago. The Ninetail whirled, eyes wide and furious, finding the girl standing at the edge. She, too, glowed with foxfire, shining like a torch against the night as she faced the monster across the field of battle.

"Kiyomi-sama," I heard her say, though she was far from me and the din around us should have been deafening. "We will avenge you today. For all the years you lost, let this bring you peace."

The Ninetail's muzzle curled back, jaws gaping as its throat glowed blindingly bright. It stepped forward, eyes blazing, as I leaped into the air, vaulted onto its shoulders, and slashed Kamigoroshi through the neck of the fox.

The kitsune staggered. For just a moment, it stood there, jaws open, staring at Yumeko. Then, the head toppled forward, leaving its neck in a spray of blood, as the massive fox swayed on its feet and collapsed. I hit the ground and rolled, suddenly too tired to spring to my feet, as the enormous creature spasmed and bled out on the stones. Its multiple tails writhed and beat the ground in a frantic, hypnotic pattern before they, too, finally stopped moving.

Slowly, I pushed myself to my feet, grimacing as all the burns, bruises, cuts and lacerations I hadn't let myself feel became loudly and painfully known. Around me, the army of demonslayers was fading, twisting into smoke and leaves that vanished on the wind. I took a deep breath, uncaring of the smoke and blood that filled my lungs, and breathed out slowly, warily letting myself believe the battle was over. That we, against a night of failure, death and catastrophe, had triumphed at last.

"Tatsumi!"

I looked up as Yumeko staggered toward me out of the smoke. Her face was covered in soot and grime, one sleeve was ripped, and blood streaked her arm and part of her robes. But her golden eyes shone with triumph and relief as she saw me and hurried forward.

I caught her as she threw herself into me, barely feeling the jolts of pain from the various hurts across my body. None of that mattered now. I was still standing, Yumeko was alive, and somehow, impossibly, we had killed the Ninetail with the power of a god.

"I can't believe it," Yumeko whispered. Her eyes were wide as she drew back, staring at the body of the huge fox. "We…we did it, Tatsumi. It's really over."

I nodded wearily. "Just one more thing to do," I muttered. Stepping around Yumeko, I walked toward the dead Ninetail, still gripping Kamigoroshi in one hand. I felt the girl's puzzled, worried gaze on my back, and heard her footsteps as she followed behind me.

"What do you mean?"

"The Fushi no Tama," I said, setting my jaw for what came next. Yumeko still looked confused, and I gestured to the motionless Ninetail. "We killed its host, but the Dragon jewel is still on the body somewhere. We have to retrieve it, before…"

I fell silent, a cold knot forming in my stomach, as another Yumeko, dirty, torn and bleeding, walked around the Ninetail's body and blinked at me.

For a heartbeat, my exhausted mind stuttered. Two Yumekos? Was one an illusion, leftover from the battle we'd just come through? But that made no sense; Yumeko would have dissolved the illusions now that the threat was gone. Why would there be two—?

"Tatsumi," the second Yumeko whispered, her voice laced with relief. Right before her eyes widened in alarm and she opened her mouth to shout something.

Pain exploded through my chest, rocking me forward. Stunned, I glanced down to see a hand, bloody and tipped with sharp claws, emerging through my middle. For a moment, I could only stare, not comprehending what was happening. Then a quiet, familiar chuckle echoed in my ear, as tendrils of white smoke coiled around me from behind.

"That was an impressive battle, Hakaimono." Seigetsu's voice was a triumphant whisper in my ear. "Brilliantly executed, perfectly strategized. It would have worked, but you and the kitsune girl made one mistake. You forgot what you were fighting. I have seen every trick, every illusion. I knew what would happen before you even thought of it. I may be a god, but I will always be a fox."

I couldn't speak. My mind had gone blank, and something was clogging the back of my throat. I coughed, and felt warm liquid stream down my jaw and neck. Other sounds seemed to have faded, though I was vaguely aware of Yumeko running toward us, golden eyes wide with horror and anguish.

"Farewell, Hakaimono." The Ninetail's voice murmured behind me again. "Do not be angry—you could not have hoped to stand against a god. Still, you fought valiantly, and the gods cannot be without mercy." I felt him lean closer, his mouth a few inches from my ear. "Perhaps I should change back?" he whispered. "Then you could at least die in the arms of your beloved."

Yumeko.

Her face swam before me, smiling, cheerful, hopeful in the face of everything. *I'm sorry*, I thought, as my vision went blurry and something hot slid down my cheek. It was getting hard to breathe, and blackness crawled along the edge of my vision. No time left. This would be my final act. *Forgive me, Yumeko. I wanted to protect you. I wanted to save you and everything you cared for. I'm so sorry. I won't…see the end with you, but… I will give you this one last thing.*

"What say you, Hakaimono?" It was no longer Seigetsu's voice whispering in my ear, but Yumeko's. "The fight is done. Just close your eyes and let go. Listen to my voice, the voice of your kitsune, as you drift off into oblivion."

I raised Kamigoroshi, flipped the blade around, and drove it into my chest, sinking it to the hilt. Behind me, Seigetsu jerked, letting out a startled, strangled gasp, and the world seemed to slow.

Something gripped my shoulder, fingers digging into my skin. I could feel the sword through my body like a strip of light, but I was beyond pain now. Images flickered through my consciousness, thoughts and feelings that weren't mine. Memories that I had never made. A world that was younger, where kami and yokai roamed freely and without fear. A world free of war and hate, where everything knew its place and was content. Until the rise of the humans, with their armies and weapons and consuming appetites that were never sated. I saw image after image of destruction, forests burning, cities in flames, fields of bodies and blood and death. The memory of a woman, tall and beautiful, with long black hair and eyes the color of jade. A pair of children scampered around her, laughing. Only the images flickered like the beats of a moth wing, and sometimes the two boys were fox kits and the woman was a kitsune with bright green eyes. Another flash, and I saw a human with a pair of dogs at his feet lift a dead fox up by the tail, smiling grimly. Horror, grief, a burning all-consuming rage, and then nothing.

I blinked. The world around me blurred, then came into focus. I still held Kamigoroshi's hilt to my chest, and could feel warmth spreading across my back, soaking through my haori. The weight behind me staggered, long fingers still digging into my shoulder, and a shudder went through us both.

"Damn you, Hakaimono." The choked whisper rasped in my ear. "Is nothing sacred to you? Those memories weren't for anyone else."

I yanked the blade free, drawing it from us both in a spray of blood, and Seigetsu gasped. Numb, I half turned, watching the Ninetail stagger back, clutching his chest. Blood soaked the front of his white haori, staining his sleeves, his hair, even his multiple tails. Though the fire dancing on the ends had gone out, and the glow surrounding him had faded.

Something glimmered through the blood on his fingers, shining briefly like a firefly. Lowering his hand, the Ninetail stared down at the pearl in his bloody palm, watching the light flicker and die, and smiled in weary resignation.

"Congratulations, Hakaimono," he murmured, as if we had just finished a long game of shogi. "Well played. It appears… the game is yours."

Stiffly, he walked a few paces away, then lowered himself to sit against a boulder, as if he was just taking a break. Blood ran from one corner of his mouth, and he gave a shaky sigh, tilting his head back.

"How unkind destiny is," he whispered, gazing up at the clouds. "A thousand years of planning, of calculating, of playing the game with no mistakes, to have my dream ruined by a demon and a girl."

His hand dropped to his lap, the Dragon jewel glinting dully in his palm, as the Ninetail who would become a god lost his hold on immortality and didn't move again.

Stumbling back a step, Kamigoroshi dropping limply from my hand, I swayed on my feet, then collapsed into the real Yumeko's arms.

28
THE PLANE OF JIGOKU

Yumeko

"*T*atsumi!"

I sank to my knees, cradling his head in my arms. He was drenched in blood; it soaked the front of his haori and streamed from the terrible wounds in his chest and stomach. Where he had plunged Kamigoroshi through his own body to impale Seigetsu, as well. Lying forgotten beside his hand, the sword flickered like a dying heartbeat, the faint purple light growing dimmer by the second.

"Tatsumi," I whispered. Helplessly, my hand hovered over the bloody wounds, shaking. "Oh, Kami, what can I do? Tatsumi, open your eyes. Can you hear me?"

"Yumeko." Tatsumi's voice was a breath, a whisper. His eyes opened, bright and glistening, gazing up at me. "Gomen," he murmured. "Forgive me, I don't think…I'll be coming back with you."

I shook my head, unwilling to believe. "You'll be okay," I

choked out, brushing the hair from his forehead. "You're half-demon—you can heal yourself, can't you? Like you did at the Steel Feather temple."

Tatsumi coughed; flecks of red misted into the air as he shuddered, then slumped against me. "I have…nothing left, Yumeko," he whispered, his voice unnaturally calm. "No tricks, or miracles to fall back on. The damage this time is too severe. This was…my last fight." One hand curled around mine, a pained, weary smile spreading across his face. "At least, to use the Taiyo's words, it was a glorious death, fighting a god."

"No." I curled over his body, my fingers tangled in his hair, his haori, anything to keep him from slipping away. "Please," I whispered. "I can't lose you. Not after everything." Tears blinded me, streaming down my face to stain the front of his shirt. "It's not fair," I choked out. "We came so far. We stopped the Wish, killed the Harbinger, defeated the Master of Demons *and* Seigetsu. We've done everything that was asked of us. This can't be how it ends."

"Yumeko, listen to me…"

Shaking, I raised my head to meet his dimming gaze. One of his arms moved, just slightly, toward where Seigetsu slumped against the rock, a glimmering pearl in one bloody palm. "It's not done yet," Tatsumi said in a broken whisper. "The Fushi no Tama. You have to…take it back to the Dragon. Before dawn… before he fades away entirely. If you can return the jewel to the Harbinger…its power…might be able to revive him."

The Dragon jewel. It had the power to grant immortality; to even bring the dead back to life. Filled with a sudden hope, I looked back at him, heart pounding. "The Fushi no Tama, Tatsumi, if you used it now—"

"No!" Tatsumi cut me off, gripping my hand. I winced at the horror in his voice as he shook his head. "I have…no desire to be a god," he whispered. "You can't use the Fushi no Tama's power without taking the jewel for yourself. It becomes a part of you. That's why Seigetsu was so eager to have it, and why he needed me to slay the Dragon—Kamigoroshi is the only thing that can kill an immortal. If you use the Fushi no Tama to save me, you would have to kill me to get it back."

I slumped, the tiny flicker of hope swallowed by blackness, leaving nothing but a gaping hole behind. For just a moment, a dark, unrecognizable part of me contemplated using the Fushi no Tama to save the demonslayer, regardless of consequence. But if I did that, I would be stealing from a god, taking what rightfully belonged to a Great Kami, and who could say what it would do to Tatsumi's soul? Especially if the only way to remove the Fushi no Tama would be to carve it out of him. It wouldn't be right. I couldn't use the Dragon jewel to save the one I loved, even as I watched him fading away before my eyes.

"Is this really how it ends, Tatsumi?" I murmured, holding him as close as I dared. "After everything we've done, this can't be what was destined for us."

"Our time was always borrowed, Yumeko." Tatsumi's voice was gentle. His gaze flicked up to mine again, intense and almost pleading. "But you can…make this one thing right," he whispered, his fingers tightening around my own. "One good thing…to come out of this night of failures. The world cannot lose a Great Kami. Revive the Dragon. You…are the only one who can now. Please." He paused, bowing his head as if speaking was an effort. "Promise me you will."

I remembered where the Dragon fell, in the center of the valley, his great body curled around the terrible pit to Jigoku. But now I was beyond fear. Beyond terror, anger, grief or determination, and all that remained was a hollow, bone-numbing emptiness. "I… I'll try," I told Tatsumi in a whisper. "I don't know if I'll be able to get there, but I'll give it everything I have." *All I have left.* "I promise."

Tatsumi nodded. His body relaxed in my arms, a tired, peaceful expression crossing his face. "Don't…mourn for me," he whispered. Slowly, his hand rose, fingers brushing my cheek, tracing the tears on my skin. "We'll meet again someday. No matter…where I end up, no matter how my appearance might change, even if I get pulled into Kamigoroshi and it takes me a thousand years… I'll find my way back to you."

I caught his hand, swallowing the tears in my throat, not wanting anything to block my final moments of Kage Tatsumi. Lowering my head, I kissed him, feeling his hand slide into my hair, sealing this memory into my soul for all time.

"I love you," I whispered, our faces just a breath apart.

His gaze went very soft. "I have…never loved anything as I have you," he breathed. "Thank you, Yumeko."

Then the light in his eyes dimmed, and his head slumped forward, his body going limp in my arms. I gave a keening cry and hugged him to me, sobbing his name, as the wind shrieked around us and the storm raged on, uncaring of the passing of another soul.

A softly glowing sphere rose from Tatsumi's chest, casting its own light into the darkness. I blinked away tears as it drifted over me. No, not one soul, but two, one bright and one crimson, merged together as they drifted into the air.

Beside Tatsumi's limp hand, Kamigoroshi flared. I raised my head, watching as the blade glowed purple, its faint, ominous light washing over my face and Tatsumi's body. I could sense a terrible pull from the sword, like a hole in a sake jug draining all its contents, and my stomach twisted in horror. Kamigoroshi was calling Hakaimono back.

For a moment, the souls in the air trembled, as if fighting the inevitable pull of the sword. The blade on the ground throbbed, a heartbeat that grew stronger with every pulse, and even the combined strength of the two souls could not prevent the will of the Godslayer. I could only watch, helpless, as the tangled oni and demonslayer were dragged ever closer to Kamigoroshi, and could do nothing to stop it.

The souls above me suddenly flared with light. I winced, closing my eyes, and for just a moment, I could see two figures hovering there, entwined, a human with dark hair and purple eyes, and an oni with onyx skin and burning ember horns. With a snarl, the demon wrenched himself from the human and shoved him back, and Tatsumi stumbled away, suddenly free of the demon's soul, floating alone in the air.

"Hakaimono..." The image of Tatsumi sounded stunned. "Why?"

The translucent oni gave a tired smirk. "Don't say you'll miss me, human. We both know that's a lie." He motioned to the glowing blade with a claw, curling a lip. "You think I want to be stuck in Kamigoroshi with you and your tiresome human emotions? There's no way I'm spending the next millennia whining about a fox girl. This wasn't a favor, mortal, it was to keep me from going crazy. So don't get too broken up about it."

Tatsumi bowed his head. "Arigatou," he murmured. "I won't forget...the demon who shared his soul with mine."

"Wish I could." The oni shook his head. "If I'd known what was going to happen, I might've let us both die the first time." A purple light surrounded Hakaimono, pulsing with ghostly flames, and he sighed, sounding incredibly weary. "No more of this. I'm done. I think I prefer the void of Kamigoroshi to experiencing that again. So...go on." He jerked his head at the sky. "Get out of here, before I change my mind and drag you into the sword with me."

Tatsumi's image became bright and transparent, and started to fade. "Goodbye, Hakaimono," he said quietly. "You were honorable, in your own way."

Hakaimono snorted. "The next time I'm free, I will remedy that, I assure you."

The oni closed his eyes as the flames spread over his body, consuming him, until at last, he erupted in a flare of violet and disappeared.

The light faded…and I was alone. Tatsumi's body was limp in my arms, nothing but an empty shell, and the storm still howled around us. Kamigoroshi flickered once and died, the blade becoming dark on the stones.

I gently lay Tatsumi on his back, pressing my lips to his forehead one last time. "Safe journey to you, Tatsumi," I whispered as I drew away. "Until we meet again."

Numb, I rose, the wind buffeting my hair and clothes, and walked to where Seigetsu slumped against the boulder, golden eyes gazing sightlessly upward. The pearl in one bloody hand glimmered dully as I bent down and picked it up. It lay in my palm, lifeless. As dead as the Dragon curled around the pit to Jigoku.

Tucking the Fushi no Tama into my obi, I turned from the ninetail, then stopped, a chill racing up my back. Kamigoroshi lay on the ground beside Tatsumi, the blade unsheathed, the steel cold and dark. My heart pounded as I stared at the sword. Tatsumi was dead, his soul departed for whatever afterlife lay beyond. But Hakaimono was still there, trapped in the sword once again. The oni had been vicious, cunning and unmerciful, a terrifying enemy, once. But…now.

I swallowed hard. He had been part of Tatsumi, part of the soul I had loved, who had loved me, as well. Even if Hakaimono was pure evil once again, I couldn't leave him here.

Heart in my throat, I reached down, hesitated, then curled my fingers around the hilt of Kamigoroshi. My hand shook, and I held my breath, bracing myself for… I didn't know what. A stab of pain? Hakaimono's evil laughter as he rushed in to possess me? But there was nothing. No pulse of a heartbeat, no consciousness that wasn't my own. If Hakaimono was in the sword, he wasn't responding.

Sheathing the blade, I walked to the edge of the cliff and looked down. The valley was a roiling mass of demons and spirits; they crawled over the rocks and swooped through the air, leaving trails of flame behind them. The scar to Jigoku pulsed red and purple in the center of the chaos. And in the center of it all, the Dragon's huge body lay in the midst of demons, giving off coils of light that spiraled toward the clouds. He was much fainter now, barely an outline of a once Great Kami, growing more transparent by the second.

And somehow, I had to get to him. Before he faded from the world entirely.

I took a deep breath, feeling my heart pound in my ears. I couldn't fail. Not this time. This would probably be my final task, but I had made a promise, to Tatsumi, to Kiyomi-sama and everyone else on this island. I would resurrect the Dragon, or I would die trying.

Alone, I made my way down the mountain, uncaring of the scrapes on my skin, the blood I left on the rocks. For a brief flicker of thought, I considered using fox magic to conjure a giant leaf to float down the mountain, but that required concentration to hold the illusion together, and I was exhausted, numb in both body and spirit. It was all I could do to keep walking until I stood at the edge of the plains.

Gazing into the darkness, I could see the ocean of demons and tortured spirits spread out before me, a vast, unending flood, and beyond them, the faintest blue-green glow of the Dragon. Flickering, fading, completely beyond my reach.

I trembled, feeling ice creep into my veins, and closed my eyes. *Tatsumi*, I thought, *Reika-san, everyone. If you can hear me, give me strength. I have to make it to the Dragon. Let me do this one last thing before I join you on the other side.*

There was a sigh in the back of my mind, a tickle of consciousness, and my heart nearly stopped. *What are you doing, fox? If you walk into that mess, you're going to get yourself torn to pieces.*

I gasped, and my stomach turned inside out. "Hakaimono?" I whispered, and felt the demon's weary annoyance. "You're here. Why…why aren't you trying to possess me?"

Don't make me answer that. The oni sighed. *You know you're not going to make it to the Dragon. Your fox magic isn't going to work here, kitsune, not this close to Jigoku. With the portal open, the spirits and demons have been driven to a frenzy. They're going to see through any illusion.*

"I have to try."

Typical. I could almost see the demon shaking his head. *Then, I suppose I'll have to help. This once.*

His presence grew stronger; I could suddenly feel it pressing against my consciousness, powerful and overwhelming, like staring into the face of a monsoon. I shivered, and heard a quiet chuckle in my mind.

There's no barrier around your soul at all, is there? Hakaimono mused. *It would be so easy to take you over and be free of the sword again. What I could accomplish with the power of a kitsune.*

I swallowed hard, knowing there was nothing I could do if the First Oni decided to possess me. I didn't have Tatsumi's training, the discipline needed to completely shut off my emotions. Especially now, when my insides were a churning mire of grief, determination and loss. "Please don't, Hakaimono."

You really are naive, aren't you? the oni replied, though his voice wasn't a threat; it just sounded tired. *Kami, I hope this fades in time. I'm never going to forgive you and Tatsumi for making me feel this way.*

I'm going to fully grant you my power, Hakaimono went on, even as my stomach twisted at his last words. *But it's going to feel strange, like you're not in control anymore. Don't resist. I'm not going to possess you, so you'll still look like yourself, but you'll need my strength if you want the barest chance of getting to the Dragon. Are you ready?*

My arms shook, but I took a deep breath and nodded. "Yes."

Power flooded me, an inferno rising up to consume me from the inside. For a moment, it felt like my blood would boil and my skin would split apart. Gasping, I sank to my knees, arms around myself, as a searing rush of heat filled every part of me.

Opening my eyes, I rose, feeling a strength I'd never experienced before, and a sudden, savage desire to cut down anything that stood in my way. I looked down and saw Kamigoroshi engulfed in violet flames, and a purple-black glow rising from my own skin.

Peering around the rock, I gazed into the valley at the army of demons between myself and the Dragon, and with Kamigoroshi loose at my side, I began walking. The snarls and screams of the demons pierced the night, and the cries of thousands of tortured spirits rose into the air, but I wasn't afraid. Or rather, all my fear had been shoved down into a tiny corner of my soul and abandoned. I didn't have time to be afraid now. Though I knew, even with Hakaimono's strength, my chances of making it through the valley to the Harbinger were slim. I would give it everything I had, but I was walking to my death, and I was… all right with that. I understood now what it meant to sacrifice everything, to give your life to protect not only the ones you loved, but their world and what they cared for, as well.

All right, fox. Hakaimono's voice was much clearer now, like he was walking right beside me. I was almost to the edge of the valley, and the wall of horrors stretching to either side. *This is suicide, but I guess we take down as many as we can. Just get out of the way and let me do what I do best.*

I gave a single nod and raised Kamigoroshi, the purple flames lighting the way forward. *For Tatsumi*, I told the demon, and myself. *For Kiyomi-sama, Reika, Daisuke, Okame… Watch over me, everyone. Let me make it to the Dragon. Just one last thing.*

Gripping the hilt of Tatsumi's sword, I started to run.

29

The Spirits Answer

Yumeko

I hit the edge of the demon wall with a snarl unlike anything I'd uttered before, fury singing through my veins as I slashed Kamigoroshi through the monsters in my path. They howled and split apart, as the sea of claws and fangs turned on me with a roar. I roared back and let the fiery hatred within carry me forward, the Godslayer a blur as it danced and sliced its way through heads, limbs and torsos. A trio of spirits rushed me, sobbing, reaching for me with grasping hands. I raised an arm, and foxfire seared forth, the sobs turning to wails as kitsune-bi consumed them.

Oh, well, isn't that surprising. What else can this do?

I raised Kamigoroshi, and foxfire erupted down the length of the blade, swallowing the flickering purple flames. With the sword blazing like a blue-white torch against the night, I gave a savage grin and leaped forward.

I lost track of time. The demons closed in, and there was

nothing but an endless sea of monsters surrounding me. I cut and sliced a bloody path through them, but there were always more, wave upon wave of them, slashing at me with weapons and claws. I struck a wanyudo from the air and felt a searing pain across my shoulder as a red-skinned demon with six arms hit me with one of its three swords. It lost two of its arms before I plunged Kamigoroshi through its middle and ripped it in half, then blasted a group of amanjaku with foxfire. They shrieked as they were burned to ashes in an instant, writhing into mist on the wind.

And then, something struck me from the side, lifting me off my feet with an explosion of pain through my shoulder. I hit the ground several paces away and rolled, somehow managing to come up on my feet, but my sword arm blazed with agony even as I lifted it in defiance.

A red-skinned oni, the thing that had hit me, bellowed as it lunged, swinging an iron-studded club at my head again. I ducked, swept low and sliced the monster's legs out from beneath him, hearing it shriek as it toppled forward. Staggering to my feet, I stared at the ring of demons and horrors around me, wave upon wave with no end in sight. I couldn't see the Dragon, I couldn't see anything except a wall of enemies, and the bloodred glow through the cracks in the clouds that proclaimed it was almost dawn.

Sorry, fox. Hakaimono's voice echoed in my head, and I felt him brace for the rush that would finish it. My arm shook; I was almost certain it was broken, and that only Hakaimono's strength and resilience were keeping me on my feet. I staggered back a pace and saw the ground beneath me was spattered with red. *I brought you as far as I could. But at least you'll be with Tatsumi in a few minutes.* I felt the oni's presence rise up, as if drawing on his last reserves of power. *And I don't plan to go down quietly. Let's send as many of these bastards back to Jigoku as we can.*

Pain clawed at me. Failure was a heavy weight in my chest,

bitter and suffocating. I wasn't going to reach the Dragon. I was going to die here, and Kiyomi-sama, if she was still alive, was going to lose everything.

I'm sorry, everyone. I tried.

With a flare of light, a small glowing ball soared overhead, lighting up the darkness for just a moment. The sea of horrors closed in, and I raised Kamigoroshi for one final stand.

Something streaked past my face, a tiny strip of what looked like paper, but glowing like a beacon in the night. It flew toward the first rank of demons and exploded in a blinding flash of light, causing them to howl and cringe back. I flinched, turning away and raising a hand to shield my face, until the light faded and I peeked up.

A ghostly, glowing figure stood between me and the horde, a massive komainu at her side. I gasped, tears immediately flooding my eyes, as the figure in white turned, giving me a familiar, exasperated smile.

"Come on, Yumeko," Reika said, holding out a hand. "Don't give up. You're not there, yet."

"Reika-san?"

My choked, ragged whisper was drowned in the snarling of demons as they surged forward, claws and fangs grasping, weapons raised overhead. As I turned to face a demon charging in from the side, an arrow streaked through the air in a blaze of white, thumping into its temple. It bellowed and collapsed, and something moved past me in a blur, cutting a spirit in two with a single, precise stroke.

"Yumeko-san." Daisuke, his hair glowing an even brighter white in the shadows, turned to smile at me over his shoulder. "Our apologies for being late. But it appears you could use our help, after all."

"Yep," sighed Okame as he strolled past, shaking his head and grinning. "Crazy fox. Leave you alone for a minute, and you go charging the entire plane of Jigoku by yourself." He raised his bow and swiftly sent three arrows into three different demons. "Well, come on then, Yumeko-chan. Let's get you to the Dragon."

A shadow fell over me from behind. I glanced back to see a massive oni, a pair of tetsubo raised, one in each claw, give a strangled roar as it toppled forward, its head leaving its neck halfway down. As it collapsed at my feet, I looked up to meet glittering purple eyes, and my heart stuttered in my chest.

Tatsumi met my gaze, looking as he had the night we first met in the forest outside the Silent Winds temple. Fully human, lacking any demonic features or hints of another soul mingled with his own. He glowed like starlight, and for the first time since I had known Kage Tatsumi, his eyes were clear of the shadows that had haunted him. He gave me a wry smile as my breath caught and the tears gathered in my eyes spilled down my cheeks.

"Go, Yumeko," he said softly, his voice a whisper into my soul. "Get to the Dragon. We'll be right beside you."

I nodded. Turning, I raised Kamigoroshi, as Chu gave a defiant roar and sprang into the wall of demons ahead.

Together, we cut our way through the endless waves of monsters. Okame and Reika stayed close, firing arrows and hurling ofuda, while Chu rampaged ahead, crushing enemies or knocking them aside. Daisuke and Tatsumi were an unstoppable force, moving seamlessly together as their blades cut apart their foes. After the initial shock, I relinquished control to Hakaimono, letting his instincts guide me forward, and joined the two swordsmen as we carved our way through the ranks of spirits and demons.

Fighting side by side with Tatsumi, I blasted a column of foxfire into a cluster of spirits, sending them reeling back, and through the sudden gap in the mob, I saw the fading body of the Great Dragon lying at the edge of a glowing pit. He was almost gone, a ghostly image with only a few tendrils of color and light clinging to the once massive Kami. Even as I watched, the Dragon disappeared, and the last streamers of light began rising into the darkness like coils of smoke on the wind.

"Hurry, Yumeko!" called Tatsumi, and cut down an oni in front of us. I dove through a pair of demons, feeling their claws miss me by a hairbreadth, slashed through a spirit that grabbed for me, and sprinted to where the last tendrils of light were coiling into the air, the final remains of the Great Dragon leaving the world.

Lunging forward, I fell to my knees in the midst of the lights, holding the pearl as high as I could. "Great Dragon," I called. "I return to you the Fushi no Tama! Take it, and be at peace once more!"

The lights didn't stop. They swirled around me, warm and bright, but continued spiraling toward the clouds. Helpless, I watched the final remnants of the Harbinger float away, growing smaller and fainter, until they disappeared.

Slumping back, I bowed my head, despair and helpless anger raging within. Too late. I was too late. We didn't make it in time, and now, the Great Kami was gone for good.

In my limp palm, the Fushi no Tama stirred. Numb, I opened my eyes as the tiny pearl suddenly pulsed against my skin, throbbing like a heartbeat. It rose into the air, following the same path as the lights had moments earlier, until it vanished into the clouds and was gone.

Hope stirred, even as I cast a resigned glance at the sea of demons surrounding us. *Maybe that was enough*, I thought as the ring closed in, despite Tatsumi's and the others' valiant attempts to hold it back. *Maybe the Dragon will revive and return to his kingdom beneath the waves. Maybe this wasn't for nothing, after all.*

Weariness clawed at me, but I grabbed Kamigoroshi and pushed myself to my feet, seeing the others falling back, giving ground before the infinite, relentless assault. The scar to Jigoku pulsed, spewing forth ever more demons to swarm the valley.

We were a tiny island in a surging sea of monsters, and that island was shrinking rapidly.

I met Tatsumi's eyes, and my heart swelled. There was no regret in his gaze, no anger or fear or madness, just a calm resignation. No matter what happened, he was at peace.

I raised Kamigoroshi and stepped up beside him, meeting the horde head-on. *Together, Tatsumi*, I thought, bracing myself as the demons closed in. *At least I'll be at your side this time.*

And then, a dozen streaks of lightning fell from the clouds, slamming into the ground a few yards away, and the world erupted with light.

30
THE WISH

Yumeko

Weightless. I felt weightless. Was I…floating?

Slowly, I cracked open my eyes, and let out a yelp.

A vista of swirling clouds surrounded me. I *was* floating, hovering in the air with the wind tugging at my hair and tail. Through breaks in the clouds, I could see glimpses of the ocean, and the expanse of the island far below. The scar to Jigoku still throbbed against the darkness, glowing sullenly even as the light of dawn broke over the horizon, ending the night at last.

I looked around and saw I wasn't alone. Five glowing balls of light floated around me, and I could feel their presence even though I couldn't see their true forms. Reika, Chu, Okame, Daisuke and Tatsumi. I knew them all, just by looking at them. The souls of all my friends.

And then the clouds before me parted, and I was staring into the face and glowing eyes of the Great Dragon.

The Harbinger of Change hovered before me, huge, terrifying and very much alive. His enormous body disappeared into the roiling clouds, his long whiskers rippled in the wind and the Fushi no Tama glimmered a brilliant white in the center of his forehead. For a moment, I wondered if the God of Tides, enraged at the indignities suffered upon him this night, had brought me here to kill me. To tear the soul from my body and drag it beneath the waves, where it would be trapped forever. I glanced at the rest of the souls around me, pulsing softly in the darkness, and felt a stab of fear, wondering if the Great Kami had brought us here to punish us all.

"Time grows short."

The Dragon's voice rumbled through the clouds, seeming to come from every direction. I felt it vibrate through me as the Great Kami rose higher into the air, fixing us all with the stare of a god.

"The night of the Wish has come and gone," the Dragon continued. *"But the summoner is no more. His soul languishes in Jigoku, torn apart by oni and the servants of O-Hakumon. But the Summoning still took place, on the night of the thousandth year, and the prayer was still recited. Mortal fox..."*

His gaze shifted fully to me, and my stomach twisted under that cold, eternal stare. *"You returned the Fushi no Tama,"* he rumbled. *"You willingly gave up the power that would make you a god. The Summoning has passed, but I will give you this choice. Make your wish, kitsune. As you returned the jewel to me, this night, I will grant you the summoner's power. Speak your wish out loud, and your heart's desire will come to pass.*

"Or, do not speak it, and I will leave this place unchanged. I will depart the mortal world, and the Wish will be unfulfilled for another thousand years."

My heart stood still. The Harbinger was giving *me* the choice to use the Wish. Use it, or let nothing change. Let the Wish go unfulfilled, or find the words to somehow make everything right. And for a moment, I was suffocated by choice. I could ask for anything I wanted, and there were so many things I wanted to change, but…we had come this far to stop the Dragon's Prayer from being used. How was I worthy of this, of speaking the Wish that would change the world? Could I even find the words to make the right choice?

"You can do this, Yumeko," Reika whispered behind me. "Your heart has always led you down the right path. If anyone can use the Dragon's Wish for good, it's you."

My stomach twisted, and I closed my eyes, hearing my heart thud in my ears. She was right. I had to do something. This was my one chance to fix things, to change the terrible events the night had brought. I wanted Kiyomi-sama to be alive and safe. I wanted the island to be restored, and the kami to return. And I wanted my friends back. To hear Okame's laughter, and Reika's exasperated voice as she lectured us again. To see Daisuke's smile, Chu's happiness, and to hear all their voices as they bickered and laughed and loved together. And to spirit Tatsumi away to a tiny grove deep in the forest, where demons and shinobi and the Shadow Clan would never find us, and be with him forever.

But I couldn't have that. I couldn't be selfish. Even though there were so many things I wanted to make right, the Dragon would honor only one single request. I had to find the one decision that would save us all.

One Wish. One chance to change fate.

"I… I will use the Wish," I whispered, and the world seemed to still. The clouds stopped moving, the lightning ceased and everything held its breath, hanging on my next words. I took a deep breath, praying that Master Isao, Master Jiro, Reika and all the mentors who saw me this far would give me wisdom, and spoke what was in my heart.

"Great Kami, save this world. Close the gates of Jigoku, and send all the demons, spirits and creatures that don't belong in Ningen-kai back where they belong!"

The world flickered into motion again. The Harbinger reared up with a howl that tore the storm apart, scattering clouds and sending lightning bolts arcing out to sea. An enormous ripple of power went through the air, like a stone dropped into a pond, and the clouds began to part, showing the sky at last. I looked up and saw we were descending, floating gently toward the valley as the huge form of the Harbinger drew steadily away.

"Yumeko," said Reika in a breathless voice, her eyes wide as she stared down. "Look."

I looked. We were closer to the valley now, and without the cloud cover, I could see the whole island stretched out before us. The glowing, ominous red scar to Jigoku was still there, but it was shrinking, growing smaller even as I watched. The army of demons and spirits were disappearing, being drawn back into the pit, like water being sucked down a hole.

Forgotten at my side, Kamigoroshi flared, a pulse that made me jerk up, and Hakaimono's presence appeared in my mind. I could feel his astonishment, mingled with disbelief and, below all that, the barest sliver of hope. Before I could ask him what was happening, something rose from Kamigoroshi's sheath, a crimson ball of light, weak and pale against the growing dawn. It hovered in the air a moment, before it flared into the spirit of an oni with ebony skin, a white mane and burning ember horns.

"Hakaimono," Tatsumi said behind me, his own voice stunned. I blinked as the demon turned, his gaze falling on the sword, dead and dull at my side. "What is happening?"

"Kamigoroshi." Hakaimono paused, as if waiting for something, then shook his head. "I can't feel the pull any longer," he muttered. "Does that mean…?" His gaze shifted to mine, hopeful and amazed. "Yumeko, your wish…"

My heart pounded. I remembered the Wish, and what I had said. Not thinking of Hakaimono, or the phrasing of the Wish, just what I had felt in my heart was the right thing. *Send all demons, spirits and creatures that don't belong in Ningen-kai back to Jigoku where they belong.*

I swallowed. "I guess that meant you, too."

Hakaimono closed his eyes, tilting his head back as the breeze rippled around us, continuing to part the clouds. "I'm free," he almost whispered. "For good, this time. After a thousand years, the curse is broken. I can finally leave this realm and return to Jigoku."

My eyes watered. There was so much longing in the oni's voice, so much hope, relief and genuine happiness. Like waking up from a long, terrible nightmare. I couldn't forget what he had done, and that he was still the most powerful, dangerous demon to ever walk the mortal realm, but in that moment, I was glad Hakaimono the Destroyer was finally free. His suffering was over at last, and he could go home.

"What will you do now?" Tatsumi wanted to know. The oni gave him a smug look, as if reading his thoughts.

"Oh, don't worry, Kage. I'm not planning a grand return to wreak my vengeance upon your precious clan. Not soon, anyway." He waved a dismissive claw. "Hanshou is dead. The Dragon is gone. The rest of the empire will finally calm down a bit with the passing of the Harbinger. And I've had enough of this realm to last several lifetimes. Besides…" His mouth curled in a terrifying smirk. "The ruler of Jigoku and I need to have a talk. I think I need to go back and see what O-Hakumon has been planning for this realm without me. Maybe whip the rest of the demons into shape, remind them who their strongest general is. So, don't worry about me—you'll all be long dead before I even think of coming back."

"Thank you, Hakaimono," I said, and I really meant it. "For everything."

"Yumeko." The oni gave me a tired smile. "Don't take this the wrong way, but I'm going to go home and do my best to forget all about you. I figure a couple centuries of slaughter and depravity should do the trick. If not, well, you're half-fox. Kitsune can live close to forever, if nothing kills you before then." The smile grew wider, and he lifted a claw. "Who knows, you just might see me again someday."

And with that faintly ominous statement, Hakaimono shimmered into a crimson ball of light and arced away toward the valley. I watched it get smaller and smaller, until it joined the flood of demons and spirits being pulled back into Jigoku and vanished from sight.

My feet touched rocky ground, as I landed on a familiar circle of flat stone at the very top of the mountain. The bodies of Genno's blood mages were gone, but the stone altar still held the remains of a shattered skull, and a long, long strip of parchment, weighed down by rocks and fluttering in the breeze. Ignoring the scroll, I stepped to the edge of the Summoning site and peered down into the valley, where the wound to Jigoku was visible far below. And I watched as the final demons and spirits vanished down the pit, the gates closing with a rumbling of stone and earth, shaking the ground until, at last, only a jagged scar remained.

Then the sickly purple light faded, the roiling clouds disappeared and the first sliver of sunlight broke over the distant horizon.

"It is done." The Dragon's voice was a whisper now, barely audible even in the sudden stillness. Overhead, the skies were clear, and the stars were slowly fading as the sun climbed slowly over the mountains, bathing everything in light. "*The Wish of this era has been spoken, and the winds of change have begun. Let no one call upon the power of the Dragon's Prayer for another thousand years."*

The presence of the Great Dragon faded away, vanishing with the stars, and the world was normal once again. I stood at the edge a moment, letting the sun warm my face, before I took a deep breath and turned.

They were all still there—Reika and Chu, Daisuke, Okame,

and Kage Tatsumi—their forms translucent in the morning light. And one more, a girl in simple robes with her hair tied back, watching me with a shy, uncertain expression. I blinked in surprise, then smiled at her around the lump in my throat.

"Suki," I whispered, and she ducked her head. "Why are you here?" She didn't reply, but it only took a moment before I knew the answer. "You…brought them, didn't you?" I asked. "When I was alone on the plane of Jigoku. You led them to me."

The yurei nodded once. "You needed them," she replied softly. "And they already wanted to help. I just…showed them the way."

I blinked, as my eyes started to burn. "What will you do now?"

The yurei raised her head to the distant sunrise. "I no longer feel a tie to this world," she mused. Turning, she gazed at Daisuke, standing quietly with Okame at his side, a warm, affectionate look crossing her features. "My purpose has been fulfilled. I think I can go now."

Daisuke's spirit stepped forward and bowed. "Thank you, Suki-san," he told her solemnly. "And safe travels to you. Do not fear what lies ahead—you will not be alone on your journey."

She smiled at him, looking peaceful and content. "I used to be afraid," she murmured. "I'm not anymore. Sayonara, Daisuke-sama. I will always remember you."

Her form shimmered, becoming a hazy ball of luminescence that circled us once, then flew unerringly toward the rising sun, and was lost from sight. I watched until I couldn't see the hitodama any longer, then turned back to the spirits of my friends.

For a moment, nothing was said between us. We knew what came next, what had to happen, and I wasn't ready. I would never be ready.

"Well." Okame's gruff voice was first to break the silence. "I guess this is it. And I hate long goodbyes, so…" He gave me that crooked, defiant grin. "Take care of yourself, Yumeko-chan. It was one hell of an adventure, one I wouldn't change for anything. Just promise me you'll keep making nobles scream at illusionary rats in their pants."

I choked on a laugh, tears nearly blinding me. "I will, Okame."

"Yumeko-san." Daisuke bowed to me, low and formal. "It has been the greatest of honors to know you," he said as he rose. "I wish you happiness, and may you never lose that light that drew all of us to your side."

"Daisuke-san..." I swallowed the lump in my throat. "Thank you. I'll be sure to write a poem for you and Okame. It will be one that the poets sing for all time."

He chuckled. "I think we would like that." Stepping back, he leaned into the ronin, who put an arm around his shoulders. "Sayonara, Yumeko-san," he murmured, as both he and Okame shimmered, becoming brighter even as they started to fade. The ronin raised his arm in one last salute, before they grew too bright to look at. "We'll be watching over you, always."

"Baka kitsune." Reika stepped forward, the hulking form of Chu at her back. "Why are you crying? This isn't the end. Death isn't goodbye forever."

"I know," I sobbed. "I'm... I'm just going to miss everyone. We came so far together. I wanted us all to be here at the end."

Ghostly hands reached out, cool, transparent fingers curling around my own. "We'll see each other again," Reika assured me. "Maybe in a different form, under a different name, but in some small way, our souls will always recognize each other. But you have an important task now, Yumeko. The Dragon is gone, but the scroll remains. It won't become important for another thousand years, but you must decide what to do with it. Whether you decide to split it into pieces once more, hide it away or some other solution I haven't thought of, its fate is in your hands. What becomes of the Dragon scroll is up to you now."

She raised her head, closing her eyes as sunlight washed

through her, causing her outline to ripple at the edges. "I have to go," she whispered, opening her eyes to smile at me. "And I'm sure you want a few moments to say goodbye to Kage-san." Her hand rose, ghostly fingertips touching my cheek. "You've made me proud, kitsune. Remember, you'll never be alone. No one is ever truly gone."

"Arigatou," I whispered shakily as, for just a moment, the shrine maiden's image glowed blindingly bright. "Thank you, Reika-san. Everyone. Thank you all so much."

The light faded, and both Reika and Chu were gone. For a moment, I stood there, shaking, tears streaming down my cheeks. Then, *his* presence was behind me, his voice low and soft in my ear.

"Yumeko."

"Tatsumi," I whispered, my voice shaking with tears. I opened my eyes but could see only my own shadow on the ground before me. "I don't… I don't want to say goodbye."

Tatsumi hesitated, and then ghostly arms rose to embrace me from behind. I couldn't feel them; like Reika's hands, they were insubstantial, only a cool tingle against my skin. But Tatsumi bent close, as close as we could get, his lips brushing my cheek.

"I'll find you," he murmured. "I promise, Yumeko. No matter how long it takes, how far I have to travel, even if it takes me several lifetimes, I'll keep looking. My appearance might change, my name might be different, but you are the other half of my soul. It won't stop searching until it's found you again."

"How will I know?" I choked out. "If you look different, how will I know it's you?"

"You'll know," Tatsumi said. "One day, you'll look up and I'll be there. And you'll know it's me because our souls will recognize each other."

I turned in his arms, gazing up at him through blurry eyes. He was nearly gone, just the faintest image against the light of dawn. I blinked at him and smiled through the tears.

"Then I'll hold you to that, Kage Tatsumi," I whispered. "Until we meet again."

He raised a fading hand and pressed it to my cheek, making my stomach twist even though I couldn't feel him. "I love you, Yumeko," he whispered. "On my honor, I will find my way back to you."

Lowering his head, he touched his lips to mine, and I closed my eyes.

Goodbye, Tatsumi. Someday, if we do meet again, I hope to hold you for real. Without clans, emperors and Dragon scrolls coming between us. Someday, when the world has calmed down and this is all behind us, we'll find our way back to each other. And when we do, I'll never let you go again.

When I opened my eyes, I was alone.

The sun had fully risen over the mountains, and the stars were gone. I stood on a rocky ledge overlooking the valley, the sun on my face and the wind at my back, watching the light slowly creep over the valley below. The long night was over. The Dragon had come and gone, and a new age had begun.

Sitting on the edge, I lay Kamigoroshi beside me and gazed into the valley, watching as the sunlight drove away the last of the shadows and darkness. I knew I should head back down the mountain, find the armies of Moon and Shadow, if any of them had survived, and tell them what had happened. And I would. The Tsuki deserved to know that their island was safe, the Harbinger had returned to normal and the Wish had been spoken. But right now, I was weary and soul-sick, and loss was a gaping wound across my heart. I needed a little time to mourn, to be alone with the memories of my friends, the human I had loved, so that when I did tell their story, it would be one of triumph and victory. And one I could get through without completely breaking down.

So I sat there, the sun warm on my head and shoulders, Kamigoroshi dead and lifeless at my side. I thought of chance encounters and first meetings: a stranger cutting down the demons chasing me through a forest; being ambushed by bandits on a lonely road; encountering a masked, beautiful swordsman on a moonlit bridge; meeting a stern, suspicious miko in a tiny shrine. I thought of Daisuke's kindness, Reika's pragmatism and Okame's irreverence. And I remembered how Tatsumi had looked at me, the touch of his fingers on my skin, his whispered promise at the very end. I thought of everything that had brought me here from the moment I'd fled the Silent Winds temple with the scroll—the danger, the friendship and the love—and several times, I found myself smiling through my tears.

And that was how Kiyomi-sama found me, several hours later.

"Yumeko."

I turned, looking over my shoulder. A figure stood several paces away, long hair unbound, sleeves fluttering softly in the wind. She looked exhausted, her robes tattered, dirt and blood spattered across her hands and face. But she stood there, steady and solid and real, gazing down at me in relief.

I blinked as my own relief crashed over me like a wave. "Kiyomi-sama," I whispered as the stubborn, persistent tears crowded forward again. "You're alive."

"Yes." The Moon Clan daimyo gave a pained smile. "We took heavy losses, and were forced to fall back several times, but the line held. The demons did not reach any of the villages, and when the Harbinger first appeared, we took advantage of the chaos and panic it caused to push them back. Still, the losses were severe. Without the aid of the Shadow Clan, none of us would have survived the night."

I shivered, remembering a wizened, twisted creature shouting at the Dragon, demanding it correct what it had done two thousand years ago. "Lady Hanshou…" I began.

"I know," Kiyomi-sama said quietly. "I was there when she

transformed. She flew into the clouds after the Harbinger and did not return. Long has it been rumored that the Shadow daimyo has slowly been going mad. I hope that, wherever she is, her spirit has finally found peace."

"What will happen to the Kage now?" I wondered.

Kiyomi-sama shook her head. "I do not know," she said solemnly. "I do not believe Hanshou had any heirs. Her adviser, Kage Masao, has taken over in her absence. He appears to have the situation in hand. Beyond that, I do not know what will happen to the Shadow Clan, nor is it my place to ask. The Kage must take care of their own. And I must do the same."

The Tsuki daimyo hesitated, then took two steps forward, watching me with dark eyes that were both conflicted and sympathetic. "Daughter," she began, sounding uncertain for perhaps the first time I had known her. "I am...pleased that you survived. I know you suffered greatly this night, and as your friends are not here with you, I can only assume..." She trailed off, her smooth brow furrowing, as if unsure of how to proceed. I bit my lip, feeling twin tears slide down my cheeks, as the Moon Clan daimyo paused to collect herself.

"But you are here," Kiyomi-sama went on. "The night of the Wish is over, and the empire still stands. Genno is gone, the gate to Jigoku sealed, and the demons have returned to the abyss. I don't know what happened, or what caused the Harbinger to go momentarily mad, but it appears that, against all odds, you have emerged victorious. I can only hope this means that the Tsuki islands are safe, that it is finally over."

I nodded. "We won," I whispered, hardly able to believe it myself. "It's over, but..." I trailed off, closing my eyes as memories crowded forward, bright and painful. "My friends," I said, my voice shaking. "I wouldn't be here if it wasn't for them. They were the true heroes tonight."

"They will be remembered," Kiyomi-sama said solemnly. "In memory and song, in verse and play, their legacy will not be forgotten." She raised her head, gazing at the sky as the sunlight washed over her face. "We will mourn those we lost, and commit them to legend, but tonight, we will celebrate with those still standing."

She looked at me, and in that dark gaze, I saw the terrible, always present sorrow finally begin to fade, vanishing like mist in the sun. "Sixteen years ago, I lost a daughter," the daimyo said. "Last night, I thought I would lose her a second time. But by fate, the Kami's mercy, or her own incredible luck, she stands before me now. We have been given another chance, Yumeko," Kiyomi-sama continued and, incredibly, she smiled. It was faint and rusty, as if it hadn't been used in a long time, but it lit up her face and drove away the lingering shadows in her eyes. "If you are ready," she murmured, and held out her hands. "I would love to show you where you come from."

Tears filled my eyes. I stumbled forward and grasped the outstretched arms, clinging to them tightly as her fingers curled over mine. "I would like that," I whispered. "It has been a very, very long night."

The Moon Clan daimyo returned my smile. With a sigh, she gazed over the valley, in the direction of Shinsei Yaju. "My advisers are likely in a panic right now," she said wryly. "And the kami are starting to return. I can feel them, the land welcoming them back. But there is much to do still. Come then, daughter," she said, and squeezed my hands. "Let's go home."

Epilogue

So began the long years of peace in Iwagoto.

For the rest of the empire, not much changed. The Shadow Clan, admittedly smaller, having lost many of their strongest warriors, returned to their lands to begin the arduous task of choosing a new daimyo. Hanshou had no living heirs, none that had been alive in the past thousand years, and though a few nobles claimed they could tangentially trace their bloodline back to one of the daimyo's children, in the end, Kage Masao proved he was the closest living relative to Kage Hanshou. Her many times over great-grandson. Lord Iesada was said to be particularly unhappy with the choice, expressing his doubts loudly and passionately. He was found in his room one morning, his face blue, his teacup smashed and shattered on the floor. It was determined he had choked on a mochi ball, a terribly unfortunate accident, and after his death, the whispers against the new daimyo faded away.

Kamigoroshi, the Cursed Sword of the Kage, was returned to the Kage family shrine, where it was sealed away and watched over by their priests. Though the blade no longer contained the trapped soul of an oni, the curse remained, according to Kage Masao. "It is a tainted weapon that took the life of a Great Kami," he told the Moon Clan daimyo before the Kage departed Tsuki lands that night. "The curse of Kamigoroshi has never been Hakaimono's presence, but the power to slay anything in its path. It has corrupted countless demonslayers and has taken the lives of thousands. It is not a blade that should be wielded by anyone in this world. I believe the Kami themselves have cursed the Shadow Clan through the years for using a weapon of such evil. Perhaps someday, when darkness threatens the empire again, Kamigoroshi will be taken up by one who can resist its pull. But for now, let the Cursed Blade fade into legend once more, and be forgotten."

And so it was. From that night on, there were no more demonslayers, no Shadow Clan warriors wielding a blade of purple fire. The story of the sword that slew the Dragon was whispered throughout Iwagoto, but in time, even those tales faded away and were lost to history.

The Dragon scroll was taken back to the Moon Clan capital, and a great debate arose around what should be done with the artifact and how its use could be prevented in the future. Hiding the scroll hadn't worked. Separating it into pieces hadn't worked, and had only resulted in more lives lost.

At last, after many days of council, the Moon Clan daimyo made the decision that the Tsuki themselves would become the new guardians of the Dragon scroll. That the prayer would remain there, on Moon Clan islands, a breath away from the cliff where the Dragon was first summoned. They would make a vow to the Kami that no Tsuki would use the power of the scroll for themselves, and they would do their best to ensure the Dragon's Wish would not fall into the wrong hands. A shrine was built within the Moon Clan palace, and the scroll would rest there, guarded by priests, shrine maidens and kami, out of sight of the rest of the world. It wasn't an ideal solution, but it was better than releasing the scroll into the wind and letting it fall where it might. Besides, who knew what the next millennium would bring? Perhaps the world would have moved on and forgotten the legend of the Dragon's Prayer.

I knew that was just a dream, that when the time came for the Harbinger to rise once more, the empire would undoubtedly descend into chaos trying to get the scroll. But a thousand years was a *long* time. There were things I wanted to do, a whole world to see, before I had to worry about the Dragon scroll again.

I stayed on the Tsuki islands for three years. After Kiyomi-sama officially made me her heir, there were a lot of things to learn. Tsuki politics, their relationship with the kami and the rest of the empire, the complicated ways of court—it all made my head spin. Still, I was happy to stay, eager to learn everything I could. This was my family; I wanted to know everything about them and where I came from. Where I belonged.

And yet, though I was happier than I had been in a long time, sometimes I would find myself on the end of a pier or on a small sandy beach, staring over the water to the place where the sea met the sky. Or sitting in the grass in the extensive gardens of the palace, gazing up at the stars as the kodama danced around me. Every so often, I would see a face or a silhouette in a crowd that would make me jump, heart in my throat, until I realized it wasn't who I thought. It was never who I thought.

One night, more than three years after the night of the Wish, there was a tap on my door, and Kiyomi-sama appeared in the frame.

I glanced up from the book I had been studying: a collection of essays from the famed philosopher-poet Mizu Tadami. It was dry, fairly boring reading, with questions that made me wonder why one would spend so much time agonizing whether a cherry blossom had a soul, but Kiyomi-sama was hosting a Mizu envoy in a couple days, and the Water Clan loved debating philosophy. A good host should be able to talk about the things their guests were interested in, Kiyomi-sama had said. Even if it made her brain hurt.

"Kiyomi-sama," I greeted as the Tsuki daimyo offered that faint smile usually reserved just for me. "Please, come in. Is something wrong?"

"No." The head of the Moon Clan stepped through the frame and closed the door softly behind her. Her hair hung loose instead of being pinned atop her head, and her robes, though elegant, were a little less fine than the ones she would wear to court. I knew I was supposed to bow, putting my book aside and touching my forehead to the floor, when the daimyo of the Tsuki entered the room, but when it was just us, the rules weren't adhered to as strongly.

Kiyomi-sama stepped daintily across the tatami mats and sat across from me, her gaze falling to the book in my hands. A wince and a faint furrow crossed her brow, even as she smiled. "Ah, Mizu Tadami. I have spent many hours debating the finer points of his work with young warrior-poets. Nowadays, however, I fear I must discuss his work over a few cups of sake, otherwise I end the night with a terrible headache."

"Oh," I said, putting the book aside. "Good. Something to look forward to."

She chuckled, and it still sent a flutter through me. Her smiles had become more commonplace, but in the beginning, it was almost as if she had forgotten how to laugh. That first year, I had spent a disgusting amount of time playing harmless pranks on the nobles, trying to coax a chuckle from the daimyo, a snort, a titter, anything. The poor nobles had suffered great indignities, from birds in their hair to having their fans stolen by monkeys, but Kiyomi-sama could either see through the illusions or was wise to the ways of kitsune, for she always seemed to know who was behind the ridiculous happenings at court. The day I accidentally let a very real wild pig into the main hall, where a troop of Noh actors were performing an intensely dramatic play for Kiyomi-sama, was the day I finally saw her laugh until tears streamed from her eyes. I got in so much trouble for that little stunt, but I considered it a victory.

"I saw you on the cliffs today." Kiyomi-sama's voice was solemn. I blinked as she fixed her gaze on me, dark eyes studying my face. "You were gazing over the water, watching the last of the merchant ships depart. And there was…a longing about you, Yumeko-chan, one I have seen before. Do you wish to leave the Tsuki islands?"

"No!" I shook my head quickly. "I'm happy here, Kiyomi-sama. I have you, the Moon Clan, the kami and all the yokai who live here. This is my home."

"I know." Kiyomi-sama nodded. "And it will always be your home. You will always be welcome here, Yumeko-chan. But I know yokai, and I have seen that look before. You came to us from the Silent Winds temple in Earth Clan territory, you have been to Kin Heigen Toshi and the lands of Shadow, you have crossed the Dragon Spine and sailed the Kaihaku Sea to find these islands. You have seen more of the empire than most of my own people, and you have witnessed things that few will ever see in their lifetimes. But that only makes it worse, doesn't it?"

I swallowed, looking down at my hands. "My dreams to see the world are strong, Kiyomi-sama. But not as important as having found my home. The empire will always be there. Although…" My hands curled into fists, and I took a quiet breath, not wanting her to see the truth in my eyes. The longing that I could not shut out. "Gomen," I whispered. "I am happy here, but…"

"Daughter." Kiyomi-sama's voice was gentle. "You are kitsune. And though it has taken me a long time, I have learned that some spirits cannot be restrained. The world calls to them, they hear its song in the wind, in the clouds, on the horizon. And the tighter you hold on to them, the louder the song grows. Until it is deafening.

"We have found each other," the daimyo continued, her voice as soft as sakura petals. "You are connected to these islands, as I am. Your home will always be with us. But you hear the world calling, and that is a song few can ignore."

The Tsuki daimyo rose, graceful and sure, to gaze down at me. "Someday, you will inherit this clan, daughter," she told me. "When I have joined my ancestors, you will lead this family, and the Dragon scroll, the pact with the kami, the responsibility to keep these islands safe—all of that will fall to you. But you are young, and I am not gone yet. I can find the strength to let you go."

Kiyomi-sama gave me a gentle smile, though her dark eyes glimmered with the hint of tears. "The name of the ship that will be bringing the Mizu envoy to these islands is the *Azure Serpent*," she said quietly. "The captain happens to be a good friend of mine. When it is time for the ship to depart for Water Clan territory once more, I can easily convince him to take one more passenger on to Seiryu City. From there, the whole of the empire will be waiting for you to discover it."

My heart leaped, but I shook my head. "I can't just leave, Kiyomi-sama," I protested. "What about the Tsuki? And the other clans? They all know I'm your daughter. If I just disappear…"

"I will tell them you are on a pilgrimage," Kiyomi-sama said calmly. "And they will not question it. Do not worry, daughter." She gave a twisted little smile. "The rest of the empire views the Moon Clan as strange and rather eccentric. It makes certain decisions easier."

Bending down, she took my hand and drew me upright, looking me in the eye. "I used to be worried," she said quietly.

"I feared that one day, you would vanish and I would never see you again. But you have grown, and you have already faced so much. If the world calls to you, I have to let you go. And I will trust that you will come back."

I nodded, feeling a lump rise to my throat, the prickle of tears in the corner of my eyes. "I promise," I whispered. "I… I think I do have to go, Kiyomi-sama. There's so much out there that I want to see. But it won't be forever. I *will* come back. Now that I've found you, nothing will ever keep me away again."

And nothing did.

From the personal journal of the Moon Clan daimyo, on the last day of summer.

They tell stories, nowadays, of a wandering fox. Most times it would appear as a humble peasant girl, but sometimes as a yokai with glowing golden eyes. You could meet her anywhere: on a bridge in the valley of Kin Heigen Toshi, in the deep forests of the Kage, on the highest peaks of the Dragon Spine. She has been encountered in caves, in tiny farming villages or walking alone on roads throughout the empire. Some stories say she is benevolent, that she travels the country looking for people to help. Other tales claim she is a force of mischief and mayhem, and will always appear when something unexpected is about to happen. But in most tales, either unwittingly, through seeming blind luck or in a baffling display of chaos, the fox ends up aiding those she encounters, and they are left confused but grateful when she departs, sometimes not even sure of what they saw.

But then one day, many years after her stories began to spread, the fox disappeared. No one noticed at first, and no one could guess the cause, though the common thought was she had just gotten bored, as fickle yokai were wont to do, and returned to the simpler life of a field fox. The wandering kitsune wasn't seen in Iwagoto again, but her stories remained, and eventually passed into legend.

A few years after the wandering fox faded from Iwagoto, the daimyo of the Moon Clan left the world. It was said she went peacefully to her ancestors, surrounded by family and clan, her only daughter at her side. Those who knew the Tsuki daimyo in life remembered a beautiful but solemn woman who never smiled, but who in her final years seemed truly happy and at peace, passing the mantle of leadership on to her daughter. Her daughter, woefully unprepared, struggled at first, but she had the kami and her people to guide her, and eventually became a leader she hoped her mother would be proud of.

Today marks the one hundredth year since the Night of the Dragon. One hundred years since we stood against Genno, the demons of Jigoku and the ninetail who would become a god, if but for a moment. Today is a day of celebration, of remembrance, of honoring those who gave their lives to stop a madman from destroying the empire. Today, the entire Moon Clan celebrates, and the empire celebrates with us, but I cannot help but feel a bit melancholy. A century is a lifetime in mortal years, and those who stood with us that day have gone to their ancestors. But I am kitsune, and my father's blood flows through my veins. A hundred years is the blink of an eye to a fox, and I remember that day as clearly as if it happened two nights past.

My friends. Wherever you are, I hope you are happy. I have not had the fortune to meet any of you again. Though I have searched the empire over hoping to see you, to catch a glimmer of recognition, it seems fate will have us meet when it is ready and not before. So be it. I truly believe we will all meet again someday, and when we do, it will be as if we never left. Though you might be shocked to learn your naive, reckless fox is now the daimyo of the entire Moon Clan. I have so many tales to tell you, my friends, but until our souls meet again, I will wait. I am kitsune, after all. I have time.

I put down my brush and stared at the paper a moment, watching the lines of ink dry on the page, before carefully closing the journal and returning it to the shelf above my desk.

A respectful tap sounded outside my door. "My lady?" came the voice of Hana, one of my ladies-in-waiting. "Yumeko-sama, it is almost time. Have you been made ready?"

I sighed. "Yes, Hana-san." I stood, turning to the door. "Please come in. Stop lurking outside my door like a yurei. The last time Misako startled me, I nearly set the shoji on fire."

The door slid back, revealing a young, pretty girl who bowed quickly and then stepped through the frame. "My lady, I have been sent to inform you your guests have started to arrive," she said, her gaze scanning my outfit as she rose. As my clan colors dictated, I was dressed in a black kimono with a gray underrobe, and the silk was decorated with hundreds of swirling silver leaves. But if you looked hard enough, you might also see a few brightly colored leaves among the swirls of silver. Five in all, each representing a different soul. I found it fitting for today.

Hana smiled, and by the wistful look on her face, I assumed I appeared presentable. "Thank you, Hana," I told the girl. "Now, stop worrying about me, and go enjoy yourself. No one is going to need their hair combed or their floors swept until tomorrow. I know Misako has already gone into town. Go join her, eat a mochi ball, fly a paper dragon. This is a day of celebration, and tonight we will honor the heroes of one hundred years ago. Do you have a lantern to float down the river?"

She bobbed her head. "Yes, Yumeko-sama! My great-great-grandfather was one of the ashigaru soldiers that stood against the demon horde. He died, sadly, but we've never forgotten his sacrifice."

"Good." I nodded. "Honor him tonight. Let him be remembered always. Now, go on." I motioned to the hallway. "Have fun. I don't want to see you back here until tomorrow morning."

"Hai, Yumeko-sama!"

Hana bowed and scampered off, her sandaled feet slapping against the wooden floors as she hurried away. I smiled at her excitement, then turned to give myself a last glance in the mirror.

A kitsune with pointed ears and golden eyes stared back, making me nod in satisfaction. The envoys and representatives of the other clans were always surprised when they met me. Not by my fox nature, which few could see. They expected an older woman, a crone, one whose face was lined with years and experience. Not a girl who could be someone's granddaughter. I refused to wear my hair up, hating the way the combs pinched and the hairsticks stabbed my scalp, and so my hair hung unbound to my waist. I did not look like a wise, revered ruler of the Moon Clan, and much like Lady Hanshou's legacy, rumors were starting to circulate. For now, given the Tsuki's isolation from the rest of the empire, they were just rumors, but eventually, it would become known that the daimyo of the aloof, eccentric Moon Clan wasn't completely human.

I didn't care. Let the empire know that the Tsuki family daimyo was a kitsune. It wouldn't make any difference as to what I did, or my vow to keep my people, my family and the kami who lived here safe.

Turning from the mirror, I stepped to my desk and carefully picked up the paper lantern sitting on the corner. Unlike the round, red chochin lanterns that hung on strings and above doorways, this one was boxy and rectangular. Its thin paper walls were white instead of red, and on each side, a handful of names had been written in the blackest ink. The five names of those dearest to me, the souls I never wanted to forget. *Hino Okame, Taiyo Daisuke, Reika, Suki.*

Kage Tatsumi.

Kiyomi-sama's name wasn't on the paper lantern, though I had briefly considered adding her to the paper walls, as well. But this festival was to honor those who had fought and died on the Night of the Dragon, who gave their lives to save the empire. There were other celebrations that honored the departed. Every year, on the night of her death, I traveled alone to a certain grove in the forest of the kami. There, along with hundreds of kodama, spirits and sometimes, though very rarely, the Great Kirin, we would honor the memory of the Tsuki daimyo, and I would pray for her wisdom to continue guiding me down the right path. So far, she had never led me wrong, and I didn't think she would mind if her name was absent from the paper lantern. Tonight was for other souls.

Satisfied, I left my chambers, and found Tsuki Akari waiting for me in the hall, along with a pair of armed samurai. My chief adviser and closest friend was a beautiful young woman with the intelligence of a sage and the wit of a monkey god. She looked like she could be my sister, and sometimes she acted like it, though I remembered when she had been a dirty-faced child running around the palace gardens. She didn't really advise me on much, but Akari had informants everywhere and knew everything that went on inside the walls of the palace; I relied on her to tell me the things I needed to know.

"Yumeko-sama," Akari said with a reverent bow and a less reverent smile that only I could see. My chief adviser was the epitome of charm and grace in public, which was also the only time she called me Yumeko-*sama*. "The sun is beginning to set. Everyone is waiting for the Moon Clan daimyo to send the first lantern down the river."

I nodded and raised the lantern before me. "I'm ready. Let us go. But first..." I gave her a shrewd look. "Were you able to obtain what I asked for?"

She gave a despairing sigh and held up a stick with three brightly colored rice dumpling balls shoved halfway down the length, a popular festival snack. I grinned and plucked it from her fingers, as the guards pretended not to notice. "When you're finished, Yumeko-*sama*," Akari said, putting emphasis on the "sama," as if to remind me that daimyo of great clans should not indulge in common festival sweets—at least, not in public... "Kage Haruko is in the main hall, and wishes to speak to you before the sending of the lanterns."

"Oh?" I bit off one of the rice balls and motioned us down the hall with the rest of the stick. "Her health has been poorly lately, or so she said in the missive apologizing that she couldn't be here tonight. I wonder why she changed her mind?"

"I'm sure you can ask her."

We walked in silence through the palace until we came to the main hall, which was emptier than normal. Most everyone was either at the festival or on the banks of the numerous moats running through the city, paper lanterns in hand.

But a group of people waited for me as I stepped into the chamber, men and women in the distinctive black and purple of the Shadow Clan. The woman in the center, surrounded by nobles and samurai, was a distinguished older woman whose hair was threaded with silver, but who was still quite beautiful despite her years. She sat cross-legged on a cushion, her back straight and her eyes closed, but they opened as I stopped in front of her, and she looked me over with a sharp black gaze.

"Haruko-sama." I nodded respectfully, and she returned it. "I will admit to being surprised to see you here. Your note said you were not well enough to travel."

"I'm not." The Kage daimyo held up a hand, and immediately the young samurai standing beside her offered his arm to help her to her feet. "I'm here," the daimyo went on through gritted teeth as she stood, "because my thrice cursed grandson would not stop pestering me to make the journey, and since we came all this way, I thought I would pay my respects." She gave me a tight smile. "You haven't changed since I saw you… thirty years ago? Before the war with the Hino that took my son." She shook her head, as if dissolving those memories. "My apologies, I am being a rude old lady. I don't believe you have met my grandson?" She motioned to the man beside her, who gave me a solemn bow. "This is Kage Kousuke."

"It is an honor to meet you, my lady," Kousuke recited.

"I would introduce you to my *other* grandson, the baka that convinced me to make this ridiculous journey, but he has apparently decided that greeting the Moon Clan daimyo in her own palace is not important and disappeared as soon as we reached the docks." Kage Haruko made a hopeless gesture with both hands. "That boy. If he wasn't such a skilled warrior, I would have sent him off to live with monks long ago. Maybe they could make sense of his dreams."

I pricked my ears, about to ask what she meant, but from the open doors of the palace, a low murmur seemed to run through the entire city, hundreds of breaths being released at once. I turned and saw.

"The sun has set," Akari said beside me in a soft voice. "Yumeko-sama, it is time."

I nodded and bowed my head to the Shadow Clan ruler. "Forgive me, Haruko-sama," I told her. "I must go."

"Of course."

Twilight had fallen over Shinsei Yaju as I walked down the steps of the Moon Clan Palace, the air cool and tinged with anticipation. It was a perfect evening. The sky was clear, the temperature mild and the breeze carried the faint, sweet smells of the festival: dango, yakitori, grilled octopus on a stick and more.

Dozens of people clustered along the water's edge as I came to the arched bridge, then carefully made my way down to the riverbank. As I knelt at the edge of the water, I could see my reflection on the surface: a girl with pointed ears and golden eyes, who looked nearly the same as she had one hundred years ago when she fled the Silent Winds temple with a scroll that would change the world.

She wasn't the same, though. She had grown up. She had loved and lost, found a family, discovered what was important. She had wandered the land, traveled to the corners and hidden places of the empire, only to find that home was where she had wanted to be all along. She had people who needed her, a whole island to protect. And, except for one tiny, nagging doubt, the smallest of holes in her heart, she was content.

The lantern in my palm glowed softly, illuminating the names written across the surface. I smiled and carefully lowered it into the water, then gave it a tiny push. The paper box bobbed on the ripples a moment, drifting lazily downstream, glowing brightly against the inky water, until the current caught it and pulled it smoothly into the center of the river.

Somewhere behind me, a drum began to sound, deep and booming. All up and down the riverbank, the crowds bent down, releasing their lanterns into the water. They floated into the river, spinning or drifting lazily, carrying the names of all the souls whose sacrifice allowed us to be here. I lost my own lantern in the flood of others, and soon the entire river glowed with soft orange light, reflected above and below like glimmering stars. I closed my eyes, sending up a prayer to the kami, and to the names drifting down the river, that they would never be forgotten.

And then, I felt eyes on me, an oddly familiar sensation, and raised my head.

Across the river of lights, a figure watched me, his eyes a brilliant purple in the hazy lantern glow. A young samurai dressed in black, with the crest of the Kage on one shoulder. He appeared to be a noble, and bore a striking resemblance to Kage Kousuke, the daimyo's grandson, but was perhaps a few years younger. He stared at me, open wonder and amazement on his face, and for just a moment, it was like we were there again, on the cliff overlooking the valley, right before he whispered his promise and faded from my arms.

My heart began an erratic beat in my chest, and my eyes filled with tears. Somewhere deep inside, part of my soul leaped up in complete, unrestrained joy, dancing, cavorting, flitting wildly from side to side. It knew him, recognized him, just as he had said it would.

Across the river, bathed in light, the samurai smiled.

"I've finally found you."

★ ★ ★ ★ ★

Glossary

amanjaku: minor demons of Jigoku

arigatou: thank you

ashigaru: peasant foot soldiers

ayame: iris

baba: an honorific used for a female elder

baka/bakamono: fool, idiot

bakemono: monster

chan: an honorific mainly used for females or children

chochin: hanging paper lantern

daikon: radish

daimyo: feudal lord

daitengu: yokai; the oldest and wisest of the tengu

Doroshin: Kami; the god of roads

furoshiki: a cloth used to tie one's possessions for ease of transport

gaki: hungry ghosts

gashadokuro: giant skeletons summoned by evil magic

geta: wooden clogs

gissha: two-wheeled ox cart

gomen: an apology; sorry

hai: an expression of acknowledgment; yes

hakama: pleated trousers

hannya: a type of demon, usually female

haori: kimono jacket

Heichimon: Kami; the god of strength

hitodama: the human soul

inu: dog

ite: ouch

Jigoku: the Realm of Evil; hell

Jinkei: Kami; the god of mercy

jorogumo: a type of spider yokai

jubokko: a carnivorous, bloodsucking tree

kaeru: copper frog; currency of Iwagoto

kago: palanquin

kama: sickle

kamaitachi: yokai; sickle weasel

kami: minor gods

Kami: greater gods; the nine named deities of Iwagoto

kami-touched: those born with magic powers

kappa: yokai; a river creature with a bowl-like indention atop its head filled with water that if ever spilled makes it lose its strength

karasu: crow

katana: sword

kawauso: river otter

kijo: female oni

Kirin: sacred beast of Iwagoto; the Kirin has the body of a deer, the scales of a dragon, and a single antlered horn that emits holy fire

kitsune: fox

kitsune-bi: foxfire

kitsune-tsuki: fox possession

kodama: kami; a tree spirit

komainu: lion dog

konbanwa: good evening

koromodako: yokai; an octopuslike creature that can grow to an enormous size

kunai: throwing knife

kusarigama: weighted chain with a sickle attached to one end; shinobi weapon

kuso: a common swear word

mabushii: an expression meaning "so bright," like the glare of the sun

majutsushi: mage, magic user

Meido: the Realm of Waiting, where the soul travels before it is reborn

miko: a shrine maiden

minna: an expression meaning "everyone"

mino: raincoat made of woven straw

mon: family emblem or crest

nande: an expression meaning “why”

nani: an expression meaning “what”

neko: cat

netsuke: a carved piece of jewelry used to fasten the cord of a travel pouch to the obi

nezumi: rat yokai

Ningen-kai: the Mortal Realm

nogitsune: an evil wild fox

nue: yokai; a chimerical merging of several animals including a tiger, a snake and a monkey that is said to be able to control lightning

nurikabe: yokai; a type of living wall that blocks roads and doorways, making it impossible to go through or around them

obi: sash

ofuda: paper talisman possessing magical abilities

ohiyou gozaimasu: good morning

okuri inu: yokai; large black dog that follows travelers on roads and will tear them apart if they stumble and fall

omachi kudasai: please wait

omukade: a giant centipede

onikuma: a demon bear

oni: ogre-like demons of Jigoku

onmyoji: practitioners of onmyodo

onmyodo: occult magic focusing primarily on divination and fortune-telling onryo: yurei; a type of vengeful ghost that causes terrible curses and misfortune to those who wronged it

Orochi: yokai; dragon serpent with eight heads and eight tails

oyasuminasai: good night

ryokan: an inn

ryu: gold dragon; currency of Iwagoto

sagari: yokai; the disembodied head of a horse that drops from tree branches to frighten passersby

sake: alcoholic drink made of fermented rice

sama: an honorific used when addressing one of the highest station

san: a formal honorific often used between equals

sansai: edible wild plant

sensei: teacher

seppuku: ritual suicide

shinobi: ninja

shogi: a tactical game akin to chess

shuriken: throwing star

sugoi: an expression meaning “amazing”

sumimasen: I’m sorry; excuse me

tabi: split-toed socks or boots

Tamafuku: Kami; the god of luck

tanto: short knife

tanuki: yokai; small animal resembling a raccoon, indigenous to Iwagoto

tatami: woven bamboo mats

Tengoku: the celestial heavens

tengu: yokai; crow-like creatures that resemble humans with large black wings

tetsubo: large two-handed club

tora: silver tiger, currency of Iwagoto

tsuchigumo: a giant mountain spider

ubume: yurei; a type of ghost who died in childbirth

umibozu: yokai; a shadowy giant that lives in the ocean and crushes passing ships

usagi: rabbit

ushi oni: yokai; a large, sea-dwelling monster with the head of an ox and the body of a spider

wakizashi: shorter paired blade to the katana

yamabushi: mountain priest

yari: spear

yojimbo: bodyguard

yokai: a creature with supernatural powers

yokatta: an expression of relief; thank goodness

yuki onna: snow woman

Yume-no-Sekai: the realm of dreams

yumi: longbow

yurei: a ghost

zashiki warashi: yurei; a type of ghost that brings good fortune to the house it haunts

Missing the Shadow of the Fox series already?

Return to where it all began with Julie Kagawa's debut novel *The Iron King* available in Paperback and eBook now!

Enter a fantastical world of dangerous faeries, wicked princes and one half-human girl who discovers her entire life is a lie…

ONE PLACE. MANY STORIES

Bold, innovative and empowering publishing.

FOLLOW US ON:

@HQStories